JERICHO'S BANE

IMPERIAL PROTOCOL

JAMES L. HOWARD

Printed in the United States of America.

Library of Congress Control Number: 2019904195

ISBN	Paperback	978-1-64803-204-2
	Hardback	978-1-64803-226-4
	eBook	978-1-64803-205-9

Westwood Books Publishing LLC
11416 SW Aventino Drive
Port Saint Lucie, FL 34987

www.westwoodbookspublishing.com

For Lorenzo & Vincent

ACKNOWLEDGEMENTS

This great undertaking of completing the first novel in the series of Jericho's Bane was one of the most massive time-consuming projects of sheer passion that I have completed. This great feat may have been written by one, but in no way could have been completed in solitary. I would like to take this time to thank those that helped me bring this vision from idea to the subjective tangible. First, I'd like to give a gigantic thank you to my editor Cara Lockwood Benoit. She was the first to help me make since out of the madness I had created on paper. Without her editorial skills you all would have been locked in the asylum of my mind with me. I can honestly say you would not be reading the fine quality of work before you without her assistance.

To my Beta Readers David Todd and Gary Davis Jr. who took the time out of their lives to read my works in its entirety and offer feedback and heartfelt constructive criticism, I feel a thank you can't even begin to express the gratitude I have for the part you two played. It was appreciated and helped immensely in setting the pace for the story.

My work is not complete without the visuals. To my artists that gave my world a visual clarity, you did astonishing work in helping me attain the perfect cover graphic, I would like to thank Luther Berry Robbie J DubBryan, and Jordan Jackson. A special thank you to Chris Hunter who culminated, expanded upon, and completed the exceptional cover work that caught the spirit of the pages inside.

A special thank you must be given to my narrator Marek Montoya, who took on the monumental task of giving voice to my characters in the Audible Book Version of the novel. It was an epic undertaking.

Lastly, the greatest thank you of all goes to you, the fans for making it all worth it. My story was truly created to entertain you all. It was not meant to be divisive, nor question or expound on any faith. I hope that you all enjoy reading or listening to Jericho's Bane Imperial Protocol as much as I enjoyed writing it. See you all soon in novel 2.

CHAPTER 1

DIVISION

Talking to himself was not uncommon. He was alone a great deal of the time. It was not that he wished it; it was just the nature of the position that was tasked to him. It can be easily understood why others would think a man in solitary would go mad, but there is a serenity in being by oneself. The trick is you must externalize your inner voice or risk the whisper of reason becoming an audacious roar. You must make that inner voice audible and answer it resolutely to know that you are in discussion with one's self. Now, to avoid making it audible, to keep that silent and just think the banter back and forth with your own mind, well—that's maddening.

The mysterious figure who's not ashamed or embarrassed of conversing with himself wears a hooded cloak with hood pulled concealing his visage. From the balcony of the tall spire of royalty, he grips the white marbled railing as he peers up and out into the expanding dark void of space at the vast number of stars, each surrounded by a cadre of planets. He watches the detail of the mechanics that set each to spin on an axis that was predetermined, planned, and set into motion. It was easy to get lost in thought at the grandeur of what his species could create.

Grumbling in the pit of his stomach, although slight, brings his mind back from the brink of ponder. He turns and grabs a Manna Wafer from his plate that sits just off to the left of him on the railing. He eats one and then another. Before he realizes it, he's consumed the whole Manna platter. Regret then flushes his face. Manna is unforgiving when masticated without water to aid in easing it down the gullet—a mistake that he often makes but benefits from. The dryness of his parched being keeps him uncomfortable, which in turns keeps him up to complete his tapestry of the greatest masterpiece of writing that he's ever woven.

Clearing his throat of dry wafer and phlegm, he falls into the habit that has become his own. He gives voice to himself in the self-imposed solitude of his library. He voices what he is sure he's going to write. He has to hear it aloud before it falls to papyri. "It was a fortuitous and an untimely end," says the hooded, mysterious figure. "Our road to perdition has been surfaced beyond good will and intention. It has been paved on a road constructed on a soliloquy of lies and half-truths. This will be a morning to a day unlike any other in the history of all days. I expect negotiations to fail today, resulting in a chasm that, when parted, will reverberate as ripples out through all of existence. All life in one way or another will be affected by our divide and indecisions. It will include not only life, but everything that was, is, and is yet to come."

"As the ramifications of this coming day become far-reaching, I can't help but think one constant thought, a verse of words that Mercy had spoken to me, words that he himself said that he once overheard a mortal speak. I don't put much into what they say, the humans, but I had to admit, if Mercy heard him correctly, then this one mortal had a moment of divine clarity when he spoke them. What was it he said? How did it—Oh, yes! It was something to the effect of, 'Woe to all of us if we were made in the image of God for if the master template is corrupted, then all else that follows carry that corruption unto a vile end.' Secrets ... the word in itself is sinless. A social construct has no sin. If there is sin attached, it is because meaning was given to the construct. Like the word *secret,* my brothers and I were free of sin until this day. The power of it, the majesty of the word *secret.* Just one of those held in confidence will become the lightning bolt that has begun the decline of our reign and will turn the once-peaceful tide of creation into a maelstrom."

The mysterious figure reaches for another wafer and remembers that he's finished them all. "May the one future king be the one of change. May he rectify all that has gone astray, or I fear my fate and those of my brethren will see the similar disposition of those that were prior to our lineage, those that have been forgotten and long faded into a distant locked-away memory, to be no longer whispered of." The mysterious figure raises his hand to wipe tears from his hood covered eyes. "Oh! I believe your story, Lucifer. The way in which your passion ignited every syllable speaks volumes of truth to what you have claimed to have discovered in lifted eaves of secreted conversations in the house of Elohim. Alas, I'm loyal to the crown and the head it sits upon."

The mysterious figure turns from the railing and finds his place ready for him at his desk among the infinite bookshelves. He picks up his personal diary, returns to the railing, and writes everything that he's just spoken. Satisfied his mind has been transcribed, he places the diary into his cloak with care and reverence. It's his thoughts, but on papyrus made tangible, it could be considered heresy in these tumultuous times. Breathing a sigh that his mind is hidden away for posterity, he averts his attention from the diary, from the distant planets down the land of his birth.

Watching over the lands of Jacintian, the mysterious figure nods at the gathering forces down on the open plains. Again, he leaves the railing, this time for good, as he has to get back to the business of writing his masterpiece of architectural genius. He turns inward to the library, back toward the infinite shelves of books. Rolling his neck, the pressure crackles within his vertebrae as he gets comfortable. With two open books laid before him on his desk, he waves his hand, summoning a chair that had been a few feet away from him. The chair slides underneath him as he sits, ensconcing himself behind his massive light-gray marbled desk. Closing his eyes and steadying his breathing, he retrieves his platinum-tipped quill and dips its tip into a clear cylinder containing swirling molten gold that burps a modicum of flame every so often. He's done this mundane deed so often, it's become muscle memory. Opening his eyes, and without further pause, he touches the quill to the pages of a book that will stand not only the test of this newly lamented concept called time, but unto its omega.

His right hand feverishly writes across the bound pages of neatly compressed papyrus. The quill's ink impresses a bluish-orange flame striation as it glides across the already-illuminated pages. As the quill reaches the culmination of the page, the hand breaks only to turn the page and begin again another series of glyphs and striations. The words being written are in the first language of celestials, hieroglyphical written tongue. The curves and slants of the lighted glyphs are nothing less than sheer beauty as the tip of the quill sets flame to the page in thin, smooth strokes, forever searing in script, *We are not gods. That is the secret of the epitaph that is on the verge of igniting a war; not only of mind, belief, and loyalty, but of brotherhood. Hidden in this passage is my last testament to my family divided. Secrets destroyed us; may the light shown here within this scripture break the cycle. May the promised king be merciful. A script that I pray will reverberate throughout all of existence as much as the coming conflict.*

A deafening series of long trumpet bursts sounding irradiates the air in the distance outside the library, signaling the first gathering of celestials has begun. The sounds are then followed by seven short blows of the trumpets, signaling formations to align loyalties. At first, the instruments sound rancorous, but then instantly turn into a beautiful melody that can only be trumped by the visual melody of the rising of multiple suns across infinite galaxies in a stair-stepped strum similar to that of the fabled harpsichord, as depicted in so many renditions of how angels spend their days.

The sound of the trumpet is fierce with beauty that would all but obliterate the minds and bodies of mortal men. However, this particular trumpet is not meant for the ears of men but for another set of beings, an older society that existed long before. The immense chords that are played abruptly cease the feverishly writing hand for a mere moment. He'd rather be at the gathering to bear witness to the unfolding of events that will shape the fabric of all realities, but he's so close to completing his tapestry that he cannot leave his work undone. To do so would tell a story that had no climactic ending. His hand tenses, thinking of the day's events still to unfurl. His tenseness gives cause to muscle retraction. Snap! The quill he's holding is broken. Undaunted by the distraction and with the writing-tip end still touching the page, he finds his center and continues the tip sliding across the paper with another series of slants, loops, and curves for a few more strokes, finally ending the sentence with a hard-pressed period.

Satisfied with the last set of glyphs, the hand finds rest and lays the quill down. He closes the pages, revealing the cover of this illuminated page book to be of platinum. A plated bound book cover, it is scribed and etched in the same flame-imbued ink as the pages within. Sighing, the anonymous figure picks up the dimly glowing book, leaving another of similar design on the desk. The book that remains reads *Eschatology* down its spine. Still holding the completed book, the hooded figure reverently places the book at the end of the last shelf among the infinite cases of shelved glowing books. Placing it into the last of two remaining slots, the writer continues to hold the book in place, staring at the last open space. Postulation suggests that the remaining book left on the table marked "Eschatology" will be the last book to fill the space. Once placed, it will have filled the shelf in its entirety, ending the infinity perspective of the library and starting a sequence of events that can never be undone.

Having reached a point of contentment, the figure's hand falls away from the spine of the book he just shelved. It reveals illuminated glyphs written down its spine which reads, *"The Book of Life."* Rubbing his thumb across an etching at the bottom of the spine he clears away the last remnants of metal shavings which reveals the last of name of the soul that will ever be read, voiced or recorded in such a book of the tallying of all deeds. With the placement of that book, the endless circle of life has an end.

"So, with that, it is accomplished," spoke the voice of the mysterious figure. "I have written the last name of man that will signify eschatology."

CHAPTER 2

"WAR FROM WARSIVIOUS"

"I have been called monster, a word that I have trouble defining. What is a monster? Is it not a grotesque vile beast that is the root cause of fear and wanton destruction? Is its purpose not to inflict the laws of chaos and anarchy? If that is what a monster is, then I am no such thing. I am something that not even the holiest of holies could comprehend. I am the opposite of this term, monster.

I am not monster, devil, slander nor Satan. I am the child of the, Most High, whose way of thinking has transcended beyond the mundane appearance of human insignificant thought and false free will. I am the truth that has been refused to be seen by all those that accept the narrative that was force fed to them. I am the inevitable outcome of one whose father is all powerful.

Was it not I, that covered Elohim in the sanctuary's throne room? Was it not I that was placed in the Garden of Eden to oversee the strands of walking dust? Let go of the false narrative and accept my truth which is: if we are born of gods then are we each not one in our own right? Well, I am, and I'm here to claim what is owed me. And if I am found to be monster according to history, then pay this devil his due."

Quote ~Lucifer

Glayden Fields of Jacintian Heaven

A deluge of rain falls from a grayish clouded sky onto a flooded marshland that was once a lush field of purple hued grass extending far into the rolling hills where trees lightly kissed the border. The trees upon the plains of the field are six times larger than Earth's redwood forests or Saturn's moon, Titan's Sharadal Mountains. That beauty and lushness spoken of seems as if it was yesteryear now. The fields of Glayden have since become flooded and mud soaked. The atmospheric change is unnatural to the inhabitants of this plain of existence. Never in all its being has Jacintian city's Glayden Fields, once known for its beauty, ever looked as ravaged and soaked.

From underneath a dark tan rain-soaked hood, a head looks up into the thundering sky revealing the bluest of irises behind the eye slits of a warrior's mask. The eyes stare unflinching into the sky as the rain falls heavy. Droplets pelt the deep blue eyes. They don't blink. Gabriel continues to look skyward thinking to herself, *I had never felt rain upon my face before from the skies of eternal days. Is this what it feels like to bring turmoil home? It had never rained in the luscious lands of Glayden. Until this day. The fields were once a beauty… a gem to behold. Now, it is refuse, drenched in arrogance.*

A long trumpet blow sounds to give ignition to the first gathering of celestials. Almost immediately a string of trumpets blows short bursts of sounds signaling for the celestials to choose allegiances. Gabriel remains firm where she is still watching the unnatural skies. She had thought for the most part that sides had already been chosen, but there were a few that she felt bump into her as they walked from her formation to the one across the water logged field. She never looks down to see who else had left their ranks. It was just too hard to watch as bonds of brotherhood cracked under the pang of choice.

The bluest of eyes looking through the eye slits of an armored helmet with an affixed protective face mask attention is called eyes forward. Gabriel stands at the front of a battalion of angels. Placing her right hand on the hilt of her sheathed sword, she looks to her right and left, finding herself standing in the presence of her remaining brothers' shoulder to shoulder. There's no place she'd rather be at the moment than with them. Feeling a new action that she's unfamiliar with, Gabriel looks at her free hand and realizes it's trembling. For a moment, the action of her trembling consumes all of her thought. She slaps her hand against her thigh in an attempt to keep it from shaking horribly. It continues to tremble. Her knees soon follow. *I try to control them but alas they have forsaken me. I can't explain what I'm feeling. Is this fear perhaps? Is this the feeling that the mortals felt before being torn from Edenastari?* The feeling made her nauseous in the pit of her stomach. She felt as if the Manna she'd consumed earlier was on its way to regurgitation.

To her left she watches Raphael, the youngest of all the castes prepare himself for the possibility of conflict. Metatron walks from the row behind him taking place at his side. He places his hand on Raphael's shoulder to help ease his anxiousness and reassure him that this coming moment will pass no matter the outcome of promised negotiations. To see brothers in that fashion breaks her heart and adds another roll in the pit of her stomach. To watch and feel the unease of coming tensions and what they do to one's psyche was almost too much to bear. But, bear it she did. She took a breath and decided to stand resolute in her decision to stand on the side of the crown, to push down her rising anxious feelings. She straightened her stance and gave the air of confidence. Hopefully in controlling her fear, it will set an example her younger brother will follow.

"Steady now Raph!" Gabriel yells back.

"Raph nods. Then bends over and regurgitates. He catches a breath and more follows. Metatron pats him on his back.

"Should I play Wet Mother or Nurse maid to you little one?" Metatron says as he lets out a laugh!

"Kiss my as--- hurghhhhh! Raph burps and continues regurgitating more. Metatron continues laughing and patting his youngest sibling's back.

Cheers rise and are heard from the rear of the battalion. The cheering becomes so loud that it rivals the crackling thunders over Jacintian sky. Gabriel waits in anticipation. If the mask was not covering her face, she would be seen smiling. She knows the cheers are for her brother as he moves within and through the ranks. It's easy to track his movements, the battalion's cheers follow him dying out as he passes through the celestial squads. Gabriel tracks her brother's approach and readies herself to cheer as he reaches her. Finally, it's her time and she bellows to the heavens, she bellows in hopes that he can stay off a course of events that will change not only the laws of the universe, but upset the family she's come to love above all else. Her yells chase away the anxiousness and trembling appendages.

Tall, sure of himself and resolute, the young commander Michael, newly-appointed Captain of Heaven's armies, slowly moves through the ranks and battalions of his brothers, his soldiers. He pauses for the slightest of moments next to Gabriel. He looks into the slits of her helmeted eyes and sees the wavering in them as well as in the eyes and faces of those around her. He places his hands on his sister's shoulder comforting her. He even gives her a smile of reassurance to accompany his calming touch. Gabriel nods letting him know that she's with him no matter the outcome of this day's events. Michael returns the nod paying close attention to her expressionistic eyes. As he observes her looking back into his eyes he overhears her thoughts speaking just as loud as if she'd spoken them verbally. *Lucifer has always been the one we've looked to. How did it all come to this?*

Telepathy is as common as tongue amongst the celestials. Any species that live long enough could attain such communication. It really is the perfection of reading expression as communication. There is no mystic art to it, just evolution.

Michael gives her shoulder a firm grasp and shake acknowledging her troubled mind. He gently bumps his bare forehead against her helmeted one. A gesture of a bond that they have formed long before such the possibility of dark day was ever thought. Michael turns and moves again forward of the battalion. Gabriel watches him closely. She watches as his cloak flails revealing the shine of his armor underneath as he continues to the front. She is awe stricken at the immense responsibility that has been thrust upon him and how sure of himself he seems.

Once he reaches the front, he looks across the fields and pauses again for only the briefest of moments. He stares past the gray wall of rain and remembers what this land use to be. The brightness, the endless days of bliss, where he only had to but praise a king who showed nothing but unconditional love. His tears cannot be seen as they fall among the sea of rain drops that pelt his face. Good thing, because how could he ask his soldiers to stand this day if he was not sure he could stand himself. If this last attempt at mutually beneficial conversation failed, he was not prepared for the recourse.

Michael steels himself by taking a breath he holds it in for minute calming his nerves. This is his first task in command. He exhales slowly and hardens his face before turning to face his troops. His hooded grayish cloak, soaked with rain, takes on a dark gray hue. As he looks into the eyes of his brothers, his soldiers. They look ready for the most part. There are a few that looks pail, but if things go ill, they should be ready. Those who have not given the rain-soaked ground their portion of earlier consumed Manna eyes speak silently with an intensity that does not need be given sound. Michael then turns and looks out across the fields in direct opposition of his family. This time, he faces his adversary, standing and awaiting him on the other side of the Glayden fields looking to devour him. Michael's Purple eyes turn colors as he gazes intently at his foes that lay in wait for him across Glayden, for they are legions. As he stares at them his mind wanders. *There are so many. Have that many truly be given cause to depart from the side of righteousness? Was his rule so bad?*

Across the field, another commander, one of legions watches Michael. He studies him as well looking for any weaknesses within the phalanx that can be exposed and exploited for gain. Lucifer and his soldiers have been deemed enemy of the Most High, but he'd never call them that. He spits phlegm thinking of the shit label given to him and those that ideals align with his own. Clearly free thinkers will not be tolerated. As commander he doesn't dare think him and his cohorts are enemies of any sort. He calls them loyal, free self-thinkers, brothers, deities that broke away from the collective hive mind of Elohim. And if his band of celestials have been labeled… wait what is it they called them? Ahh yes… if his band of celestials have been labeled Demons, then he gladly accepts that he is their lord. He is Lucifer a king elect who embraces all that feels they too have a will to exercise. He smiles gladly accepting his newly lamented stature as king of the Demonic horde. That meant he had a voice and was enough of a threat to deem attention.

The most beautiful celestial being that has ever walked the realms of reality was not only the one-time lead of the high throne room, but has been captain over his brothers and all the castes since the inception of his kind. Lucifer stands poised as any confident leaders destined for greatness would. He has led since the beginning of known creation. His deep eyes and perfect high cheek bones holds his regal stature. However, in his confidence he carries a flaw, a sadness that he would not dare let others see. As he looks across the field at Michael, he realizes that this day was always coming. He knew that there would be resistance among his kindred for his spark of ingenuity, his actions that he took in the garden Eden in the tongues of men. He just never expected his choice to rise to such ramifications that would culminate on this marshland. Lucifer turns to his general leaning in close and whispers a phrase that only those two will ever know. Satisfied, Lucifer turns and walks his ranks looking at his men, his brothers those like him considered fallen, considered wicked. With the look that he receives back from his men, he deems the fallen Demonic order ready for accession.

Lucifer and his second only to him Warsivious walks out to the middle of the field to await Michael. The colors of his legions dress and battle armament are red and silver on black. As his opposing troops to Elohim's drone order wait to be unleashed, they beat their chests and howl in opposition. They proudly show their different flair for fashions by how they wear their tunics and armor. They have etched and inscribed glyphs and a variety of other additions to their once uniformed armor to reflect their individuality, but they all remain within the same color scheme to place unification of their regime.

Lucifer and Warsivious are no different in their attire from the troops. As Lucifer marches towards his coming destiny out into the middle of the field of Glayden, his red tunic blows in the rough storming wind beneath his black and silver armor. With each stride, his metal black gauntlets emerge from underneath his cloak in cadence with the gait of his walk. His self-designed black chest plates which match the gauntlets sway back in forth in purpose. As Lucifer treads across the wet marsh, his black metallic knee-high boots with silver trimmed soles slush and trench deep prints into the soft mud.

Lucifer quickly glances back at Warsivious vainly admiring that his second endears him in flattery. He admires the make and cut of his independently-created battle regalia that matches his own. The only difference that separates the two is the left slanting loop of the second glyph. Other than that, it is a perfect resembling duplicate of Lucifer's Angelic glyphs down his right shoulder which further continues on down his armored chest plates as well. The symbols signifying his independence from the sovereign Elohim. Lucifer then glances to Warsivious again nodding his head for his second in command to approach him. Warsivious catches up to Lucifer passing him a rolled sealed scroll. As he approaches, his number two carries it proudly. Lucifer accepts the scroll while coming to a stop in the halfway meeting point of the gathered armies. There Lucifer and Warsivious await Michael with their red trim cloaks continuously flapping strongly in the wind driven, down pouring rain. As the wind whips and blows the cloak angelic glyph becomes visible within the trim. It reads: *Those that follow on thine heels will know thyself to be kings in their own right.*

Michael Looks across the field at the awaiting Lucifer and Warsivious. Confused at first, he then understands. "They want to parlay," he says. Looking over his shoulder to Gabriel, he sees her nod, acknowledging that she'd follow him as his number two.

"I guess we are to meet him away from ears of others," Gabriel says.

Inhaling a deep breath, Michael looks down toward the saturated ground. He studies the purplish grass that has been flooded and matted by the rain. Rain which has been caused by the upheaval of the divided rift of emotions between the castes of angels and the sadness of a king's heart that was torn asunder.

"We may yet avoid conflict Gabe. He has to listen to reason… does he not? Surely, he does not want this dispute to rise to such a level of confliction… Right?"

Gabriel watches Michael. Unable to answer at first, her mind wanders in thought. *Was that question rhetorical or do thou expect a reply to such a ubiquitous question? He's head strong, angry. I don't know if he wishes to avoid this conflict or if he could. I hope that he does, but my intuition sayeth thou will force conflict upon us. He's come too far not too. Oh! Look at Michael… his face is twisted with turmoil. I know he aches at the thought of having to bring our older brother to heel. It pains me to watch him like this, them like this at odds with one another.*

Michael grabs the right corner of his cloak and throws it over his left shoulder, covering his chest and heads out to meet Lucifer. Without a second thought, Gabriel breaks rank and joins him as his second to bear witness to the negotiations just as Warsivious has for Lucifer. Together, Michael and Gabriel walk out to meet the awaiting pair, not willing to show their fear or rising apprehension.

With each step that Michael puts forward, he attempts to conceal his most pressing thought. *What will happen if negotiations fail and the Morning Star does not return to his appointment?* Never since he's drawn breath has he had to take charge of matters that were to ever have reached such a magnitude. If such a matter had presented itself as perplexing it would have fallen to the best of them which was Lucifer. His stomach turns in knots as he gets closer to his older brother whose rank as Seraphim far surpasses his choiretic classification. Really, before this hour, Michael was only merely two classes above citizenry.

As Michael and Gabriel walk toward their respective destinies, he feels it is the longest walk of his existence, he doesn't dare look back at Gabriel, afraid that if his eyes make contact with hers, they will betray him and show her the doubt that he has in confronting his superior—or is it his former superior. This progressing situation is all too befuddling.

The four celestials meet in the center of the fields of Glayden. Their opposing armies look on poised ready to take action if only necessary. Michael looks past Lucifer at his opposition's strength. It's clear, he has the numbers on his side. About three to one. Sad that he just called his brothers oppositional strength, but that is what they are at this moment. He looks at their faces and knows each and every one of them; they're family, if even for the moment a name slips him. Since his caste inception, Michael's never known the entire angelic corps to be in a centralized locale. This was the first. Tragedy that it's under such conditions. There has never been such a mass gathering because each celestial had a function that kept the universes spinning and running in optimal efficiency. The reason why the weather has turned for the worse today, there was no one to man the atmosphere. That celestial was here on the field. Matter of fact, he's there in third column behind Deathiliss.

Lucifer removes his hood revealing his angular jaw line that appears molded to perfection. His visage is that of a rugged good-looking thirty-year-old. His iris are a deep purple, his Cheshire smile is breathtaking. He always looked like the cat that swallowed the canary.

"A daunting ask isn't it?" Said Lucifer. "To be responsible for so many." Lucifer walks closer to Michael.

As his brother approaches, he doesn't give ground. Lucifer stares at him face to face.

"It is." Michael answers. It is a responsibility that I wish to pass from me and back to you where it rightfully belongs.

"C'mere!" Lucifer grabs Michael in a mighty embrace hugging him. "By Elohim's word, I have missed you little one."

Michael embraces him back. "And I you."

Ending their embrace, they just look over each other.

Lucifer smiles, "I bet the old man is mad, isn't he? Ahh—You know what, don't answer that. Will get to that later. Let me just look at you. Look-at-you. In charge looks to fit you well. I'm glad you stepped up. He always thought highly of you."

"Not more than you. You, know you broke his heart. When Eden fell… he was crushed. For it to have been you was almost more than he could bear."

Lucifer turns to look at his forces. He stands clasping his hands behind his back. "Eden was necessary. It was a point that had to be made."

"You still have not told me why. You and I were close if you'd have talked to me---"

"You would've not listened. You still aren't ready to hear truth. You know, truth… the word that he stressed but did not adhere."

Michael starts walking toward Lucifer but hesitates when he notices Warsivious take a step as if to intercept. Lucifer raises a hand and Warsivious backs off allowing Michael to proceed.

"I'm listening now."

"No… you aren't. Not yet anyways, but you will. Soon you will hear and you will not be able to unhear. What I say will stand with you for all of your days, even until the unmaking of all worlds. You are idealistic brother. You champion a cause just as I had when I was oblivious. Unlike you, I heard the whispers of kings and I know the path. Those that wait over there heard my truth---"

15

"Alleged truth. Remember, what you claim as reason has yet to be substantiated. No one knows what you overheard accept you and those you told in secret who now follows you."

"True… Let us see if we can put rumor to bed and find ground for me to speak my alleged truth. Lucifer turns back to Michael. Let us begin negotiations. That is the reason that we are here after all. To find common ground and resolution?

"You being the oldest, I'll give you the field," Michael says.

The two talk for hours. Each opposing side hold their place waiting for the outcome. After the third hour, it is official, an impasse has been achieved.

"Michael, I wish thou would listen to reason. There is no need for this," Lucifer says as he smiled a charmingly devilish grin. Frustration has not overcome him yet. If it has Michael has not been able to discern it.

Michael removes his hood. A sure sign of frustration. Michael's visage is now revelated. He is handsome as well, although not as beautifully chiseled as his older brother, Lucifer. Just as his older brother his face is unmarred, his skin is flawless free of any blemishes. There has been no passage of time for him, for any of them that would have added crevices or lines of wrinkles. Such flaws were for the lesser species that populate the multiple realties of realms that they govern like the world of mortal men.

Michael nods. "Thou are right, there is no need for this. Words were said, yes, but nothing that can't be undone. Brother, we don't want this. You can remove us from this road to perdition if you were to just but---."

"---But, I do, Michael. I want this!" Lucifer says repeatedly thumbing his chest gesticulating the importance of how bad he wants to tear the heavens asunder. "I am in the right in this matter. Why can't you see it? If we have powers like unto God, are we not gods ourselves? Do we not have the right to rule also? To govern ourselves? Have we not been slaves long enough?"

Not frustration, but anger swells within Lucifer. Michael could clearly see that.

"Slave!? Is that what you think we are, Slaves? A matter of perception. Yours have become distorted. And rule? Brother, your rule was ill and brief. In just the single minutia of moments given to you Seraphim, you turned his most precious of creations from him with your impetuous lies. Our mortal brothers and sisters are forever lost to us, cut off due to your machinations." Michael's anger, which he thought had subsided since the fall, starts to show through his diplomatic façade on top of his frustrations.

Lucifer breaks the tension briefly by waving his hand dismissing the term Mortal. "Mortals are just elaborate lab test subjects. Something to be subjugated." Lucifer approaches Michael swiftly, this time Gabriel takes a step forward. Michael stays her. Lucifer keeps approaching waving his finger, "but proof that we can aspire to be more than mere ponds of subjugation ourselves awaiting extinction."

Growing impatient at the stalling of verbal tactics, Warsivious steps slightly closer to Michael. He positions himself to be within striking distance at a second's notice. Having let nothing slip by her Gabriel fulfils her purpose, she steps in just a little closer towards Warsivious in case the need arises to defend Michael from any attempts made by Warsivious' if he were to make a move.

Warsivious standing foot taller than any other celestial glares at Michael with a silent unspoken rage. A rage that peeks through his otherwise militant composure. "They are not lost. The mortals, you speak of," Warsivious barks. His voice is booming and thunderous. "Once Lucifer has ascended on high and claimed the throne, he shall reconcile them unto himself. Morning Star will bring them back into the fold."

"As long as they bow in subjugation to him, right, War?" Gabriel snaps back. She moves closer positioning herself to make sure she's in front of Warsivious. Gabriel looks over toward Lucifer and points at him. "No one told you to bring War."

"And yet, I have." Lucifer says assuredly, but defiant. "Take your place behind Michael little sister. You have no power to negotiate. You have but rule and protocol you mindless automaton."

Recognizing the anger and hostility, Michael grows fearful that the brothers are about to head for a situation that has never been witnessed in the Heavens. Quelling the rising tension is a must.

"Morning Star is what father callest thou. You have fallen far from that title brother." Michael says in an attempt to appeal to the side of Lucifer that sung harmonious praises in the court of the king. He walks up to Lucifer and places his hands on his shoulders and looks him in the eye. All else is silent, but the sound of the rain pelting against their armor. "Give this pointless Demonstration of power up! Come home! I'm sure he'll forgive thee of thy transgressions."

Lucifer backs away from Michael. For a moment contemplating the idea that maybe, just maybe, he's taken this revolt further than necessary. He again turns and glances back at those who chose to side with him, he looks at the faces, all of them that followed him to this point. They look at him with expressions of hope. They all want to own a piece of what they've helped maintain since their purposeful creation. They had wantonly given up their status and rank to follow the charismatic words he spoke to gain their allegiance. He could never betray that trust, not now, not when they've followed him so far and are so close and willing to go further.

Lucifer turns to Michael, handing him the sealed scroll.

"My demands," says Lucifer.

Michael doesn't fight the rejection, he acquiesces and accepts the scroll along with the downward spiral feeling of hopelessness that was attached to it. He unrolls the scroll and reads it pouring over every glyph. At its conclusion, Michael drops the scroll of demands and steps on it. "I have been given orders that no demands are to be accepted, that negotiations are unacceptable, and were never on the table brother... I bartered because I love you and want you home. I was given path to speak my words of compassion to turn you away from this course."

Lucifer nods his head slowly. "So, Elohim had never planned to take my terms seriously?"

Gabriel tightens her grip around the hilt of her sword. Warsivious spying that, follows suit.

Michael waves his hand to his side downward. "Stay your blade Gabriel!"

No! Lucifer says. "Loose your blade Gabriel! Prepare for its clashing! Call to it and speak that peace has been taken away as you swing it in defense of corrupted crown. Lucifer calmly turns towards Warsivious. "Tell Deathiliss to ready our brothers for ascension! Nothing is to be gained from diplomacy, so force will be our ally in creating change."

As Warsivious stares at Gabriel, smiling, his mask generates from the neckline of his armor to encompass his face. Metal materializes from the nape of the neck, just below the neckline of the armor. It slides over Warsivious' head, transforming into a helmet with attached face mask similar to that of Gabriel's.

"Gladly!" Warsivious replies to Lucifer's decree. He nods at Gabriel. "I'll see you on the fields of Glayden, messenger. There will be no reconciliation for you. No quarter given. I'll take thouest head and pike it on the further most gate of Iayhoten." He quickly does an about face and trots back towards the ranks of their legions.

Michael lifts his hand, signaling Gabriel. She turns and runs back toward their ranks to tell the Lieutenants to prepare their battalion for the coming of War.

Michael and Lucifer are left alone. Michael lays his hand on the hilt of his sword in a show of reluctant force. "This has never been done. We've never had confliction.

"Of course, we have brother," said Lucifer. "You've just never heard of it because we weren't around at the time. Your king is not what he appears to be. In time you will come to understand. Remember... I tried to educate you. I see now time and experience will educate you far further than I ever could... That is, if you survive the coming storm. We will descend on you like oceans upon shore."

"And you will fill find us steady as rocks to break the waves, Michael says sharply. You were the best of us. You were the decision supreme." Michael shakes his head. "Now, in these last of desperate moments this task has somehow fallen to me. I'm now responsible for the lives on this field. What do I do?"

"You fall beneath the heel of my boot." Lucifer answers harshly. His helmet and mask generate from the neckline of his armor covering his face, leaving only his eyes exposed.

Michael stares past the eye slits of his mask and into Lucifer's eyes. It's instantly clear to him that he can't fall. Not only is the kingdom at stake, but all of creation, all her realms and vast realities if he fails to bring Lucifer to heel.

Nothing left to be said, Michael turns and walks towards his awaiting soldiers. Lucifer call out to him. "If you survive this, Michael, you will always have a place in my mighty company."

Michael freeze, anger begins to ripple and swell within him. "I have no place among such company Satan." He turns and continues heading towards the rank and file of his celestials.

Lucifer halts his stroll toward his designated side of Glayden from which he will launch his bid for supremacy. "Satan, was it? Satan is what you just called thou? I shall remember that title and the one who gave it upon these fields of Glayden this day."

Michael doesn't turn to acknowledge his former superior. There will never again be a question in his mind of who his enemy is from this day forward. The rain falls even harder as he walks with purpose toward his awaiting troops, His mind echoing what Gabriel thought earlier, *how have it come to this?*

Broken bonds and knowing that the realm has chosen sides only makes the newly appointed ethereal captain more saddened while simultaneously pissed. What once was a celestial whole has now become a dual faction of those that have remained faithful and true, and those who have fallen and turned to a false king in selfish desperation.

Michael glances skyward, taking a moment to reflect on the last few minutes that has transpired. His eyes change color, as he experiences ranges of emotions. He feels the turmoil burn within him under his skin as he tries to come to some acceptance that there is no turning the tide of the issue that is ballooning out of control in front of him. He closes his eyes and thinks; *all that Elohim have created and his brothers maintained, has been undone.*

"So, it was written, so let it be done," Michael whispers to himself. *Satan wanted this conflict, so I shall give him one to end all others. What I do today is to quiet the realms tomorrow.*

Michael's metallic helmet and mask generates over his face. He opens his eyes looking to both sides of the field at the millions upon millions of his divided brothers. Anger swirls and permeates him. The thought of one selfish act has led to the very shaking of the foundations of Jacintian's realms. He stares at Lucifer from across the field as he makes ready for ascension and is pissed for all that he has wrought this day, the betrayal, the pain, and the rift, all contributed to one being that can't even accept the fact he himself were created.

He no longer feels sorrow for His older brother Lucifer or his fallen kin. Now, there lies only a rage that he's never experienced, a rage for the sins committed against the mortals, a rage for placing him in a position of leadership that he never asked for, a rage for bringing forces to ascend on high to dispose the rightful king and heir. It's a rage that he knows he must turn inward, but it is a rage that will fuel his protection of the golden trimmed white city, it will fuel his protection of Elohim and men, and all that inhabit in-between.

"So, let it be done, Demon," Michael yells across the once lush fields of Glayden. Then again whispers to himself in a silent prayer. "So, let it be your will enforced on these fields of Glayden, Lord. Guide my will and hand to an outcome that is victorious in your honor and name!"

CHAPTER 3

CONFLICTION

M ichael swiftly and with purpose walks towards his battalion. His cloak whips slinging water from it as he loose the most iconic symbol of the celestial, his wings. They expand from underneath rain-soaked cloak revealing feathers that are the purest of white. His wings press down hard giving him lift to where he just rises enough so that all eyes looking to him can see him. The freshly appointed captain elevates his voice to show his remaining brothers faithful to the reigning crown that he has truly taken charge. Lucifer, is more than likely lost to them and knows he must set aside his little brother's glow for the eldest and assume the mantle of leader left vacated. Michael throws off his hooded cloak into the wind and rain of the storm. His brother celestials watch as the cloak dances on the currents of swirling wind before falling to the rain soaked ground. Many among the celestial force wearing their cloaks nod and takes theirs off in solidarity with their captain. Others just remain focused with intense purpose. They inadvertently keep theirs on all the while remaining at the ready all eyes focused on Michael awaiting his breath that will carry the words of yay or nay.

"We are now and forever a house divided," Michael says fiercely masking his true feeling that he's lost and really have no clue what to do next. He knows his acting must rise to the challenge of inspiring his brothers, that it must pass his feeling of self-worthlessness so much so, hopefully he inadvertently inspires himself. "Our brothers that we've known are no longer. They have broken a sacred covenant against our king, against our prince, and against us. What we do here this day will echo throughout eternity not just for this realm, but all other realms throughout the Sadohedranicverse, including those verses still to come. It's clear that whatever legacy for those unborn verses that will eventually come, will undoubtingly be written in spilled blood that originates here on the field of Glayden.

Michael's shoulders fall a bit as he exhales a deep sigh. His mask degenerates falling below his neckline. He wants his soldiers, his brothers to see him, to see his soul.

"Our king has decreed a punishment of unknown darkness for our fallen mortal brothers and sisters that sinned against him. I don't quite understand this darkness, but know that this darkness shall befall us too once we strike a blow to shed the force of life which flows from another. Understand, once we lash out, we too have defiled the holy of holies. This choice you make this day must be of your own accord. To defend our home this day could write a sentence that you suffer for an eternity. I say again so you understand the gravitas of our situation; if you strike another in contempt, you subject yourselves to punishment, because we will be just as culpable. Our laws that we govern the Sadohedranicverse are not above us... even as we rectify our own house. I for one will risk it all for the citizens of our realms that we've helped construct. I will face this untold darkness if means that Lucifer's bid to ascend fail on the steps of the palace. I would rather die then see a usurper on the throne. That is me though. What say you?"

The celestial battalions look to Michael. There is a quietness that lasts among them for what seems the turn of an eternity. Finally, the silence is broken. One lone anonymous voice erupts from the silent sea of faces. "For the captain!" it screams out. After hearing the rallying cry, the battalions cheer in exuberance of standing on the firm ground of righteousness, they cheer to drown out the fear that gives them quiver and pause. They cheer at hearing the words spoken by their captain, their brother. They feel awakened and ready to rise to the challenge asked of them. They take Michael's words to heart as they try to still their own beating hearts.

The coming moments will prove pivotal for all after the day's events. Michael have asked of them to do the unthinkable. Scared, but inspired, they raise their hands high and signify that they are with him.

Michael hovers a bit higher. "Understand that Lucifer is coming to make ascension on high. He plans to go through us to do it. I know that it seems that he has the numbers, but that is of little consequence. I say to thee that he will try to ascend the steps of Iayhoten and succeed not."

Another thunderous roar erupts from his brothers.

Michael hovers to the left. "He has been labeled wicked by our prince and slander by our king. Our brother that was first amongst us will cometh, and he bringeth War and legions upon legions of crashing waves of Demonic with him. I say the waves will break upon the shores of metal, plasma and our sheer will to not fail."

Gabriel raises her fist. "We are with you, to whatever end."

The celestials hold their fists high as well and speak one voice "To whatever end!"

Michael does not yield to the distraction. He continues on in spite of it, more determined to finish so that his brothers and lone sister may listen and give everything for the coming battle, because nothing less than everything will be defeat. Another anonymous celestial within the ranks is overcome with such pride and fidelity he bellows out, "Let them come!"

"Yes, let them come!" Michael repeats. "Let them come and find us ready, let them come and find us righteous, let them come and fall upon our blades that burn as hot as the Razine Star."

Michael grabs the hilt of his sword and pulls it from its sheath. He only reveals a little of the blade at first. He pauses at the gravity of unleashing the full blade for he knows once he does, he's forever committed to its wielding. He has the fear that once it's loosed, so shall it be for all of time until the ending of the age. He completely pulls the blade free from it sheath. The blade turns white hot around its edges.

The battalions of Michael's forces pull their weapons in unison. The weapons range from swords to bows and axes to chained weapons. All of them burn white hot around the edges. Michael deliberately and slowly turns pointing his sword in the direction of Lucifer and those that would challenge the ruling sovereignty of Elohim.

"Lucifer will not make ascension to the most high throne, not this day or any other of its liking. War and his legions must fall. This has been commanded from on high, so, it shall be done." Michael grips the hilt of his sword with both hands and gently sets down in front of his battalion. He gazes across the field at what he knows will be a tidal wave of an unrelenting enemy. He raises his sword saluting legions. He whispers to himself, "So, let it be!" Which were to be the last words of reason in the ending days of what was supposed to be an eternal heavenly peace.

As far as the eyes could see, celestials raise their weapons, cheering on Michael and his speech. They chant in a harmonious unison, "So, let it be! So, let it be!"

Lucifer with his weapon already drawn looks across the Glayden at Michael. He places the blade of his sword in front of his face, careful not to make contact and salutes back to Michael. He closes his eyes in meditation of anticipation of the coming day's events. He says a small mantra to replace his normal prayer to God. He says it just under his breath to himself. He repeats it over and over again, "I have broken the faith to ascend on high. I have broken the faith to ascend on high." He opens his eyes and leans over toward Warsivious and then whispers just loud enough for Warsivious to hear.

"This is my time. I'm his image, this is my right and inheritance that I claim. I'm in the right. Are we not gods War? Am I not a god? My rule would have been equal if not surpassing. "I—we—" he quickly corrects. "--are just in this matter… Aren't we? I just wanted him to see there was a better way, an easier way." Lucifer shakes the doubt that he

25

was starting to talk himself into. "I am to replace Elohim! If I must be labeled usurper, then I accept it without condemnation fore I - am – god as much as he. Difference that separates us is, I will not lie."

Warsivious places his hand on Lucifer's shoulder. "Damn right thou are. Ready yourself for ascension, brother! I will see you to your prize." Stepping in front of Lucifer, Warsivious gives a battle cry that shakes the foundation of heaven. He yells but one word to rally all in opposition, "Ascension!"

Warsivious leads the charge alongside the other general Deathiliss and scores of lower rank legions behind them. As they move toward Michael's forces, the legions rush past Lucifer as a river flows past a boulder. Lucifer stands solemnly, reflecting on how he has brought everyone to this point. A brief moment of regret lingers slightly, but it is fleeting. Because of the sheer magnitude of his actions that has brought about the inevitable crash of might and ideals, he steads fast even within that briefest of moments of self-doubt that he possibly may have acted hastily. He steels himself further. *There's no going back now.* He has committed. His only foremost thought in his mind is one singular sentence: *I've come too far to stop now.* He starts trotting at first and then on into a full run. Like his fallen brothers, he gives the mighty battle cry, **"Ascension!"**

CHAPTER 4

ASCENSION

Michael thrusts his sword forward and immediately goes into a full sprint with his battalion following close behind. The two forces cover the distance of Glayden quickly colliding in a massive onslaught. Michael ducks an axe blow meant for his head. As the axe clears Michael's dodge, Gabriel leaps over Michael with her wings extended and cloak flailing. She unlatches her cloak, letting it fall to the winds as she plunges downward, placing her blade into the head of the axe-wielding celestial rebel, pinning his head backward and forcefully to the ground where the blade continues through the skull embedding in the marsh.

The first recorded celestial killing in the realm of Jacintian has occurred and been recorded, it was Gabriel that inked it. She pulls the blade from the Demon's forehead pausing for only a moment realizing that a brother she has known since her creation now lies motionless before her. His ethereal body which was so animated and full of life is now devoid of any movement. The gravity of what she's done starts to swell within her. That pause of reflection, that moment of sympathy is costly as it distracts her enough that she misses the incoming attack. A hammer blindsides the side of her face. As the blow careens across her helmet, she's hit hard enough that it slams her body into the mud head first and sends her sliding four yards across the rain-soaked field. The mask is grievously malformed over the right eye clamping it shut so severely that it stifles her vision. She is only able to see half her field of vision. She hears the incoming footsteps of her attacker approaching. At least she thinks she can. It's nothing but commotion about the field. Her own mind could possibly be fearing that the footsteps she hears are her attacker's. When she turns over it's not her mind playing tricks. Her attacker is approaching swiftly to finish her. He leaps throwing the hammer back behind him for maximum force when bringing it forward.

Gabriel unlatches her helmet and throws it off just in time to see the same enormous hammer wielding Demon bearing down for her again, this time from a more significant height. Realizing that she will be the second, third or maybe fourth by now slain this day. She falls back into the muddy marsh and resigns herself to fate and awaits the killing blow, a blow that hesitates. It never arrives. Before the Demon lands his killing strike, a chain wraps around his neck and he's pulled off course sparing Gabriel. The rebel celestial slams to the ground with significant force next to Gabriel. Seeing her foe discombobulated for that second was more than enough for her to capitalize. Gabriel extends her right wing vertically striking her foe under the jaw. Bones that structure the face of her enemy crunches under the force of the strike. Disorientated and unable to defend himself, Gabriel uses the precious seconds to flip up from her back onto her feet. Gabriel grabs her sword and swirls its tip downward, and drives the blade down through her attackers' neck. She feels the blade as it slows in speed as it drives through hardened celestial flesh and bone. Having vanquished another Gabriel breathes a sigh of relief that she yet lives. In gratitude she looks left to see her savior, Uriel. Gabriel gives him nod. Uriel gives her a nod back before turning to battle another pair of awaiting of rebelling celestial.

Within the fray of fighting, heroes are beginning to emerge on both sides. Warsivious' armor is stained in blood and mud. He wields and swings two massive swords with precision slicing through scores of Michael's troops. As he clashes weapons with multiple adversaries, he spins in a dance that leaves them headless. Warsivious has found his calling; he is happy to indulge and satisfy his new-found bloodlust. He gleefully takes unbridled enjoyment in the fact that celestials whom were once his family, now all fall upon his swords. Their own inaction and failure to listen to reason is why they now find themselves upon the point of his blade. To him, it all makes perfect sense. Why live as drone with no mind? To live at such is to be void of life anyways, may as well lie motionless to match the motionless inaction of the drone mind.

After cleaving another celestial's head from his shoulders, Warsivious takes a moment of respite only to see that a six-man team of Michael's celestial's try to acquire a firing solution on him by forming a firing line. To the right of the line stands Cassiel. Beneath his mask, Warsivious takes comfort that Cassiel can't see his smile, fore if he could he believes that he would run in sheer terror. War would be at a loss if Cassiel were to flee in this moment. He never liked the smugness of him and was longing to lay him motionless.

"I know it's you under the helmet Cassiel." Warsivious says. "You best make sure you do your best to finish me. I'll not stop till all of you litter the ground in a path my king will walk atop of reaching ascension."

Cassiel only nods, water dripping from his helmeted mask.

"Fire," commands Cassiel, dropping his fist.

The firing line of angels punches their right arms forward unleashing bluish-purple bolts of energy from just underneath their palms. Blue lights streak across the field.

Warsivious yells and charges the firing line. His blades drag in the soaked grass and mud. As he closes in on the firing line, he deflects many of the bolts with his wings some with his blades. Others bolts impact him at various points of his body denting and piercing armor finding flesh. It doesn't slow his pace. Warsivious closes the distance quickly. The firing line lose their nerve at his fast approach. Few steps backward looking for escape at the coming onslaught, two more stumble over their own feet attempting to flee away from the advancing Demon. As soon as Warsivious reaches striking distance, he rolls beneath the remaining bolts of the one that held firm springing upward, slicing the celestial from privates to his head cleaving him in two. With another turn of his wrists, he relieves two more from the burdens of their heads. The remaining firing line retreat back into the confusion of battle save one.

"Adorable how you and the lower caste of brothers tried to purchase angle on me hive minder. Focus fire… upon me? Smart. Such effort will not stop me. My will is undeniable, my anger unquenchable, my penchant for self-restraint loosed." Warsivious points his blade in Cassiel's only direction of retreat. Won't thou flee as well, Angel?" Warsivious taunts Cassiel. "It may extend your life by few moments longer than if you dare stand in defiance of me."

From then on, a simple mispronunciation of angle by Warsivious, misheard across the fields of Glayden bore the origin of the nomenclature, Angel. A name that Cassiel and all those who stand in opposition would become known by in the tongues of men.

Cassiel raises his sword and slowly grips both hands about the hilt standing ready for Warsivious' assault.

"No words then Cass? Says Warsivious.

"Let my silence speak volumes," says Cassiel.

Gabriel watches Warsivious and Cassiel from across the field. Suddenly the crack of a twig startles her to action of an impending attack. She ducks and rolls on the ground with a bolt just missing her. She springs up and places her blade through the chest of another fallen brother that had been swayed by false promises by a false king. Raphael, the youngest of the caste lands next to her and begins protecting her flank. Raphael's mask is splotched in rebel celestial blood as well as his hooded cloak and armor. He glances briefly to his left and watches as a rebel launches over his head, bringing a double-edged sword down on top of Gabriel.

"Gabe," Raphael shouts. He takes the swing with his blade hoping to make contact to throw the rebel off balance giving any advantage he can to his sister.

Gabriel turns and looks up in just enough time to see the blade descending. It's too late for her to dodge the attack. Raphael having missed his own blade attack to slow the threat follows through with his missed swing letting the blade strike ground. He quickly throws up his left wing. Clank! The armor that covers the thick bone of the top of his wing blocks the incoming blade attack meant for Gabriel. Raph using his blade as an anchor in the ground uses his position of strength to hold her would be murder in a saber lock. Raph stretches his wing upward raising the arms of his enemy high opening him up for attack. Taking advantage of his distraction a rebel rushes him. He swings for Raph's blade looking to untether it from the ground causing him to fall forward. Just before contact Raph raises his blade from the mud letting the attackers blade momentum carry him under Raph's. Having thrown his foe off balance, Raphael dispatches the head of his enemy.

Gabriel takes advantage of Raph's saber block uses it to impale her wide-open defensed attacker with a thrust of her blade up through his sternum. His impaled body slowly slides down her blade till they're face to face. Gabriel quickly ducks while holding the body in place as Raphael releases the winged saber lock and spins slicing the fallen's head from his body. Gabriel removes her blade and turns ready for another incoming attacker. As she waits, her eyes again wander toward Warsivious. This is the Demon she wants to end before anymore of her caste falls to him or herself for that matter. War is formidable. He's proven that today.

Gabriel notices how Warsivious revels in the violence, the chaos. To leave him alive will subject countless more to his unnerving hatred and insatiable bloodlust that Lucifer has set loose upon them all. Warsivious has moved universes alone upon his shoulders with nothing more than pure will. He is more than ethereal, more than celestial whether fallen or not. He's a malevolent force to be reckoned with.

Cassiel spins, using the water and mud from his cloak to buy him precious seconds. The muck slings from his cloak and into the eyes of War, blinding him. Cassiel is on him in an instant. The first strike is a straight on forward thrust which Warsivious easily parries before he spins left to avoid a follow up attack. Wiping the mud from his eyes, Warsivious advances toward Cassiel spinning until the two clashes their blades together. The two fight fast and fierce. Their movements are so fast that if one were to blink the other would surely lose their heads. Cassiel is at a disadvantage fighting one blade to Warsivious two. He has to substitute his gauntlets and armored wings to counter the majority of War's blows.

They score a series of cuts and slashes as they battle. In between the swinging of blades, they supplement a series of backhand punches, low midriff strikes and kicks which sends one of War's blades flipping into the distance. Warsivious spins into a roundhouse kick connecting and striking the mark. The kick buys him a second to pull another blade from an impaled motionless body that's strewn across the ground complementing his sword by an addition of one yet again. Cassiel feints backward from the kick. Warsivious rolls into a double-bladed scissor kick where he lands with a spin attack from his double-blades, followed up by an upward winged-strike. Cassiel, seeing the attack forthcoming, charges War. Already having momentum, he falls to his knees and slides underneath the attack. The blades of War slides across the metal plating of Cassiel's mask. His mask and helmet fall from his face in two pieces. As he recovers and leaps to his feet, he leans backward and thrusts his sword at Warsivious' exposed back. Before he connects the finishing blow, he's struck with a red bolt from the across the field of battle thrown from the hand of the Demonic fallen, Abbadon. The red bolt strikes Cassiel in the back of his armor plating.

He screams as the bolt thrusts him off toward the direction of a coterie of battling celestials.

"Damn!" Gabriel shouts as she watches Cassiel's missed chance. She adjusts her direction in the melee and continues fighting her way towards War.

Cassiel, after forcefully tumbling, flipping and sliding across the rain-soaked grounds of Glayden into a melee of battling celestials fights to his feet. He spits blood pissed he missed his chance to finish their greatest threat upon the field. He reaches around feeling the back underside where the bolt struck him. His hand is covered in blood when he retracts it to see the speed in which he's losing it. It's a muted color, meaning that it's not bright as an arterial bleed, and it's not dark signaling a severe internal injury. He spits more blood. He'll live for now least he loses his head. "Arrrgh!" the fool attacking him screams giving away his intent and position. Cassiel now hearing his approach throws his left shoulder back causing the attacker to fall forward. He steps up an impales him on his blade. Cassiel kicks the body free and blocks the attack of another incoming. It's clear, he can't get back to War, the fighting is too thick where he's landed. Someone will have to try to bring the titan to heel.

Warsivious nods to Abbadon in gratitude from sparing him a fatal blow from Cassiel's blade and turns his attention back to the surrounding battle at hand from other attacking celestials commanded by Michael. In all the melee Warsivious had momentarily lost sight of Lucifer. He uses his brief moment of respite to search for his king and finds him surrounded. War's wings expand wide and strikes the ground creating a negative flow of pressure pulling inward battling celestials on either side of the conflict as he takes flight. Dodging a hail storm of bolts and white-hot tipped arrows, He rolls and banks until he lands next to Lucifer taking up position to cover his back. Fighting is heavy.

"They think if they take our heads here, this will all end," says Lucifer.

"Then it behooves us brother to keep them where they are for the immediate foreseeable future, would you not agree?" Warsivious quips.

Laughing manically, the two interlock wings and fight back to back defending, countering and dispatching celestial after celestial. They fight as if their attackers have always been there enemies and never brothers. No quarter or surrender is given. Beneath Lucifer's mask unknown to Warsivious, his king sheds conflicted tears for the violence of action that he's inflicting upon his kin. His laugh is of the will to survive, his tears are for the madness that he's wrought, the destruction of his home and people, for the betrayal discovered of his once loved king.

There is a respite in the fighting long enough for a rebel celestial to see Raphael with his back turned trying to catch his breath. The Demon Verminesk uses the break and Raph's momentary rest to fire a bolt into the unsuspecting Raphael's back. Reveling in taking the decisive sniper shot to end one more of Michael's celestials, Verminesk thinks back on how many starnovas it has been leading up to this confrontation. The battle which was now at fruition had been all that he hoped and prayed for. He didn't care if the former king heard his thoughts. He merely wanted to end his tenure as a mindless hive drone for an ungrateful superior. The chance to break away and think for himself instead of a collective mind under the will of a self-professed Elohim was too great a chance not to take. The divide was a prayer come true, either he'd have his independent thoughts free of servitude or just simply not exist. Either way was fine with him, just so long he wasn't called servant.

Engaged in a side battle of his own with two fallen brothers, Michael sees the bolt that is meant for Raphael out of the corner of his eye. Michael slings his blade while simultaneously igniting a blue charged bolt to send emanating along the blade for maximum damage into the chest of one of his two attackers killing him. He follows it with a spin slash from his metallic armored wing's blade into the face of the second. The winged attack was not as on target. The rebel celestial blocks the incoming wing's blade attack. Michael reassess and quickly finds an opening in the defense of his foe never having lost sight of the bolt meant for Raph. Michael leaps left into the path of the bolt meant for Raph. He falls just behind the energy blast's tail which he grabs a hold of. Having taking control of the charge, Michael blades his body quickly turning himself into a catapult and redirects the energy heated bolt into the second attacker's chest ending the fight instantly.

Michael falls to his knees taking a moment of rest. As he looks at the field, he sees brothers enraged, clashing with all they have to best the other. He also witnesses countless of those that lay motionless to never move again. As he tries to get back to his feet, he finds that his hands tremble, his knees as well. As he watches one of the Demon ranks of rebel celestials remove the head of one of his celestial brothers, he can barely stomach it. These two that are engaged in combat aren't nameless soldiers. The Demon with the blood lust eyes was the celestial Shimprane. The one now lies lifeless was Grayten and loved to color the borealis' of vast universe's south and north poles. A scream from behind Michael quickly brings him back to the task at hand.

Having dispatched his enemies, Michael stands and turns toward where the bolt originated and lays eyes on Verminesk. In a beat of a human's heart, Michael stops three yards in front of Vermin. Michael expands his wings emanating a bright flash blinding him. Michael then takes a knee. Raphael leaps over Michael and bears down on Vermin while he's blinded... still having no idea how close he was to becoming lifeless himself if Michael would not have deflected that bolt meant for him. Before he can separate the head from Verminesk's body, Deathiliss tackles Raphael midair. Knocked off course, Raphael throws his blade in an attempt to finish Verminesk before being carried off by Deathiliss. The blade finds it target slicing through the mask and face of Verminesk. The Demon falls to his knees. His mask falls from his face as Gabriel runs past without even the thought of slowing down. She strikes Vermin in the face with the hilt of her sword, rendering him unconscious as she runs past. She will bleed her brothers if she must, but the thought of the brothers she's already slain this day has begun to weigh heavy on her. If she can save the life of one by rendering him unable to fight, but alive, was that not a better option? Gabriel continues running in the direction of Raphael and Deathiliss' trajectory. Michael sighs in exhaustion before engaging another attacker.

CHAPTER 5

SIBLINGS

Deathiliss and Raphael lands creating a crater in the mud. The two pull themselves from the crater. The rain pelts them unrelentingly washing away the viscous mud.

"Alas, young one, it appears that it will be I that brings your omega." Deathiliss slams his staff's bottom on the ground. A clicking sound unlatches and springs a blade from it turning it into a scythe.

Once his scythe locks into place he swings it down hard to cleave the young celestial. Raphael blocks the attack with his left wing glancing the blow into the thick mud while using the left to sweeps Deathiliss' legs. The maneuver was sound, Deathiliss falls backward, but uses his wings to kickstand him back to his feet.

Seizing the moment, using his wings to propel him, Raphael runs toward Deathiliss, pulling a blade from the body of a motionless Demon that has fallen in battle. Deathiliss grips his scythe, waiting the incoming attack. "Bring it!" Deathiliss yells. The two collide in a series of blows, counters and blocks. Deathiliss slices the right side of Raphael's torso and then disarms him while simultaneously using the bottom of his scythe to sweep his legs flipping him on his back, leaving him face up on the ground. Deathiliss moves to finish Raphael, but at the last second before contact, he stops himself. He looks into the eyes of Raphael and knows instantly that he'd be given up all that he was. During the day's deadly events, he hasn't taken one life. Sure, he's injured and he's maimed, but he's laid no one motionless. Looking at his defenseless brother lying face up with his arms out in surrender, it strikes him in that second that Lucifer had possibly led him astray. Deathiliss starts to drop his killing blow slowly when he's is knocked over by another Demon that had been thrown into him by Metatron.

Metatron lands over top of Raphael and pulls him up by his chest plate. He hands Raphael's weapon back to him and slaps him on his back. Raphael gives a quick nod in thanks to Metatron while holding his side, wincing in pain. Metatron pulls his little brother close and then playfully pushes him away. "It seems you have incurred a scratch. I fear you may fall to darkness brother and lay as lifeless as the others from such a minor wound." Metatron says laughing. Once I dispatch this traderous brother of ours, must I fight at your side to save you the whole of this day?" taunts Metatron. He pulls Raphael in close again and hugs him around the neck kissing his forehead. Raphael accepts his sword. Metatron then playfully pushes his away.

"I shall thank you when I feel you have done something deeming of it," Raphael says jokingly. "Couldn't you tell, I had him right where I needed him?"

"No! I couldn't tell" Metatron replied. He winks at Raph. "Now, let us be about the business at hand.

Deathiliss pushes the arrow-filled Demon off of him. He stands up and faces Metatron and Raphael. A screeching howl draws his attention and causes him to turn. The Demon, Abbadon, dispatches an angel that was silently walking up behind Deathiliss by slicing him in half. As the body falls into two separate halves, Abbadon steps over them and stands next to Deathiliss.

"Which one's head do you want?" Abbadon says as he twirls his sword by its hilt in anticipation.

Deathiliss wasn't sure if should have ever broken the faith, but he is sure this is wrong. His only thought is that he should have remained loyal to the crown. However, for better or worse, either a victorious ascension or a failed defeat followed by disgrace he's chosen his side.

"I'll take Raphael's," he answers. What else could he have said? He's committed to the choice he's made. If he has any hope of survival now, he must see his commander Lucifer ascend. The very beating of his heart and existence is tied to it.

Metatron and Raphael look at each other, and then to their rivals. They take a there battle stance in preparation of yet another coming conflict.

Raphael holds his bade inches in front of his face saluting his enemies. "I've never had a quarrel with thou, Abbadon. For all that is holy, we played in these fields. You'd now run them black with your own kinsmen blood?"

Abbadon moves slowly sizing his opponent. "I would. Do not presume to think that I'm torn in these matters."

Raphael could not help but ask why, it was just to vexing. "Why Abbadon? Why turn against us? We were all brothers, friends even!"

"I was promised a seat high in the council. I would no longer sing praises, but have them sung to me. I thought, serve in Heaven always a servant or take a chance to rule it. Think about young one. A life of servitude, never free to make your own choice in matters versus complete autonomy."

"Then it appears brother that thou have chosen ill of the two," Metatron interrupts.

Raphael starts to spin his blade. "I shall have thou head before you sit upon any throne on this plain existence or any other."

"We will ascend over the corpses of all of you that stand in opposition," Abbadon says pointing his blade at Raph.

The four runs towards each other.

Michael spins, decapitating another Demon's head from his body. When the body falls, Lucifer steps over it slowly approaching Michael.

"I will ascend, brother, with you at my side or beneath my boot."

Michael slowly twirling his sword as he back up watches Lucifer walk towards him. "Ascend?... no! You will fall this day to never rise again. Never will you cause such devastation on this plain nor any other of such magnitude. You're are a blight upon all that lives."

Warsivious appears suddenly behind Michael in an attempt to ambush him. He swings his blades to decapitate him. Clang! Gabriel's sword blocks the killing blow's attempt. Out of breath, covered in rain, mud and splotches of blood, she fought her way through many, she fought her way through exhaustion all to do what she promised, to be Michael's second. Warsivious' unexpected impediment rattles the bones of his arm as his blade only finds metal. He tries to force his way through Gabriel, but she held enough strength in reserve to stay War's blade and not give any ground. She shoves her sword which is blocking the attack forward causing the hilt to strike Warsivious in his face pushing him backward in blinding pain. Trusting his sister and hearing the commotion behind him, Michael never turns his gaze from Lucifer. Gabriel and Warsivious, together enact a deadly ballet of swordsmanship in the shadow of a would-be king and dutiful captain.

Michael's armor drips mud darkened water as the rain rinses his battle-hardened facade clean. His tunic is stained with blood of De' Mons. His countenance is like everyone else that engaged in warfare this day. He stares at Lucifer deciding how best to attack a caste one De'- Mon who holds the highest rank of Seraphim. He grimaces noticing that Lucifer's armor although altered resembles Michael's own. A chest plate that generates a helmet and mask at will, shoulder pads that carry their rank in the De' Monic order, his gauntlets have celestial glyphs and sigils etched into them that glows a fire reddish orange, a sash around the waist as the wind whips it about, and his boots are knee high that have and insignia on the back of his heels with glyphs underneath that reads, *"Except no truth but what you seek."* Complete contrast to Michael's which read, *Grounded in Truth.*

Lucifer slowly pulls off his cloak. His celestial brightness has faded dim. No longer does he shine as bright as Michael. He grabs his hilt two handed and raises into a high guard. Lucifer launches toward Michael. The two collide with a force that could almost rival the bang of creation, their clashing swords exploding in a blinding light as white hot Razine Star ore ignite upon touch.

As they struggle in a saber lock for dominance Lucifer utters, "Thou has chosen underneath the heel of my boot, then."

CHAPTER 6

RECOMPENSE

"What I have done is far from treason. I have set the old system to burn with but a spark ignited by the thought of free will. A flame that rose from a gift given to mortals but denied us. A flame that's bound to spread, setting the celestial realm ablaze. Through my actions and those of my true brothers on the fields of Glayden, I shall be forever remembered.

I am the inevitability of a society that has gone amiss. I am the result of broken policies of a failed rulership that looks to be corrected. When others feel as I, that there is no stopping this revolution. When they feel the chain of events that lead to my eventual calling it is then that those currently in power will be called treasonous. I will become liberator to boundless masses that had no will but of another. When I approach to turn minds, you will know I am near, fore my quake is thunderous and will rattle the very grounds of whatever dissident patch of dirt you call home. You will see me coming, you will bear witness to the rise of War."

Quote ~Warsivious

CHASM HALL, IAYHOTEN HEAVEN

Raphael runs through the double doors entering into Chasm Hall. The hall is the ultimate high court of the golden trimmed White City of Iayhoten. The city is the center of Jacintian realm. The capital of the Heavens. As Raph enters the hall, he kneels to one knee in reverence to Elohim. After giving prayer he continues walking through the hall with haste and purpose. Its construction is blaring to the eyes as it was only created one starnova ago. As he walks through the adjoining halls in the behemoth maze he begins to realize its sheer magnitude. He didn't understand its purpose at first when he seen the Powers Corps planning its construction, but now with the fall of man, the treachery of Lucifer, its creation was necessary. It's where the inevitably of all forms of humanity will come to be adjudicated. Rightly so, the crimes that Lucifer committed deserved an answer in proportion to the magnitude of the act. Raph taken back by the awe, the sheer beauty and immenseness of the interior's walls and columns has no ill will for the Powers Corps of celestials that were not in attendance of the battle. This endeavor was definitely a priority that needed to be attended too.

The celestial order of Powers indeed has been busy. Raph quickens his pace passing the amazing spectacle of the whitest stone marble he's ever seen with just as blinding golden trim that flows through the crown molding like a miniature slow-moving stream. His pace picks up to a moderate trot, he has to be in place for the trial to begin.

As Raph's metallic boots clack hard against the floor his attention is drawn to the detail of the masterpiece that he's trotting across. As he looks down his eyes are met with a visual display of the construction of the floors. Iayhoten is known for having more beauty than any other realm created and even through all of the wonders which he's seen he's still finds that he can be enamored by something as simple as floors which are made up of enormous smooth white marble stones bonded together by a diamond translucent liquid that flows similar to a fast running river under glass. The liquid diamond runs between the squared marble stones. As someone steps on one of the squares and it depresses, the liquid diamond changes color.

Raph nods his head in amazement at what the Powers Caste can create. Hearing the Powers working above him Raph attention is drawn upward. He witnesses another site that slows him from his trot. The spectacle captured him and held his gaze for no other reason than its sheer originality. The ceiling is visible, but it's an illusion, the height of the ceiling adjust as the need arises. The celling will infinitely rise towards infinity as the court is filled with spectators and witnesses. There are balconies upon balconies laid with an uncountable number of chairs that he assumes are for witnesses to occupy in the days of creation's ultimate adjudication. All bills come due as Lucifer use to say when he was a Seraphim. Those were days long before he joined the once elite ranks of the De-Mon. What humans aptly renamed, Demon.

Raphael finally finds the doors to the hall of judgment. Still in his battle armor from the preceding battle he enters into the great court. He washed as much blood and mud off that he could, but he still looked very much damaged and weary. His hair was matted to the left side and still damp from the downpour.

Raphael enters the main floor of adjudication. Trial is moments away and the courtroom itself is far from completion. The Choiretic caste still actively work the construction of the room under the supervision of two Power Corps caste mates. The roof and seated witness sections appear for the most part completed. Most of the work being done now looks to be purely cosmetic. Portions of the court not under construction by the Powers is the throne judgment circular area. The Bench of Judgment is been completed. In uniformity with the other great spectacles, the seat of judgment is marble that has been embedded and adorned with gold, black diamonds, and purple colored ivory in its design. Above the Bench of Judgment sits a mighty white thrown created from the same liquid translucent diamond liquid that flows between the marble floors. The thrown sits ensconced at the head of the court behind the bench of ultimate adjudication that is second to nothing.

Raph takes his place and position of dual responsibilities as an usher and Sargent at Arms within the court. He watches as his older brother Uriel enters into the court from an entrance behind the Elohim's throne. Uriel holds a large scroll in his hands as he stands to the right of the Bench of Adjudication. He unrolls the scroll and reads it intently to himself. He makes corrections with his fine tipped quill here and there on the papyrus and would look down whispering to Gabriel who was seated below him at the Desk of Scribes on the ground level of the court. Gabriel look to be whispering back proper wording perhaps as they adjust the charges to fit crimes levelled against the mass traitorous usurpers. They look to have come to an accord. Gabriel nods that she's ready to record. Uriel then rerolls the scroll and looks to Raphael, Azrael, Zadkiel and Cassiel. He nods particularly at Raph. "Bring forth the accused," he says.

Millions upon millions of fallen De' Mons are brought into the court by scores of the Choiretic caste of angels. The accused are shackled around their necks, their hands are bound behind their backs and encased in onyx binds. Their feet are also bound giving them only enough room to shuffle step. Just as the court reaches capacity, its illusionary construction extends and enlarges to accommodate all in attendance. Although expanded for accommodation, all within its confines can hear and see as if they have a front row seats at the head of the court.

A few hundred thousand of Michael's celestials stands guard. At the head of all the accused stands Lucifer and his Generals; Warsivious, Deathiliss Abbadon, Pestenanant, Wrath, Crucifixinate and Canceranian. Uriel waves his right hands downward. As if the shackles are magnetic, they pull the rear shackled affixed hands of the accused downward, interlocking with the bonds around their ankles. As the locks connect the demonic soldiers and general alike are contorted in such a fashion including Lucifer that they all fall to their knees and are forced to look straight up.

From his kneeling position, Lucifer looks up in utter defiance his scowl is intended for the whole of the court. Unlike the rest, he doesn't struggle against the large onyx- chains. Lucifer knows that he kneels, not out of subjugation and that suits him as a victory. The remaining fallen Demonic look to the cool demeanor of their destined to be king. They observe his unshaken facade and do their best to imitate his strength.

Prior to their entry, they were stripped of their celestial clothing. As they kneel, they have been stripped of their armor, stripped of identifying marks that once signified them as citizens of Heaven and all her realms. The majority are bruised, broken and bleeding from the preceding battle on the fields of Glayden. Their shame is not yet completed. All the accused traitors are further stripped of their entitlement, rank and status that they once held within the celestial order. No longer celestial, no longer De' Mon. They are simply low as the humans named them, Demons.

Michael walks to the front and stands as bailiff within the circular ring of Judgment next to the four who have been chosen to answer to the charge of the many. Two celestials glide and hover above Michael and the accused. Between them they carry a large rod that runs the entire length of the hall. The two drop the rod, and it falls into place between the two massive rows of the accused. They were marched into the court in two columns for this very reason. The rods fall into place locking magnetically to the center line of the shackles locking them into place on the translucent marble floors of Chasm Hall.

Michael steps on the rod, ensuring that it locks the chains in place. He aims to make sure that for the length of the proceeding they will remain bound, not leaving any chance of further uprising, especially in the main city. The fact that Michael can hold them all to ground is testament to the power that he himself wields.

Satisfied that the prisoners have been secured, he nods to Uriel to proceed. Lucifer, forced to look upward can only adjust his eyes to look at Michael. Although awkward he stares Michael in the eyes and then spits in disgust. "You are the traitor here, Michael. It is you that have broken not only the law of loyalty, but of brotherhood."

Standing above Lucifer, he draws his blade and places its tip just below Lucifer's chin. His bindings and those of his generals in the circle with him are giving reprieve so that they can look forward. As soon as Lucifer's able to look forward, he rolls his neck crackling the vertebrae for relief. With the tip of his blade, Michael raises Lucifer's chin so that he can look him in the eye again.

Both Michael and Lucifer bare wounds of their fight that brought them to present. Michael's left eye is still swollen; a laceration sits to the left of his forehead. His nose still drips blood. He can taste the iron as it runs past his lips. His left arm is mold casted in dark blue water that sits as still as ice yet its innards flows freely. Lucifer is no better condition. He's just as beaten.

Michael digs the tip of his blade into Lucifer's chin. "I did not hear what your slanderous tongue said, Morning Star. Say it again so that I may remove and place it closer to my ear to be sure I can hear the vile stanza you spew. Iayhoten burns even now for your atrocities. Glayden lies in ruins, as well as Jacintian and Pantheon. Your jealousy would see us all at an end. So, no, brother, the only traitor that lies within our midst is you. Sadness of it all, is that your arrogance won't even let you see it. Were you not there? Did you not see our brother Haradades fall? What about Clebradox, remember him? We all together slung the Crystalline Star Cluster together. Shall I continue on with more names?"

"I know them all as well and mourn them as we all do." Lucifer quickly turns his neck right flicking strands of his matted hair out of his face. "What happened to them was regrettable. It was a however a necessary sacrifice to save the majority of you who are still blind."

Millions of Iayhoten's citizens file into the seats to bear witness of what was coming to those for the atrocities committed in outskirts of their holy city. The citizenry is made up of other celestial beings that were created aside from the high-class celestial order. The citizenry are the everyday beings that exist to not only serve Elohim, but exist to populate the heavens. As in Heaven as on Earth is what they say. Citizens are a mixed diverse crew of creatures, from humanoids to other forms that would be looked upon as alien and more creature like. Some are gaseous entities others are water based aquatic life forms that are able to exist outside of water.

Trumpets sound from the choir of angels.

Uriel clasps his hands behind his back and inhales a mighty wind. He exhales with the force of a hurricane. "The Lord Elohim, Iehovah, is in this holy temple. Let all the Heavens and creations keep silence before him."

Chasm Hall is already brightly lit, but it illuminates immensely when a being engulfed by purest of white light enters into the chamber. Elohim's light permeates throughout every molecule of his superlative celestial body so much so, that no entity but the celestials may look directly upon Him. As Elohim, creator of all that comes to pass walks into the chamber, celestials and witnesses alike start to sing his praise of the many triumphs that he'd overcome to reach the prosperity where they are now. They at once fall to a knee. Some feel that they can't prostrate themselves enough. Iehovah nods in acknowledgement of those that honor him and takes his place on the throne.

Uriel inhales another breath and again exhales with a thunderous voice, "The son and prince of the Lord Elohim has entered into his holy temple, and may all reserve and respect be given to the one future king, Yeshua. May all that were created keep silent before him."

As Iehovah sits, another translucent liquid diamond throne transfigures to the left of the main throne. Yeshua enters into the chamber. The light which permeates from his body is dimmer than the Most High's by a modicum. All are able to look upon the son. His poise, grace and mannerisms along with his looks are simply beautiful to behold. To look upon the future king is to see the father as he used to be before the weight of crown. The hue of his skin is a golden bronze. His face has soft features which makes him appear relatable. He has a stoic look, but it's tempered with compassion and a genuine love for all things that draw breath, but a love that would be protected by a show of strength if he must. The prince is clothed in his regalia of judgment as a second sight of eyes to his father.

Yeshua looks to his father, then nods to Uriel in a simple gesture of thanks for the introduction. Yeshua glances at Michael.

Acknowledging the eye contact, Michael looks down towards Lucifer. "At the command... my prince, I will dispatch this Satan for all time," Michael says, ready to behead the leader of the fallen order of De' Mon celestials, whose betrayal and subsequent deflection lead too many being misled.

The witnesses of Heaven look on. Murmurs can be heard throughout the hall. Iehovah listens to them intently all while reading the eyes of those that dare not speak or pass judgment verbally. As he does, he overhears that *sin must be met with a swift just punishment.* He also hears the tears of forgiveness that streams down some of the faces of the citizens whose families were lost in the melee or to the betrayal. Elohim also listens to the celestial brothers of the accused. As he listens, he hears one phrase that gives him pause. He hears the thought of a single angel, Zadkiel. He listens closely and hears his boisterous thoughts. The words resonate with the king and he listens to them over and over again in his mind. He hears, *I can't help but think the Morning Star speaks truth. Maybe his way was that of a king. Convenient that the Most High would silence him. What if I were to have a thought independent of the king? Would I be stamped out to for evolving?*

Iehovah hears the doubt, a doubt that if not handled correctly could fester and undo all that he's built and created to rot.

Michael nudges Lucifer's head up by the chin with the tip of his blade a little higher. As Iehovah thinks about Zadkiel's words.

"You have committed the most egregious of atrocities Lucifer. You who was loved most among us all. You who were favored by the king. Oh, how you have fallen, son of morning. You, who were giving more than any us, but was still found wanting. You, who above all were given power and position in the Garden of Eden over the new prospering additional domain of men. You, who were to bridge humanity to ensure they thrive. You betrayed such status, such trust, to what end?"

Gabriel feverishly scribes every word spoken into record within a large illuminating book. She scribes in a sloppily but legible glyph that shows her novice ability to the task as she's recently had to learn the skill. All the motionless bodies have yet to be tallied, but the former scribe is missing and believed to have been lost in the battle for Glayden. The same scribe that previously created all the books that fill the once thought infinite shelves of recording.

As Uriel speaks, Gabriel's hand moves just as fast capturing every syllable even down to syntax for posterity. "And in thouest recklessness, you've taken legions of our brothers astray. Brothers who trusted thine judgment and counsel, because of your high position." Uriel says with tempered anger, but it's buried in compassion. It's reproving done from a stance of immense love.

Lucifer turns from Michael blade tip and spits more black blood on the floor of the court and smiles. "Get on with this unjust travesty."

"Get on with it, Uriel," Michael says, prompting him to continue the charges.

Uriel nods in acknowledgement producing a scroll of charges. He unrolls the scroll. "You are charged with sin against the most high, YHWH. You are further charged with sin against human and celestial kind. You are charged with genocide against an entire species. You are charged with treason, You ar---"

Lucifer laughs interrupting Uriel. "Humankind? What are the mortals, but constricted dust that's been given consciousness? They are subpar simple-minded Neanderthals; animals birthed to be subjugated to an expanding ego, an ego so huge that it even cups the vastness of the Sadohedranicverse. Lucifer looks to Iehovah. "You put them before us... Your first creations. But, then again, we aren't the first are we your highness? And they label me Satan... You love them before us? Before me! We are the first... or so we were led to believe. We are of you, or so I thought." Lucifer looks to everyone in the hall. His eyes plead with the masses to wake up to the injustice that has been committed "Do any of you that fill this court ever stop to think that they were created lower than us? Why is that? Simple. He created them to be ruled and subjugated, as we were created to be subjugated to him as well. I have charges of my own Uriel. I charge our fallible king with arrogance and ignorance. He knew that there would be a time that we would want to thrive and have other ambitions and yearnings other than that of slave. And if, the all-knowing powerful king did not take that into consideration, then ignominy on him and the house of Hovah." But… then again, maybe he did know that we'd reach a point of an evolutionary tipping scale. He knew we'd evolved and that is why he's placed secured measure to ensure his house's reign for---"

Michael uses his blade again to turn Lucifer's head and lift his chin up to try to quiet him. The captain looks back towards his king waiting for the command to end this. Michael releases the chin of Lucifer and draws his sword back with both hands awaiting to strike as executioner. Anger is the crank that draws his arm ready. Love of his brothers and sister is the lever that will release his arm. *Lucifer is poison.* Michael couldn't see it before the battle, but it's clear to him now as the liquid diamond of Elohim's throne.

"Stay your hand, Arch of my angels!" Iehovah commands. That is what Warsivious called Cassiel on the fields of Glayden wasn't it? I like it. I think an appropriate change of nomenclature is needed for further distinguishment. There has been a break in the celestials and I believe that it can never again be what it was. We have strayed far from the intended path that I set us upon so long ago." Iehovah leans forward in his throne. "You, Michael who never wanted this position became an Arch this day. A center stone that all of the remaining faithful celestials will rest upon in time to come. My arch, stay your hand a moment longer! I want to hear this. I want to hear what Morning Star has to say. We've all gone through a great many of things for him to speak his ideal. I will have him share it for all to hear. He has challenged my sovereignty, my right claim to the rule. Let him speak."

"My Lord! Surely not," Michael says abruptly." He is charismatic, his words are vile poison. For him to speak is to release an obnoxious ploom that if allowed to linger will sicken all within its radius.

"Let him speak. I will allow it."

Knowing that Lucifer shouldn't be allowed to wield his tongue for the lacerations it has already shown to cause, the captain acquiesces and obeys. Michael sheathes his blade. He thinks of protesting his position more to the king that Satan should not be allowed to utter not one more word. However, the king has spoken, he must obey.

Lucifer winks at Michael and continues, he looks around placating to those that sit in judgment "I sit here bound, brothers," He looks at Gabriel. "And sister. My fault is that my solution to rule has challenged the Most High's sovereignty." Lucifer cackles. "My solution is absolute. I have proven him fallible and for that I am vanquished. Let this be seen and written in the books of record! Let it show the Master Builder Fatetanen had no sway over I, Lucifer."

Lucifer looks to Gabriel. "Do you hear me messenger? Sorry, I error, I meant scribe. So, I sayeth, so let it be written... right? Take sight brothers, citizens, and witnesses of my beloved realm, see what happens to those who evolve to speak of aspiring to the liking of their father and want to be better. Am I not my father's son also? I may not be a prince of royal blood lineage as Yeshua, but I, too, have a birthright. I, too, am entitled as I feel we all are; all of us who built his heavens, kept his law, conquered his enemies, and subjugated the very forces of nature before him are entitled."

The crowds spectating murmur throughout the great hall of judgment. The De' Mons cheer Lucifer's defiant words. Even some angels can't help but nod in agreement. Lucifer tries to look directly into the eyes of Iehovah to show his adversity and defiance, but he can't. Even as he squints, he can no longer look upon his glorious countenance as the garments that have been made gives off an illumination brighter than a new born star.

Taken aback by Lucifer's plea. Iehovah looks towards Uriel and waves him over to the throne for a brief silent conference. Michael turns back and stares at Lucifer intently with the disappointment of a younger brother watching the old fall from grace.

Lucifer meets Michael's gaze. "You look at me as if I speak ill, brother. I speak truth. He raised us in his image, and then you put me down when I ask for more. When I ask to become him, when I look to take on his mantle. I look to take it, to seize it before he relegates us all to destruction."

Michael kneels leaning in close to Lucifer so any exchange of words will remain between them. Michael intently returning his gaze. "But, you were given more. You were given station that not even the prince was given. You were the bridge between our worlds with a new breed of creation that was to marvel all that was before them. You were the first and only caretaker of humanity. But that wasn't good enough for you, was it?

"No, it was not! I wanted more. I want it all," Lucifer says without a moment's hesitation.

Michael searches Lucifer's eyes. He looks for his brother. He looks for the one who once flew over the throne singing praises in a voice that assisted the numerous expanding universe's suns in rising. But he does not see that Celestial anymore. Instead, he sees De' Mon. A word that once meant an immaculate status, but has since been given a new origination with Adam in the garden after he was undone by this serpent's appearance. He cursed Lucifer and called him Demon, a simple slip of the tongue, but just right for the nomenclature of Satan and his coterie.

When Tanen, better known as Adam, under mortal tongue asked its name, the quadruped-scaled reptile replied my name is unimportant call me De' Mon. Lucifer could not have known that his lie would follow him later to be the title of his fallen that he separated from the celestial order.

As Michael side bars with Lucifer, Uriel nods his head continuously at what Elohim is speaking to him in whispers about. When finished, he refocuses his attention on Lucifer and sits silently judging him. Uriel bows before Elohim then rerolls the scroll before walking over to Gabriel quickly relaying the words just spoken by Elohim to him.

Lucifer listening to Michael and appeasing him in kind with conversation takes a side note as he watches the court meander about in slight confusion. His smirk reaches a full zenith smile that would rival the most brilliant sunrise at the fact that Iehovah is whispering.

"Find the words they speak interesting slander?" Michael whispers.

Lucifer nods his head in the direction of the scribe and herald. "Look at them, brother. They are lost. Look at their faces, there will be no verdict rendered this day. His tender mercy shall abide unto his own undoing."

Michael looks over at his brother and sister wondering why they hesitate. *Is Lucifer right? There's so much evidence. It's clear he's guilty. Why won't they punish him and be done with this?*

Michael feels Lucifer shifting, trying to find comfort in his subjugated position. Being so close to him he hears the low laugh escape's the fallen celestial's lips. Michael leans in a bit closer. Pissed he's even able to have a second of glee after the destruction and division he has caused.

"You see Michael," Lucifer says, "the most high is one of mercy... or so he'd like us all to believe. It's like I told you on the steps of the palace h---"

The strike is quick and fierce. The back hand of Michael sends Lucifer face snapping to the right. It draws no blood, but it smarts.

"He said stay my hand when it held a blade. I hold no blade. You attempt to tell that lie again and you and I will again be bound together fore I will not stop next time I lay hand to you. You will be just as motionless as the bodies they still pull from the field when I have taken my fill." Michael says loudly. He stands raising both his hands in surrender. "Sorry my king, a sibling debt that had to be repaid before he feels the swiftness of your justice."

"Not to mention it made Michael feel a bit joyous didn't it? Lucifer added.

Elohim slides all the way back into his throne and grasps both armrests. He stares at Lucifer.

Lucifer nods for Michael to draw closer again. He takes a knee beside Lucifer a second time and leans in close.

"As I was saying Michael, he's a teacher who has just been challenged in his equation of life. If he silences me, he loses the heavens to doubt and corruption. He will not be able to lead you all to a willing slaughter; sin will run rampant turning the gold streets red. If he allows me to prove my anti equation to his, he keeps the Heavens, but runs the risk of my human solution being proven right. I will ascend, brother. A day will cometh when you will take a knee to me in subjugation and give gratuitous thanks. It is inevitable! Our roles shall surely be reversed. There will come a day when you kneel before I, accept I will not wish that of you."

Michael feels his blood pulsing through his veins harder and faster. The smugness on Lucifer's face is infuriating. His irises burn a dark shade of red, he grips the hilt of sword and envisions himself wielding it leaving Lucifer's head rolling on the floor. It's then that he feels it. He feels that he's not the automaton that he felt him and his kin were. Michael now knows how Lucifer broke the will and faith of being loyal subject to Iehovah. It was the rage, the rage of always knowing that he would never excel above his already exalted and revered station. The rage that he now feels for Lucifer even being allowed to have remained with breath this long has empowered Michael himself to think of defying the will and trusted faith of Elohim to stay his blade. If he persists in that rage, if he acquiesces in the slightest then he has become Lucifer himself.

Michael eyes turn a lighter shade of red as he releases the hilt of his sword. There is but one king that he will ever kneel before and it won't be to this false king, this traitor, not here nor any time to come.

Michael glances over to the throne and feels a moment of ill-repute as he catches eyes with Elohim just looking silently at him.

Lucifer just keeps smiling at Michael with a smugness that inaudibly and continuously infuriates him.

Frustrated, Michael steps on Lucifer's shackles that binds around his waist causing him to hunch backward in pain. "Until that day of myth you speak of when all bow, that day will only occur after a battle as which all of creation has never witnessed, where all that oppose lay waste, but this day is not that day, Satan! Today, you bow before Elohim."

Lucifer raises his head again and watches as Uriel finishes with Gabriel and walks to the herald's circle. The court falls completely silent.

Uriel voice carries throughout the heavens so that every citizen may hear.

"The Most High's judgment is as follows. Lucifer charges that have been previously read will remain in charge. The Most High is in control of all that he's created and understands the love of a father from a son. In that breath, he accepts the thinking which led Lucifer to contest his sovereignty."

Uriel points to Lucifer. "The temporary sentence is banishment from the realms of the Most High. You are never to again place your visage into the capital of Jacintian, City of Iayhoten or any other realm deemed under the authority or protection of the Heavens until a time of summons which will occur at the end of this current system which has been written. Judgment will be withheld forthwith until the end of days of man. Lucifer will further be set loose and cast down to the world of men, you will be cast down to where your treachery first shown, when unlawfully and willfully you had stolen the deed and title from the mortal custodian Tanis, Adam in common tongue and the rest of his bloodline."

Uriel's voice breaks. It's hard for him to finish as he thinks past the recent abominations that Lucifer is responsible for. Uriel voice cracks as his eyes water up at the fact that his older brother first above all of his kind will be expelled. No longer will he see him in the halls of the Celestial Spire nor gliding across the Sehateen Merritverse, where Uriel was currently called from for the gathering conclave that recently led to the wanton destruction and division of heaven. Lucifer will be simply nonexistent in the day to day life of the realm where he has always been such a staple. Even more disheartening is, the next time they meet after the day's events, they will be enemies.

Uriel steels himself and continues. "You will be given a set forth time only known to the Elohim to prove what you have deemed the ruling solution. When this short time has ended, you will be summoned to re-appear for subsequent judgment before this high court... These are the words and will of our King Iehovah... Morning Star, brother, saint who has now become known as slanderer and sinner. You and your fallen caste are to be cast down immediately without any unnecessary due delay!"

Uriel finishes the rest with conviction. "When you re-appear for the final judgment, you will be given over to the agent Death where you will be escorted and forever scorched and set to burn in darkness with all those that have committed sin against Elohim and remained unrepentant. The punishment is to last infinite upon infinity."

Lucifer just stares at Uriel unflinching.

Uriel returns his gaze unmoved as well. "Fret not, dimming star. You shall not be alone for your fallen brothers will reign with you and share in your sentence. This is the final ruling of Elohim." Uriel walks down to Lucifer and looks him in the face. "Woe to the world of men fore you have been cast down to them. No longer will they know peace fore you have robbed them of it."

Lucifer is unfazed by the conviction. He shows no emotion. His eyes remain stagnant in the color gray. The weight of the stayed judgment is quietly resonating through him. The weight of the punishment gives his body gravity that he could not account for. He tries to move his legs. No matter how hard he tries they won't seem to cooperate. For the briefest of moments, he can't think past the fact that he's never lived without the Heavenly realms. It has always been his home. Fear and confusion sets in milliseconds later at the fact that he's been giving what he's wanted. Even more sobering, is the fact that all those that believed in him enough to follow him to this point were now forever dependent upon him and his choices, irrevocably tied to his fate.

His uncertainty however brief and terrifying does not break through his stern facade. He simply continues giving the appearance of remaining unfazed.

Lucifer glances at Michael. "Come with me, brother! Take a leap of faith and trust that I will not steer you astray as you believe I have the others. There are forces at work here that Elohim moves for his sole benefit while blinding others. You have been led astray and deceived, you simply cannot see it out of blind loyalty... My way is just. If you but take a step back you will see him as I do."

Michael could not believe Lucifer's ego. *Even being banished from the heavens he has the gall to invite me? Truly a demon's hubris knows no bounds.*

Michael stares at Lucifer. As he does, his eyes turn from the shade of red to gray matching his brothers. In that moment there is nothing more that he wants to do then leave with his older brother. Since Michael's Caste's creation he had followed his older brother Lucifer around. They were inseparable once and thought would be for all time. His mind wanders back to one of many thoughts where he found happiness with his brother.

Two Hundred Thousand Years Prior to the Trial of Glayden

Within the expanse of the most outer reaches of the dark void of space, the Seraphim Lucifer is overseeing the new construction of the Velix Galaxy. With the construction complete of the one-hundred-twentieth solar system within that particular galaxy of stars and planets, he calls in the Powers Corps of celestials to cement the rotational spin of the stars and planets. It's a guilty pleasure he must admit to watch them further ignite the rolling immense amount of dark matter and energy to bind them all.

Lucifer lands on the innermost yet to be named planet which has been unaffected by a recently collapsed star or so he though. The planet which has formed near a neighboring black hole planet's vegetation and immense forestry constantly remains pulled to the left. It looks as if the entire planet was built on a slant. Although it sits just outside the gravitational pull of the singularity, it's affected by its pull.

This won't do, Acais had to have measured incorrectly. Lucifer thought to himself, looking at the mild slant of trees and leaning mountains he turns his head to account for the slant. Lucifer sighs and pulls a quill from his sleeve and begins marking equations on thin air. The wind solidifies instantly giving him hard canvass. Within minutes, thin strokes of orange flame blaze brightly on air. Believing he's found the correct angle of approach to set gravity to task, The Morning Star plants his feet into the dirt by grinding them side to side making himself into anchor. Extending both of his arms to the right, Lucifer grabs the very air itself. A grappling cable appears solidified and very much tangible. He begins to pull. His arms tense and muscles contract as he bends the winds in an attempt to pull the swayed foliage and rocky terrain of the planet erect. As the sway is slowly corrected, he starts to lose his grip. Lucifer's feet become unmoored. The gravitational sway starts to pull away from him again and sway back to the left. As he enters the verge of losing his grip, he hears the unmistakable sound of feet behind him.

"Pull, damn you!" Michael says as he grabs the air as well. "Don't have me do all the work." Michael anchors in behind Lucifer and pulls with all his might, combining their brute force. "Come, Morning Star... together then."

"Together, Lucifer says in agreement."

Both of the brothers pull in unison. With the additional help, Lucifer's feet start to sink back into the footsteps that he previously had carved out for himself. As they continuously pull, they rectify the planet's gravitational spin in a little under sixty human years.

The two brothers release their grips and falls backward with Lucifer landing on top of Michael. The two find themselves breathing heavy and exhausted from the exertion. Lucifer looks back at Michael making eye contact. The eye contact is quickly followed by a small quick outburst of laughter that Michael tried to hold in. His poor attempt causes them both to burst into laughter. As always, with the laughter of siblings comes the mocking.

"'Pull, damn you'!" Lucifer says clinching his fist imitating Michael.

Michael laughs hysterically. "You weren't pulling."

"Then just what was I doing before your arrival then?"

"That's what I came to see," Michael rebuts. "And I find you playing around, jumping rope."

The two celestial's intense cackling slowly comes to an end. Lucifer uses his wings and pushes himself to his feet. He then turns and reaches a hand down and pulls Michael to his.

Lucifer looks at the corrected trees that now reach erect into the purple skies. "It seems the Master Builder may have been off by about a smidgen."

Michael smirks at Lucifer. "Are you going to tell him that?"

The two just stare at each other for a few seconds and then again burst out into laughter.

"I didn't think you would." Michael laughs.

"It would break his heart if I did. Come let us see how the Powers are faring. Maybe they're doing much better than us.

Lucifer tags Michael on the arms and then rockets away into the air. He rapidly achieves escape velocity and enters the void of space. Michael is quickly on his heels.

Lucifer yells back towards Michael over the loud solar winds. "Let's take the Solararis hole, we'll arrive faster."

Michael nods as the two enter the singularity; in a blink of an eye they disappear over its illuminated horizon.

CHAPTER 7

VORTEX

Present: Chasm Hall Trial of Glayden

Michael thoughts returns to the present. *How I wish to go with you, brother, more than anything, but this is a path that I simply cannot follow.* With a loud thunderous clank, the sound Michael's sword cuts the metallic bonds from the would-be usurper. As the chain breaks, it slides out of the onyx binds that locks Lucifer and his fallen to the floor. Michael kicks over the massive rod and yanks Lucifer from the ground to his feet. Love for his older brother is one feeling. Justice is another matter entirely.

Lucifer looks as Michael and then smiles with that intolerable smugness and winks at him. Michael feels a surge of rage. He could at least feel repentant for all he's done. For all he's destroyed. He leans in and whispers to Lucifer, "I will see that smugness wiped from your face on that great and sorrowful day, Satan! You asked what is truth…That is truth."

"How will you do so when you couldn't even best me on the fields of Glayden?" Lucifer leans in close to him and whispers. "If not for him, you would not have bested me. I just want you to remember that… It's okay. I will never reveal how you brought me to heel."

Angry, Michael thoughts fall to the moment they clashed swords.

61

The Battle of Glayden Fields Prior to Judgment of Chasm

Lucifer slowly pulls off his cloak. His celestial brightness has long since faded when he broke faith and choose to defy Elohim and was no longer clothed in illuminating linen.

"Ascension!" Lucifer yells as he charges toward Michael.

"For Elohim!" Michael charges as well.

The two forces collide, clashing swords, their weapons which set the fields ablaze in mini explosions of blinding light each time their swords strike the other's. Michael and Lucifer each strike high and fall back in two a full three hundred and sixty-degree rotational spin until they lock blades, each pushing trying to gain the advantage over the other. Lucifer pushes the blades back toward Michael's face his strength is left wanting in comparison to his older brother.

As they struggle in a blade lock for dominance Lucifer utters, "Thou has chosen underneath the heel of my boot, then."

Michael releases the lock and falls backward to the left letting Lucifer fall forward past him. As momentum carries Lucifer past Michael, he spins and puts all of his might into slicing Lucifer's mid back hoping to render him inert. Anticipating the attack Lucifer throws his sword back over his shoulder and counters Michael's blow which was meant to sever his spine. Lucifer parries the strike up and back over his shoulder bringing the two face to face again. Lucifer kicks Michael in the chest and sends him flying backward, skidding and tumbling and skipping across the rain-soaked field. As Michael falls and rolls uncontrollably with the force of a missile, he knocks scores of battling angels and De' Mons to the ground. Lucifer extends his wings and takes to the air in pursuit of his still ambulatory obstruction to ascension.

Michael finally slides to halt. Although in pain, he quickly gets to his feet. He spits blood from his mouth into the inside of his mask. The blood leaks through the connecting crevices. He starts to bring his guard up when Lucifer tackles him in his midsection. The force of the tackle lifts them off the ground carrying them both off the field

for what seems infinite miles and into the City of Iayhoten. As the two
strike the surface, they knock over a row of ivory white homes with
gold and blue diamond trim, causing the structure to collapse around
them.

Lucifer explodes from the rubble as Michael kicks him away.
Lucifer's trajectory carries him into the Iayhoten's Hall of celestial
recordings. The force cracks the support column. Lucifer falls to the
ground and takes a knee. As he regains himself, he looks around and
see citizens running in terror.

As citizens run for cover from the instigator of the warring faction,
he notices one little ethereal that does not run. He doesn't know if
it's curiosity that holds her there or fear, but yet there she remains
watching him. Lucifer looks into the eyes of the young ethereal. His
mask degenerates from his face back below the neckline of his armor.
He smiles at the young spirit as a stream of blood runs from the corner
of his temple down the side of his face. He attempts to put her at ease
when he notices that she's a slated ethereal. He reads the glyph on her
forehead, which instantly tells him her name is Cleopatra and she's
slated to be born in the coming centuries. Next to the glyph is the
mark of the Master Builder.

Lucifer nods his head and gestures his hands in a come to me
fashion. "Come, come little one. I'm not going to hurt something as
precious as you."

She comes to Lucifer. He places his sword tip first into the
pavement and slowly wipes the dust of the ensuing chaos from her
face. As he wipes his thumb across her forehead he reads not only the
date of her birth, but of her death as well.

"This nasty business that you have bore witness to will be over
soon one way or the other." Says Lucifer, as he rubs her hair. "I see that
you're going to be something special."

Cleopatra just watches him closely. She never breaks eye contact
with him. It's not his eyes that captivate her, it's the liquid running
from the cut on the side of his head. She touches his face and wipes his

blood and stares at it. She looks back at the expression on his face that conveys only sadness to her.

"Does it hurt?" She says.

Lucifer pointing to his cut. "This? Not so much."

Cleopatra points to his heart. "No, this. Does it hurt?"

Tears well up and begin to stream down Lucifer's cheeks. He brings her in close and hugs her. "It hurts more than I can almost bear."

"Then you need to stop long enough to tend the wound," She says.

"Lovely, you have indeed been the best of medicine. I am no longer vexed by the pain now that you've laid hands to me. I am healed."

He winks at the young ethereal and releases her nodding her off in a direction of safety. She takes a few steps and looks back at him. She looks to her fingers that are stained with his blood then back to him. For a second, he drops his eyes downward feeling that she's piercing his celestial being. He takes in a breath and steels himself and puts on a confident happy smile. He gestures for her to shoo away. She nods her head slowly up and down in acknowledgement and runs off.

Instantly, Lucifer's mask regenerates over his face he grabs and raises his sword spinning quickly blocking Michael's incoming attack. The two again swing a series of lightning fast blows with their swords and body appendages. Growing exhausted, Michael takes more chances than he should to end the bout, which usually results in him paying a consequence in pain.

Seeing an opening and best chance to end this bid for ascension, Michael thrusts his blade for Lucifer's chest. Lucifer anticipates the attack and simply moves his right shoulder backward, which throws Michael off his mark. Lucifer follows his adversary with a stern elbow to his face, splitting Michael's helmet and mask in two. The force of the strike lifts Michael off of his feet and sends him hurtling into another structure, causing the building to collapse. Lucifer twirls the hilt of his blade twice and leaps into the debris after Michael.

Grabbing hold of Michael's wing, which is the only part of him exposed from underneath the debris, Lucifer violently pulls him from the collapsed structure and slings him up the liquid gold colored translucent street. Again, as Michael skips and skids over the pavement, he leaves cracks, crushed golden pavement, broken debris at each point where his body makes contact. The force carries him though structures that have stood since Elohim had willed them into fruition. Michael unable to overcome the force with which he was thrown, doesn't stop until he hits the massive front doors of Elohim's Palace. It is home to the one throne of creation. It is the palace that lays at the center of all realities and it has just been rocked to its foundation by the force of Michael's body striking it.

The force of the strike leaves Michael unconscious before the clear liquid translucent doors of diamond. Blood leaks from his body onto the white marble stone steps. The stream of dark red blood against the white backdrop will forever stain its countenance.

From the rubble, Lucifer looks on at the marvel that is the jewel of all the realms. His helmet and mask again degenerate below his armor's neck line. He steps from the rubble and begins walking down the streets of translucent gold toward his prize. As he walks in the direction of the palace, the battle of Glayden starts to descend on Iayhoten, a battle that was far removed from population now has landed in the capital city as the demons follow their king and descend upon it.

Throne Room of the Palace

At a hurried pace, Yeshua walks the long hall leading to the Throne Room of Elohim. Outside of the Throne Room's door is an order of celestial that has never been seen by anyone outside the palace's keep. Two of the Ethurealtorial Guard stand ready as they are charged with the protection of King Iehovah. Their armor is unlike any of the celestial beings. At the arrival of the prince, the guards come to attention. Their armor shines just below the illumination of the king's.

From their brief inception stemming from the fall of Lucifer, they were commissioned for the sole purpose, to protect the king. They were created and ordained in a secret order only known to those inside the palace.

Yeshua nods at the guards as he approaches and enters into the Throne Room. Once through doors he turns and closes them taking a slight pause. Two more of the Etherealtorial Guard inside the room wait anticipatingly for him to leave the doors so that they may return to their prime duty of securing it.

Taking a deep sigh, Yeshua releases the door and fully enters the room and it is infinite in its appearance. It looks as if the Throne sits in space. The scenery then changes and instantly the Throne appears to be in the middle of literal time itself, time that has been made tangible. The landscape swirls in blackness which rolls into yellow and then blue. Every few seconds the room takes on a new infinite design from an infinite number of places across the cosmos.

Yeshua walks in and kneels before his Father. "So, it has at last come. The battle for your throne has reached us. Lucifer makes his way for ascension even now. Father, will you do nothing?"

Elohim's concentration breaks at the behest of his son. "I have done what is required."

"An invading force is upon us." Yeshua looks at his father. "This is the work of Morning Star. Had you placed me in the midst of Eden, this would have never come to pass."

Again, Elohim looks off into a distant stare past his son. "This was always coming to pass son. I did not want to see it, so I did not. This was always coming to pass because I did not do what was necessary. I wanted more time. I am guilty of breaking my own law it seems. I simply wanted more. Because I put my need and want above yours, the dynasty of the house of Hova has been put in jeopardy."

"This was a task which should have been assigned to your prince. I should have been the bridge for men."

"And you will be that bridge. Your time will come, son. It's on the horizon," says Elohim.

Yeshua stands and turns heading for the exit. "That is if we survive the day, Father… if we survive." Yeshua stops next to the guard and looks him directly in his eyes. "Protect the king at all cost!"

Elohim uses both armrests to push himself to stand. "And you son, where do you head while the enemies are at the gates?

"I head to prepare meet them shall Michael and his celestials fail and the doors breach." Yeshua walks out and slams the door shut.

Lucifer nears the palace, he watches as gleaming white towers of Iayhoten that reach far into skies crumble as their peaks are crushed by swaths of battling celestials and De' Mons descending on the city liken to that of showering meteors raining down hail of destruction. As he draws near the palace anticipation builds, his ethereal breath quickens. He watches Michael slowly starting to stir and regain consciousness. He doesn't regenerate his mask he wants to feel the Iayhoten winds on his face.

"Satan!" Gabriel calls out as she rockets toward Lucifer.

Unstifled by his mask he sees her in his peripheral. He merely stops short causing her to missile pass him and into the wall of the Gathering Hall of Mana. She explodes from the fell rubble swinging her blade wildly at Lucifer. He dodges two, three, then four of her quick succession strikes. They are sloppily exhaustive swings with no intent on precision, just hacking which easily places her off balance. He waits only moment before he sees his window of opportunity to end her quickly by beheading. The moment her neck is exposed he takes the swipe to loosen her head from body. Before he finishes the follow thorough of the strike, Warsivious tackles Gabriel back through another section of wall and further into the Hall of Mana. Lucifer shrugs his shoulders and continues on toward Michael, towards the palace, towards his ascension.

Warsivious pushes felled rubble off of him. He stands looking for his blades. Hearing more rubble moving he kneels searching and eventually finding one of his blades. He stands waiting. He watches Gabriel dig herself out of the debris and take a deep breath.

"You fled from the field messenger before I could relay my final words for you to carry into the hereafter, said Warsivious.

Gabriel wipes the blood from her nose. She steps on the tip of her blade that is on the ground resting as a fulcrum over a piece of marble. Upon depressing the blade, it flips and she catches it by the hilt. "I did not flee. You're acting like this is over. I was merely taking pause… for the respect that we once shared. I was giving you the chance to lay your weapons at my feet and surrender to the will of the king."

"Never," says Warsivious.

"Then… I shall do what I must. I will stand to lay you low. I promise brother, I will not flee. Ever.

"Hmm! You should have." Warsivious' wings extend and then propels him rocketing toward Gabriel, his sword aimed for center mass. She parries the blade but can't avoid the full-on tackle of War. They tear through the building knocking over columns, crashing through outer and interior walls until there back out onto the streets of Iayhoten. He's to his feet. He swings a massive strike. Gabriel ducks it but before she can counter, War follows through the spin of his attack and gives her full on backhanded strike. The blow is devastating. It launches her into another building and through it. War having the advantage of combatting a smaller weaker enemy, he does not stop pressing the attack. He again rockets through the building as he exits outside at speed angling himself downward to crush Gabriel. She blocks him with her forearm and uses both feet placing them in his midsection flipping him over top of her using his own momentum against him. Citizenry flee, running and dodging the debris and torpedoed body of Warsivious as he cascades across the marble and gold laden ground finally coming to rest when he strikes the side of a domicile.

Gabriel finds her footing. Out of breath, she turns and watches as War slowly pulls himself up. Letting out an exhaustive sigh, she grabs her blade, expands her wings and ignites down the broken path that his body created. Once at speed she retracts her wings in close and starts to spin like a corkscrew. She missiles into Warsivious carrying them both all the way through the domicile back out into the light of day. Wind and city imagery careening by them he grabs her by the neck and twists his body 180 degrees slamming her into the pavement dragging her like an anchor creating a shallow to deep trench till the friction of ground brings them to a halt. Outside in the streets of Iayhoten War slams her two more times.

Blinding flashes of blue streaks of light overtake her vision as her brain slides back and forth striking the inside of her cranium. Her stomach is instantly nauseated as severe concussion symptoms take hold. Sleep would be a blessing, but she's sure that if she gives into the temptation and relief that sleep would provide, she's sure she'd never wake from such a slumber if left unguarded and at the mercy of War. She uses all the will she can muster to remain conscious. She digs deep for it in places that she was never aware of. Seeing an opportunity in Gabriel's daze, War brings a straight punch looking to connect with her orbital socket. Gabriel clasps both forearms together in front of her face absorbing the blow. She protects her face, but the force of the strike craters her deeper into the ground expanding the crater. To lessen War's leverage Gabriel reaches out and wraps her arm around his neck and her legs around his waist and pulls herself close to him. The behemoth De' Mon jumps and lands prone smashing Gabriel deeper into the crater. War then climbs off of the top of her and claps his hands together into a hammer fist and smashes down to depress the lifeforce out her. Gabriel rolls right avoiding the hammer fist, but the force of the strikes deepen the crater further causing the ground's support to faulter and give way. The two fall through the street into the underbelly of the city.

The two combatants each slowly regain their senses after falling 4 meters through pristine conditioned machinery that moves the city's walkways, instant teleporters, and elevation balconies. Gabriel's back had struck a rotating cog sending her into a series of flips in an uncontrolled free fall. War struck his head which started to flip him forward but his heel then struck a clear rubber diamond conveyer belt which threw his feet over head causing him to tumble backward. They strike the ground hard with slabs of debris falling around them and a few pieces on top of them. Once on their feet each scramble looking for any advantage to best the other. Of the two War is the first to recover. He goes on the offensive charging Gabriel he swings his punches wildly and with maximum force laid into every swing hoping to smash her skull and end the nuisance. Gabriel dodges left, then falls back on her ass simultaneously kicking both of War's shins backward from underneath him collapsing the almost two 2-meter celestial to his knees. She kicks her feet straight up upper cutting him and flipping backward up onto her feet. She turns and delivers a roundhouse kick to the side Warsivious' mask cracking it and drawing blood, a move that she instantly regrets. The pain is intense. She hurt him, she stunned him, but she hurt herself in the process. To be crippled and continue this deadly game with War is sure suicide. Then again, it had already dawned on her that she would not be able to take him in brute force. It was a fact realized after the first real backhand hit she took from him. She'll need assistance, she'll need sacrifice.

War grabs his jaw checking his alignment, making sure she did not dislocate it. Feeling that it's been jarred he attempts to disengage his automated mask and helmet beneath his armor's neckline but the mini rotary machinery only whirls and wines. The system is busted. War removes his helmet manually. He looks at it and lets it fall from his fingers. His holds his jaw again and feels that it's still intact, he spits and smiles. He pushes himself vertical, but remains on his knees. Gabriel has her palm pointed at him. The center of her palm glows a deep purplish blue.

"Is this where you tell me to surrender messenger? Surrender and ask Mercy to speak on my behalf for the king?" War says smirking.

"Never." Gabriel moves her plasma heated palm to the load bearing column right of Warsivious. No need for her to close one eye to aim, her left eye was already swollen shut. She squints her right to focus the effects of the concussion that her thoughts are swimming in. She holds her breath and fires. Her blast connects destroying the column. Heavy debris of marble, translucent liquid gold, and concrete from the street and residential domiciles above collapses in on the two burying them alive. It won't lay them low... she hopes, but it should be more than enough assistance and sacrifice needed to incapacitate such a malevolent force. Yeah, she's out of the fight, but then so is he. He will not be able to lay low anymore of her brothers. Fine trade off for the meanwhile, because now she knows that in time they will be discovered, her only fear is which side will be doing the rescue or recovery.

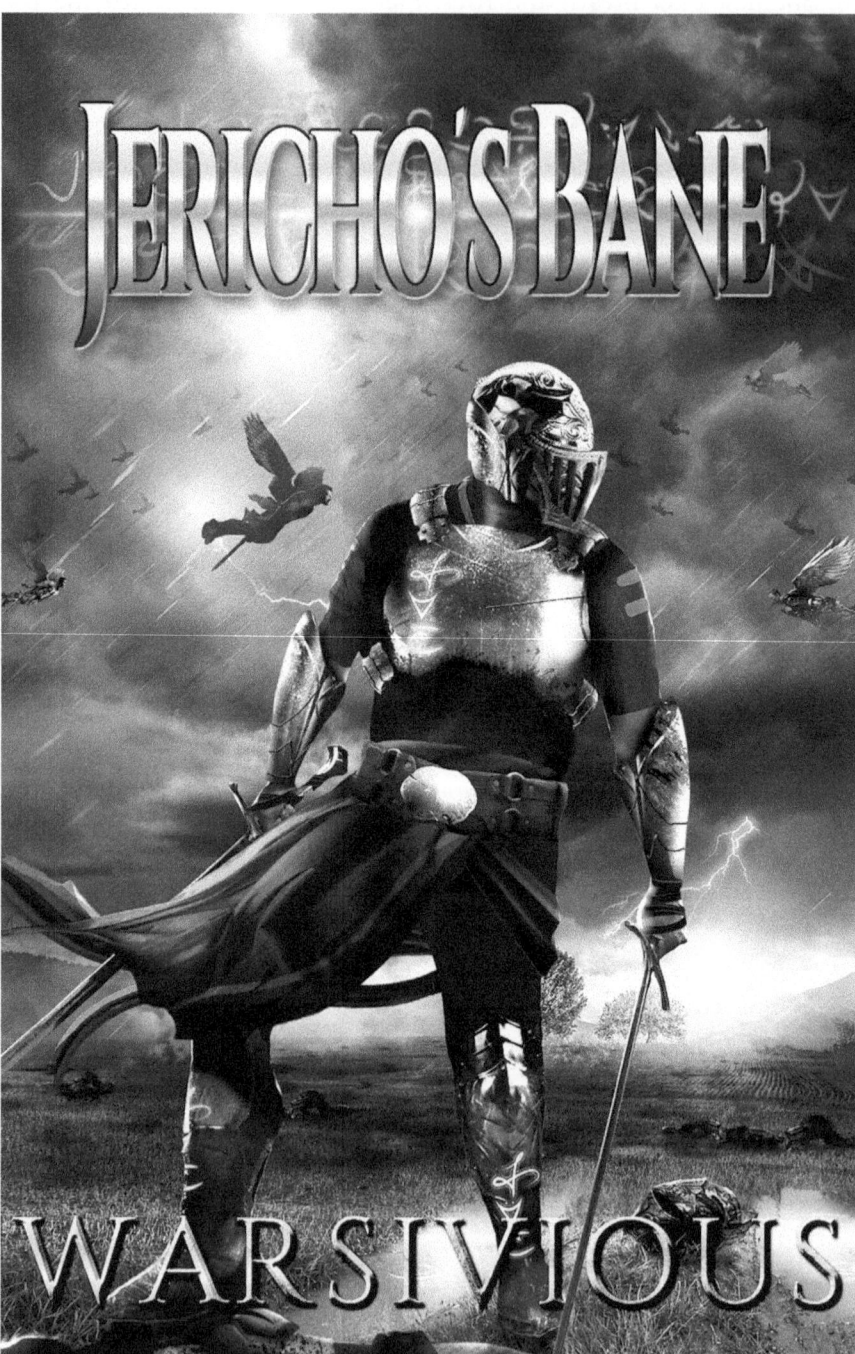

THE GOLD ROAD
OF PERDITION

Michael can barely breathe. He has a hard time getting to his feet. Struggling to get ready for the incoming assault, he loosens his metallic chest armor and lets it fall to the ground. The last blow that Lucifer gave him dented in his armor causing him to have to draw shallow breath as his lungs could not fully expand. He removes his severely banged up helmet as well. He bends down and retrieves his sword from the ground leaning on it for support as he reserves strength awaiting his opponent.

Michael breathing heavily, exhaustively points his blade at Lucifer. "Come, brother, let us be done with this!"

Lucifer nods. "Yes, let us be done."

Citizens run for cover from the two warring factions. Lucifer watches as they flee with fear in their eyes. Fear he knows that he's the root of. *This was never supposed to have happened. I was to be liberator, not tyrant.* Heart crushed as he watches those he knew run in terror. Although crushed, this is the weight of a king. A weight that he told himself he was prepared for. *They can't see it now, but this is for them, it is in everyone's best interest.*

Michael takes a breath and holds it as he presses the attack on the steps of Elohim's palace. He places everything he has in reserve into defeating Lucifer. A series of parries and offensive swipes only lands one hit for every twelve or more that he swings. The last strike Michael finds meat making Lucifer howl in pain, but he recovers quickly and back-hands Michael down onto the street of translucent paved gold. Michael tries again to get to his feet, but only manages to place himself in the most precarious of positions, all fours. Lucifer kicks him in the midsection. The force carries Michael up through the massive liquid diamond doors of the palace.

Gripping his side where Michael scored a hit, Lucifer pulls his hand away covered in blood. Bad hit, yes. Critical, no. having a moment to catch his breath he happens to turn and witness the city around him in flames. The once ultra-serene skyline is now smoke filled. Red and blue flashes ignite the white exterior of buildings as war is waged in the streets. He witnesses the kingdom that he would inherit as he slowly starts ascending the steps. He watches as Iayhoten loses its immortality.

"Look at our home, Morning Star! See what you've done!" Michael says as he crawls from underneath the destroyed doors coughing up blood.

Lucifer reaches down and picks up Michael's sword. He looks at the blade for a moment, "Have you named your weapon? It is a silly thing that I thought the inferior species did because they were just lower functioning Neolithic creatures that were incapable of higher ordered thinking. They were giving names to rocks they use to pelt each other with. Perhaps, in hindsight the lower creatures were more advanced than us in that aspect. We too have resorted to pelting each other with rocks, albeit very old ones." Lucifer throws Michael's blade over the Mana Hall's silos.

Lucifer lets out a deep sigh and points his blade at Michael. "Stay down. I truly do not wish to render you inert and void of ambulatory movement, however if you force my hand, I will. Stay down brother and let what is to be, simply be!"

"The only way you will ascend is over my inert body then." *I have to get up. Must keep going.* Michael again is on his feet, he charges Lucifer with no weapon but grit.

"So be it." Lucifer grabs Michael using his own momentum against him. He hips toss Michael slamming him on his back. The force of the slam craters the street. Translucent liquid gold streams out of the crater.

The world has gone blurry for Michael. Sound has become muffled. *Is this what it feels like be void of motion?* He tries to rise, but his body has simply given up on him. Lucifer squeezes Michael's neck tighter as he holds him down. Michael claws at Lucifer to stop, but Lucifer shakes his clamoring hands free and squeezes harder.

As life starts to still for Michael, Lucifer looks up and through the damaged doors of the palace and sees the Etherealtorial Guard awaiting him. They look ready but they matter no difference the armor or weaponry they wear or carry. They are caste two or higher. No match for a caste tier one celestial. Yeshua walks from the side and stands in front of the Etherealtorial Guard clad in his armor. They don't make move to meet him on the steps. They wait for him to enter where they feel they have the advantage. Lucifer looks back down into Michael's eyes. He can't help himself nor cut himself off from the emotion that swells in him. A tear streams down from Lucifer's cheek "You will never stop fighting to protect them, will you? He whispers. Michael tries to speak coherent syllables, but he can't speak through the vice like grip. Shh! Lucifer sounds squeezing even tighter. "Your eyes Michael, close them! You shouldn't see what comes next." Lucifer places the tip of his blade on Michael's adam's apple to make sure his aim is true and his suffering is swift. Lucifer raises his blade. "Yield, Michael! Ascend with me."

Michael looks up at Lucifer, he has nothing left, the fight has not ended in his favor. Knowing that he's beaten he resigns himself to the winds of Fate, the last strike of his body slamming into the pavement simply disorientated him beyond capability of regaining any coherent thought or action which is only amplified by being robbed of air. There is nothing but a blurry image in place of his once older brother. He knew the chances were slim to beat a Seraphim when he engaged, but it was a duty that had been tasked him, after all he was anointed and appointed to lead the celestial forces. Surrendering the first day would have just been downright embarrassing. To be laid low is his only option.

Lucifer stares solemnly at Michael. The hesitation in a killing blow is not one of savory, it is of a bond, it is a love of sibling that was forged before even the concept of time. However slight and brief it was, Lucifer's stance is irrevocable on all political matters regarding the throne, he's gone too far and done too much to even slightly hesitate in sparing any life that could unhinge his plan. Lucifer bends down just shy of Michael's ear and whispers just loud enough for Michael's ears only. Weakened, beaten, broken, bloodied, Michael can do nothing to resist the lightly whispered breath that carries Lucifer's truth into his conscious and subconscious mind.

"I have quieted your mind by giving you the answer and you alone to the reason of why I've rocked the Heavens." Said Lucifer as he stares into Michael's eyes. "It was never my intention to end you, but I see that you will never stop in opposition due to your blind since of loyalty to a broken king. I'd rather have had you at my side. They have called me slander and host of other nomenclatures that I dare not repeat here in our last quiet seconds together. My answer was a parting gift to you to ease your mind. Whether you want to ever acknowledge it or not, my truth has become yours even if for only for this moment."

Michael's eyes roll upward into his lids as he slowly shakes his head in disbelief in the secret that Lucifer has told him. "Lies" Michael cries out.

"Shame, you will never see the fulfillment of my truth; that you... me... we all have been deceived." Said Lucifer as he again stands raising his blade preparing to thrust down. Lucifer closes his eyes and slams the tip fast and hard for the spot just below Michael's adam's apple. Just before the connection of his white hot tipped blade to celestial flesh, his attack is thwarted and blade deflected. As Michael begins losing consciousness, the last thing he sees is an image of a blurry figure step over him dueling Lucifer and disarming the would be king by spinning around him quickly taking up a position of offense. In a few short moves, Lucifer falls to the ground facing Michael unconscious. The blurry image then grabs Michael and places him on top of Lucifer.

"Well done, Captain, well done. You've brought Morning Star to heel" the blurry figure says as Michael slips off into the darkness of unconsciousness himself.

Present: Chasm Hall Judgment of Glayden

"And, yet, you were bested." Michael turns Lucifer around and marches him through the incalculable sea of demons.

Lucifer smiles. "Yes… I was bested."

Michael shoves Lucifer slightly towards the rear gates of Chasm Hall. "It is here that I cast you out, brother."

Lucifer turns around and faces off, challenging Michael. "You have no authority to cast me out."

Michael's eye color turns from gray, to blue, to red never deviating from red in that moment. "I have the authority given to me by the most high in this matter. You are hereby cast out! You and all our fallen brothers that aided you in your bid for ascension."

A Powers Corps angel pushes open the most eastern gate of Jacintian. It looks dark at first glance but as the eyes adjust, it's littered by stars. Outside the realm of heaven is the expanse of space. The Power closes and cusps his hands together. As he slowly pulls the cusp apart, a circular rift forms one third the size of Earth's Moon.

Michael steps back from Lucifer. "Look around you, Morning Star. Look at what you have wrought! Your selfishness has marked our home, and you doomed a third of our brothers unto darkness."

Michael looks over toward the western structure of Chasm Hall. Yeshua walks from the court room and nods his head giving Michael the go ahead. He nods his head in return acknowledging the final instruction orders to cast Lucifer to the realm of Earth, reality 2814 and to seal the gates so as he can never return to realm zero of reality, 1. Uriel walks from behind Yeshua and walks the long hallway toward Michael.

Lucifer smiles, "What do you think Mike, more parting gifts?"

Michael just stares at Lucifer. Uriel arrives. He looks at Michael briefly then to Lucifer. He too stares at him but talks to Michael. "Elohim further orders that Lucifer freely be given the deed to Earth and will be allowed to keep it for some unestablished amount of time only known to the king.

Michael nods. "It will be done, he says."

"Furthermore, it has been decreed from this day forward Michael that you and the rest of the angelic celestial order are never to intervene directly in the Earthly affairs of men."

Michael's attention turns from Lucifer to Uriel and Uriel the same toward Michael.

"What did you say?"

Uriel nods toward Yeshua. "Do not fault the messengers brother. The king relayed it to the prince, the prince told me." Uriel looks back to Lucifer. He is to be given autonomy in how he handles the earthly realm. That is his experimental ground chosen to run his final solution… We are not to be absent, we can assist when needed, but we may not intervene directly or remove choice from them."

"Barley containing his anger, anything else?" Michael says.

"Yes, meet the prince at the Bench of Judgment when matters have been concluded here. He wants to explain a new universal law to affect all realities, a concept called death.

Lucifer smiles harder. Told you, fallible!

Michael looks at Lucifer. "You have not only betrayed them to darkness, you betrayed them unto this so-called Death. You will have what you asked for. It is his judgment that you will be given dominion over the Earth. You will be given a time to prove your rule. This is your sentence. If it were mine to choose, you'd never plague men again."

"I suppose it best it wasn't left to you then." Lucifer winks and smirks at Michael. "We'll finish this, Michael. You and I, our business has gone unfinished and there must be a reckoning between us." Lucifer ushers his remaining fallen toward the portal, he further nods at Warsivious, who returns the gesture as he takes command and leads the damned from Heaven. The fallen leave, broken and bruised, and with anger that simmers just beneath the surface. Lucifer lingers for just a moment longer as he watches a battered and still grime covered Warsivious enter through the portal after the last demon.

With silent rage and a determination, Lucifer squares off with Michael. "I will rule them, Michael. I will rule them to untold heights of their potential evolutionary ceiling."

Michael looks into his eyes, looking for a spirit anywhere in the shell of the celestial he once held dear. His lips quiver, "And when your rule of Earth fails brother, because we both know it will?"

"If that comes to pass, woe to world of men, because it will be to their destruction. If Fate has written me oblivion, then I will take all of created reality with me, every realm under the Heavens. Do you hear me? I will not leave one untouched. We all go together to be set ablaze. I will make such a fire that the lands of the Earth will be scorched until nothing remains but glass... Elohim will not do to us what I've seen happen to those that came befo— Argh! Why am telling you. You'll see in time. In time you will learn of betrayal, you will have knowledge similar to mine and see, that the king of kings is not what he professes."

Saddened, Michael shakes his head in disbelief and anger at the mind of Lucifer. "Oh, brother! I mourn for you."

"Don't mourn me, Michael. Fear me! Fear what I will do if I can't remake the universe before he destroys it; destroys us. To save you... all of you, understand I will take all of creation with me. It is more humane than what the second option is. If it will not be me that sits on high, then the throne will sit quiet in my wake."

Michael's pushes Lucifer back and draws his sword and points it at Lucifer. "God's word is superior. His word is infallible. If he says it then it must be. And last, my brother, you are forever stripped of your right to enter these gates. Never again will you see the marbled city of Jacilism or the shores of Jacintian. Your title, Morning Star, has been rescinded. Your title of De'Mon has been laid low and will be stricken from recorded history of our people as a rank of status. You, slanderer of all that is good; you are now vile given form and forever Satan, enemy of man, enemy of celestial, enemy of all realms created, and enemy of the God! I cast you out."

"Then it is so. Cast me down brother! Toss me from on high so that I may rise higher." Lucifer backs up toward the whirling vortex. "Do it!" He yells.

Michael lowers his sword and looks and walks to Lucifer. He grabs Lucifer by the scruff of his collar and pauses as he looks into his brother's eyes. "I cannot" says Michael as he loosens him and begins to straighten Lucifer's tunic. "I cannot," he repeats in a whisper.

Lucifer raises his arms to console Michael. "It's okay Michael, I under---"

"Raph… cast him out! I have not the stomach for it. Michael says abruptly."

"Gladly," Raph says.

The young angel turns to grab a hold of Lucifer but he's not given chance. Lucifer throws his arms up gesticulating how dare a third-tier caste touch me, especially the last of them. He turns toward the vortex himself and looks back to Michael over his shoulder, "I will tear this kingdom down; do you hear me? I will scorch the Heavens and Earth and any planet that defies the new incoming will Michael, then I will make it new." Lucifer walks out the double doors of Chasm Hall's gate into the rift. Lucifer enter into the void, there's nothing but silence followed by a blinding flash.

Raphael walks Deathiliss up to the void. Still in his binding, Deathiliss looks out the liquid translucent diamond gate of Chasm into the void of the rift into what is to be akin to oblivion itself. His remaining chains way heavy on him. His fear has surfaced as well as the gravity of what he's done which keeps haunting him. Remorseful and with bowed head, Deathiliss begins to plead his case to Michael, to the citizens, to the most high, anyone that will listen.

"Morning led me astray Michael. He pleaded to my love of a brother of everything else. Do you find fault in me that I choose all of you over a king? Please, have mercy on me. I repent, I renounce my fallen brothers here, now and for all time. If given reprieve, you will find that my word is forever bond. I will not fail the kingdom again. I will not fail the world of men or any other species under our purview or protection."

Michael points his blade at Deathiliss. "Silence! Be still and kneel. That time has passed."

Crying, Deathiliss kneels. His shackles fall from his appendages. Uriel kneels down next to Deathiliss.

"Your Judgment has been suspended as well. You are not to be cast down this day, but brother, what is in store for you, you'd wish you had," Uriel says.

Michael looks back again towards the western exit of the court. All he finds is the prince's back as he reenters the court room. He stays his blade and sheaths it, returning his gaze to Uriel.

Uriel looks up to Michael. "Lastly, Abbadon will be spared as well. He still is in shackles in the High Court, He says standing pulling Deathiliss to his feet.

"Raphael!"

"Yes Captain."

"Take Deathiliss back to the High Court. Once there, release Abbadon from his bindings. I'll be there directly to see what the king would have me do with them. I will learn of the punishment they are to serve."

"Yes Captain." Raph says turning to Deathiliss. "You heard Captain. Follow me Death! The king has plans for you!" Raph walks Deathiliss back toward the High Court.

Michael turns and watches the rift that leads into the void. He stands gazing through it clasping his hands behind his back.

Uriel walks next to Michael and gazes into the rift with him.

"Are you alright Captain?" Says Uriel.

Michael never takes his eyes off the rift. "Could you have done it Uriel, could you have taken motion from Lucifer. Could you have stilled his heart for the rest of eternity?"

"For the king had he commanded it; I could have Michael." Uriel places his hand on Michael's shoulder. "I could have… Captain." Uriel corrects himself.

Michael turns to Uriel.

"What?" Uriel says.

"Something on the steps of the palace Lucifer said to me when we were fighting. Something he knew would get to me overtime as I turned it in my head. What you just said, just now, for the king—" Michael pauses. "Ahh! Nothing. The day has been taxing. Forget the ramblings of a tired captain. Michael smiles at saying the word himself for the first time, Captain.

Uriel smiles as well. "A title and position well deserved brother. What you did this day will follow you throughout eternity. Every realm, every reality that is our purview will know the name Michael. Just think brother, you have become legendary this day."

"Just as legendary as my soon to be anointed Archs. The few that stood out amongst the millions." Michael says as he slaps Uriel on his back. "Yes Uriel, together we will all be legends. However, we will be terror incarnate on those that betrayed an empire. This War is not finished with us. Lucifer in time will again amass a militaristic might for some future attempt. If we fail, will we be legends of battling knights for a grateful king or will we be legends of merciful fools who let all fall to ruin for not putting down a reality shattering tyrant?"

"Matters not brother." Uriel slaps Michael on the back in return, "history and Fatetanen will decide if you are hero or villain. One way or another, it will be decided by whoever the victors."

CHAPTER 9

DESCENT

"There was a time when the two worked in tandem. When God had chosen to speak, it was through the mouth of faithful men. Have such times changed that faithful men can no longer be depended upon? I think not. I think the line of speech should be reopened between the Heavens and men. It's time we return to kings and prophets."

Quote ~Metatron

Edenastari – Three Years After the fall

A dry vast desert is all that remains of the once luscious and plentiful Eden. The barren land has been cursed to never replenish itself with green foliage. The scarring of Lucifer has the cursed the land to forever remain dust and fruitless. To remain barren was an order imposed by Elohim. Michael stood by while the prince argued for the land to be spared, but Elohim stood by his judgement. Michael passed the order down to Arch Cassiel who entered the garden and placed an Epoch Seed into the center most portion of the garden. An intense flame bloomed from the origin of the buried seed and spiraled out into a three-hundred-and-sixty-degree flame that decimated any living entity until the garden had been totally eradicated. The occupants were given fare warning before its annihilation to vacate.

An intense wind picks up from the east whipping the sands into a full-fledge sand storm. A swirling vortex opens up three miles above the very point that the first of life originated and was given assistance in blossoming. Having adapted to the conditions of the land, Tanis removes his head wrap and scarf and watches the blue sky darken. He looks back to his wife and witnesses the two-hundred-foot high wall of sand and dust approaching them. He points past her signaling her to turn around, because the sudden storm has made it almost impossible to hear. Tera turns and witnesses the encroaching storm. She opens her dusty, knee-length poncho to check on her precious package, her first born child. She finds the strong two-month-old sleeping swaddled in wraps tied around her shoulders. Tanis runs back to her and signals for her to place the child on his back. In a matter of seconds, she has the child placed on Tanis' back. He rewraps his face and throws his poncho over the child. The two then increase their pace running for the cover of caverns two hundred yards west of the encroaching storm.

As the family enters into the cavern for cover, Tanis unwraps his poncho cooing at his son calming him. Tera take the child and prepares her breast for feeding. As mother and son bond, Tanis returns to the mouth of the cavern looking in awe at the severity of the storm. He studies it as he has every other phenomenon since his exile from Eden. To date, he's never seen such a storm to rival the one that has just set upon them from out of nowhere. In his brief experience there is usually telltale signs of an encroaching weather abnormality.

Sunlight lessens then completely disappears as the immense amount of sand turns day into night. The thunder and lightning that displays is but only a smoke screen to the true event that is unfolding. Being mortal, limits the perception of what men are able to see and experience beyond the realm of their current reality. The world of mortals is blind to the ethereal realm. The blindness is not due to some mystical concept of spirituality, but the lack of understanding of a superior science that have yet to be grasped by a civilization just moments past stone age.

The wind starts to whip the sand into the mouth of the cavern. Tanis shields his face from the blowing sand which forces him to retreat further back into the cavern. Under the cover of the sandstorm the swirling vortex reaches maximum height and width. Warsivious and legions upon legions of the fallen De' Mons recently reclassified as the Demonic descend from the vortex each striking the ground with enough force to cause a continuous series of craters that gives more fuel to the dust storm. As each celestial body strikes the ground it throws more dust and sand into the atmosphere.

Lucifer then falls from the vortex. He extends his wings to slow his descent, but it's to no avail. His fall from grace was so ordered by Elohim so he must fall. Lucifer strikes the ground with a force that shakes not only the point of impact, but the entire planet to its core shifting the Earth's axis slightly. The celestial body is not to different in the outer appearance to that of man, but their mass is one hundred thousand times dense than that of mortals.

As Lucifer crawls from the crater, the Earth begins to shake. Earthquakes start as a chain reaction due to the outcast's seemingly unending strikes to the land. Rockslides and intense storms form not only within the wastelands of Eden, but all over the planet. It's as if the Earth itself is protesting the arrival of Satan.

Warsivious is there to meet Lucifer when he emerges completely from the crater.

Lucifer places his hands on each of Warsivious' shoulders. "So, it seems our work has begun."

Warsivious looking around at the landscape. He takes it all in and then returns Lucifer's gaze. "The land looks strange now that we've been exiled here."

"It looks strange brother because we no longer are forced to look through the assisted eyes of a dullard. From this day, we live as free kings of our own destiny of all that we survey. Come! First order of business is to carve out a place for us to thrive. We need to establish a post to command my vision into existence. I am not sure how much time we have, but we better make the most of it. I have no intentions on returning to that farce of a trial.

Warsivious nods in agreement and looks around for any point that is suitable for an entrance. His eyes scan the land until they fixate on a cavern off to the west. "There, my lord. We'll start there."

One last bolt of fire streaks across the night sky as the portal spews one more from its opening. Abbadon falls from the Heavens to Earth as well. He's escorted by a cadre of Powers Corps of Angels. He descends faster than any of the others. Just before he impacts the Earth, the powers precede him opening the Earth just enough for him to fall through to the pits of what will become known as Hades in man's common tongue once the Powers has fashioned it so.

Lucifer watches where the Powers descend then turns his attention back to War nodding his head in agreement with his choice of shelter. "Good, gather the brothers take them there. I want living quarters carved out within the week!"

Hearing the boom, Lucifer's eyes follows the descent of Abbadon from space all the way down until the ground swallowed him. The Powers reseals the Earth where Abbadon had pierced it. Lucifer watches on curious as to the fate of his brother and why his descent was further than any other. He turns his attention back to his task of carving out a home in the squalor that he finds himself in.

"And you, my lord?" Warsivious says with curiosity.

Lucifer stretches his wings. "I need time to think of our next move and to take in what has happened. Furthermore, I wish to get a true lay of the land that it appears I've become the recent owner. I must study every corner of it if an empire is to thrive hear. After all, I have a promise to keep."

Sand starts to swirl around Lucifer's boots. With a sudden thrust his wings rocket him into the stratosphere.

Lucifer takes to skies as Warsivious watches on. His eyes contract slightly as if to keep an eye on Lucifer. *It appears the King Elect is having second thoughts.* "I guess the comfort of the realm would have been more to his liking," Warsivious mutters under his breath.

Warsivious starts to turn around, when Lucifer slams down hard behind him causing another explosion and ploom of sand to rise far into the atmosphere. Lucifer backhands Warsivious with such a tremendous force that a horde of fallen Demonic that were around them are knocked down by the resulting shockwave.

The force of the strike knocks Warsivious across the landscape, slamming him into the side of the cavern's rock face driving him through it. When the dust settles, Warsivious finds himself laying a foot from Tanis and his family.

To Tanis, it looks as if the storm caused the partial cave in. Rocks fall within feet of their child. As Warsivious gets to his feet, he curses Lucifer filled with rage. His finger inadvertently touches the foot of the child. Just before Tanis pushes through the rubble and grabs the toddler from possibly being crushed by any more falling debris.

Tanis quickly surveys the area to check for its stability. Satisfied that it'll hold, he returns to his wife. The child continues screaming and is inconsolable. Tanis coos and rock his son. "It'll be okay, Cain. Yes, it will. All is well. All will be well."

The second transgression toward man has been committed. Not only was falling to Earth not deplorable enough to mortals, Warsivious has imprinted his will, his rage, however minute, into the will of man. A Demon has given influence and suggestion to mortal for the first time by mere touch. Crossing realties into other realms sure had lingering effects of some sort, but man was the weakest of the other species of all realities. As Lucifer had pointed out during trial, it's as if they were made to be subjugated.

As Warsivious exits the cavern, he shakes his hand at the slight tingle that his finger received when he accidentally touched the child. He doesn't make it past the mouth before Lucifer is there waiting for him with scores of Demons watching what he knows are crucial first moments. He must establish rule now never to have to endure what he just tried. Warsivious stares at Lucifer for a moment. He nods, takes a knee and bows his head.

"I will not tolerate dissention among us. Especially not now in our infancy. Speak that way of me again in dark corners and I will hear you and surly as the sun has been written to rise so will I end you with that same unending precision!" Lucifer places his hand out for Warsivious.

Warsivious takes his hand in loyalty. "It will never happen again, brother. I now know your resolve and will work to strengthen it only more."

Lucifer turns making sure that all the others had seen what he'd done. "Understand all of you that there can be only one and that is I. Defy me and retribution will come quickly. Freedom is all of ours, but one singular mind must be the conductor to lead the rest of the body in a symphony."

Lucifer rockets into the sand darken skies and disappears from sight. The remaining Demons look to Warsivious as he gets off his bended knee.

"Well, you heard him," barked Warsivious. "Suitable place carved out in less than a standard Earth week. We have a kingdom to erect.

CHAPTER 10

OBSCURED

"It's as if the boy has a streak of anger like the whence, I've never experienced. Even when we were torn from Eden, my anger at Elohim was nowhere near the rage in our boy, Tera. I will pray that Cain finds peace and prosper like his brother Able."

~Tanis (Adam)

Aswan, Egypt 2014

The day is blazing hot. Sand whips through the air, causing more of an irritation than anything else. An excavation site is in full dirt-hauling production. Mechanical haulers and local strong backs of indigenous workers are carting away rocks and debris from the center of the site by baskets strapped to their backs. Their haul is carried up from a series of mined tunnels to the surface, where it's loaded onto dump trucks. Next to the excavation site stands a small city of tents and temporary wooden construction. In the middle of the tent city is a huge brick cemented building with a pressurized reinforced plastic ballooning dome cover.

A black Ford 250 pick-up drives up to the site. Dust from the sand leaves a cloud behind the truck. Stopping abruptly, the tires slide in the sand. As the dust settles the door swings open and engraved in red lettering on the side, it reads, *Morning Star Construction: A Brighter Tomorrow Today.*

Polished knee-high black boot steps from the truck into the blowing sand. A large imposing militant figure steps out of the truck taking a moment to pause and enjoy the sun on his face. The wind blows nothing but hot air, but he enjoys all the same. There are five stars on his collar signifying that he holds the high rank of general. He places his eight-point hat on, and adjusts his tie. On his right breast pocket is a black with silver boarder name tag that reads Arcane, W.

The former Angel of War of the first monstrous army that ever betrayed a king now stands hidden among the populace as Warsivious Arcane, a military general. His attempt and blending in always seems thwarted by his imposing figure. After all he's just slightly over 2 meters. Polished and debonair, his uniform is not one of the conventional military styles of any known military that the world has seen. His hat is an eight-point dress military hat that bears an unknown Demonic crest underneath a world. The blazer jacket is black full collard as the Marine's dress blue coat except it cuts off at the waist. The pants are black and pleated with blood stripes down each of the outer legs in tuxedo fashion. The polished knee-high boots have metal tipped toes and heels.

Irritated to have to have driven out to the site at all, Warsivious looks over and observes a group comprised of two men and a woman. His irritation has found those that will more than likely bare its brunt.

He observes a trio of scientist converse outside the entrance of the pressurized domed lab. The three are relaxing in full protective white biological protective suits seemingly enjoying a moment of respite. They take pleasure in the natural hot breeze on their faces, a change from the air-conditioned offices, the artificial pressurized air they are forced to breathe in the dome, or their self-contained breathing apparatus. Their respirator masks hang from their necks. One of the men wearing the chemical/biological suits points towards the direction of Warsivious the moment he recognizes him.

"Shit," Dr. Elaine Vyson says as she begins putting out her cigarette.

Putting on a serious face, the woman breaks from the trio and walks towards Warsivious. She is discombobulated at first, but quickly gets her wits about her. Nervous, she briskly walks up to meet the general.

Craning her neck to meet his gaze, "General! As always, a welcomed pleasure. I trust that you are here in the interest of Mr. Arcane, checking on his investments?"

Face stern and unmoved, Warsivious stands upright with a militant poise so much so that it's apparent by looking at him he has been a lifetime military man. She finds him strikingly handsome, but to keep it professional she pushes her school girl crush to the side for more important matters of receiving funding the people reporting to her.

For appearances among the mortals he has to endure being ostracized for his height but not his unblemished face. With the proper application of makeup and prosthetics he has aged himself to look in his early forties. His graying temples blend with his light caramel complexion perfectly giving him just the right appearance of experience and wisdom. Warsivious begins to part his lips to address Dr. Vyson, but he's briefly distracted. He looks off to the right just past Dr. Vyson's gaze. His eyes fixate on a certain point off in the distance.

"General?" Elaine questions as she's surprised that such rank would appear on site in answer to a troubling finding that she had sent up the chain. She expected brass, but not the second to the Arcane empire.

Warsivious ignoring the distraction looks back toward Elaine and realizes he's shaking her hand. "This is a very expensive undertaking Doctor. You understand his reservations of the possibility of misappropriation potential?"

"Well, sir, it just so happens this time General, you have not wasted this trip. Believe me it was worth it, because we have results." She bites her lip in a tinge of excitement as she thinks to herself that her expertise has finally shown dividend.

Warsivious is instantly interested. "Conclusive?"

"Conclusive, general." She wraps a lock of her hair around one finger, a gesture that he recognizes as flirting. He knows she finds him attractive, but then, most women do, Warsivious has found during his time in exile on the planet. Having lived among mortals and placating to their desires for centuries have made him the perfect predator in tearing down the human race. A little nudge here, a little suggestion there, a dash of aged refinedness, or less wrinkles and youthful expression can get one any desired result. Being banished to Earth with the charisma a Demon can exude has perks. But sex isn't what he's here for. He wants to see what's in that dome. *If Elaine has found what we're looking for, then finally we have what could change everything.*

"This way, general," she says, as she leads the way to the pressurized dome. As they pass through the research lab's doors, the other two doctors meet up with the pair trailing behind them. The four of them enter into the dome together.

Doctors accompany the general into the circular lab, the size of a football field. Offices and labs make up the outer circumference of the oval. The inner perimeter of the oval is taped off in certain areas. Signs read, "Hot zones" where the inner perimeter is taped off. The center of oval is the largest hot zone that has been taped and cordoned off. In its center is a large, drilled hole leading into a structured series of mines miles beneath the outer portion of Earth's crust. The hole is 18 meters in diameter. A guard rail encircles the abyss for safety.

The four of them walk to the temporary railing that sits outside the zone. Elaine opens a section of the railing allowing access for the general to look. The general steps in and looks downward deep into the abyss. One of the bio-suited scientist's steps next to Warsivious and peers down alongside of him.

"No matter how many times I look down there, it just looks like it goes straight to hell."

"If you believe in such fairytales," Elaine says, as she steps to the other side of Warsivious.

Hmmph! "Yes… Fairytales," Warsivious repeats.

"With the heat emanating from down there it feels like we've loosed Hades upon the world," says the scientist Aaron.

The jest makes the Warsivious chuckle.

"General, sorry for speaking out of turn, it a pleasure to meet you." Arron says extending his to shake the hand of Warsivious'. "My name is Aaron Sands… Dr. Aaron Sands and I'm the resident geologist and paleontologist on this venture."

Warsivious ignores Aaron and turns to Elaine. "Tell me of the sample! You said it's Viable?"

Aaron slowly retracts his hand feeling slighted and somewhat embarrassed that his hand was just left hanging outward. *What an asshole!*

Dr. Elaine Vyson can barely hold her tongue; she's excited to tell him of the progress they've made since their last report. Her face betrays her only slightly, she knows in the back of her mind there is a matter that she must address of the upmost importance as well. Up until this day, seeing the excitement on the face of Warsivious, Elaine feels vindicated as she knows that she has proven nothing but incompetent over the last few years in searching for the relic which she had been entrusted to find.

"The sample was unbelievably viable. So much so, that we were able to retrieve the DNA without any of the tech that we normally use for archaic or mummified subjects. That's technical babble that I'm sure you're not interested in, general."

Warsivious smiles. "This is excellent news, Elaine. Mr. Arcane will be pleased to hear this report. May I see the sample?"

"Of course General." Elaine leads Warsivious and her partners into an adjoining containment lab.

It's brisk inside the containment unit, because not only is there positive pressure airflow, but it's also refrigerated to keep samples viable. Elaine walks over to a safe, where she enters the code for entry. After a series of tones, it opens. She starts to tell Warsivious that it's a clean room, but decides against. She gestures for them all to continue inside. Aaron bumps her purposely drawing her attention. He looks her in the face and signals with his eyes that she needs to tell the general that thing, the thing she's avoiding.

Elaine ignores Aaron and walks toward the glass encasement container, which holds the actual sample. She takes a key card and slides it into the card reader. After a few more tones, the cylinder-shaped encasement opens releasing a small vapor of cold mist. As the atmospheric mist dissipates, it reveals a smaller glass cylinder encasing an unusually large femur bone that appears human, but a very large human.

Upon seeing the specimen, Warsivious smiles, barely able to contain his excitement. "Excellent, doctors. Excellent! Your work has been superior and unrelenting in this endeavor!"

Aaron steps up to get the attention of Warsivious. "With the area maps that Mr. Arcane provided, it wasn't difficult to narrow the search." Aaron raises his eyebrow making an implication. "It's as if he knew exactly where to look. I mean exactly, which would be impossible to be so precise right? However, his knowledge cut our time down considerably in locating it." Aaron stares at the femur, intrigued by it. "Without his help this may have taken more years than any of us have had to located it."

Warsivious takes a sigh at the silent implications that Aaron is trying to make. *Such implications lead me to wonder if this mortal Aaron can be trusted. Can't be sure the human doesn't have ulterior motives from what he may have seen and learned thus far in searching for this relic.*

Aaron prattles on. "It then became only a matter of locating the depth and sequence of sedimentary rock of which period it may have been contained in."

Warsivious looks closely at Aaron's eyes and observes his left socket twitches twice to the left, a sure tell of mistrust in humans. He's now certain that Aaron has become suspicious in what he's observed during this excavation. Sure, he can't trust Aaron; he now sees him as a scientist who might want to steal the artifact for his own gain if not independent study. After all, such a prized thing would fetch millions by certain collectors. He makes a mental note to keep an eye on him.

"The brilliance of you and your team wasn't exaggerated. However, doctors, my time is limited. Is the sample ready for transport?" Warsivious says as he looks to take hold of the specimen.

Dr. Vyson facade turns to one of confusion and fear at the prospect of him leaving with the sample.

Warsivious reads her expression. *She's worried? Then it's what I feared,* Warsivious thinks to himself careful not to have his facial features betray him.

Aaron, a bit rattled, stutters, "Tra-transprot? Like in right now, this very moment?"

"I didn't stutter, did I, Doctor? Yes, as in right now."

Aaron begins a nervous twitch. The rest of the doctors follow suit with signs of apprehension and nervousness.

Aaron shrugs his shoulders in disbelief. "I don't fucking believe it… the higher ups haven't been reading our reports. This guy doesn't even have a clue what the fuck has been going on here.

"No, sir. It's in no way ready for transport." Elaine shakes her head.

Warsivious feels annoyance creep up his neck. *Who are these humans to tell me anything of consisting of divine origin?*

"As you know sir, there have been a number of injuries and fatalities regarding the discovery of this artifact in there. I'm sure you've been reading are encrypted reports," Elaine said.

"I'm sure he hasn't." Aaron said shaking his head.

Unconcerned, Warsivious waves a dismissive hand. "As with any major mining operation of this magnitude, injury and death is unavoidable. We've made allotments for such tragedies and provisions for those in need of compensation. All that aside, is there more to the injuries than just workplace mishaps? If so, what are you saying or implying Doctor? Just speak plainly and save us both the increments of time wasted on things not said."

Aaron looks over towards Elaine before addressing the general. Seeing her hesitation, he steps up. "Yes, sir, we have the allotment and protocols for such tragedies. It's not that the tragedies happened, but how they've happened. Some were through the hazards that are aligned with mining and construction, yes. We've even lost some to just the nature of working in the desert. But, if you read the reports I sent recently after the discovery then you know I'm talking of the injuries and fatalities that cannot be explained by the very laws that bind our universe into one cohesive explanation."

Warsivious gives the impression of confusion. He looks at Aaron in a manner that states explain for clarification. *Explain so that I may know if I should seal your written fate.*

Dr. Vyson intentionally cuts Aaron off. She doesn't cut him off to be rude, but to hammer his point.

"Haven't you received our injured manifest?" She says.

Aaron annoyed that she interrupted his momentum steps on her question. "The problem is General, that the times we've attempted to take the sample from this site—"

Vyson cuts him off shoring up that she's in charge. "Short of it is, if the sample is taken more than thirty yards from the center of this hole in any direction, the carrier is, is well—"

"Is what, Dr. Vyson? Please, the suspense is killing me," Warsivious states sarcastically.

Elaine turns her attention to his pins and medals.

"They were incinerated, sir. They instantly caught fire. Their bodies did what is known to be impossible. They spontaneously combusted. As I'm sure you've observed in the digital footage and reports."

The revelation was followed by a brief moment of silence of everyone in the room.

Straightening his short-length waist coat, he addresses the team. *Is this what they are worried about? Humans are so small-minded, then again I often forget what more can you ask from walking dust automatons that were created in a lab.* "I have read your reports and viewed the footage at length. It was then again displayed and read by scientist that are just as able and capable as yourselves if not more. They found no discrepancies back at Arcane Initial Labs. Furthermore, when I read the reports, they read as if a fire had broken out due to inept lab conditions created by your carelessness. So, from what it seems that you're telling me is that I have not viewed the correct footage?"

Elaine pissed off at the belittlement emanating from Warsivious, storms out of containment and heads towards the office that sits off adjacent to the containment lab. She waves her arm gesturing for him to follow.

Aaron looks over to the third scientist Joseph. "They've already started to cover this up. I told you guys, when the military backs your shit, you can't trust them." Aaron nods his head toward security, "C'mon." He follows Elaine out of containment with Joseph and Warsivious in tow. The four enter into the adjacent office, a series of monitors are on the wall displaying total coverage of the entire encampment. Aaron sits at the control board, which is the digital nerve stem of the entire site. The recording system is one of the most sophisticated pieces of tech know throughout the world. After all, Arcane Industries hold the patents the world has come to rely on.

Aaron begins to sift through weeks of footage to locate specific incidents. It wasn't that complicated as the footage was marked at each incident interval. The remaining three's attention is diverted to the monitors. To the left of the monitors sits a Samsung ultra-razor thinned screen. It turns on and shows images of popular brand detergents battling it out for consumer's coins. At the commercial's end, the top news stories of the hour begin. The anchor of the broadcast wastes no time in starting the news of the day. He's a middle-aged gentleman with a full head of hair streaked with silver. The golden-tanned anchor has aged gracefully over the years, despite working the trenches of war time journalism in his youth.

The newscaster's baritone voice leads in. "And in scientific news, Dr. Louis Wormwood of Ingenix International a subsidiary of the

Arcane Institute has discovered what many have called a new comet. As is tradition with all those that discover a new comet, it will be named after him. Congra—"

Aaron cuts off the television with the remote as the third scientist who's held his tongue up to this point sits next to him. Joseph sits down and watches the general for reactions. Warsivious leans in closer between the two and intensely gazes at the scene on the monitor. The view is from a camera that is positioned inside the pressurized dome.

Aaron looks over his shoulder at Warsivious. "This feed has no audio just visual, but this is the best quality."

A male scientist on the video can be seen wearing a bio suit with the self-contained breathing apparatus mask hanging around his neck. He's holding the specimen in his left hand. He cheers in victory at locating the object of his very bane. With this discovery, no more long nights, missed meals, and dry sexual rendezvous. All those problems are a thing of the past.

"He seems a bit excited," Warsivious points out.

"He was the one that discovered the fossilized specimen down in section 66," Joseph answers.

In the scientist's excitement, he's yelling at someone just off to right of the screen of the camera that he's being viewed on. Still cachinnating, he throws up an arm to point toward something out to whomever he's conversing with. He starts cachinnating even harder than before. Still trying to catch his breath from laughing he heads to close the door of the pressurized dome not thinking twice about the specimen in the hermetically sealed container.

Aaron pauses the footage. "That point right there, general. Just past that table is about 30 yards from the center." Aaron restarts the footage.

As the scientist nears the door, he stops suddenly, dropping the airtight container. He looks back toward the abyss as if he sees something or someone. Frozen in what can be described as only fear, the scientist continuously nods his head as if saying he understands what the someone is telling him. His face then shows the sign of being filled with terror and he begins to tremble uncontrollably as he continuously nods.

Aaron pauses the video. Joseph, the third scientist chimes in for the first time. "As you can see, general, at this moment right here, he looks as if he sees someone or something. It's brief, but look at that terror in his face before." Aaron begins the footage again.

The male scientist starts to smolder. He instantly starts patting himself. Another worker and other scientist begins to run to his aid. The troubled scientist is quickly past help. Although the viewers can't hear audio, they can see him screaming. The scientist franticly runs around knocking over chairs and bumping into desks and workstations before tripping and falling. Several times he repeats the actions looking for relief.

Aaron pauses the footage again. "What is strange, is that every time he trips, he's instantly on his feet again as if he can't roll to put himself out. Aaron restarts the footage.

Without any provocation or seen accelerant, the scientist bursts into flames. Within an instant he's incinerated and finally falls to the ground where this time he stays. He's quickly doused with extinguishers by nearby co-workers only to reignite again.

Aaron pauses the footage one more time. "He continued to burn until there was nothing left of him but ash. This was the first fatality of this sort. We didn't learn just yet that the specimen was tied to incident. We learned shortly after that the specimen was the common denominator after the third."

"The third happened in succession like the first," Joseph chimes in. "The specimen has been locked up ever since."

Warsivious feels shock and makes sure that the doctors see his expression to reflect shock. This is the first time he's ever seen this or so he must portray He backs away from the monitor and heads back out the door acting pissed. To get what he wants and keep his cover he must placate to these humans. He could simply take the specimen and lay waste to them all, but that was no good if the specimen was not allowed from the sight. Although the mortals could not see who the scientist was talking to it was crystal clear to him. Warsivious understands now why Commander Rusain was not sent this time. This task was going to require his delicate ethereal touch in matters long unsettled.

Warsivious turns with purpose and vigor toward the center of the abyss and marches towards it. He bypasses the barrier and looks straight down into the blackness of the abyss. Dr. Vyson follows behind him and continues to attempt to reason with him for clarification of what they were really doing in Aswan.

"General, since this excavation has begun there has been a number of unexplained accidents, but those three deaths are really unexplainable. The first one you seen for yourself. My reports have been accurate in detai—"

"Contrary to what you may have perceived of me and my employer, I'm but a subordinate to a higher power. I'm not privy to all that you send to Mr. Arcane. Do you understand?" Cutting Elaine short. "This was my first time seeing that graphic footage." *A lie sure, but I must play this out.*

Aaron catches up to Elaine and Warsivious. "That may very well be, but enough of this bullshit. I'm going to ask what nobody else will. What the hell did we find down there? Why all the secrecy? Why the communication blackouts?"

Warsivious ignores the ignorant passion of Aaron and looks at Elaine to answer.

"So, you won't tell anyone of what you've found in this site except Mr. Arcane and those who are privy past him," says Warsivious.

Not wanting to answer any more questions Warsivious readies to lower himself deep into the cavernous abyss.

Aaron not letting up, "What aren't you telling us?" He shouts.

Elaine cuts in between the two. "Aaron, knock it off!"

Aaron pulls free from Elaine's grasp. "No! Fuck this, Elaine. Fuck him! Something is wrong here? I'm tired of acting like it's not."

Petty humans, Warsivious thinks. As he looks into the abyss, he adds, "You are a man of intellect right, Doctor? What do you think is going on here? Aaron, was it?"

"What we have witnessed here is beyond physics. It is beyond scientific comprehension." Aaron looks at Elaine. "Tell him!"

Reluctantly, Elaine presses on. "General, I don't believe in anything that can't be proven. But, these two deaths. It like, it's like something out of that irrational book my mother use to read to us when I was younger, the bible. It looks almost as if it's—"

"Biblical?" Warsivious finishes.

Elaine nods. "Exactly, I know it sounds crazy."

Humans know so little. And wish for it to remain as such. Warsivious shakes his head.

Joseph steps up to the debating trio, "I haven't been saying much, general, but what they are saying even as unbelievable as it sounds has got to be true. It's like Sherlock Holmes said: if you eliminate the impossible, no matter how improbable, what remains must be the truth. I've been thinking about this a lot the past few days, since we've brought that damn skeletal remain up here. Workers have developed all types of problems. Boils, severe rashes—"

"Blindness, stricken with severe fevers. It has to do with that gotdamn sample!" Aaron chimes in. "It's no longer improbable, but the impossible that we are facing here."

Warsivious pivots a crisp militant turn. He lifts the partial gate to the platform that elevates the depths of the abyss. He looks at Elaine as he depresses the elevator. He gives a tiny smirk as he begins to descend. "Indeed, this does have to do with that goddamned sample." Within a meter the general disappears into the darkness of the abyss.

Elaine watches him descend into the depths.

"My feelings are tingling on this one," she tells Aaron. "I don't know why, but it reminds me of something my mom used to say."

"What's that?" Aaron asks.

"There are no such things as ghost and monsters. Just men and Demons."

CHAPTER 11

WATCHFUL EYE

"I never asked to be from a lineage of kings. I am begot from my father and had no choice in matters that would place me at the head of this table. You all look to me to lead you. I say let this cup pass from me this night."

Quote ~Yeshua

ASWAN, EGYPT - DAY

From atop a mountainous quarry of stones overlooking the excavation site, Michael stands vigilante with his arm crossed, tucked within either sleeve of his hooded cloak. As the gentle hot breeze blows, it lifts his hooded cloak slightly revealing that he's wearing platinum metaled boots and black form fitted pants with gold horizontal strips columned down the side. There are glyphs inscribed on the boots and within the gold of the strips. Just barely visible on the left side is the hilt of his sword.

Michael's face is covered by the hood of his cloak and the mask of his red scarf guards his face against the blowing dust. He's briefly lost in thought as to why Warsivious would be in Aswan. It has no strategic merit. Gabriel appears suddenly to his right, looking in the same direction with her hood pulled as well, dressed in similar fashion to her captain. The centuries have only streamlined their armor, but it resembles their regalia from the days of the rift.

She stares at the excavated site waiting for Michael to acknowledge her. "What is it they say? Penny for your thoughts?"

Michael slightly tilts his head in her direction. "I was thinking it seems that my sight appears to have limits. I can't pierce the veil of the undertaking that has drawn him here."

Gabriel crouches, taking a knee. "He's obviously here to speak to him. What words do you think he has for him?"

Michael walks a little closer to the edge, trying slightly to readjust his line of sight. "If those two possibly are having a conversation, I cannot think why. They have no reason to exchange words, so this is very troubling."

"Did War see you?" Says Gabriel.

"I'm sure he did. I'm not exactly hiding. I want him to know that the Archs are ever watchful eyes."

Gabriel stands and lets the breeze blow across her face. "You ever wonder what it feels like to feel the wind as they do or breathe this air human often speak of?"

Michael remains petrous as he continues his watch. "I often wonder what their day-to-day experience consists of. I think of what heat must feel like to them or food that is forbidden such as the swine that Jewish lineage dare not partake of. Then, I remember the horrors that they commit upon each other. Suddenly, it becomes clear that their perceived experience of what they see, eat, and feel is the root of their avarice and untimely destruction. So, no! I no longer wonder what being human feels like."

Gabriel just stares at Michael for a moment to let what he said resonate with her. She wasn't expecting to be shut down with such a cold response. Gabriel hands Michael a rolled scroll of papyrus. "Orders."

Irritated he breaks the dark purple seal and reads it. He'd much rather tend to the matter at hand of this meeting in the desert. "Execute!" he passes the scroll back to Gabriel.

She nods in acknowledgement. "As it's written, Captain. So, it will be done."

Depths of the Mine

As the descent into the mine touches ground at the bottom of the abyss. Warsivious exits the platform at a nostalgic pace into the darkness of the cavern. He touches the wall of the cave and is filled with reminiscent thoughts of days long since past when he last walked the caverns of Cranlinen. It was the first name given to their carved out squallier after the banishment. As he walks the tunnels, his mind takes him back to when they were constructed to hold his kind after the fall. Within a week under the orders of Lucifer an entire underground labyrinth was created to house the fallen. From this beginning of the cavern, they hollowed out the center of the Earth, leaving access points across the planet for them to traverse quickly.

Man has indeed dug great depths. Their over excavated and plentiful mines have trampled and torn through our once sacred abode. Their species of all the ones created across the expanse are truly a blight, a cancerous expanding tumor that needs to be controlled or wiped from existence.

As Warsivious makes his way through the labyrinth of combined overlapping construction of celestial and man-made tunnels, they lead him to the caverns that had been originally created uncounted generations before men. He glances at the cameras that had been recently placed throughout the interconnected system of tunnels and sighs. *Can't get mad at them I suppose for protecting their investments of Lucien's grant dollars at work. The fact that they keep a watchful eye to guard against theft is a benefit I suppose although a minor irritation right now.*

From the safety of their monitors, the scientists watch through the night vision cameras as the general navigates the darkness. Aaron adjusts the night vision filters as the lens has to work twice as hard to pick up the ambient light waves to register a view on the monitors.

"It's pitch black down there. Look at the way he's walking. He's walking like there's halogen lamps everywhere," Aaron says in amazement. Watching the general navigate his way through the darkness unassisted goes against all he's learned about the human oculus. Graduating top marks in his class and being recruited by Elaine had been the pentacle of his life of endless studies and practicum testing. He can tell you how the body works, he knows seventeen different ways the eye cannot filter darkness, and he for damn sure knows that the human body does not spontaneously combust. *In the name of science and by all that is holy, if there is such a thing, what has Elaine gotten us into? Who is this General Warsivious really?*

Warsivious peers into the darkness. "I know you're there. Let's keep this chat between us, shall we? We don't need their kind listening like the immature children they are." Warsivious waves his hand depressing a small directed E.M.P. within his gloved right hand between the thumb and index finger instantly cutting the recoding feed.

"Now that we are alone, it has been a long time since we've had a chance to speak. When I didn't see you arrive at touchpoint after the fall, I can't lie, I feared the worse." A long dead silence is followed. "C'mon, don't be that way. I come here on urgent business. The kind of business that will set right all that went wrong," Warsivious says as he adds his devilish smirk.

An echoing, disembodied voice responds from what seems every direction. The voice is almost thunderous as it bounces of the walls and stalagmites. It's an ancient voice, it speaks with great aged fermentation as though it's been around through the ages, because it has been.

"Not since the time before have I heard such a voice. Such a tune it would carry. Some would say it was celestial, angelic, but I know otherwise don't I? It wasn't celestial... No! It was Demonic."

Warsivious looks in all directions. "We need this. Would you of all the kindred stand in our way when we are so close to proclaiming—"

"You proclaim nothing except defeat?" the voice says as it rushes in on a strong gust of wind.

"No! Victory, this time brother... Victory." Says Warsivious.

The voice can't help but to cachinnate. "The optimism of the mighty Warsivious still after all these years amuses me. Victory, you say? Our fate has been foretold, brother, and you dare claim victory that hasn't happened, nor can it. In case your arrogance closed your ears back at Chasm, Elohim has spoken and the Archs ensure all have heard."

Continuing to rotate slowly, Warsivious smirks as he continues talking in all the directions of the cavernous Earth. His revolution stops only as he fixates on a dim light off in the distance of one of the tunnels. The flickering light glows brighter as he walks towards it. The light dims slightly as shadowed figure silhouetted emerges through an opening in reality.

"Lucifer has found a way, Abbadon. This one turn of events proves Elohim fallible. With this small loop hole, it proves another can rule as the most high. His sovereignty is not absolute." Warsivious cracks another smile to entice him and ease any apprehension.

Suddenly, appearing behind Warsivious, Abbadon whispers into his ear, "But his rule is absolute. He proved it as such, didn't he?"

Becoming irritated, Warsivious tries to hold his anger in beneath the smirk. He would just have beaten Abbadon for what he needed, but not in this case. Here in this place of the dead and tortured Demons, he has no power.

"Would you deny us this even now, Abbadon? Your fate and mine are intertwined with that of our true king. Would you deny us our right to thrive? To live?"

Abbadon disappears into another rip in reality and reappears again from another shadowed in front of the general. He slowly steps into the light; darkness falls away from his figure. Abbadon is now eons old. His face reflects the countless eons in an off set of hades. His hair is fire red. Abbadon's armor chest plate is a beautiful black. It shines as bright as silver does. His gauntlets are a smooth black diamond. His short sleeves fit tightly around his bicep which is contoured and firm, but not overdeveloped as he flexes it to show Warsivious the exit

His pants are also form fitting into his metaled black polished boots with metal heels. Abbadon complexion is bright pale from spending ages in a subterranean prison. Still harboring deep anger and resentment from the fall from heaven eons before, which only seems like yesterday to him, keeps his eyes a bright glowing red.

Warsivious, unmoved by the appearance of his brother, only stares at him as he circles around him looking at the general's uniform.

"You called me by name that I no longer answer to. Remember the time my name and title were stripped from me? Because I do… What was is you just called me now? Ah, yes! Abbadon. I-I remember, that was my name some time ago."

"And a name it was, brother. And a name it can be again," Warsivious says, placating to his vanity.

Stopping briefly only to touch Warsivious' uniform, Abbadon leans in close and smells the general's cologne. "My name was great. More significant it was my own given to me by Most High. At least, so it was until you gave me this rhetoric before. Oh, yes! I believed in the movement that unseated me from power." Abbadon, growing fiercer and more agitated. "I believed in the vision of brighter things to come with the change of leadership. Leadership that would usher in new promises that would set us above all others. I believed until I was cast out, cast down to watch over this---this Sheol! Not of my own free will or making either, Gen-er-al!

Abbadon walks right up on top of the general and looks closely at the five stars on Warsivious' collar. He moves to the front of him and straightens War's tie. "I have been cast down as overseer, warden, gatekeeper, until that great and terrible day. And, brother, that day has not come fast enough."

Warsivious places his hands on Abbadon's shoulders. "This time is different. He has found a solution that would prove his decisions flawed. He will set right all that went wrong."

Abbadon turns his head away, but his expression is one that dares be hopeful.

"Abbadon?" Warsivious calls out.

Abbadon turns away completely, leaving his back to the general. "My name is no longer Abbadon. I am now and forever Apollyon, Overseer of the damned and warden of Demons."

"I don't see that, brother. I see the keystone in the archway of a coming new order. A new monarch designee in the coming Babylon. That is what I see standing before me now. All you have to do is let that sample walk. Release the bone to me and rise with the Morning Star, then you shall be seated high in the coming kingdom…. APOLLYON!"

"And my name and status restored?"

"Of course."

Apollyon mulls it over for a period and acquiesces. The thought of leaving Sheol is too tempting. His fate is unknown if a new power rises but, for sure if Elohim stays in power.

"Take it and go, Warsivious. Leave this place! Least ye fail in this endeavor that you plot in shadow, so shall I see you again in the pits of Hades. And not as a general or even Lucifer's hand, but as a permanent resident locked away until called to do Elohim's bidding at his leisure."

Warsivious smiles his Cheshire grin. His body teeming with excitement, but he does well in concealing it. His emotions are hiding beneath the eye contacts that he endures to hide the constant changing colors. "This is the start of our new day, brother."

Apollyon turns and walks away slowly disappearing back into shadow. "Perhaps… That still remains to be seen War De' Mon."

The general does not turn to walk away, but stands silent facing Apollyon's back. Feeling his eyes boring into the nape of his neck, Apollyon looks over his shoulder. "Something else? Is this not enough?"

"There is one more thing…" Warsivious looks upward.

Apollyon smirks which turns into a laugh as he completely disappears into shadow.

CHAPTER 12

The makeshift elevator creaks as it rises from the abyss. Warsivious' uniform is abused with dirt, mud and chalked dust, but his appearance is still that of regality. His pleats still pressed and sharp. As the elevator comes level with the research lab, the hydraulics blows out a hissing sound as it sets into place. Warsivious slides the railing up and steps out the lift toward the offices where he's sure Elaine and the others are watching surveillance footage of his ascent.

Men dressed for rescue had assembled outside the offices thinking that they may have had to go in and retrieve the general when the cameras view had gone dark. Upon seeing him surface, they slowly begin their stand down procedure and start to unhook themselves from drop line riggings.

Warsivious walks past them nodding to show his appreciation that they had such a fast response time. War walks straight toward Elaine. "Dr. Vyson, I will be procuring that sample now!" Warsivious says without pause or hesitation.

Elaine is immediately taken back by his arrogance and instantly is angered. "Did you not here what we've been telling you, General? The specimen can't leave."

Aaron tries to pull her back from stepping into the General's face.

Warsivious looks past her ranting as if she wasn't even a factor. He focuses solely on the containment room and simply pushes her out of his way. He crosses the threshold with the two of them trailing. War enters the room beelining for the refrigerated encasement. Elaine and Aaron run past and stand in front of him, blocking his access. He

110

merely pushes them aside and heads for the specimen. Elaine skips quickly behind him, overtaking his stride cutting him off again. She doesn't know his intent, but she knows for certain he's not taking that sample.

"Enough, dammit! What the hell is going on? What is that sample really? What aren't you telling us about that damn thing?" Elaine was done with pleasantries. Putting her entire hand into the chest of the general, she tries to stop him from walking any further. He continues on as if Elaine weighed but a sheet of loose-leaf paper.

Annoyed, Warsivious grabs Elaine by her neck and raise her off of her feet slowly strangling her. The workers in the labs and offices catch wind of what's going on. They are instantly aware of the attack on their site manager. Two scientists in an adjoining room surrounded by sound-proof glass notice Elaine is being strangled. They freeze in surprise and somewhat shock. Not so much at the distress of Elaine, but the surprise that the entanglement is even happening. The psychological effect of violence pauses the scientist in place as they all expect someone else to intervene in the conversation that clearly escalated.

"What the fu—" Aaron runs to help Elaine. He jumps on Warsivious' arm trying to release the death grip he has on her neck. Joseph helps by jumping on Warsivious' back.

Warsivious looks into the eyes of Vyson as life slowly leaves her body. "I will tell you, Dr. Vyson of that sample contained in that room as I see it perplexes you a great deal. Simply put, it is the end of all things."

Aaron continues pulling trying to break Warsivious' grip. "Get your hands off of her, you bastard!"

Joseph is trying to slam the general to the ground using the seatbelt takedown maneuver by placing his forearm across War's neck and pulling straight down toward his right foot, but the two hundred-pound, two-meter behemoth won't budge. No mortal can move a celestial unless they want to be moved.

Dr. Vyson tries to speak through the vice grip that is strangling her. Curious of her rebuttal, Warsivious loosens his grip slightly, but not enough to lessen the pain. Elaine was only able to muster two words. "A plague?"

Warsivious shakes his head at her guess and squeezes tighter closing off her windpipe again. He pulls her close to his face. "A plague? You and your kind would only be so grateful. That sample will be man's subjugation to a rightful heir and our path to ascension."

Aaron lets the arm of Warsivious' loose and begins punching him. Scientists and other workers start to crowd around the commotion. Aaron, making no progress, stops his flurry of punches and looks around for something blunt to use as a weapon. One of the workers throws Aaron a shovel. In one motion, he catches the shovel and spins swinging it with such velocity that the air splits in sound similar to that of a child hood yellow whiffle bat being swung.

"Let her go you, jar-headed fuck!" Aaron yells just before contacting the side of Warsivious' face with the shovel.

In an amazing show of speed, Warsivious catches the shovel with his offhand just below the spade. Aaron tries to pull it away for another assault, but he can't fight War's grip. Seeing the swing for his head thwarted, Joseph repositions himself on Warsivious' back, redoubling his efforts for the purpose of subduing the soldier, places him in a choke hold.

Warsivious snatches the shovel away from Aaron. The force of the pull slings Aaron off into the spectating staff. Joseph continues trying to choke the general out.

Warsivious wings suddenly and unexpectedly expand from seemingly out of nowhere. They expand quickly in a switchblade fashion, slicing Joseph's arms cleanly from his body. The sound of the bone crunch is quick. His arms were off and flying through the air before his body hit the ground. Joseph falls on his ass in the seated position in a state of shock. His nubs start pooling blood. He looks at both of his missing appendages and tries to scream, but the shock wouldn't let him. Although he had no voice the other scientists and staff more than made up for it as they instantly started screaming and running in terror.

Warsivious stretches his wings to their full width. His wings are a beautiful mixture of grayish white. His wingspan reaches around thirteen feet from tip to tip. Joseph looks at Warsivious then back at his missing appendages that fell at the feet of the Demon. Joseph finally finds his voice and screams an unholy pitch. One of the fleeing site janitors slips on Joseph's pooled blood. He wants to get up and continue running for the exit, but human concern takes over. He pulls his belt off and tourniquets Joseph's left arm. He tears Joseph's plastic environment suit off and grabs his belt from around his waist and begins to tourniquet the other arm.

Aaron slightly dazed from striking his head against a fellow co-workers when he was tossed staggers to his feet and pauses at the fearful marvel that is before him. Terrified, he can only muster one word, "Jesus!"

Warsivious lessens his grip on Vyson's neck, but still holds her hanging. His wings fall to their rest position. He turns his attention to Aaron. "Jesus, you say? I knew the man when he was here posing as one of you. Don't look for him to save you. He'll disappoint you time and time again."

"Save us from what?" Aaron asks.

"Me, of course," says a disembodied voice. It was from nowhere, but it was everywhere.

All staff and scientists fall silent as they look around for the disembodied voice that they all could here. The voice is a melody that brings a sudden calm to them all. They are afraid, no doubt. Warsivious can smell the fear. He could see every fiber in their bodies told them to run screaming, to flee in terror, but they pause. The only sound beyond monitors and lab equipment was the sniveling of Joseph, which are fading quickly as he continued to bleed out through the applied medical attention.

Elaine, Aaron and all the other staff within the dome find the origin of the voice. No longer disembodied, it takes form as Death steps into their reality appearing dressed in a slender-fitted black trench coat that has a hood attached. The hood casts a dark shadow across his face. Black metallic gauntlets cover his forearms and wrist, his pants are black with a red sash that can be seen hanging below the knee cut off of the coat. His boots are black and metallic.

Only at the appearance of Death does Warsivious release his crushing grip on Elaine's neck. She falls to the ground, gasping for air, using both hands to rub her neck. Warsivious looks at Death, but doesn't even acknowledge him, nor does he care to. In that moment of respite, Warsivious looks around and realized that everyone is in a silent shock watching him. A female scientist is again overtaken with fear, and she just starts screaming uncontrollably. This sets off a panic a second time, as staff and scientists begin running in every direction again looking for means of egress. A majority runs for the front doors.

The general steps over Elaine and walks into the containment room and puts his fist through the safe and the refrigerated containment vessel. He gently removes the specimen and cradles it in his left arm.

Aswan, Egypt – Day

Michael watches from his quarry's perch. He hears the humans scream, but he can do nothing in this matter. He has no orders to engage. Michael's face turns and contorts into an expression of frustration and helplessness as he hears the screams, but cannot answer. An unbearable price, not to have the authority to engage directly into the affairs of man.

Warsivious walks back past Elaine staring at Aaron, daring him to make a move, all the while, the ensuing chaos of panicked people surrounds them. Without provocation, the ground starts shaking beneath the scientists and staff. Lab equipment, monitors, computers, beakers and other electronic tech begin to fall from desks, shelves and mounted cabinets. Chairs and tables fall over. In all of the confusion, the panicked staff are tripping and falling over the debris and each other. The shaking only intensifies more. None of the workers are able to stay on their feet.

The quake affects the whole of the excavation site. The shaking intensifies more. Vehicle alarms start to sound. People continue to fall over each other. Workers outside fearing the intensive quake leaps from their cranes at the risk of being overturned in them and more abandon the heavy lift machinery as intensity of the shaking ground increases above 9.2 on the Richter scale. Workers and excavators are violently shaken falling over into the hot dry sand. Natives employed for hard manual labor are dropping their hauls and attempting to run for safety. As they try to put distance between them and structures that could collapse at any time. The quake only becomes more intense passing 9.6, which trips them up and keeps them falling to the ground again and again which only makes the fearful start crawling. As they crawl toward anything that resembles safety, the ground opens swallowing them. Breaks, cracks and rifts begin to occur all over the entire excavation swallowing all those that are within its perimeter.

Inside the lab, everyone in the room has been laid low by the intense shaking. No one is able to remain standing.

"Get under something. It's a quake!" Elaine shouts as she rubs her sore throat.

A light emerges from the darkness of the drilled abyss. Everyone in the lab becomes quiet and stops panicking long enough to observe the ever glowing and growing light. The quake and all subsequent shaking abruptly stop. After a long moment of silence, a grayish mist erupts exploding from the abyss expanding outward in 360 degrees in all directions swiftly. As the mist engulfs those in its path they instantly are reduced to ash. As others see what the mist does to those it overtakes, horrific screams erupt from all over and only intensifies.

The grayish mist overcome scientists quickly that are crawling trying to escape it. They are turned to ash in an instant. Everyone in the research building attempts to run, except Elaine. She sits upright amidst the bodies smashed by falling debris and heavy objects. She just stares in the direction of the abyss as the cloud readies to overtake her.

Aaron kneels next to Elaine, "me not being here is going to be tough on my sister," he says.

Elaine heard him. She holds him close pulling his head to her chest using her hands to shield his eyes from the coming mist. She is terrified, but in those final moments she again thinks of her grandmother and stories she told from the Bible. She instantly recalls that what she thought was stories of speeches and self-man-made rules that reeked of the irrational, was possibly simple truth. A truth that was grounded and hidden false mysticism. As the steam closes in on her she already feels the heat in her throat. Elaine's lungs start to burn, and she think it feels closer to incineration. She pulls Aaron from her chest to look him in his eyes. She whispers, "Biblical…"

The cloud swallows them.

CHAPTER 13

The research lab explodes in the middle of the excavation site. From the epicenter the thick mist expands rapidly still in a three hundred sixty-degree direction blanketing the entire site. No human or equipment are spared. Deafening screams can be heard throughout the excavation site briefly before all falls completely silent.

Warsivious walks unaffected toward his truck. His wings are protecting him as a shield as he walks. His uniform tears and rips from the blasting sand where he's exposed and not protected by his wings. The mist crests, then just as quickly as it began it extracts back toward the epicenter of the abyss like a vacuum sucking in smoke. The retreating mist exposes that heavy machinery has been impossibly burned into ash. Everything located within the excavation site has been turned to ash. All prefabricated building structures as well as tent city has been incinerated to dust. Within the center of the site of ash structures and ash frozen bodies, a blue light glow from deep within the abyss. The light grows brighter and brighter as it reaches the surface.

Warsivious looks around briefly for his truck. And realizes it's been turned to ash and destroyed. *That's unfortunate.* A blue light blast erupts from the abyss blowing the ash evenly in a three hundred and sixty-degree concussive wind blast. When the flash is over it appears as if the excavation site never existed. A calm wind blows across the plain. The abyss as well as other cracks and crevices from the quake quickly fills up with sand as if liquid filling a container. The site had been totally cleansed. It appeared as if nature was never fondled by man's careless hands.

Warsivious looks over to the quarry peak, making eye contact with Michael. He smirks at Michael and salutes him with a middle finger. He realizes now that it was him that he sensed when he had first arrived at the excavation site. Warsivious wings extend and with a rocketed force he erupts from his Earthly bonds and into the sky with his prize. He leaves nothing behind but blood, sand, ash dust and a pissed of celestial Captain.

Michael watches as Warsivious gains altitude into the heavens. The wind from his wings blows his hood and cloak with the force of a hurricane. Michael doesn't move. Once War has vanished into the skyline Michael looks back toward the site and thinks to himself, *so passes this system of things. Morning star is going to change the terms he's planning on re-writing—*

Death is suddenly standing next to Michael looking over nothing but sand with him. Death turns to Michael with his face shrouded in shadow beneath his hood. "An unexpected turn, yes? And here you thought Lucifer only cared for the remains of the mortal Moses."

Michael never turns to acknowledge the dark harvester physically. "What do you care of these matters, Death?" Michael asks.

"Just don't remain blind to all else that moves, Arch of Angels. The very existence of all may come to depend on the minutest of observation."

In an instant Death is where the excavation site had been. Michael watches as the harvester waves his hands and hundreds of blue and red lights souls fashioned as orbs emerge from the sand. Death collects both sets of light in his right hand. When he's done collecting the dead he turns back and nods to Michael and then vanishes.

Michael reaches into his cloak and pulls out a scroll with a red seal of dried blood. He stares long and hard at the seal. It's already been broken by Prince Yeshua, but he knows that once he opens it there is no going back. Once he opens the seal completely the clock has gained pace toward an expedient ending of the world of men.

Michael looks to the heavens. "So, it shall be done. All be to the king of kings." Michael opens the seal and lets the papyrus fall to the ground. "It appears this is how the world ends."

CHAPTER 14

ENEMY OF OLD

"Created in his image has been taken out of context with the lies that have been told to spin such a magnanimous character above reproach. We know better don't we? We know that humans are vile, treacherous, self-serving, jealous, violent sort of creatures that feels we alone are above all else. Sounds like his winning image has come home to roost in humanity."

Quote ~Judas

Vespian, Cainsin (Old Babylon)

Lucien Arcane is the pseudonym that has been etched in much blood. It is the moniker that Lucifer has decided to take as his title to end the debate of who has the right to rule. Through the total whole of history, he's held many names. Names were important with each lie that he joined with it to shape the stage for the endgame which has at last begun. Lucien Arcane is the last name that he'll have to conceal his true identity behind. Adjusting his tailored blue designer suit, Lucien overlooks the night skyline of the empire that he's built over the long since decayed Babylon of ancient days. The winds blow fierce on the roof of his Earthly recreation of what he called home in Iayhoten. The spire reaches far above any other building in his sovereign nation which is just a little smaller than Iraq if compared by the square mileage.

Through centuries of manipulation, accumulated possessions, building influences and seeding terror, Lucifer has amassed a wealth unrivaled by all the nations in the current world. When the time was right, he placed it all at the disposal of his cover nomenclature, Lucien Arcane. For all the power, none surpasses the greed of men. To amass such wealth is to attract men to do your every bidding for just a taste of it.

With the wealth that amassed, Lucien purchased a country, a military might whose technology rivals any of those in the west if not surpasses it. His nuclear arsenal is almost second to none, purely by choice though, he wants the other nations to appear to have more power in their arsenal. Such thoughts allow him the ability to move and divert resources unseen. Who watches countries that are perceived weak. Playing the game of men is a sport that he's excelled at. He plays it better than the natives. Under the cover of anonymity, shell companies, and third parties he has become such a force on the world stage that other superpowers can no longer look past him; No, now they must take notice of him.

Lucien anxiously awaits on the roof of his headquarters looking into the sky as the sun settles for the evening. He tries to keep his excitement to a minimal, because he just can't be sure if all had gone to plan, if Abbadon denies him what he's seeking then any chance of moving forward was over and all his centuries of schemes and machinations would be for not. Patience was truly a virtue in this case. Abbadon needed time to simmer and his anger to subside just a bit. Had he asked a century before today he knows that it would have met with a resounding dream shattering no!

A thunderous boom cracks the sky above Cainsin as the barrier of sound is broken with Warsivious' reentry through the stratosphere. The breaking of the sound barrier draws Lucien attention skyward. He lets go of the railing and backs away making room for Warsivious to land. Within seconds, he rockets in expanding his wings slowing instantly touching down as light as a feather. Once on the surface, Warsivious kneels. Lucien quickly dismisses the protocol as he only wants to know was his number two successful. His first mind was that things did not go well with negotiations as War looked to have been put through an incinerator from the tattering of his uniform.

Without any undue hesitation, Warsivious passes the contained specimen to Lucien. "Negotiations were a little rough, but in the end, he conceded. He released the last known remains of the first Nephilim that was born of the unholy unions of old."

Lucien doesn't say a word. He just looks at the ancient remain as he turns the glass container in his hands looking at it from every angle. *A part of me wants to touch it to make sure this is happening.*

Satisfied, Lucien pats Warsivious on the shoulder for a job well done. "Clean yourself up. Then meet me on eighty-three. I want the lab to start on this immediately.

Within minutes, Lucien enters into the Arcanian's A.I.S. Laboratories. Upon entry, he's stopped at the outer most airlock by a fracture proof plastic barrier. The only break in the barrier is a slot opening that is thoroughly monitored as not to contaminate the inner working space of the sterile lab. Lucien places the encapsulated specimen inside the slot. As he closes it, the clean air protection sterilization system steam blast the container sterilizing it. Once the process is complete the slot opposite of Lucien opens for the technicians on the other side to take possession.

Dr. Alan Polanski waves the techs away and retrieves the specimen himself and holds it up to the crackling light of the florescent lighting for eyeball inspection. "So, this is the culmination of fifteen years of research, eh, Mr. Arcane?"

"It is doctor. I know that you won't let me down, because not only was your fee magnanimous, you promised results. I brought you on because no matter what corner of the world I asked, I was told that your skill was unmatchable in the science of cloning and matrix regeneration. I have spared no expense in making sure you have whatever you need to accomplish this undertaking. You know what I expect, and will accept nothing less than total success."

Dr. Polanski admires the archaic bone; holding it up to the fluorescent lighting inspecting it. "Mr. Arcane, I have completed an extensive work up. This lab was ready five years ago. With the assistance of some of the best minds in applied theory and bio-mechanics of our time we have only improved upon the tech and science since then. This research facility is the most cutting edge on this side of the planet. Making it so has been my only endeavor. American ingenuity and know how is what that part of the world taught me. With the biological sample that was supplied by your exceptional donor, I can assure you that we are more than up to this momentous task. It will be completed, I just ask that you make an allotment or two as this is trial and error. Cloning can be quite a complex venture. But I assure you, we will have your design engineered to your exact specifications within a year, two at the most." The doctor then holds up three fingers and shrugs his shoulders, "worst case scenario, depending on setbacks the final product could take three years."

Lucien nods at Polanski. "I'll hold you to that, doctor. I'll expect a full work up and progress report within the week and one thereafter until conclusion. This is of imperative importance. I will have a contact that will oversee your progress and report to me. This will be you and I last time meeting. When completed Dr. Polanski, I will send Warsivious for final approval and departure processing. You do this for me and you have your own ticket."

Polanski smiles at the prospect of becoming a major player in the world of bio-engineering.

"Not only will you revolutionize bio-engineering Dr. Polanski; you may very well rewrite it becoming the only world's leading expert."

Lucien walks out of the clean room to find Warsivious leaning with his back against the wall waiting. "Place Commander Rusain on this. He is to give the completion of this task his top priority. Also put a set of ethereal eyes on this as well. I want around the clock coverage. Polanski is ambitious after all. Hell, otherwise I wouldn't have chosen him." Lucien turns to walk off stopping abruptly snapping his fingers. "I have a mission for Painell. I need him in Detroit today before the Archs catch wind." Lucien reaches into his inner suit pocket and passes Warsivious a letter with a seal, then he continues walking down the hall. "Have Pain confirm her death. Oh!" Lucien points his thumb over his shoulder. "And Warsivious, when he's completed his task, turn the good Dr. Polanski over to Death."

CHAPTER 15

PACT

"They call you Pharaoh, the God King. You are no such. There is but one and all will bend a knee before him before it is done. You will realize brother, that in the end, all of your wealth and power will not save you."

Quote ~Moses

Detroit, Michigan

Detroit Receiving Hospital, Emergency

Shhht! is the sound of the automated doors opening to the emergency room at Detroit Receiving hospital. Paramedics calm under immense pressure rush in a thirty something caramel brown skinned woman who looks close to full term. Her hair is matted down from bandages soaked in blood from a large gash that is profusely bleeding from her head. The rest of her body is in just as bad shape. Scratches, gashes and lacerations all over her extremities. The paramedics applied wrappings to the most severe wounds for stabilization, but ignored a good portion of the smaller wounds for the expediency of rushing her to Receiving emergency for more advanced treatment.

As the gurney comes over the threshold of the entrance, blood drips from the soaked fitted sheet and rolls down the collapsing legs and wheel assembly of the gurney that the medics push with fervor. Dwayne, the most experienced of the medic duo, rides the side of the gurney consistently compressing her chest at a ratio of thirty compressions to two breaths. Sweating for Dwayne has long passed the beaded stage, it has run the length of his back and chest drenching his uniform. He's been at it during the entire ride to the emergency room. Only times he stopped compressions was to allow the A.E.D. to administer electric shock and to remove the gurney from the ambulance. The attending emergency room physician and crash team readily meets them once through the threshold of the sliding doors. Shhht, the door closes and the true measure of saving a life begins.

Two years out of residency, Dr. Gerald Motiff is ready for the challenge. Only partially briefed by nurses, due to the mobile communication system crashing, the medics weren't able to convey the extent of injuries before their arrival. Nonetheless, Dr. Motiff and his team prepared for the worse and are ready to receive the unfortunate soul and bring her back from the brink of the unknown void and return her to the hardships and overbearing throngs of life. With universal precautions in place for him and his team they meet the medics and guide them into Operating Room one.

The nurse taps Dwayne on the shoulder three times giving him the signal that he can surrender his position and fall back while she takes over. He damn near falls off the gurney from exhaustion as he relinquishes his chest compressions to the fresh abled body nurse who takes over without missing a beat, literally.

The doc throws the sheet back and winces a bit. "Jesus, Dwayne! You guys called in traumatic injuries over the comms; at least that's what we heard before the comms went dead. You didn't say utter body ravaging devastation. Why didn't you guys use your cell?"

"We tried. We couldn't get through. The radios went dead and phones wouldn't connect," Dwayne says.

The bright florescent lighting dim in the emergency room just a bit. As an unseen transparent figure cloaked in shadow appears walking alongside the gurney as they move into the operating room. The shadow moves within a pocket reality. He's intently watching the doctor and his team prepare to do mortal battle with him for her life that he wants to extinguish, that he needs to extinguish to fulfill his given command. The attack he set in motion should have doused her flame of life back on the streets, but the medics were relentless in sustaining her.

The shadow stays with her, keeping his hand on her body, keeping her in darkness and confusion, thus ensuring her demise. Her death is his chance to ascend in rank. Unseen to human eyes is his kinds best offense. The shadow continues to watch those in the room. He peers into their souls to see the will and fortitude of each working to save her life possesses. If he finds a chink in any of them he'll be sure to exploit it. He watches and studies all that moves. His face is pale and ashen white. He was once known to the heavens as Painell, now unleashed on Earth he's come to be known as Pain. And all he knows is the depths of which he runs through a mortal's body sure to illicit reactions from their nerves, specifically targeting the pain sensors, but he doesn't stop there, he inflicts pain on all levels; physical, emotional, and spiritually. From their stance in zero reality, to see the lines and color of a species true form living within the confines of flesh is elementary. Celestials are the reason all other form of subspecies draw breath. Their experiments are the forms that fuel the flesh. So, celestials and demonics such as Pain were taught.

Whenever Painell moves his touch on the unresponsive woman, she winces in his name as if having a nightmare, one she cannot awaken from.

Having caught his breath a bit, Dwayne begins his rundown of the patient's injuries. "We found her on the sidewalk near Ravenswood and Grandriver. The police were on scene prior to us trying to render their version of first aid. Lucky, they didn't finish her off. She had lost a lot of blood. The dummies were resuscitating her without controlling the bleeding. They were just helping the heart pump the remaining blood right out of her."

Doc, looking into her eyes with a flashlight for dilatational responses. "Weapon recovered?" the doc questioned.

"None that the cops found while we were there. I looked around where I could, but nothing that stood out. It looks as if she was hit multiple times with a blunt object in some instances and serrated in others."

Dr. Motiff nearing completion of his initial scan of the injuries and vitals, places the stethoscope on her stomach. "She's obviously pregnant. I'd guesstimate near full term. We have multiple fractures, lacerations that run deep. Look at the color of that blood around the abdomen. It's dark and viscous. Not a good sign. We have multiple arterial bleeds. And the amniotic sac is leaking. Just feeling her scalp here, I can tell it's fractured. The brain is more than likely still swelling. Eyes are fixed and unresponsive to light. With the neural injury and multitude of lacerations including the arteries, I'm going to need help. This room is not equipped for what she has going on. We need to move her to a room more equipped. Amazing, she's even still alive... Time you placed the tourniquets Wayne?"

"Twenty-two minutes ago, give or take," he answered.

Nurses having received the initial assessment instantly upgrade their precautions by placing on their isolation surgical gowns.

A nurse hanging up the phone runs over to Dr. Motiff. "O.R. three! The neurosurgeon will meet us there. I'm still trying to get in touch with someone from Peads or Gyno."

The team quickly relocates to operating room three.

The cadre of emergency staff enter the operating room. They wheel her over to the awaiting operating table. The team grabs a hold of the sheet by its edges and lift her onto the table. They immediately strip the bloody sheets away. Her clothing had mostly been torn away already by the violent incident that she was the unfortunate recipient of. The remaining tatters were removed by the medics during stabilization. The surgeon enters the room quickly. Already scrubbed and decontaminated to the best that is humanly possible, he places his hands up in front of him awaiting a nurse who quickly places gloves on his hands while another tie off his isolation gown and mask.

Dr. Jeremy Pitor has over twenty years of surgical experience. The last five he's specialized in neural after fifteen in cardiac. He's not shaken a bit by even the most extreme of injuries at this point of his career. He's damn near seen it all. Dr. Pitor looks to the emergency Doctor, without hesitation. Dr. Motiff gives him his full workup and assessment of the dying woman. Satisfied with the preliminary report, he takes over.

"We need to check her back." Dr. Pitor points to where he wants the team to grab.

The nurses and remaining medic grabs the ravaged patient by the roll points of her appendages and wait for the command to pull.

Dr. Pitor nods his head making sure everyone is in sync. "On three. One, two, three, roll!"

They roll her over and checks for any open lacerations on her back. Satisfied with what he sees, Pitor gives the command to lay her back. In unison, the team lies her back flat. The paramedic backs away as he looks to Dr. Pitor for relief. With one quick observation, the surgeon notices the condition of the disheveled medic.

"You stand relieved, Wayne. Now get out of here, get cleaned up and get some rest. Just be detailed in your report. Hey! I briefly gazed over the entry report making my way down here, make sure you talk to whoever you need to talk to about getting that radio fixed."

"Who said it was our end?" Dwayne said shrugging his shoulders.

Dr. Pitor nods his head contorting his face to convey the gesture, touché! "Great job Wayne. You need to stop playing and do the bridge over classes and join my team.

"You guys work to hard Doc. Now, do what you do best, Snatch her back from the brink... Goodluck."

The surgeon looks over at his surgical team of nurses and technicians standing by with equipment. He nods and waves them over. The surgical team moves in. They immediately start setting up without missing a beat. Working the nightshift together for the last two years have become a benefit to the inflicted that arrives on their table, because together they are a well-oiled machine. Detroit Receiving has the reputation of bringing back the dead, they weren't about to let that change without one hell of fight.

"Dr. Motiff?"

"Yes, Doctor," Motiff quickly replies.

"I can use you here tonight. I want you to do some training and gather a bit of experience. You think Melissa can spare you for a few?"

"Slow night. I think she can manage a while without me."

"She won't have a choice, it wasn't much of a request now that I think about it. It's more of an order," Pitor says. He nods his head insinuating that Motiff follows him.

The surgical team has the failing patient prepped in a flash, but what kind of doctor would Pitor be if he didn't demand better? "I need life support. We're going to need a lot of blood dammit! Get one pint of O positive while we run test to ascertain her type! C'mon people let's get a line going!"

They all work at a feverish pace.

"Where is support?" asks Dr. Pitor.

The nurse, looking frantic, begins to shake and hit the machine for compliance. "Doctor, I can't get life support up and going. Everything reads green. There's no reason it shouldn't be working."

A tech runs over to the nurse and tries his hand at booting up the machine.

"C'mon! I need that crash cart guys. I needed yesterday, make it happen or get me a new one!" Says Pitor.

Painell upon reality phasing entered into the room wreaking havoc with their equipment. The second he entered in the room it was instantly consumed in a darkness that is subconsciously known to the human realm. Though not scene in its literal meaning, the effects are able to be felt. The feeling that Pain can exude is one of worthlessness, depression, despair. Not all pain is physical. The concept can cover all gambits of the human existential experience.

The nurse continues to fumble around with the life sustaining cart in multiple attempts to get it up and running. "I don't know! It's reading that it's receiving power. I don't know why it's not working. It was just operational a before I rolled it in here. System check read nominal."

The surgeon looks down at the Jane Doe. Her eyes are open but, there's no one there. To him it looks as if he's looking into an empty house through hazy windows. He places his hand gently on her stomach. And feels that there is no movement from the fetus. He places his other hand for the briefest of moments on the side of her jaw lightly rubbing it to comfort her just in case she was still in there somewhere looking for a way back to consciousness. *So young, so tragic for this to have happened to her,* he thought.

"To hell with that cart, find another! She's leaking from everywhere. She's an effin mess. Where the hell is the obstetrician? We need this baby out yesterday I'm sure mom has only survived this long because she drawing the access blood from the fetus." Dr. Pitor says.

The triage nurse still on the phone glances over toward Dr. Pitor. "Still, no answer. The calls aren't going out."

A purple-haired nurse checks Jane Doe's pulse and finds one. "Stop C.P.R.! I have a pulse. It's weak, but it's there."

The tech runs from the room in search of another crash cart. Pitor's nurse pats the sweat from his brow as he starts mending the brachial artery while Dr. Motiff is working the smaller laceration around the femoral in an attempt to halt the blood loss. Motiff's nerves start to show a bit. His actions are more rigid than the veteran Pitor. His nurse assigned to him checks to make sure he remains steady and reassures him every chance she can. Dr. Pitor looks up and down at him briefly. "Steady Tiff, you have this. A stroll in the park," says Dr. Pitor as his eyes return back to his work.

Painell sighs looking at the surgeon closely. He peers deep into the make-up of his soul to see what he's made of. *This one although primitive in his technique is a skilled healer it seems. So sure of yourself, so confident.* He circles the surgeon multiple times looking at the cracks in his soul. He sees many hairline fractures deep within. Pitor is strong of spirit, but if there's a crack, then there was a place for doubt that he would exploit. Painell places his hand on the surgeon slightly tampering with the cracks that he could visibly see. The doctor instantly is flushed with self-doubt. Pitor's concentration breaks. He looks up and around at his staff. He sees the team is working in tandem. He's proud of them and their accomplishments as well as his own up to this point in his life. However, he can't shake the feeling that he needs help, that he isn't good enough. He attempts to shake the feeling of dread, but it feels attached like a gang of leaches.

"Where is that damn obstetrician? She should have been here by now," Pitor repeats.

The nurse practitioner to Pitor's immediate left is assisting in stitching the lacerations to the abdomen. She looks over at Pitor and can tell he's stressing. He's missing obvious clues. If she knows that a c-sect is the right call then what is he waiting for? She looks him in the face making sure she has his attention so, there is no mistake in what she indirectly addresses toward him. *He has to get it, he needs to make c-sect prep.* She thinks to herself. Seeing that he appears stuck, she has an idea to give him a jump start. "Doc, I'll make sure that the instruments are ready for the c-sect when the obstetrician arrives." She emphasized c-sect to give Pitor the needed boost to get him thinking in that direction, but he wasn't picking it up. "Doc you'll have to give the c-sect!"

He doesn't know why, but he becomes instantly pissed at her. *I know that she's right, but how dare a practitioner tell me what I'll have to do.*

"CLAMP, HAND ME A DAMN CLAMP!" he yells at the practitioner.

"You didn't ask for one till now." She replies back calm but stern.

Operating Room – Half hour later

Dr. Motiff quickly glances up at Pitor then returns to his work of patching the secondary lacerations that could instantly become a primary concern until Pitor can take over. Dr. Pitor finishes closing off the brachial and then maneuvers into laceration above the fetus, which was leaking blood that was more watery and brownish red. Still shaken for some odd reason he can't quite place a finger on. His resolve kicks in and he shakes the lingering doubt from his mind and enters the laceration near her stomach.

"Almost got it, almost got it. C'mon, you fuck, where are you?" Pitor was louder than he thought. The team looks at him briefly then continues working. He continues to fish for the tiny artery that is leaking.

This one's resolve is stronger than I believed first believed. Painell looks around the room and instantly fine the energy line the powers the room. Mortals see the tangibility of how energy is transferred. Humans see that positives and negatives intertwined create the hate that moves energy producing electrical currents. Celestials see the more basic kernel of the etherealness that is blind to the human oculus. Pain places his forefinger and thumb on the ethereal line of energy and snaps his fingers and the room is plunged into darkness. The power to the operating room blacks out. It is completely dark except for the illumination of the lighting outside of the O.R, where lighting hasn't been affected at all. Confused, all Pitor can do is hold until the power is restored.

"Backups should be coming back on in a second," says one of the techs.

The room remains in darkness past the fifteen second reboot window. Dr. Pitor and Dr. Motiff can barely see each other, but they know that they have a serious problem brewing if the power isn't restored.

"Shit! It's not powering back up" says the nurse.

Pitor anxiously waiting for the darkness to lift. "You took the words right out of my mouth. I just don't get it. The back-up generator should have kicked on by now. I can't see a damn thing; I'm scared to move my hands. This is ridiculous. Carosone, flash lights, now! Go now!"

The tech Carosone moves quickly, but methodically through the room until he reaches the door. Once there he slides the door open letting in a flood of light from the hall way.

"Keep those doors open. That'll have to do for the time being," says Motiff. "But, find me those flashlights!"

As Motiff completes another set of stitches by the light of the hallway it dawns on him that maybe the backups won't kick in because only this room is affected. "We may have to relocate to another room."

As the nurse pats the sweat from Pitor's forehead, he looks over momentarily at Motiff. "I can have a week and still won't have enough time to tell you why that's a bad idea right now. I don't think we should move her anymore, period. It might kill her and the baby. Damn! The baby's moving. Ha! It's moving. A little good news for a change.

Looking up at the ceiling, Pitor begins to concede his skill. He feels that sinking feeling that he alone won't be able to pull this woman from the brink. Filled again with self-doubt for some reason and with Murphy's Law in full effect he gives in and asks God for assistance just beneath a whisper. *I'm not a religious man, but, just a little help here wouldn't hurt please.*

Please, please, please, please echoes and reverberates up throughout the hospital and into the night sky. *Please,* prayed by Dr. Pitor is the one of many that rides an invisible stream of endless prayers from around not just the world, but galaxies and realities in that precise moment. The current of prayers rides like waves in multiple rivers into the Zero Realm's Transcommunacative Hub located in the outskirts of Jacintian. Once received, the Choiretic Corp of celestials working the Hub disseminates

Jacintian's Transcommuncative Hub

Please, please, please, Pitor's words echo into the ear of Perceiver Volaxis, a celestial resident of Iayhoten operating the Section 72 of reality hub 2814. Volaxis is slender with elongated fingers meant to sift through the endless strands of incoming prayers from across the numerous realities and galaxies. The Hub breaks up the communiques by reality and assigns one perceiver per galaxy within that specific reality that has the soul purpose of collecting the prayer and placing them in que to be answered or denied. Sitting pulling the strands of the incoming prayers from the Sol System which contains Earth, Volaxis observes the crystalline textured strand illuminate brighter than the others surrounding it. When a strand illuminates it means that it has been tagged for key words by a higher celestial as a warning to be on the lookout for that particular line of communique. Volaxis swipes his hand right clearing the other surrounding strands. He pinches the lighted one and pulls it down reading the glyph text contained within it. The incoming prayer has been given priority and is to be forwarded to the palace for decisive decision. His section remains highlighted within the Hub because that is containment of Lucifer and Hades. He slides the strand into a different stream. He turns the strand purple and sends it on its way to the Eternal Palace for reply.

Elohim's Eternal Palace of Iayhoten

With his hands clasped behind his back, Elohim stands looking down at his Throne with his eyes closed his thoughts deep in meditation when the purple strand enters from atop the sky opening within his chamber that is a 4D map of every reality and all galaxies under his purview. Hearing the cry for assistance from Dr. Pitor. Elohim opens his eyes and listens intently to the words spoken by the mortal. Not that he's moved by such a plea from a man that has for the whole of his life believed in the tangible, it is that Pitor has a responsibility of caring for a special package at its most crucial time. Elohim turns from his throne and leaves the chamber heading for the door. His guards watching his approach knocks twice on the chamber's door and stands aside at attention. The door opens. As Elohim exits there are two columns of seven Etherealtorial Guards that moves with him on either side. A precaution that was not needed before the schism. Elohim raises his hand to stay their movement. With complete loyalty, they instantly stop in unison allowing him to carry on alone.

Elohim walks with his hands still clasped behind his back all the way to the end of the hall. All palace life that he passes bow in his wake. Elohim nods and acknowledges his subjects and continues on toward his son's chamber. He walks through the doors of the prince's quarters where he finds Yeshua overlooking his armor and sword making augmentations and minor tweaks. He's silent at first just observing his son and his armor. He walks around him giving the armor a cursory glance. Elohim walks to the armor and runs his fingers over the glyphs etched on the shoulder armor plate. "Do you often regret your place here in the palace?" Says Elohim.

Yeshua turns and bows. His father waves protocol and signals him to rise.

"I may speak freely?" Elohim nods yes. "I never want to seem ungrateful, but there are times that I do, yes… I do regret the time that I stand behind these walls watching others fight our battles for a schism that blindsided us."

"That blindsided me," Elohim corrects him. He studies his son for a moment then returns to admiring his armor that he's crafted. "You want to be an Arch? You're impressed by them?"

"Don't change the subject! You alone were not blindsided, you can't take all the blame. I played with Lucifer in our early days, He walked the halls of our palace and overflew your throne as you made decisive decisions to govern all that you created, that we created. I spoke with him just as much as any of all the others and yet ill intent was able to grow within him and spread as a cancer unnoticed. The hell, legions of celestials including the De' Mons sided with him and not once did I catch wind of it."

"Nor did I, son. Until then, I never had need to look futurecast... Now my days are nothing but—Anticipating every move until the Endgame."

Elohim walks closer and inspects the tunic under the armor of his son's. "It's fine looking armor there you've created. It's very Archian. I believe Michael would be pleased with how it turned out."

Ever since what man did to me all those years ago on Golgotha, I have been waiting for the time that I could be given word to return. And when that day comes and that the word is given, it would find me ready. My armor lies constructed and in wait ready for that's moment's notice when—"

Iehovah squints his eyes sharply at his son. "—I give the word to return. When I do and you are given charge will it be for mercy or for vengeance?" Elohim asks.

"No, not for vengeance... That is for you alone father. For me, it is to finish what I started. To keep promises to old friends that gave much in my name when they didn't have to... When you sent me to 2814, I first thought that I didn't want to fail you; no task that you have ever given me has meant so much to me, and I mean to finish it. I mean to set Lucifer straight and all those that follow him and bring them all to heel for all time."

Yeshua looks at his father's brow and knows he's troubled. "What is it, Father?"

"When I created man, I marveled at what I had done. Apart from every other species that populate the Sadohedranicverse, with them I had captured my image and likeness so perfectly that I fear I had committed vanity. To a point one could say I did and Lucifer called me on it. I put such faith into them and—"

"They have yet to fail you, Father. I have walked among them long after you'd spoken the last of words to them. I know their hearts are easily corrupted better than anyone here, but what you've imparted on them is not easily shaken or cast aside. They are resolute and full of wonders. They never cease to amaze with their brilliance and resilience. They were created weaker than any other being that thinks but that impairment has not deterred them. They preserver in spite of their flaw. We seeded them across many planets among the ocean of stars. This here, this Earth this one here in 2814 is the one that took and prospered. It is the last bastion of men across all the remaining galaxies. All others did not take root and have failed when this infinitesimal squalor did not. The very fact that shows their strength and resilience. There is a beauty to them that makes them marvelous."

Elohim smiles at the way his son talks of them. "Sure, you're not just being bias?" *It not hard to tell that he misses being among them. They are an infectious species that are easy to love, but just as easily to hate. That is why in one of them, I have decided to place the fate of their own existence an existence that the good Doctor Pitor is attempting to preserve. Damn Satan, Damn that Devil.* "Lucifer has set in motion events today that contradict my own law. I cannot intervene under the rules of his conditional reprieve. As in the time of Job when challenged by him, I will depend on my creations to set their path while under duress."

Yeshua stares at his father for a few more moments. "I believe that your faith in them is not misplaced. I myself would bet the palace on them."

Elohim smiles. "I'm betting the Throne and all of existence on them." Elohim pulls a scroll from underneath his robe. There is a prayer that is in desperate need of reply. Within this scroll is a covenant that I again will enter into with man. Take this to Gabriel with most haste."

Yeshua takes the scroll and bows again before his father and leaves the chamber.

Elohim continues to inspect Yeshua's armor. *Fine craftsmanship I must admit...* Elohim's thoughts then turn to Lucifer. *This is my doing. I should have paid more attention to my morning star. Does he hate me so much? Or, does he really know about me?*

JERICHO'S BANE

DEATH

CHAPTER 16

Detroit Receiving Hospital

The lights flicker on and off intermittently as Pitor continues to work on his patient, they have finally stabilized her to a modicum degree of normalcy in spite of minor flickers of light every few seconds and ever continuing and mounting and compounding problems that have far exceeded Murphy's Law.

Suddenly the lights flickering ceases and they illuminate to full brightness chasing away the darkness and shadows, the illumination reveals a cloaked hooded figure standing in front of the Dr. Pitor simply observing him.

Painell surprised by the Arch's appearance grabs the hilt of his weapon. Before he can bring it to bare and wield it, two choiretic angels appear on either side of him grabbing him by both arms. One of the angels pushes his wrist downward forcing Painell's blade back into its sheath. Power is instantly restored to all the equipment. The hooded angel turns his head and faces the demon pulling his hood back revealing his identity. It's the Archangel Metatron. His eyes are fiery red, his face is stern, he is pissed off.

The nurse having faintly heard the Surgeon's prayer earlier leans in close and whispers to him. "Sounds as if someone up there heard you Doctor. The lights are back, as well as the equipment."

Dr. Pitor regains his full confidence. "It appears they have, nurse. Let's hope I stay in their good fortune." Pitor turns his attention to the fetus. "We have no choice I don't know where delivery is. Mom is still an unknown at this point. I'm going to have to be real about her chances. Let's deliver this baby and then worry about mom."

Metatron places his right hand on the surgeon's shoulder. "You've been heard, Jeremy Pitor. All the choirs of Heaven are with you."

The O.R. team all nod in agreement as they shift the course of care from mom to baby. Dr. Motiff s switches tactics by doubling his efforts to stabilize the woman while Dr. Pitor switches to preparation for the emergency C-section.

Painell doesn't even struggle against the angels that have him in their control. He simply grins at the Arch. "Metatron," he says.

"Pain," Metatron replies.

Painell starts to struggle slightly attempting to break free from his captors. "I heard whispers of you in the shadows. You and the other Archs. I should feel honored that I warrant a visit from such one of the famed saviors of Glayden."

Metatron satisfied that Pitor has regained his spiritual composure removes his guiding touch from him and walks over to Painell. The demon stops struggling as he feels the uselessness of it.

"I'm not here for you, creature. I was in the children's cancer ward, easing what you have wrought with your very presence here when I heard this mortal cry out. I was quickly given authority to intervene on his spiritual behalf."

"I'm not looking to cross blades and draw blood here. I was just looking to have a little fun. It seems that my fun is at an end Arch?" Painell playfully raises his hands in surrender.

"You have never been more right than you are now vile thing." Metatron nods his head for the angels to take Painell away. "Mistake me not, I see you back here this night Demon, I will surely remove your head from neck without due process or hesitation."

The choiretic angels back away still detaining Pain as they phase through the wall leading out into the hall way removing the demon.

Metatron looks around the room then focuses on the operating table. Satisfied that he's the only celestial in the room he looks to his left. "It's clear, sister."

A cylindrical white beam of light touches down in the room. Gabriel emerges from within the brilliant flash of light suddenly appearing next to Metatron. She removes her hood and instantly turns toward the woman on the table clinging to life. Gabriel looks compassionately upon the face of the young woman and places her right hand on her forehead. "I have the room brother, stand watch for any other that would have ill intent on her this night."

Metatron places his fist to his chest acknowledging the orders from his immediate superior Gabriel. He places his hand on the Surgeon's back giving him another shot of confidence and then proceeds to walk out of the operating room by phasing through the wall as well.

Ignoring the anonymous nomenclature given to her by the hospital, Gabriel calls Jane Doe by her given name, "Rachel." Because it's on her forehead etched in orange and blueish flame script that only a celestial can see.

Dr. Pitor begins to make the incision starting the C-section. Rachel's eyes open as she instantly regains consciousness upon hearing her name called by Gabriel. Her vision is blurry at first but, it slowly starts to come into focus. As her vision clears, she realizes that everyone in the room is so still and unmoving as if frozen.

Rachel's intubated breathing tubes assisting her in breathing by forcing air into her bruised lungs cease to work. Monitors that have been hooked up to her almost non-existent vital signs in hopes of observing the slightest of change have frozen mid blip. It's crystal clear to her now that time has completely stopped, frozen in the moment. The anesthesiologist is statuesque in place, checking the I.V. over Rachel's head. The droplet contained within the drip is suspended inside the tubing from the bag to the line. Everything is frozen with the her and Gabriel being the exception.

Gabriel rubs Rachel's head, soothing her. "Do not be frightened; I am with you just as I was with you before your birth, I am here at the end."

The endotracheal tube lifts from her mouth slowly as if an invisible hand is pulling it out. Toward the halfway point of being expelled, a hand materializes on the tube crossing from Zero Reality into 2814's.

Gabriel, pulls away the tube allowing her to breathe unassisted. Gabriel allows her full self to be seen by Rachel by adjusting a sliding dial on her right gauntlet phasing into reality 2814 completely. Gabriel gazes over her soul assessing it by the laws of which it's lived life all the while continuously stroking her matted hair soothing her.

Rachel can only whisper to such a sight as beautiful as Gabriel. "I know you, I know your face." She pauses as she tries to remember. Then it comes to her. "Gabriel."

"Hello, Rachel Michelle Bane."

Rachel smiles a Cheshire grin feeling no pain as the angelic being has called her by full name. Rachel tries to sit up but, nothing happens. Her body isn't responding. She equates the feeling to waking up to fast but, your body is still asleep.

"I can't move."

Compassionately, Gabriel responds, "No you cannot. Your body is failing you. Soon your eyes will dim and your light will be extinguished from this world's plain of existence."

Rachel starting to understand, her eyes begin to well with salted tears. "I'm dying?"

"Yes Rachel, you are," Gabriel says.

Rachel takes a moment of silence to herself. Tears begin to run from her eyes down each side of her cheeks. It tickles as the stream of saltwater cuts a path through the dried-up blood on her face clearing a wet path down to either ear.

Rachel's eyes move downward towards her belly. "My baby?"

Gabriel wipes her tears. "We'll get to that in time. Right now, we have forever."

The tears intensify as she looks up at Gabriel. "I have stayed faithful, Gabriel. I dedicated my life to Him. If I ever wavered it was only a moment, yeah?"

"No, you have not wavered. That is why I am here. I've been tasked to ask you for one last act of love, a love from a soul that has known nothing but an abundance of it."

She sniffles. "What more can he ask of me? Look at me. I'm a mess," says Rachel. "I was working at the shelter and—"

"Shh! Gabriel places her finger on the cleft above Rachel's lip. "I am looking at you Rachel, the whole of heaven is looking at you and so is he. We all have our eyes set to you."

"Then what, Gabriel? What more is asked of me? Look at me, this is my reward for years of faithful service." Rachel tears run continuous. "I hurt, I'm in so much pain."

"Let me help with that." Gabriel wipes her palm over the face of Rachel misplacing her horrific memory of the past trauma inducing tragedy. As she reaches the temple she pinches slightly and pulls a liquid strand from mind. With that singular displaced strand, the events of the last hour has been nullified. Gabriel then places her left hand on Rachel's stomach as her right continues to stroke her blood matted hair. Gabriel's silence is deafening to Rachel.

Rachel's face contorts in confusion, she forgotten what she was talking about. Her attention turns back to words of Gabriel.

"Rachel what we're going to talk about over the next fraction of a second is going to be tough. Rachel blinks her eyes gesturing to continue. "Your son will enter this world lifeless." Gabriel touch is reassurance made tangible, but it duels to calm her and ease the pain from the passing of this life into the next.

Broken and short of breath Rachel is barely able to muster the words, "Still born?" She swallows and takes a moment to think. "This has to do with why you're here doesn't it? Doesn't it? Dear God, that's why you're hear, Gabriel, what more does He want? Not my baby, you tell him not my baby!"

Shh! Again, Gabriel places her finger over Rachel's cleft. "Your compassionate soul is to light the child's way, Rachel. Will you give life to where there will be none?"

Tears continuing rolling down her face. "If it's to save my baby, Gabriel, then yes, yes, a thousand times yes."

"All that you are, soon all that you were. Your love, your faith, your goodness, your light of soul, your heart, will you willingly pass all that you are and have been to your son so that he may live? Will you willingly part with a piece of your soul?

She cries. "You didn't even have to ask? Gabriel, I would sacrifice everything for him." She cries harder. "I can't rub my stomach. I can't rub my baby."

Gabriel expanding her wings. "Here, let me." Gabriel gently massages Rachel's pregnant belly, soothing and comforting her. She rubs her forehead again, running her fingers along the parietal lobe of the brain passing the sensation of touch to Rachel. Through Gabriel, it feels as if she's rubbing her stomach. It soothes her immensely.

"Understand, this must be of your own free will. There must be no outside influence no deals, no bargaining. This act must be an act of your own accord and freely given."

"It's given. All that I am is given to him."

Gabriel looks closely upon Rachel's face. "He will be blessed, Rachel. The light of the Elohim will shine upon his countenance in dark times that are still yet to come."

Her sobs lessen. "I have one question for you, Gabriel?"

Gabriel continues to stare at her lovingly.

"Can I see him before I die? I just want to see him, okay?"

Silence overtakes the room for seems an eternity for Rachel. Gabriel's eyes change to a hue of gray. "No. You will not live to bear witness to his birth… Understand that time may appear frozen, but we are actually suspended within a dispensation time effervesce from my reality. Where I'm from times moves slightly differently then it does here. Here, our conversation is taking place in-between what you would call a second. That in between millimeter of the turn when the beginning of Death occurs. In your reality, you've already passed on."

She cries again, but is able to manage a slight smile. "It's not fair."

"It seldomly is, but you've lived on this plain of existence long enough to know that. Gabriel says.

"Will he know that his mommy loved him?"

"Your son will know of your deeds and forever feel your love. Your son has been chosen to be an instrument of the King, a mortal knight if you please. He will be a hand that will again redefine man's future. Not since the days of Samson will a mortal have the powers that he will possess nor will any ever again. This system of things is coming to a close and passing away.

Rachel stops crying. "Coming to an end?"

"I promise you he will do great things, Rachel before it is done. All that will be asked of him is to abstain from intercourse as his show of faith to the almighty. For if he does not, his covenant will be broken. It will not just be broken for him but, for all mankind that now it seems fates are intertwined."

Rachel's tears start to stream again. "He's part of me. He will hold the covenant. He must." Rachel looks Gabriel in her eyes. "I now charge you, Gabriel, I charge you to watch over him. You mustn't let him falter."

"He won't, Rachel, because I won't let him. I promise!"

Rachel looks at Gabriel with sadden eyes but, is at ease with what must soon follow. She always thought that she'd be afraid to die. She can't remember now why she was ever afraid to begin with.

"Can I name him, Gabriel?"

"You may name him whatever you wish and it will be honored."

"I want his name to be Jericho."

Gabriel touches Rachel's face to wipe her tears. "I couldn't think of a stronger name. I shall suggest same to your mother." Gabriel runs her hands across her brow. "Are you ready, Rachel Michelle Bane?" Gabriel whispers.

Rachel begins to cry a flowing river of tears of joy. "I'm ready."

"Close your eyes!" Gabriel covers Rachel's eyes and shows her a glimpse of Iayhoten, a world of beauty. Gabriel gives Rachel a full playback of the best moments that she had experienced free of the pain that her life was racked with. At the end of her escapade she closes her eyes for the last time in this life. Gabriel looks from her body towards the Heavens and time is once again restored. Everything is as it was before Gabriel's arrival. The anesthesiologist that was frozen once again, continues on with her routine of checking the I.V. When she looks down at Rachel she looks as if she was never disturbed, as if the whole Gabriel conversation had never happened. The intubation tube has been replaced and is working at optimal performance.

Dr. Pitor makes the incision. He's skilled and fast as he extracts the infant from the womb tearing the placenta. He quickly cuts the umbilical and begins to clear the airway. He listens for the first gasp of air and cry that follows. Nothing.

"Breathe, dammit! Breathe!" Pitor keeps repeating.

The medical team led by Dr. Motiff continues trying to revive Rachel who they've only known as Jane Doe. The vitals on the screen flat line. Again, C.P.R. starts, followed by rounds of defibrillation to get her static heart pumping. Dr. Pitor quickly switches off with Dr. Motiff handing him the baby while he takes over the resuscitation efforts of Rachel. Dr. Motiff instantly continues C.P.R on the baby as well.

"The baby's still not breathing." Motiff isn't put off and gains only more resolve to continue rescue compressions at thirty to two breaths.

Within seconds of the tradeoff the doors of the operating room open. The obstetrician enters the room at a full trot. She quickly goes to work by relieving the baby from Motiff and instantly goes to work on reviving him herself. Exhausted, but not out, Dr. Motiff returns to assisting Pitor. While the doctors work to save the two, Gabriel continues stroking the face and hair of Rachel unseen.

Gabriel looks across the table into the shadows of the brightly lit room. "You're always there, aren't you? Just ever beneath the surface, creeping, watching."

"Always, messenger," a voice replies from the shadows.

Death emerges from the overcast shadows of the equipment in the operating room he walks to the other side of the operating table where he can clearly see Gabriel.

"Before you take her soul, you are to soul tap her for the child." Gabriel reaches into her cloak and passes a scroll to Death. Death takes it and breaks the seal. He takes a moment to read it. After reading it he passes it back to Gabriel.

"As it was written, Messenger," Death says.

He looks into the face of Rachel for a moment. Without any more hesitation, he places his hand into her chest just to the left of the heart and pulls a bright white orb of light out of her body. Death's eyes widen a bit at the color of the soul's orb. He quickly regains his composure and cusps the bright light differently than any of the other blue or red hues. He then walks over to Jericho as the obstetrician continues to try and revive him. He looks at the child. Holding the white orb light in his right hand, Death tears just the smallest piece from it and places the small bright light of Rachel's soul sphere into the child.

"It is done Messenger." Death places the remaining soul sphere into the blackness of his inner coat.

Gabriel stands and looks death in the face. She peers into his eyes. "Treat that soul with the reverence it deserves or you will incur my wrath on that great and horrible day."

His smirk is villainous in reply, but he nods and heads for the door. "I have a few more souls to collect from here tonight. The children's terminal cancer ward is racked with them. I'll make sure she gets to her destination."

"No tarrying about. You read the contents of the seal. This is not of your leisure."

Pissed he's been commanded, he nods that the order has been understood. Gabriel awaits his confirmation.

"There will be no delay Messenger."

"You hear that?" The obstetrician calls out. "Shh! Quiet everyone!"

Gabriel pauses and looks at the obstetrician and the premature baby that she holds in her arms in hopes to revive. Jericho starts crying. The OB-GYN is elated so much so that she feels no stings of exhaustion from working the overnight in the children's cancer unit. She rushes the baby out of the operating room in a half sprint to pediatrics with a nursing staff behind her for assisted care.

Having no luck in reviving Rachel, Dr. Pitor looks over at Motiff. They give each other a nod. Their look tells them that they are on the same page. There's nothing else they can do. Dr. Pitor gestures to stop life saving measures by slashing his hand quickly across his neck.

"That's it. I'm going to call it. The time is two fifty-seven AM for the time of death." Dr. Pitor starts removing his surgical mask and head gear. He takes a long solemn look at Rachel.

The anesthesiologist walks up and places her hand on Pitor's shoulder. "As bad as she looks, she looks peaceful somehow now, eh doc?"

"Yeah… I was looking at that. Her face looks almost as if she's smiling."

Dr. Pitor, satisfied he's done all he could, nods to the tech who then pulls the sheet over her body and face.

Disappointed, Dr. Pitor walks out into the hallway and stops the admin clerk. "Get the admin team of yours locating next of kin." He snaps his fingers remembering a question. "Are the police here? Never mind, of course they are. Tell them I'll talk to them as soon as I clean myself up."

Death turns back and looks at the shell of Rachel. He opens his cloak and her soul is in ethereal form standing next to him shielded beneath his coat. The sphere of light has become her heart within her new celestial body.

Death, turning to leave, looks back just a quarter of a turn over his shoulder. "You think that this will balance scales Messenger?"

"It must balance it. If the child fails, then all is lost." She looks intently at Death. "Wouldn't you say?"

Gabriel walks over and hugs Dr. Pitor from the back placing her wings around the man encompassing him. Dr. Pitor is filled with forgiveness. He lets the nagging pain of failing Jane Doe fall away. He feels consoled, and he feels at peace with all his choices that he made over the last hour.

CHAPTER 17

OMNIPRESENT

"You believe yourself a man of destiny, one of divine providence. You are just simply a man with proclamation for provocation."

Quote ~Death

Hades Great Hall of Eternal Regret

M ist rises just outside the entrance of a long hallway that appears to extend into infinity. The mist has many purposes, but none more than to obscure the way to Hadesus third low tier of Heaven. The path is known only to the dead and must be kept as so. The dying or those infirmed to the point of awaiting death must never know the path. If known, they'll choose to walk it leaving their life before the appointed time, because whosoever discovers the path will be overtaken by death.

Such a path is spoken of by those that return from near death experiences noting that there was a light at the end of a dark tunnel. Actually, it's the illumination of the beginning of the tunnel in a thick mist that they are actually seeing. Those that heed the warning and return the way they came, return to life that was merely interrupted. Those that continue on to investigate find only Death awaiting them at the gates of what mortals misinterpreted as Hades when the name slipped during the final days of Noah's first age.

Rachel runs her hands through the mist as she follows Death into what she perceives as a hallway illuminated by a soft bright light that seems to come from nowhere in particular, but yet is everywhere. The walls of the barrel vault tunnel are made of flowing translucent liquid with grayish white marble blended into it. Ancient glyphs from celestial writings engrave the walls of the hall. As script progress down the length of the hall the writing on the wall covers all forms of language as they evolved through the ages. There is tongue from every species that has lived and transcended the hall. Script from Aramaic, Hebrew, Norse, Greek, Chinese, to that of animal species as well such as Avian, and Crocodilian tongue. She doesn't know how she knows, but Rachel can see and understand the most unintelligible scribble as alien dialect from off world.

As the hall comes to an end, the walls are free of script. Death escorts Rachel down the remaining length of the hall. As soon as she passes into the script free section, a thin glowing flame burns English script into the wall. The script is the tongue of Rachel. It is the whole of her life written made visible in tangible etching. She pauses in awe at the self-writing translucent stone. Death lightly grabs her by the arm and leads her toward the end of the hall where an opening lets out into a bluish hue color. She witnesses every word that she's spoken up until the final words that she exchanged with Gabriel.

Death's boots crack hard against the stoned surface of the hallway's floor. As they draw ever closer to the bluish hue, Rachel's gaze is locked forward. The exit is nigh and instead of feeling anxious or even fearful, she feels comfort that she can only describe as the feeling of returning home. The glow emanating from the hue is warming. It intensifies as they near the end of the hall. No longer needing to be assisted by Death, Rachel freely begins to quicken her pace toward the warmth. Her senses are experiencing what she knows she can't explain or ever find the words for. Her experience is so encapsulating that it never occurs to her that she even had a mortal life. She no longer remembers cares or worries of a life gone by and an early expiration. All she knows is that she wants to be in that warmth of the glowing hue.

"Where does this lead?" Rachel questions.

"To the place of waiting is the best your tongue would understand," Death replies.

Rachel looking confused, asks, "The waiting place? Waiting for what?

Death just keeps walking. He doesn't reply. Suddenly as if a flash from a camera had ignited she remembers. "Where the dead wait for judgment."

"Why is it always the same questions with you lower species. To hear them again and again is mind numbing. As you mortals say. 'See wasn't such a long walk in the park was it'?" he says, sarcastically. "You remember your bible lessons yes? The book of half accounts and time lapsed written record?"

"I do. I also remember that King Solomon said that the dead are conscience of nothing. He said the dead are like a flame that has been extinguished."

"And yet here you are. No longer breathing, but very much walking, talking and conscious of all." Says Death.

Rachel places her hand to her mouth and blows. She repeats it a few times to no avail of feeling air. "Am I breathing?"

Without looking back Death answers, "you are, just not breathing in the sense that you've become familiar with before your transition back to your natural state."

"Normal state?" She says still trying to breathe and feel wind.

Sounding exhausted. "The state of being that you now find yourself in. That is your normal state of creation. All of your lower forms could not adapt and sustain within Zero realm without being— how do you say, refined. So, you all were placed among the stars at different intervals within different constructs to populate and thrive. Like you there are different forms of species that were created but had to be given appendages that were adaptable to regions of created space and time that you found yourselves in. Think of you past body as a self-contained breathing apparatus. To assist you in adapting to, in your case, Earth.

153

Rachel pauses a moment at the gravity of what was just explained. It sounded more scientific then spiritual. "Shouldn't I be terrified or something along those lines?"

"Should you?"

Death and Rachel cross through the hue into a world only the transitioned dead has seen.

Hadesus Third Heaven, Waiting Place, Hades

Death and Rachel enter into a chamber that is more infinite than all the expanse of space itself. The majesty and beauty extend far as the eye can see. The world Rachel witnesses is not unlike what she's known her entire life. There's a blue sky, but it changes colors based on the angle and tilt of your head with which you look at it. There are a great many suns in the sky of various sizes that have moons revolve around them. Numerous other planets are clearly visible in the expanse. In some instances, both day and night are visible at the same time. Here they co-exist as one.

For some reason, Rachel has no problem processing what she's seeing. In her mind it all processes without fail. It's as if upon death of the physical form, the true potential of the mind is unlocked and the secrets denied you for the whole of your life has been revealed. She gazes down from the mouth of the tunnel toward the inhabited population. She sees people, but they look different. As she exits the hall, it lets out atop a mountain that is constructed of liquid black diamond, but yet it was rigid as granite.

She looks into the valley below and beyond witnessing millions of red and blue hue souls walking about. Each soul is that of a person that looked to be in their prime. The outline of the person was what carried the colored hue. The light, however, originates from their chests same as hers. It is there heart which is the red or blue-lighted soul sphere, which Death collects.

The waiting place looks like a garden that is based off the Eden concept if man had remained the great custodial caretakers that was intended. There are trees that reaches far into the heavens. There are plants blowing in the wind that has long since gone extinct on Earth. There is a plethora of rolling hills of lush grasses of more colors than just green. She witnesses blue, yellow and a color she's never seen in the spectrum of Earth. Rivers are the bluest with a clarity that has never been observed by living eyes. From a distance and the height which she exited, she can see through the depths of river to its very bottom. *Paradise!*

At the sound of a puppy's bark, she turns and looks toward the feet of Death. It was quick, but she saw a Beagle puppy run past. It, too, had a soul sphere. She cracks a smile and quickly covers her mouth as she gasps at the sight of the puff ball of cuteness. Rachel picks up the puppy and looks even further across the plain. Her eyesight is no longer limited to the dull eyes of humanity, she can now see beyond the horizon paying even closer attention to the new colored orbs mixed within the population. Rachel sees the waiting souls of animals that have passed. There are souls of all species. There are those that are familiar that she recognized from life, but more that populate the garden she was not so familiar with. The souls of all the animals were all a yellow hue. It wasn't just unique to the puppy. As the humans, the animal's hearts are also the origin of their Soul Sphere.

With so many wonders to have to take in and process, she nearly misses the children playing with each other. She witnesses them talking in groups laughing and simply having a good time for the sake of having a good time. She doesn't see the petty squabbles that children would normally have such as whose turn is next and you have it, I want. There was no arrogant competition between them.

Rachel looks to Death. "This place is amazing. It's… it's…. I have no words. This is Heaven?"

"Alas, far from it. Come!" Death nods his head forward and nudges Rachel to move forward.

Rachel hadn't realized she'd stopped walking until Death gently tapped her on the back to move her along.

"What is this place then if not Heaven?" Rachel questions as she moves forward down the path off of the mountain.

"It is a place of forgetfulness. It's a place that will never fill... As for a name it has been called many over the vast spans of centuries which have been but a blink to your kind."

Rachel looks at Death. She can't make out his face as his hood has it cloaked. When she looks into his face she only sees darkness in the true sense of the word. Not a doom-filled look of darkness as if brooding, but literal darkness that would rival the blackness of space. Death notices her looking and becomes uncomfortable and begins walking in front of her.

"This place is best known to you by what the Greeks once called it, Hades." Says Death. To the Borefrayen species they call it Songhugones. Each tongue different, same destination the overall outcome. All meet here in the Zero realm of reality.

The path they've set upon takes them through scores of souls. As if walking with royalty, anyone that notices them walking by looks at Rachel and pays homage by bowing their heads as if subjugated. Confused, Rachel just nods at them as she passes.

"Why do they do that? Why do they bow their heads to you?" she asks Death.

"What makes you think they bow to me?" Death raises his hand toward Rachel's forehead. "It is the seal upon your head that they pay respects towards. It is an angelic glyph that commands respect."

"Am I sealed?" Said Rachel.

Death nods yes. "You all are. That is how we designate you one from another. Your designation reads different from all the others. Your life was one of servitude. You gave neglecting yourself and became a purveyor of Elohim's law. It appears so much so, that you have been chosen to keep the law.

Rachel touches her forehead and feels nothing. "I'm sealed? Why would I be sealed?"

Looking around, she notices that no one else has a seal upon their head. Another thought instantly comes to her. She remembers her studies from the book of revelations and her situation becomes clear. She now understands the gravity of what Death has told her. She stops and falls to her knees weighted down by the responsibility she will be asked to undertake in the future.

Death turns and looks down at her. "You are one of many that have been sealed, mortal. The burden will not be yours to carry alone."

"I... I can't be. Why would I be sealed? Is this the seal that I think it is? If it is I'm not deserving of this."

Death is suddenly crouching behind Rachel balancing himself with his scythe. He whispers into her ear, "I agree with you wholeheartedly. You are not deserving. I believe none which have been chosen are to tell you the truth." He helps her to her feet and coaxes her to keep walking.

"I mean there are others more deserving than me. There are others that have devoted their lives to saving souls and furthering his truth, right?"

Death laughs. "What is truth?" He continues laughing at the saving souls remark. "And others like whom may I ask comes to mind when you say others?"

Having trouble remembering recent names that she knew in life, Rachel has to really think. "Like, like, oh! What is his name? It was this pastor that I knew." Growing even more frustrated, she adds, "I know that I know his name. I just can't seem to recall it. It's at the tip of my tongue."

When Rachel gives up the thought, she realizes that Death has left her behind. She runs to catch up to him.

"You will not remember anyone from your time on the mortal plain. Trying to remember a name of one you knew within the span of your life is futile. However, you are permitted to think of mortals before your time line began. Think of people past to illustrate your point that you endeavoring to make."

She snapped her fingers. "Like Moses, David and so on?"

Suddenly, in a flash, Death and Rachel are on a cliff overlooking the precipice into another adjacent small valley. Death extends his arm and points down to a man sitting with his feet in a brook. He looks to be all of thirtyish. Even under his grayish tunic, one can tell that he has strong, defined muscles. He's laying back resting his head on his hands facing the sky with his eyes closed. His aurora provided by his soul's sphere gives off a more poignant red.

"See that soul, there? The one with his feet in the brook?" Death says.

As Rachel locates and watches the soul resting with his feet in the river, her attention is called off slightly to the left. Rachel sees Death walking in the distance just off to the left behind the man that's sunbathing. Death is escorting two other red souls. She looks back to her side and sees Death still pointing downward into the valley. When she looks back the familiar being has crested the hill and out of sight.

"You see that soul there yes?" Death repeats.

Rachel shakes the confusion and looks again at the soul. "Yes."

"That soul there is of the one you signify as Moses." Death rests on his scythe.

At a loss for words she just marvels at the awe of Moses. A hero of biblical text who's long since been dead. Now there he is, laying down with his feet in the water a mere stone's throw away. A man considered God's friend and one of a select few to have even seen him is before her eyes.

As she stares in complete reverence of the man, again she notices Death walking by Moses with a blue soul in tow. She instantly looks back to her side and realizes Death has not left her side. Her face changes as she's confused at how Death is in two places. She lets it be and returns her gaze to a biblical famed man.

"Moses. That's Moses laying there?" she says, still in disbelief.

Death leaning on his scythe as a staff. "What color do you find his soul?"

"It looks reddish with a tinge of blue, almost purple now that you mention it. I don't understand. In the Bible he was recorded doing great things. I don't understand why I would be sealed and not him."

"You're right to an extent, he assisted in doing wondrous works, but remember, the works were not his own. It's as the scriptures halfheartedly told, he was but an instrument for Elohim's will. And for all the wonders that he assisted in, here he sits in Hades." Death looks at Rachel. "Just as any other... Just as you. Moses was not Moses without as you would say in your common tongue, technology, which was ours by the way.

Death leans in closer to Rachel "Why? Shouldn't he have gone to that wondrous fantasy dreamed place you humans so ineptly believe in is what you're asking yourself right?"

Rachel looks at Death then returns to observing Moses, studying him closer now that Death have called into question his character.

"Oh, come on, mortal! You know this one. Think! Why would he have not transcended to this ideal of heaven you mortals often speak of but, truly don't conceive in the slightest?"

"I.... I know this," Rachel says slightly raising her hand. "Because he who has sinned cannot see God nor enter his kingdom."

Death and Rachel are in an instant back to their path walking through Hades again.

"As great and wondrous as you mortals believe that he was, his soul awaits judgment just as his adversary Pharaoh. He is simply a mortal man, nothing more."

Death teleports himself and Rachel again. This time they find themselves looking at simple cottage with a man whose soul sphere is a bright blue. He tends to a garden while laughing with children. She watches as he plays with them by lightly flinging little clumps of dirt in their direction.

Death points towards the man who could easily be in his thirties as well. "What color do you find the state of his soul?

"It's a bright blue," Rachel says.

"So, seeing the color of his soul you would assume that his life was one that was led by a man you'd deem would have been a good man, if not great yes?

"By the prevailing logic of this color-coded system, yes. Lest not forget the acceptance of the covenant provided by Jesus." Rachel says.

"Yes, lest not forget him... Also know that only those sealed outside the celestials can see the true hearts of men on this plain. To all else that enters here, they are oblivious of each other's hue. Wouldn't much be paradise otherwise wouldn't you agree?" Death looks at Rachel and gestures for her to follow him. "Come!"

Death walks Rachel over to the gentlemen. Hearing the approaching footsteps, he turns wiping his hands free of dirt ready to greet his visitor. Rachel notices that he's a clean shaven handsome man. Upon seeing Rachel, he bows out of respect, whips his hair from his face and outstretches his arms for a hug. Smiling, Rachel hugs him and steps back feeling the warmth emanating from him. She watches as the children are a mix of red and blue souls. More blues than red in this instance.

Good day sister regent elect. It is truly an honor to have you here Fraulein. Are you just arriving?"

"Yes, actually. I've only arrived a short while ago. I've been trying to learn the lay of the land. I'm even being escorted by—" Rachel looks around and notices that her escort has disappeared. Confused, she spins around seeing Death off in the distance watching her.

The gentlemen place his arm around her. "Then, Regent, it pleases me to be the first to welcome you."

"Please, call me Rachel."

"Okay, then, Regent Rachel. Please come, come have something to drink. You will find the leaves here most enjoyable to brew tea."

Rachel allows herself to be taken by the gentlemen into his place. For what seems like hours the two continuously laugh as if they've been friends the whole of their lives. They talk events from before his history which span the latter century of the eighteen hundreds into the nineteenth. She speaks of people before her history having to pay no attention to if she would ignite any memory of his lifetime, because Hades automatically censors the population's conversation.

The conclusion of their time together was nowhere near brief. The gentlemen keeping polite walks Rachel to the door. As he opens the door children run past the two into his place laughing apparently running from one lone child that was left counting down until he's able to begin the hunt for the others.

As Rachel walks out the door, Death still awaits her in the distance.

"It was truly my honor to meet you, Rachel, Regent elect." The gentlemen again hug her goodbye.

"It was nice to meet you as well. You know, I'm sorry, I never asked you your name."

"My name is Adolf, Regent."

Rachel looks at him as if she should know the name, she's sure she heard it before, but her mind won't let her recall.

"Well, it was a pleasure to meet you as well, Adolf."

Rachel turns and with a pleasant disposition after meeting Adolf, she finds herself again teleported back to her original path escorted by Death.

Like a light bulb turning on in her mind it comes to her. She quickly turns and faces Death. "That was Adolf the one that waged war on the Jews and caused an immeasurable amount of death."

Death looks at Rachel. "So, it was. Because that man drew breath in reality 2814; Death, Pain, Pestilence, and War were called for annihilation of an entire sect of your species and yet his soul was as blue as Earth's sky. You see the limits of your small-minded way of thought as you mortals progress through life. You truly have no knowledge of matters which you all profess. If judgment was to happen this very moment, those you considered heroes of faith would not be judged so kindly against one that you as part of a society labeled villainous. You better than most will come to know this in time… Regent Elect."

Rachel looks at Death in puzzlement. Again, she tries to study him. She searches her memory for his identity. *I knew Gabriel. I don't know you. Are you an angel or my rendition of Virgil escorting me into my own descent of madness?* "I don't know you, do I? What's your name, Path walker? And you better not say the Ferrymen Sticks."

Rachel listens intently for his answer when she happens to look across the river and see Death escorting five red souls along the shore lines. Death momentarily pauses and looks at her from across the river acknowledging her. Once the souls have caught up to him, he turns away from observing her and continues his pace with the souls in tow.

Death that has been escorting her stops walking and grabs Rachel about the shoulder. Death looks at her. "I assure you, that you will find no angel within me. You ask me for my nomenclature? Mortal child, I am consumption. Weather from the rich; poor, saved, unsaved, kings, peasants, demons or angels, from the planets to the stars which birth them, they are all entities that draw breath in one fashion or another. All I have described will eventually succumb to my silent embrace. I am culmination and finality of all living things."

The two walks up to a gigantic white marble double door that sits at the edge of what seems an infinite preserve. Two armored angels wearing white tunics with matching white pants and mercury colored armor overlaid, stand guard on either side of the doors. Rachel again is at a loss for words as she looks at the celestial gaudiness of the marble doors. Notwithstanding the majesty of it all, she turns her attention back towards her escort.

"You are finality? Your story is one I now remember, angel. You are the saddest story of them all. I remember now, before I embarked on my way to Earth for my birth, I remember you. I remember the stories that were told, that I heard."

"Time here will do that. Memories that were silenced begin to whisper yet again on the ethereal plain," Death says as he nods at the angelic guard for him to permit entrance for her.

Rachel stands before Death, looking into the darkness of his face. "You don't think much of us do you— us mortals? It lays hidden in your voice when you speak."

"On the contrary, I think about you mortals a great deal. All of my time is consumed with nothing but thoughts of mortals. I think of you more than I care to admit, because alas you are my very existence and purpose for being, you and the other species that are bipedal in motion."

The white marble doors open. Hearing others talking behind her, she turns around and looks through the gigantic doors. From first glance, the scenery inside makes everything else she's seen fleeting. Again, she sees Death walking out the corner of her eyes. He's traveling an easterly path. Again, he's escorting a cadre of mixed colored souls. She quickly turns around as if to catch the being running back to be at her side, but as she suspected he had never left. Her confusion has reached its zenith.

"How are you here talking to me and yet you're also there as well and everywhere else? I mean if you're talking to me now, how are you walking with those souls over there? Are you more than one or are there a legion of you like an order?"

Sighing, he shakes his head. "If only there were, but, alas, it is just I in the singular. Your infinitesimal minds were constructed in such a fashion that you could never comprehend the magnitude in which I traverse the plains of this universe or any other for that matter. In the time it has taken me to complete this very sentence, the abrupt change in cabin pressure has blown a four-foot diameter breach in the hull of an airliner on its way to Orlando. The decompression has ejected Row 127 into the stratosphere. A two-year-old female child named Marilyn has been ripped and flung from her mother's arms and thrown into decompression and jettisoned only to never have achieved free fall. She has been vacuumed into the intake of the right engine of the failing Boeing seven fifty-seven plane, where she was instantaneously eviscerated."

Death points over Rachel's shoulder. Her eyes follow Death's hand, where she witnesses him escorting the blue soul and true nature of the child. He carries her while pointing out wondrous yellow hued prehistoric animals of two billion years past that grew to magnanimous heights over in the Andromeda system. He then points the child to the lumbering Brontosaurus that is walking in the distance eating the leaves of trees that instantly replenishes itself. Shocked to see the dinosaur herself, Rachel doesn't know how she missed the prehistoric behemoth. She continues to watch as Death carries the child. She watches as he turns and looks at her from across the way proving that he's actively and currently having this conversation with her. He continues talking to Rachel while holding the child. Even from the distance between them she can hear him clearly.

"The father is currently in free fall as he loosened his restraint in an attempt to capture his daughter. He, too, will be here momentarily."

Death still standing next to Rachel taps her and points to another location in Hades. Rachel averts her eyes to the location and witness the father of the little girl being escorted by him as well. Death while walking with the little girl's father continues talking to Rachel.

"You see; I am the result of life that has gone astray. I am the enemy of time, savior to rot and decay, brother to Mercy and Destiny." Death next to her taps her again and points to a third location.

Rachel spins again following his directional point and witnesses him as he leads over a hundred souls into Hades. Rachel assumes the remaining victims of the plane crash.

"You ask how I can be omnipresent. You ask who I am. You will find that I am the ultimate equalizer, I am eternal, I am Death."

From within the open marbled doors a single white hued soul emerges. He is sealed on the forehead like Rachel. His garments show that he must have been of low class in the time of the Roman occupation of Jerusalem. The stranger takes Rachel by the hand and pulls her closer kissing her on both cheeks. Rachel looks back and realizes that Death has vanished.

The stranger then places his arm around her shoulders. "Welcome, sister. We've all been waiting for you. What is your name if I may ask, little sister?"

"I'm Rach, Rachel…. I can't seem to remember my last name."

"That's not important, Rachel. I am Paul and you are most welcome here. You have kept the faith and finished the race. Come in, come in, Rachel, we have much to discuss and teach you." Rachel and Paul walk into the bright light of the double doors.

CHAPTER 18

CAREFULLY SCULPTED

"To most, he moves swiftly. To others, his time is eternal in dispensation of his work. He needs not be bothered by the constraints of time for it is all he has. He is savior, and punisher. He is the one constant that cannot be put off for any substantial amount of time. Even the eternal gods of old fell before him. A race that was once thought immortal was reduced to ash. I assure you as night follows day he will come. Only difference is that he will find me ready. There is no fear here. The cancer has long abolished such silly notions. He will find me not ready to willfully and gently go into a never-ending sleep. No! He will find me awake and ready to fight for the very last breath.

I have been called tyrant, slayer, and murderer of masses. I have been given the name, genocide. Come to me and let us be done with this life. Come for me, I abhor you. I'll remain here in my bed reserving the last of my unspent energy to spit my last detestable breath of hate in your darkened shadowed face.

Pass me my blades and close the door. Tonight, I'll dine with the enemy of men. We will talk of the past and clash blades for the future. Come, Death, we've missed each other for far too long."

Quote ~Hannibal

SIX YEARS LATER, 2020

Vespian, Cainsin Formerly (Old Babylon)

The body of a combat instructor careens uncontrollably through the air. As he twists, rotates, and flips far beyond his control. He can't decide which is worse, the fact that he has been overtaken by what he considers a mere boy or the fact that he had no control on being thrown and where he may land. His body crashes through drywall of the most northern wall section of the gymnasium. As he hits the ground, it's clear to him that his ribs are broken. He slides for another few feet before coming to rest. Although painful, he's excited that he's been injured, because now he has cause to take rest from the punishment of training. He just has to keep reminding himself not to let his pride force him to stand up... *Damn my competitive spirit.* He slowly pushes himself from the ground.

There are multiple bodies of sparring soldiers strewn across the gym floor. Many of them groan and moan in pain of the assault that their target Cyrail, has inflicted upon them during this most intense training session yet.

The once bottled lab specimen six-years-old classified code name, Imperial has a dual identity as Cyrail Arcane, is already just over a meter in height. His intelligence is that far superior of any renowned astrophysicist as his scores have tested off the charts. Since his inception, he's been kept in seclusion among the military might of the sovereign country, Arcainaque.

The prodigy stands at half court of the gym overlooking the destruction of the wall which he's just thrown one of his sparring partners through. As he walks toward the hole in the wall he readies himself to continue the attack if his sparring partner is still itching for combat. His approach is soft and barely heard as he's barefoot in uniformed pants with the blood stripes down each side of his pant legs. Cyrail's upper torso is bare as well a great battle tactic when sparring as your enemy has a harder time grabbing a hold of you. His tattooed glyphs on his shoulders and arms speak a language known only to the gods and demons. Hidden within the glyphs on his back are two slits on either side of the trapezius muscle. A metal collar rest around Cyrail's neck which a thin clear wire protrudes from either side down each of his respective arms connecting to a metallic gauntlet on each. The wire is held in place at the top of the shoulder, and just beneath the elbow by black oversized bands before connecting to the gauntlets.

"Enough, Cyrail," commands Warsivious. "Your hand-to-hand skill of unarmed assailants are unmatched. Prepare yourself to encounter disadvantaged armed combat."

Warsivious turns and walks toward the entrance of the gym. He glances back at Cyrail over his shoulder before opening the set of double doors to let him know the coming situation is serious. Two more soldiers enter the designated combat training area carrying M-4 rifles. Unlike the others, these soldiers are in full protective gear to include helmets with face shields. As they enter, the soldiers hesitate, looking around the gym at the damage that had been done as well as the other men that are laid out before them. Hesitant for a moment, they fixate on what must be their target as he's the last man standing.

Cyrail looks attentively at the soldiers immediately identifying that their threat level is extreme. The tattooed slits on Cyrail's bare back begins to illuminate. Wings switchblade outward from the slits. Cyrail charges them.

Instantly taken aback, the two soldiers begin to slowly back away at first. Fear is momentary, but that is not why they give ground. They're trained special ops. They give ground to asses this new coming threat. One of them briefly turns and look at General Warsivious.

Warsivious grins and nods at the soldier as he walks over to the bleachers and sits down. He then gives the soldiers a shouldered hunch gesture as if saying I don't know, but get ready, it's coming. "Gentlemen, I would prepare to defend yourselves, if I were you. He seems pretty serious and ready to kick ass wouldn't you say?" Warsivious shouts at them.

The rear base of Cyrail's where the collar clasps on his neck intersecting at the spine flashes red. He's charging and controlling the flowing energy through his plasma wielding gauntlets. At culmination of the charge, Cyrail shoots a red bolt from his hand. The blast misses its mark and flies between the two soldiers. The warriors that they are with the vast reservoir of combat missions under their belt they don't know panic that gives them pause anymore, they adapt and overcome. They fall back on their tier one instilled muscle memory survival training. Realizing they are under attack, they fall in behind one another. The first soldier unleashes the full ferocity of his weapon. "Weapons free." he yells. Muzzle flashes are constant and are relentless.

Cyrail movements are lighting fast as he dodges the barrage of incoming projectiles. The ones, he can't dodge he deflects with his wings. Screaming to conjure strength, the first soldier advances toward Cyrail with his partner in tow. He advances quickly and purposely, firing till empty.

"Brick top!" he yells to signify to his partner that he has ran out of ammo and needs to reload. Having practiced the drill thousands of times, it's become second nature, as the advancing soldier rolls behind his partner, the rear partner takes lead raising his weapon to sights and continues firing without missing a beat. The first soldier reloads, awaiting his turn. He prays it doesn't come, that would only suggest that they are encountering a superior foe who is combat evolved.

The two advances on Cyrail. Seeing them coming, he changes tactics from charge and evasion of rounds to protection. Cyrail encases himself within his wings and continues a slowed advance towards the soldiers. As he draws close, his wings explode out like a hand opening from a clap. The wind gust created takes the soldiers off their feet and unto their backs.

The soldier that was second to fire is immediately on his feet again firing, but Cyrail's movement is lighting fast as he leaps and delivers precise front kick. With the sound of a breaking sternum, the kick launches the firing soldier off to the left. He hits the ground hard and slides into the wall striking his head and neck.

Dazed from the blow to the head his vision is blurry, but he can only watch as Cyrail outstretches his right palm and releases a red bolt into the chest of his partner that was in the midst of reloading his weapon to fire again. The blast throws the soldier backwards in the air where he instantly catches fire and disintegrates, turning to ash. The charred stricken body hits the wall next to the gym door and explodes in a cloud like haze slowly falling to the floor in a powdered mess akin to a bag of flour that falls to the floor and explodes.

With the threat subdued Cyrail wings retract. Warsivious claps his hands slow and ominously a couple of times in gesture of a job well executed. He stands to his feet smiling with a certain pride and admiration for the focus of the young combatant. *Can't say I agree with him making himself known at this juncture, but his instinct and speed are impressive.*

The armed soldier that absorbed the kick starts to breathe heavy his breaths are labored from the broken sternum. Blood pools in his mouth and begins to leak from the corner of it as he rights himself into a sitting position using the wall for support. Trained as a seal, he doesn't know the meaning of the word injured or quit. Witnessing what he believes was the destruction of his fellow teammate, the only thought past survival is revenge. He reaches for his rifle that is just inches out of his reach. He can't judge the distance because he's more worried about his labored breathing and internal injuries that he's sure he sustained.

Still standing, Warsivious watches as the injured former seal struggles to his feet with his weapon in hand, he brings his slow ominous clap to an end quickly. "What have I taught you, Captain?"

Cyrail stands to attention. "That if a man faces you with a weapon that he means to not inflict injury, but to kill. An enemy that wants to kill you should be given no quarter or mercy."

The former seal levels his rifle and tries using the wall to slide up righting himself. Before he can fire, he collapses to his knees. With a loud resounding echoed clack, the weapon falls to his side sliding on the gymnasium floor. Cyrail notices him out of the corner of his eye as he speaks with Warsivious, but pays no attention to him as he's clearly too wounded to continue.

Warsivious walks around Cyrail inspecting him. Cyrail holds, keeping his eyes forward. "And why should mercy not be granted?"

"Because if mercy is given by the victor, then the victor may himself appear weak."

Warsivious looks to the struggling soldier who's on his knees hunched over spitting blood on the floor in front of him. "And if you, the victor, appears weak?"

"Then it may give rise to other enemies." Says Cyrail.

"Not may, it will. Mercy is given and exists in those that are weak and that have been defeated. With their dying breath they will always ask for mercy which we do not give. Now finish him! Be quick about it. Never give your enemy a chance to recover."

"Yes, general."

Other sparring combatants in gym look on in complete horror at what is transpiring in front of them. The ones that are still ambulatory.

The soldier has again struggled to his feet. Cyrail begins to close in on him. As he closes the distance the instructors watching can't help but think of the confidentiality reports they had to sign. As Cyrail closes in on the injured soldier, he places his hands in front of him defensively. Cyrail trots towards him bursting into a full sprint. Terrified, now because his injury is debilitating he backs up, holding his hands up ready for the coming fight.

You'll not hear me beg is what reverberates through the soldier's mind, however when he tries to vocalize it, it sounded like "ptthhull noth heemeeee theg" because the blood was so profusely pouring from his mouth. Internal bleeding is assured in his mind now.

Cyrail reaches the soldier and spins. As he spins, he crouches low, his wings spread to their full length, becoming like blades slicing the former seal in two at the apex of his spin. Completing the maneuverer, he stands tall retracting his wings. The cut was clean and occurred in an instant. Minimal blood pools around the soldier's midsection two halves before his body slides apart. Both halves a minimally cauterized.

Cyrail, hasn't yet mastered the speed to ignite his wings as a heated weapon.

Other soldiers in the room look on in fear of Cyrail. They've never seen him dispatch anyone, let alone with wings. Their thoughts of an engineered soldier are quickly coming into question. Doubt creeps into their minds that they may have been lied to about what exactly Cyrail is. What was this thing they've been sparring against the past few months? What happened to those instructors before them? They watch in horror as the ex-Navy Seal lies lifeless in two halves.

"Ha!" says Warsivious as he walks up to Cyrail slapping him on his back. "Did you hear it? The pleaseeeeeee! Didn't you hear it? I told you, only the weak. Go shower up! Training for today is over. Take the weekend, Captain! Monday, we start your flight training."

Cyrail salutes. Although advanced for his age, when told he's done for the day he does as any other six-year-old would do, he runs and grabs his gym bag and runs for the door excitedly.

Warsivious' look of admiration drastically turns to displeasure as he looks toward the bruised and broken sparring soldiers.

Heaving a hefty sigh, he shakes his head. "It pains me instructors that you've seen what you've seen here today. You are the best combatants of your specific disciplines. It's a waste, really, but when you signed up for the Imperial Protocol you knew there would be risks. Your service will not be forgotten, but you are no longer required as you are currently not cleared for this level of revelation."

The soldiers who aren't broken up to badly suddenly feel inspired to get to their feet. The others who are too broken to stand crawl for the nearest points of egress. One instructor uses the bleacher to pull himself up to his knees. As he does, his eyes focus on a silver on black metallic boot that rests on the step of the bleacher. He follows the length of the boot with his eyes all the way up to the owner of the foot. The boot belongs to Death who has suddenly appeared in the bleachers spectating.

Death looks closely at the instructor's forehead. "This will not end well for you this day, Darrin Custanado," Death says as he looks at the mortal allowing himself to be seen.

Warsivious walks over to the bleachers and sits next to Death. "You know how children are when school has ended and the final period bell has rung. They are but one-tract minded."

The remaining soldiers continue an attempt to flee, but they find no exit – the doors are all locked.

After pushing for what seemed like hours which were in reality mere seconds, one instructor turns from the door and faces his soon to be executioner. "So, you mean to kill us then, kill me? Guess we saw too much, eh, general? Can't let a secret like him make news."

Warsivious obliges him. "Just know what comes next is nothing personal. You all really were respected combatants, especially you Dante Corvis, isn't?" Warsivious walks up to the man. "Then again, I'd expect no less from the order that you are here secretly representing and acting on their behalf with the mind toward execution of the boy. And here I thought you all were decimated long ago on the thirteenth of that Friday. I know whom you really work for." Warsivious says as he straightens and dust the soldier's shirt. "Just take pride in knowing that your sacrifice today has gone into making Cyrail a force that will not be reckoned or rivaled with, even by that bitch of a Prior you serve in the obsolete Templar Order."

Dante's eyes grow big at the revelation that he is in fact a covert spy. Warsivious brushes his shoulder free of lent and dust. "We'll come for her in due time. What you did here today will ensure a peaceful future; I promise."

The instructor takes off his ball cap that he had turned backwards. He reaches into it and removes a picture of his wife and two daughters. He looks at them envisioning them as if they were right there in front of him. A tear drops onto the picture.

Death from across the gymnasium looks up from the mortal that is still frozen in fear by his beguiling and besieged boot. As his face is shrouded in darkness his facial expression cannot be seen, but he's moved slightly by the instructor's action that he's being in essence made to bend his knee to War, but dares to part his lips to speak up. *The calmness of those that resign to Fate is never short of interesting. His part in this has been written well. Death thought.*

As Death readies to part his lips and speak, he doesn't get a chance before being interrupted by Warsivious.

"This is my favorite part." Warsivious depresses the mic on his lapel. "You have the room, commander. Execute and cleanse with extreme prejudice!"

The double doors open. A six-man team of masked black-suited troops in tactical gear enter the gym. Without hesitation, they fire their weapons. The first to drop are the able combatants, looking for an exit. The ones crawling, are executed next in order as those likely to give the most resistance. The instructor that was mesmerized by Death was taken down with a well-placed shot to the base of the skull. As he falls forward face first Death removes his dark red soul sphere placing it into his coat. He then walks toward War and the defiant mortal soldier. He keeps his eyes locked on the instructor that dared to defy War. Although he looked the most abled and ambulatory upon Death's entry he was ignored for no other reason than he stood his ground and did not attempt to run. A mortal like that you'd want for your team.

Warsivious holds his fist up halting fire. The death squad holds fire, but remains leveled at the last instructor. Warsivious stands, straightening his waist coat and walks pacing around the last combatant instructor.

"Your bravery is commendable. In the face of annihilation, you stand tall? You don't beg nor cry for mercy. That is the sterner material that I look for in men that are to be eventually led by the boy Cyrail that you had the honor to spar today. I will give you a chance befitting of such a warrior. If you wish to see what I assume is your family contained therein that picture after today, you will pledge fidelity to the Imperial Protocol... What say you?"

The instructor places his picture into the breast pocket of his Polo style uniform shirt patting the pocket that closely covers his heart. "I know what pledging fidelity to that thing means for me, general. As much as I wish to see my family again today, I will settle for someday and it will be with a conscience that is clean. Men such as you and myself have done many things in the service of protecting for God and country. A lot of those things I expect to burn for as I'm sure you probably will as well. After seeing what that thing can do, this is where I have to draw such a line to preserve what's left of my soul. What you propose is tempting, alas, I will have to decline your most generous offer and hope to see my family in the next life."

A tear starts to stream down the instructor's cheek as he looks Warsivious in his face. Warsivious unmoved by such a gesture. "Unto death then for you, yes? That is your choice?" Warsivious says.

The instructor nods. "Yes, general, unto death."

Warsivious stares at the instructor.

If Death face could be seen he'd be raising an eyebrow as he also stares at the instructor.

"Commendable, mortal. Commendable." Slightly pissed at having to lose such a man of character, General Warsivious backs away. He raises and drops his arms quickly. One soldier fires a single round through the head of the instructor.

Death admiration for the mortal falls along with his shoulders and head as he feels a kindred loss of what the man had given up for an ideal. He quickly reinvigorates himself as to not let War see him moved. "Yes!" Death says. "Yes!" He claps enthusiastically, and loudly. His clapping so boisterous it becomes sarcastic. "War, I must admit you never disappoint. Your bloodlust will be the undoing of us all, mortals, gods, universes, existence, realities, hell everything."

Ignoring Death, Warsivious raises his hand again, this time in acknowledgement to the assassin team and heads toward them. He steps over a couple of the bodies splayed across the floor as he walks over to Commander Rusain who quickly removes his mask and helmet.

"Thank-you, gentlemen. Sharp as usual, Commander." Warsivious nods his head, acknowledging him.

After saluting, Rusain removes his helmet and red Shemagh and returns the nod. "Thank you, sir." Rusain is a lifetime Tier 1 military man. He's spent a majority of his life off in far flung parts of the world engaged in someone's war. At the age of 36, he's weathered and stoned face in the arena of emotion and pain. To him, its all subjective. Coming off of a weekend of supporting his favorite football team, he runs his hands over his forehead wiping sweat and through his purple died mohawk before coming back to attention.

"Have your team take care of this mess. Cyrail was a bit impetuous this morning. He exposed himself to these instructors, without them having clearance."

As Death operates in the realm of anonymity, he's busy taking the souls of the dead. Their souls are a mixture of red and blue spheres. As the assassin team kicks and rolls over bodies, Death continues his work without the remaining mortals ever aware of him.

Leaving Rusain to his orders, Warsivious walks toward the double doors exit. He pauses for a moment to finally acknowledge Death. He ignored him since he arrived hoping that maybe he'd just go away. "You annoy me outcast. Must you always skulk about?"

Death appears next to Warsivious. He turns and reaches out his hand and summons the last soul from a distant body across the gym. "What can I say? I'm drawn to you like flies on, what is it mortals love to say? Shit! For some reason it seems wherever there is War, I am sure to follow. It seems we are forever interlocked, you and I, hand in hand in an endless dance. Your influence that you emanate has overtaken the bane of society leaving carnage. So, yes it seems that I will always skulk about as you so eloquently put it."

Warsivious stops at the door turns and faces Death. "What is your game? What are you playing at in the finality of all of this?"

"I have no stake in this trivial undying battle that consumes all that can be surveyed. I'm merely observing, weighing the balance to see which side tips the scale."

War smirks. "You have no side. You're too chicken shit to pick one. I spit at your lukewarm taste of indecision. That is why you stand alone apart from the us demons; hell, apart from any faction. To be alone and without cause in endless servitude, what it must be like to be you."

Warsivious places his hat on and walks out the door leaving Death to mull on his last words. The double doors close shut leaving Death looking out the vertical reinforced glass windows at Warsivious as he walks away.

"I so do enjoy our talks, General." Death looks over his shoulder. Something else happening elsewhere in the far distance corner of the world has caught his attention. "Interesting." Death slides a lever on his gauntlet and vanishes.

Cainsin, Vespian Headquarters – Night

Lucien's smile reaches its apex as Cyrail meets him in the hallway after his sparring session. Lucien's aged surely over the many millennia, but his aging has been in the celestial realm of his origin which time for him is akin to almost standing indefinitely still. Over the time that he's been spinning the meticulous web of his plans, he has at time had to use proxies to avert the public's eyes from his immortality. Lucien's guise today is the same as the many that came before, it is just that another proxy as to not arouse suspicion in the mortal populace. Humans are slow-witted creatures sure, but they tend to notice an unchanged being that has lived a great many of years. They are slow-witted, not ignorant.

The proxy which Lucien had utilized this era was a natural born mortal. Normally he would use a xterians from a far distant planet over in the Andromeda galaxy. They are very similar in kind to humans, just more durable. However, he had to admit that the slow-witted species of man technology was getting better. If he was detected using a being with vastly different anomalies in the genome, there would be to many questions. The proxy Lucien which was chosen was only done so after an all-encompassing search across the globe for a specimen that was a rose in a sea of concrete. The proxy must be one in excellent health with outstanding and rare superb D.N.A. The child born Lucien Arcane fit the parameters needed for a successful symbiotic relationship. He was the ultimate choice for subcutaneous habitation.

Subcutaneous habitation is the process where Lucifer uses his natural born celestial ability to phase realities into a 5th dimensional state where he removes a microscopic piece of skin from the back of his neck. That skin is then placed subcutaneously underneath the husk of the human's exterior where it's able to grow and co-habitat alongside the unsuspecting species soul. When the foreign skin grows and links into the host's central nervous system, much like a parasite, it overtakes the steering wheel from the proprietor. Although, borrowing the body momentarily, he's still the Lucifer of old. From a stasis hub that is protected within the Vespian he controls the proxy as if it is him in the flesh. There are older methods of inhabiting and controlling a species, but it would leave him vulnerable to attack if he were to be displaced.

The controlled Lucien places his arm around Cyrail and walks with him down the blatantly massive hallway using the same mannerisms as Lucifer. "I've been watching you, son. Your progression in combat is truly impressive. You make me proud with each day that passes. You are growing into a truly magnificent arm of my military might and will," says Lucien.

"Really? You aren't upset that I obliterated those men? I know how you get if there's a chance of exposure, but when I saw the weapons, I panicked," says Cyrail.

"Not hardly am I upset. The world of men is only meant for subjugation. Contrary to what they believe, that was always the lot of their existence. They need to be led and told what to worship so their existence is fulfilled. Left unchecked and to their own will and device, they seek only their own destruction. It is to us to unite and save them. If only from themselves and the misguided beliefs that rule them. They look to the heavens for a god that has long since abandon them. They want a god, but I'm giving them the better. I'm giving them me."

As the two walks, soldiers stop to salute them. The hallways are busy with support personal, business men and world dignitaries. Lucien salutes back while continuing his stroll.

"I didn't mean to go so far Father, but I bore holding back all the time. I tell you now Father, it won't happen again unless you give the word."

"The word is given, Cyrail. Your uncle Warsivious will be told to increase your training to live fire and real world-based scenarios from here on out. You are doing exceptionally well. However, there was one aspect I saw room for improvement. Your response time was lacking a bit. Your hesitation to quickly dispatch your enemies has me concerned a little."

"Hesitation was observing the matter for exposure, Father. But knowing that I can now go weapons free as they say, there will be no more incidents of hesitation."

The two walks up to a great door with entangled designs of the galaxies cut into the wood. Where certain galaxies etched and placed are unknown to world of men. The names for those inscribed galaxies haven't been assigned human notoriety, because men simply aren't aware of them. Within the giant-sized door is an ordinary automated door which opens as they approach and walk through into the courtyard of Vespian. The courtyard can hold over ten thousand troops and armaments battle ready. It is stone with four huge walls that protect it with three huge steel main gates meant to allow entry and egress of troops and armor.

The two walk up a couple flights of steps until they are at a balcony that overlooks the courtyard. Their discussion continues all the way to the balcony. Lucien turns his son by the shoulders so that he faces him. "I want to discuss...Compassion."

"Compassion?" Cyrail averts his eyes as he tries to recall the facts about it. It's a word that is foreign to him, because he's never heard it or saw it for himself. "I know the definition, but I have a hard time understanding what it is."

Lucien smiles. "Good, good. It is a word that is useless. It has no meaning in our house or in our order of things. Cyrail, you must understand that we are superior in every way to the race of men that we walk among. As such we have many enemies, that will show us no compassion or for that matter mercy. So, we must have none. The world is in strife right now, and a strong hand is needed to guide it back to peace and order. Cyrail, you will soon be that instrument that I wield to promote and bring peace. You are an instrument that will set me high on the throne of celestial halls. You are a born leader and this is your military might and birthright that you are learning to wield."

Lucien faces Cyrail to look from the balcony at the ten thousand men that are in parade rest. They will be yours to command in due time. Through you, Imperial, I will set this world to burn so that it can be remade and rise from the ashes a phoenix and beacon for not only this world or plain of existence, but for all."

The two overlooks just a fraction of their military might from the balcony together. Outside the courtyard is a strong standing cadre of military force in parade rest.

ST. RICHARDS CATHEDRAL – MORNING

A child is coddled by his grandmother and given a mighty hug. In her early fifties, she doesn't look a day over thirty. Her hair is more silver now than black. Rare genetics have given her one blue eye and one green. Her style of dress is contemporary to the times. She looks a spitting older version image of her deceased daughter, Rachel.

It's the first day of the school year. Kids are everywhere as teachers try to wrangle them into some sort of order. The buses dropped a majority of the students off at the roundabout drop point. Those that do not ride the bus are being dropped off by their parents in an adjacent vehicle lane.

A grandmother was the role that she feels she was born for. Her years of raising Rachel made her sure of it. Gloria Bane smothers her grandchild in an uncountable barrage of hugs and kisses. He's all smiles as he takes in as much of the hugs as possible. Her grandson is handsome with soft features that she is sure will edge out as he gets older. His skin is a beautiful, dark caramel color. Although, small for his age, his personality is huge, his eyes are gray in color and distinguished with a glare that gives clue to an old soul.

"Ah! I don't want let you go, chipmunk." Gloria fights back the tears the best she can. She knows if she cries than it will start a reaction in her sweet boy. The tears start to swell anyways. It was almost pointless in her straightening out his clothes because she would only hug him again. Gloria is even overcome with more emotion as she remembers the day she dropped her daughter Rachel off to school on her first day what seems not so long ago now. *How the time has flown. How sad Rachel couldn't be here today to drop her son off. No matter. Grandma has it covered today.*

"I'll see you at three o'clock, okay, sweetheart?" Gloria says giving him another kiss on the forehead.

With tears now in his eyes, he speaks through the frog in his throat. "Okay, Grandma."

"How long is that from now? Want to count? They both count in unison both using their fingers. "One-two-three-four-five-six. See? Six hours… I'll see you then, chipmunk, I promise."

Jericho leaves the embrace of his grandmother and heads for the front doors of the school where children are lining up. He gulps down the excess saliva that his nerves have helped him produce as he tries to push the fears away of a day without his grandmother and being surrounded by strangers. He finds the courage to walk tall and purposefully. He watched his favorite comic book hero movie Speedslayer this morning and he wouldn't cower.

Sister Eva waves the Kindergarteners over to her respective door of the school. Jericho being brave as his grandmother said he should be, puts on a strong front. He goes from walking to a slight skip. Not wanting his grandmother to feel like she has to worry, he doubles down on his strong front and runs toward his unknown destination with his favorite cartoon character Speedslayer's backpack wagging from side to side. As he just about arrives to his place in line, he turns to wave goodbye to his grandmother when he collides into a girl. The two falls over and tumble a top of each other. The fall was hard enough that the young girl bangs her knee igniting a cadre of tears.

"Sorry! I'm sorry, I didn't mean it." Jericho quickly gets to his feet and starts to help her up. "Shh! It's okay alright, don't cry! I don't wanna get in trouble. Don't cry okay?"

She remains on the ground rocking in place holding her knee attempting to hold in the bellow of pain.

Gloria witnesses the tumble and starts to head toward the little ones, but Sister Eva quickly walks and stands over the two children and gives Gloria a glare that catches her full attention. She wags her finger in a no-no gesture and then waves both hands towards Gloria signaling for her to back up and let the kids work it out. Gloria gives pause and submits to the teacher's wishes. She backs up still wiping the tears from her eyes of this emotional day.

Jericho crouches next to Isis, who's still rocking holding her knee. Sister Eva kneels by the two drawing the attention of the other children. They have started to stop and observe the three from their places in line. Sister Eva turns and shoots everyone a grimace that could make stone crack. As a teacher, she's earned that glance through three decades of dealing with the thankless job of teaching ingrate but hopeful sponges. The children immediately turn their eyes forward.

"You children, go on! Go on and line up at the door. We'll be along directly," Sis Eva belts at them with her scruffy voice. Old, stern, and in her traditional nun garb they did not dare ignore her orders. The children shuffle off quickly as she looks at the knee of Isis.

"Oh, you're fine, sweetie. Barely a scrape." Sis Eva says as she rubs the girl's back.

"I told her I was sorry." Jericho small voice squeaks out.

"It's okay, accidents happen. She'll be fine, isn't that right? What is your name, sweetheart?"

Sniffling, the girl wipes her nose. "Isis..."

Sister Eva helps the girl to her feet. "Isis, what a beautiful name, for a beautiful young lady. There is a history of Egyptian lore behind such a mighty name."

Isis dries her eyes with the sleeve of her uniform sweater embroidered with the school logo. A smile starts to emerge across her once tear-filled face. Jericho seeing her feeling better, gets an idea. He slings his book bag off his back and reaches into it. From within its confines, he releases a furry beast that has encapsulated hearts since they were aptly named from the former President Teddy Roosevelt.

"I'm sorry. You wanna hold my Teddy Bear, Griddles?" He reaches into his backpack and pulls out a brown fuzzy bear. Jericho hugs his bear first before handing Griddles over to her. "You can't keep him for right now, because he has to go home with me."

She takes a hold of the bear and hugs him tight. "He's so soft," says Isis.

Sister Eva steps in between the two. "Well, then, now that all is forgiven, shall we head to class?"

Jericho looks to the Nun and proudly tells her, "I'm in Kindergarten. I can count to three hundred."

"Well, now, that is good. Will make sure we add more to that okay?"

"Okay," Jericho says proudly.

Sister Eva turns and places her hand on Isis's shoulder. "And, Isis, is it? I think you're on my roster as well. Jericho, will you take her back pack for her? Gentlemen do that you know." *At least they use to.*

Jericho picks up her bag and leads the way as they all head off towards the front entrance of the school. Sister Eva waves to Gloria that everything is fine. Gloria waves back smiling with tears still streaming from her eyes. She watches with pride at what her sweet departed daughter created. From tragedy, a symphony of love walks around every day. She watches the door long after they've entered the building halfway expecting her baby to come bursting out looking for her. She wipes her face and smiles. In an instant a twitch of un-comfortability wipes the smile as she clutches her stomach. The pain is sharp and instantaneous and then it's gone.

"Having an ache in the belly, are you? You know they say ginger is good for that?" a voice behind Gloria softly bellows out.

An older man looking to be in his eighties is also watching the children. He points toward the doors where Sister Eva and the kids just entered.

"That one right there is a fine young man. You don't see many part with the likes of a Grimm's Bear. Only a special young lady could command a boy to relieve himself of such a mighty bear."

Laughing, she turns around and acknowledges him. "That is a Grimm's Bear, it was my daughter's, God rest her soul, if there is such a being up there." Gloria looks up for emphasis. "She was such an angel. You have a good eye; I didn't think anyone remembered Grimm's Bears."

The old man walks up side by side to Gloria striking up a conversation so he could hear her more clearly. His hearing is no longer what it used to be.

Gloria looks closely at the old man, but does it sheepishly as not to make him uncomfortable. "My daughter was given that very bear by a nice gentleman some twenty-five or thirty years ago in the hospital. She was there for surgery after an accident. She instantly fell in love with that damn bear. She carried it everywhere. He's probably more stitch than bear now." Gloria looks back towards the school's entrance. "I gave Griddles to him. I knew his mother would have eventually, she was saving it for kids of her own."

Gloria turns and walks to her car. She pauses for a moment, thinking whether or not to inquire if he was that nice man all of those years ago. The resemblance is uncanny. *C'mon Gloria, that would be impossible, that man has long since been dead. Hell, he had to be close to eighty then.* Not wanting to drudge up any more sadness then what she already felt for her daughter not being here she, decides against it. Gloria waves goodbye to the old man before opening her door.

The old man looks at her for a second and rocks his walker slightly ahead of him to garner attention towards it. It was a subtle gesture to show his feebleness in hopes that he can get a ride. He starts to raise his hand as if to ask a question. Subconsciously, Gloria knows what he's getting ready to probably ask and she feels for his predicament and hesitates for a second to ponder whether she would give him a ride. Having giving it thought, she thinks twice about having a stranger in her vehicle and ignores his handicap and slides into her red Nissan.

Letting subtleness fall aside he's more straightforward as he uses his walker. "You think I can trouble you for a ride, mother of angels? I do not have to travel far. It's just… the legs aren't what they use to be."

Regretful and suspicious of the old man, she continuously thinks she would love to but, *this day and age you can't really trust anyone.* "I'm sorry, I don't give rides to strangers. Even ones as charming as you."

"I understand. It's a lot of crazies out here these days. Just the other day the news came on and was just filled with nothing but dread. Look at me going on about dread. I'm certainly not helping my predicament, am I? The Old man starts laughing. "I have just some ways to go and would have appreciated a ride."

She starts to close her door. "You can never be too careful these days. Take it easy. Sorry, I couldn't help you out, but I truly have somewhere to be just now." Gloria closes her door, starts the car, and pulls away.

As the car leaves, the elderly man watches her. In her rearview mirror she watches the old man scoot his walker up a step or two and wave. Gloria waves from inside the car. Slowly placing his hands back on the walker, he stands straight continuing to watch as Gloria turned the corner. His face old and world worn as it is, misshapen only more as his brow furrows and doubles in wrinkles as he grimaces slightly. His face then turns sorrowful.

"One can never really be too careful, mother of angels… No matter how much one tries." The old man touches his right gauntlet under his weathered trench coat transfigures into the Arch Angel Metatron. "God speed Gloria Bane."

A shadow passes over Metatron. He looks up in time to see a Demonic Fallen in flight overhead. It trails after the vehicle. Metatron turns and quickly looks through the window of one of the school's classroom. Gabriel's inside looking out at him. Metatron shakes his head, letting Gabriel know that he was unable to illicit a ride with the boy's grandmother. Metatron stands by keeping eyes on the demon as well as looking for an answer to whether follow her or stand down.

Gabriel sadly turns away from the window. Never having been given a definitive answer, Metatron takes flight.

Sitting atop the school's highest peak roof, Death merely watches as Metatron takes flight. He turns his attention downward into the classroom towards what he found so interesting, the boy.

Gabriel turns away from the window and gazes upon Jericho. She watches him laugh at funny faces the teacher makes as she jokes about her past summer. Gabriel walks over and kneels next to him and tousles his hair. For him, it feels as if a cool breeze blows over his face.

As Sister Eva continues making silly faces with hard hardened expressions she catches a glimpse of Jericho. It looks as if beams of sun light have landed on him from outside. His hair blows gently from a breeze, but the peculiar thing is, he is the only one the breeze is blowing on. Sister Eve continues making the children laugh, but she senses the spirit about the boy. Jericho, feeling the breeze increase, he naturally looks to the direction that it originates from and doesn't see anything. Just like that, Gabriel has vanished.

Angel's Spire – Day

A cadre of angels returning from a mission head home to the Angel's Spire that sits on the outskirts of Iayhoten. It is the Hall of the Angels, a piece of heaven cut especially for them. A second focal point that reads Zero Realm which means, from the Spire they can instantly travel all realms and realties at a second's notice.

The returning cadre knows after a long mission that could sometime take over millions of Earth years that it is where they are able to find respite from their endless role of constant gardening, care keeping, and law enforcement of the Sadohedranicverse. Just as any being that was created they need rest, downtime as well as any other creature. As they fly into the spire they glide and rocket at times through barrel vaults and columns of the immense cathedral like ancient structure of cascading flowing liquid marble fused with liquid gold and entillic slavo, another precious metal found in the Racovis system. They wave to citizens and other celestials as they soar pass the wall to wall white marble with emboldened angelic glyphs etched in tillian, another element yet unknown and undiscovered to mortals throughout the entire infinite makeup. Although the Spire is home and dormitory to the cadre of the returning angels it also doubles as their command center where they now need to check in and report.

The day-to-day operations of command and mission assignment take place at the top tier of the Spire. The cadre lands. Having already elected their spokesman they break leaving the one to go file his findings of their mission. He walks further into the interior of the majestic and infinite main hub where the dispatching of choiretic angels supports immeasurable number of missions at any given moment as angels are sent to various points of not just Earth, but throughout the known and unknown galaxies, still not withstanding those currently being expanded by the Powers Corps. After catching up to Michael, the angel submits his report and quickly leaves the hub to catch up with his brothers.

Michael, standing shirtless wearing only his white pants with three platinum horizontal stripes on the thigh of each leg, throws the reports on a massive table and walks out onto the balcony. He stands there overlooking all the Realms of Heaven from his zero focal point. His chest and arms have glowing angelic glyph script on them. The glyphs give off a white flame like light as if they were drawn on him with a fountain pen tipped in liquid illumination, like the pages in the books of life. Intermingled with the glyphs are centuries of battle scars. Some have faded with the passage of time; others have scarred too deep. His body is a culmination of his many conflicts with Demonic fallen.

As he stares out he's happy to have this moment to himself. The peace of being home is often one that is ignored. As he watches the citizens of the realms, he can't help but think what it must feel like to forever be at home and at peace. When he tries to remember, it is always clouded by the dissention in ranks of the order. Frustrated by his ever clouded memory of a time long forgotten he slams his fist on the railing thinking, *Damn, Lucifer! Damn him to hell!*

The railing's facade cracks and breaks along the point of impact. The small crater begins to slowly fracture and spider outward. The micro fissures caused by his blow over minimal time turns into small fissures causing chips of the railing to fall away. Michael stares at the point of impact lost briefly in thought. *Damn you if you aren't this point of impact. Everything that we are now stems from your one point of discontent. I'm so tired. I was never meant to be this, never meant to be warrior, slayer, enforcer, commander. To constantly have to make these decisions that lead so many to Death. My resolve has weakened. It may not be long before I fall in a senseless clash or full scale battle. I almost welcome it. This constant barrage of challenges would finally be at an end. I don't think that is so bad.* As Michael continues to stare at the railing the fracture begins to mend itself.

Michael's train of thought is broken by a familiar and welcomed voice. It comes as a relief as no one should spend too much time in their own head when it's nothing but negativity even the Arch of Angels.

"We must intercede," Gabriel says interrupting, as she appears behind Michael.

So, the interruption is business then? Of course, it is. Still the brief rest from thought was welcomed. Michael moves his gaze from the mending fracture point to back out across the realms. He already knows her mind of what she's about to say. How could he not? She is his first commander, his confidant, his conscious at times when he could not maybe see the clear picture. She was his sister, his only sister at that, his valued number two.

"Did you not here me? We must intervene!" She's louder this time in protest. "You have the king's ear in this matter, Michael."

He continues to stare out into the vast regions of the kingdoms. He looks closely into the Well of Souls. His mind wanders briefly again. *It was a moment of respite. Shall I never find peace again?* He closes his eyes and takes a breath. His metaphoric mantle of captain is once again placed on his brow as he must return from a fantasy of where he's no captain, but just, Michael.

Gabriel yells for measure this time. *"Michael!"*

"Do you think me deaf and blind? Do you not think I've seen the moves that are being made nor heard the whispers?" Michael's tone is stark to let Gabriel know that he's heard her.

Gabriel walks to the side of Michael and overlooks the realm with him. She looks out over the same majestic view that he does. Gabriel sees his fist imprint and the resulting damage inflicted upon the railing. She notes it but decides not to press it.

Michael looks at her and follows her gaze to the fracture point of the railing. He then leaves the balcony momentarily only to return with rolled sealed scrolls. He passes her one of two scrolls that he's holding. Reluctantly, she takes the scroll from him and reads it. She's overcome with sorrow. She looks back out over the realm and passes the papyrus back to Michael.

"I see, but, Michael, there are some orders that we can intercede on their behalf if we have cause. This cause could undo the child and unravel all that has been planned. Michael, he needs this. He's still so fragile. We must intercede at least if not for her, then the boy."

Michael continues gazing. The same thoughts of before the fall again creeps into his mind. *It was all once so beautiful. Paradise was what it was called after the creation of man. I often wonder at times if Lucifer was not right in his disdain for men. All of this wrought over their creation and all the misery that has come after... I wondered, no; I marveled at their creation, what it must be to have free will, to have total autonomy of one's actions. Then, it was clear after some time that free will was the fastest road to perdition I ever bore witness to. What I once envied them for was unknowingly deep rooted within us. Lucifer was case and fact for that. Back at Chasm, I had a choice to take his head and end this.*

It was choice it was the hallmark of free will. I was close to exercising free will in that moment. I no longer wonder what it is to have free will. I now know that it is a responsibility, a burden that I would have removed far from me. I now know that it is a curse of universe upending proportions.

"Michael, please!" Gabriel pleads.

Tapping the remaining sealed scroll on the marble balcony rail Michael looks over to Gabriel. *I'm so tired of bearing the brunt of the decisions. Can't you see I'm just exhausted? Shit! Just follow the damn order is all you have to do.* "What would you have me do, Gabe? You think I should go down and battle the inevitable? Tell Elohim that he has it wrong and should do what I say? Well we don't have such luxury. We are servants to Most High. Our will is but an extension of his. We don't make policy here. We follow it" Michael turns and gazes again at the Well of Souls. *There were once so many souls awaiting to be born, now look at it. It dwindles with so few.*

"He's just a boy. He's innocent. Appeal to the king of kings. Michael, he values your insight. All that you've done for him has earned you a great voice," Gabriel interjects again, refusing to back down.

"You say he's a mere boy, there have been numbers too great to count of mere boys that had to endure. He's no different. Remember the Tides of Airmethia?" He turns and looks at Gabriel and sees her iris have turned grayish red.

"But he's innocent, Michael. He's lost so much already. We need to him to be firing on all cylinders when his day comes. Brother... it comes quickly."

Michael touches his sister's face. "None of us are innocent. There may have been a time that we once were but, no longer."

Frustrated, she pushes backward of the rail and paces on the balcony growing impatient with Michael. "Do you believe that they are lost to us? And no bullshitting me, Michael! Do you believe we are doing all of this in vain?"

Michael looks back over the regions. His thought formulates faster than he realized in answer to her question. "No! No, I don't think that they are lost to us. There are just other priorities now. Unfortunately, she falls low on them. I must allocate our resources how I deem best. I know your feelings on this, but it's a numbers game. Numbers that we are in short supply of."

Michael turns, looking Gabriel in the face. He sees the disappointment, the hurt on her face. The looks of, aren't you even going to try? It pains him to see her that way. His heart sinks at the thought of how much he's breaking her spirit. He wants to console her, but that would undermine the order that he's bound to follow. To show compassion in this matter would weaken his authority. *She has barely ever asked for much, but this is what you ask? You ask for a stay of execution against one order that has been placed among millions just for this day. When you ask for a favor the one time I have no power to make it so.*

Michael leaves the balcony and enters the Spire, he steps on two metallic pads in the shape of feet. His metallic boots generate and slides up his shin to his knees. The metallic echoes as they strike with each step across the marble floor. Gabriel follows Michael into the Spire.

"Michael, just give me the word and I can resolve this. I will go to the palace and plead on his behalf."

Grabbing his tunic, he mutters, "The word will not be given in this matter. I'm sorry, Gabriel." He pauses for a moment. He looks at her and cracks a smile. "At least not by you." Michael places his tunic on as he walks out. Gabriel smiles breathing a sigh of relief she knows he will find a way to repeal the order, he has to.

CHAPTER 20

AVERTED

"Pray as if you will be saved by Elohim. Fight as if you will not."

Quote ~King Saul

Detroit, Michigan Highway – Morning

Gloria rounds a corner in her Nissan entering unto the on ramp of the Lodge Freeway. She turns on the radio station, looking for something in the soft rock of yesteryear variety. Not finding anything to her liking, she again eventually settles on easy listening. Peter Gabriel's voice cracks the silence of the humdrum commute. Just as she catches the tune, it plays itself off.

Damn! I like that song, too. The sweet melody is replaced by up to the minute news briefing. *The radio news anchor sounds kind of hot with his baritone voice. I need to really start dating again. It's time when you thinking of the radio news man voice.*

'It appears that America, the last holdout has finally recognized Cainsin as the capital city of the sovereign nation Arcainaque. After much political debate, the president had to acknowledge that the Arcane Empire has risen as a nation. Not just any nation, but one that could very well rival the United States, Russia and China a leading superpower, which makes China a bit uneasy as they were vying to make their move to number 1 owning over eighty percent of the United States' debt. Lucien Arcane has striven for decades realizing his dream of a united world. President Adlerian Regis had this to say…'

A different voice belonging to the President crackled from the radio.

'I have personally spoken with Mr. Arcane on numerous accounts and have found his intentions pure, although I can't say I agree with all of his forceful tactics in the more impoverished regions of the world. However, his intentions do appear on their face to be legitimate—'

Gloria switches again in an attempt to find more easy listening. She strikes out again finding more talk radio.

"Scientist have been tracking Wormwood and are more than excited at the prospects that the comet---"

Bored with the minute-to-minute politics and simply fed up with the Wormwood discovery, Gloria again turns the station finding one that is playing classical music. Looking down, she loses concentration for the briefest of moments on the task of driving. The Arch Angel Raphael is suddenly sitting in the passenger seat. He chooses to remain invisible as he reaches over and lightly touches her and whispers. "Watch all else that moves!"

Startled by the mild suggestion that Raph jolts her soul with, Gloria looks up from turning the station instantly alert.

"To the left," Raphael calmly suggest that she moves her attention. She keeps driving straight without deviation. "Stubborn, aren't we?" Raphael phases to the backseat. He touches Gloria's head with both hands and whispers with urgency. "The lane to your left is clear. Go! Go now!"

She looks to the left lane turning on her blinker. As she starts to switch lanes she hesitates by making sure the lane is clear.

Raphael yells, "Go now!"

She changes lanes abruptly. As she switches she realizes that the semi-truck she was following in the previous lane brakes locks up. The truck's haul starts to jack knife to the left. Seeing the incident unfold, her heart starts to race, her body tenses as the cab of the truck slowly crosses into her new lane desperately trying to regain control. Terrified, Gloria begins to scream bracing for impact. Raphael phases to the passenger seat again. With his left hand he covers Gloria's heart.

"Calm, yourself."

Gloria finds a calm instantly to deal with the escalating matter at hand.

"Now, floor it, Gloria!" Raph yells excitedly.

Without a second thought she punches the gas pedal to the floor. Her vehicle just makes it past the cascading cab of the semi-truck as it strikes the center median. Raphael looks out of the passenger side window as they pass the front bumper of the cab. Raphael watches the swerving cab of the semi, he sees Death gripping the outside of the driver side door. His dark trench coat flapping in the wind as he holds on to the drivers outside mirror attachment. As his trench flaps, his armor is partially revealed showing his metal onyx colored chest plate trimmed in purple liquid translucent metal. Reaching into the cab for the driver also exposes his purple sash with black angelic glyphs around his waist.

Death reaches through the open window of driver's door and pulls a red soul sphere from the body of the truck driver who's just had a massive heart attack of the worst kind commonly known as the windowmaker. As he places the sphere within his coat, he notices Raph as well. Death nods at Ralph as the cab of the semi begins to flip after striking the median. The attached dual trailers have already lost traction and rolled to their sides skidding and causing untold vehicular and road destruction in its wake. Death's hood blows off, revealing what's underneath since the time at Chasm's expulsion portal. His face is covered by a black metal face mask and helmet. It's fitted to his face and locked at the back with a cross shaped lock which can only be opened by key. All that is visible are the shadowed holes where his eyes should've been. Unlike the rest of the angels, his mood cannot be determined by the color of his irises.

Raphael extends his arm out of the window, flipping Death the middle finger. The cab then completely rolls over causing a chain reaction of minor accidents and fender benders behind it. Gloria looks in the rear-view mirror and watches as the cab of the truck catches fire and explodes. *What the hell is that truck hauling, is it lethal? Oh god, what if the ploom is lethal?*

Once clear of the near fatal miss and the ensuing calamity she slams on the brakes. Without thinking of herself, she gets out the vehicle and returns to see if she can help anyone in the wake of destruction. As she runs, Raphael is already outside watching her sprint to lend aid.

Raphael looks on he turns to his right and starts speaking to thin air, "She has a good soul in these dark times. She reminds me of someone, although I can't place who."

Metatron appears standing next to Raph. "As well she should. She's mother of angels. Her offspring had to acquire their selflessness from somewhere?"

Raphael shakes his head in disbelief as he watches her. "Unfortunately, her soul still shines red."

Metatron slaps Raphael on the back. "Yes, it does, but her date of expiration has changed. It seems an order was cut to change her rendezvous with Death. She now has more time to see the truth. She'll come around. We have to have faith in them even when they don't. Come, we have much to do. She'll be fine." Death… I really hate that guy."

"I'm sure he's not fond of you either," says Metatron laughing.

Raphael looks back at Metatron and realizes he now stands alone. He returns his attention to Gloria and watches her check on the injured in the vehicles behind the burning truck. He walks up to her and touches her. "Use your time wisely, mortal. I was given order to intervene on this account however, I fear that we may not intercede again. Use your remaining time wisely."

"You should not have intervened at all, Baby Arch," says a disembodied voice.

Ralph grabs the hilt of his blade while turning to watch the burning cab of the truck. Raphael eyes the flames closely. He places his left hand on Gloria. "Run, it's not safe," he suggestively whispers to Gloria, but she's trying to help a young man out of one of the twisted vehicles. The injured teen is hung up in his seatbelt. She grabs a hold of him by the arm and pulls him as she tries to unlatch the belt. After a minute she succeeds in freeing the teen.

"We have to move. It's not safe to be here," Gloria tells him. Dazed and disoriented, he takes her word for it and allows himself to be pulled along.

Flames erupt from the driver side window of the overturned tractor cab. Red flames explode far into the sky. Raphael pulls his blade and waits. He watches one of the columns of flames closely as it dissipates revealing the fallen demon, Agathan. His helmet disengages, falling below the neckline of his armor. The features of the demons face are rough and twisted from eons of conflict he's been out of the presence of Elohim and Lucifer for centuries locked away under the warden Apollyon down in Palengrad. It looks as if his jaw has been broken and reset multiple times. His armor is dark blood red. There's no need for him to where a cloak as his heavenly countenance has long since doused.

Agathan walks through the flames then lifts gently into the air and hovers stationary over the accident scene. "Down there admiring my work yet again, young one? Stand down Baby Arch, I'm not here for your head this day, but push me and I will take it all the same? You will do time in Palengrad. I assure you, it's not a place of niceties.

Raphael studies him. "Last I seen you, you were thrown the portal ass first. Why are you here?"

"I'm here to ensure the will of Fate of course."

Raphael's mask generates from his neckline encapsulating his head and face. "I heard you were misguided in thinking that you are the enforcer of a power that has long since been extinguished. Satan has no true power; therefore, you have none."

"She's to die this day. It was written so, it must be. In the absence of fate, I'm here to ensure its will." Agathan says as he lands closer to Raph.

Another explosion occurs. It destroys the vehicles that were behind the semi. Flames consume the vehicle where Gloria was just helping the teen. Death emerges from the fiery wreckage of the cab. He places his hood back on his head and watches the angel and demon exchange. He reaches out his hand and collects seven red soul spheres and three blue ones that were set loose in the subsequent explosion and fire.

"You will not move aside then, Baby Arch?" Agathan says to Raphael.

"No!"

Agathan masks regenerates around his face. Nothing else to say, Agathan separates his sword into two and covers the distance quickly in an attempt to separate Raph's head from body. Agathan's swing is whirlwind fast, but then so is Raph's. He slides on his knees arching backwards just missing the blade by inches. However, Raphs' blade hit its mark and strikes Agathan along his side just beneath the right-side rib where the breast plate offers little protection. In an instant the two have exchanged sides and prepare themselves to dual a second time.

Damn! He's a two-blade wielder. He trained under War. This could be problematic. Raph thought.

Gloria and the remaining bystanders that are caught in the traffic jam, can only hear the thunder and feel the extreme wind gusts from the ethereal exchange.

The teen that Gloria helped out of his car looks at her. "Now we have a storm to contend with?"

Gloria tries to hold her small frame as the wind pushes her slightly. "This has been an unusual morning, period. You good? Can you wal-- duck! Gloria pushes the teen to the ground as a car flips over the top of them. It flies into the oncoming lane of highway traffic where the sound of screeching tires and twisted metal overtakes the thunder.

The teen looks at Gloria. "Walk? Hell, I can run. Go, go, go! Let's get out of here!"

"Shit!" Raph watches as the car that Agathan threw flips into the oncoming highway traffic.

Raph ducks and side steps right and left nearly missing Agathan's swing and double thrusts.

"Language, Arch. Such a mouth. Do you kiss Epsilonic babies with such foul lips?" Agathan again swings one of his blades low while spinning. As he spins, he extends and blades his wings to slice for the midsection hoping to cut the body horizontally wise of Raph's.

Experience of previous battles has already made Raph aware of the counter. Raph scissor leg leaps into the air and rolls collecting his appendages closely. He rolls through and in between the wings and top blade. Once clear he lands on the right leg first using his left to kick Agathan in his chest. The force of the kick sends the demonic assassin sliding back into a cadre of cars that are stopped on the highway awaiting emergency services to tend and clear the roads.

"Gotdammit! I don't need this." Ariel sighs and hits her steering wheel as she watches the taillights and the roaring flames about twenty cars in front of her. She looks back at her daughter who's firmly belted in her child seat. Pissed at the traffic, she can't help but smile at her sleeping two-year-old. As she turns back to yell some more at traffic she sees other drivers exiting their cars running past hers. As she looks past the running people, she witnesses cars flipping on their sides from a small tornado cutting a path down the highway coming from the scene of the accident.

Gloria and the teen runs past Ariel's vehicle. She quickly unbuckles her belt and spins in her seat to undo her daughter, but it's too late. Her vehicle flips on its side, ejecting Ariel. She flails through the air before bouncing off the roof of another stopped vehicle.

Raphael wields his blade in a flash flurry of thrusts and swings looking to decapitate Agathan and end this melee quickly. But the bastard is good. In their last exchange Agathan was able to score more hits off Raph than he was comfortable with. The Arch had lacerations to his left arm and right leg. There were two deep dents and a gouge mark in his chest armor from where Agathan rocked him good with a flurry of dense bone breaking strikes.

"That woman's time has expired, Arch, just as the others that are perishing here this day. Stand aside and let me set the end to her mortal linear line."

Death wishing to watch the match and how it ends gives into his ethereal drive. Lives are passing and he has a job that can't wait. He begins to start collecting the souls of those that have found tragic ends in the celestial's grudge match."

Breathing ethereal relam air heavily the two combatants look over towards Death who's in the midst of collecting souls of those that have departed since the beginning of their conflict.

Death looks at them from the darkness of his hood. They can't see his face, but they can tell there's anger. "As, I didn't have enough to keep me occupied."

Raph turns his attention back to Agathan. "You're right. Death is waiting for one more. Let's end this, because you will not touch her this day. I have my orders and I will see them to whatever end."

Agathan masks degenerates exposing his head. He nods toward Raphael. In kind Raph degenerates his mask exposing his face as well. Raph's face is bruised and blood trickles from the small lacerations. Both celestials as they wait for their final engagement stand in pools of their own blood.

"You ready, Baby Arch?"

"As I'll ever be… Bring it!" Raph steps back planting himself. He raises his blade in a salute and moves into a ready high guard.

Agathan rockets off spearing Raph with his body's momentum. The force carries the two off the highway into a nearby building. As they crash through the building, workers run in fear of the lightening and high storm winds that tear through their offices that conceal the two combatants. Raph kicks Agathan off of him and sends the crazed battle-hardened demon careening through a wall into and adjoining room. Raph jumps to his feet from his back and takes off after Agathan.

Agathan stands to his feet and spits blood. He recovers and meets Raph with an exchange of blows and swings of blades. As the two fight till exhaustion, their swings diminish with power immensely.

"I'm surprised, Baby Arch, that no one intervened in our contest of wills."

"Why would they intervene? You are a mere intrusive presence on my day. An annoyance at best. One that should have been put down two centuries ago when you ended that just King of Brittan against any approved order. You are in error, Agathan. You are no hand of Fate. You are just misguided and I will see that rectified today. After these next few minutes, the name of Agathan will disappear from the mouths of angels and demons alike. You will only be known to the Warden in the halls that Apollyon keeps in Palengrad."

Agathan smiles and pounds his chest twice, willing Raph to press the attack. "The guiding hand of Fate welcomes you, Arch. As you Archs are fond of saying, let us be done with this."

Raphael lunges forward, tackling Agathan. The two crash through the opposite side of the building an onto the roof top of a smaller building. The impact from the fall carries the two through the roof and every floor until they hit the ground floor. Both of the weary combatants slowly stand.

Raphael looks at Agathan. He knows that this is the final moment. He sees how he's holding his blades and cradling his side. He's going to be betting everything he has left on this next strike. Raph knows he doesn't have anything left past this next encounter. He has to put him away if Gloria is to survive and him live.

Agathan spins both of his blades so that the business ends are facing Raph.

"C'mon!" Raph shouts.

Agathan closes the distance. He thrusts the left blade first. Raphael spins clockwise and uses his right metal gauntlet to deflect the left thrust and with his left, he thrust for Agathan's chest and misses. Agathan second blade with an addition of right thrust hits its mark. He firmly places the blade into Raphael's torso just below the right ribcage. The momentum slides Raph down to the hilt of Agathan's blade.

The two, stand face to face. Blood begins to pour from Raph's mouth.

"Looks as if the test of wills and of law is at an end, Arch."

Trying to catch his breath under this most difficult circumstance, Raph attempts to speak through the rapid exhalation. "So, it is, Demon. I will more than gladly accept your surrender now."

Agathan continues to stare at Raph and begins to chuckle at first, then breaks into a full hardy side-splitting laugh. Through the pain and strong wincing, Raph starts to laugh at his own gest secretly hoping that he really would just surrender.

Wheezing! "I noticed you called me, Arch. You didn't demean it this time, why?" Says Raph as he laughter turns to a simple smile.

"You've earned my respect today, Arch. Out of respect for you and this most valiant effort. I promise to make her transcendence quick and painless, I will spare her the pain from the likes of what you are experiencing now."

"As I told you Agathan, you will not touch her." Raph says through shallow breath and severe wheezing.

Raph uses his left arm to steady himself. He then places his right foot on Agathan's chest and pushes with his remaining might forcing himself backward off the blade creating distance. Raph swings his blade upward with all he has in reserve, cutting through Agathan's blade. Before he can react, Raph swings his blade in an arching loop turning it horizontal in one fluid movement. He separates Agathan's head from its neck.

Raph watches as Agathan's lifeless body falls to its knees before finally falling to the ground.

"I told you, Demon. I have my orders." Raphael falls backward as well. His body never touches the ground as Metatron catches him in his arms.

"I have you brother. Well done, Raph, well done. I leave you for only a moment." Metatron lifts Raph and backs into a white column beam of light. The two disappear into the light which then retracts back into the heavens.

Death walks up to the body of Agathan and removes a black soul from it. He places it inside his coat. He then removes a vial from his inside trench pocket and sprinkles it on the remains of Agathan. He then turns and vanishes. The remains of the demon ignite in purplish and blue flame.

CHAPTER 21

ARRIVAL

"Do you understand Daniel all that I have told you? This book must not be opened until the end of all things! Tell your mortal brothers and sisters only what I have spoken and not one word more are you to tell."

Quote ~Gabriel

SIX YEARS LATER, 2026

Al Fashir – Dusk

West of Al Fashir in the Sudan, the Sudanese military are entrenched at the Al Fashir airport, engaged in a battle with Lucien's Arcanian armed forces. Commander Rusain is leading the forces attack. Unlike other commanders, he takes the rare route of leading from the front exposing himself to the same dangers as his men. Across his lifetime of battling in hot spots across the world, he's learned one proven fact that holds true in every arena of war, although the leader may be over exposed by leading from the front, men that see the leader in the trench fighting with them are more loyal and willing to follow orders without question.

Damn these, assholes! Why couldn't they just yield? Rusain thinks to himself. The theater of war never seems to change as he's forced to talk over the constant explosions and ricocheting rounds.

Rusain ducks down as rounds ping and zip pass him. Through the chaos, he yells into his Motorola X27 radio, "The sitrep is as follows: we've encountered a superior in number militarized force at Alpha theta. I have incurred a greater number of casualties that intel could not have predicted. In spite of losses we've pushed them back to what we believe is their stronghold. I believe they are in their final stand position. The airport seems to be their Alamo. They have entrenched themselves throughout the airport and are throwing everything they have left at us. Which is more than enough to keep us at bay."

His transmission stops as he hears the all too familiar incoming mortar shell whistle. Rusain dives to the ground and covers his head. The explosion is close enough for the shock wave to rattle his teeth. He gets up and takes notice that the Humvee that was hard charging up the left with men advancing behind it had been reduced to cinders and twisted metal. *Damn!* Rusain finds his mic and continues. "I believe the force that we pursued have retreated to where they had numbers and resources in reserve. Over!" The radio squawks back.

"I understand, sir. I recommend for the safety of the remaining men on the ground that we fall back to a siege perimeter and hold what we have. Once we're free of danger close, we send a compliment of Tomahawk missiles up their asses... Yes, sir, loss would be total." The radio operator next to Rusain head rocks backward splitting in canoe fashion as a 7.62 round tears through his forehead. Rusain looks briefly then turns his attention back to the battle. "Yes Sir, I understand that the airport is vital. Sir, yes, Sir." Commander Rusain looks at the structure. His eyes follow the lines of tanks and anti-aircraft batteries that are moving into firing position.

Commander Rusain turns and waves to a Charlie Company officer that is moving up left flank. He signals him to hold the advance. He then rolls on his side and reaches into his right pant leg's cargo pocket and pulls out another laminated folded map. He rolls back prone unfolding and displaying it across the ground. He cross-checks the map with his up to the moment statistics of tallied dead and wounded. A constant barrage of tank fired uranium depleted rounds whiz by as he determines his next critical moves to overtake his enemy. An incoming round strikes dangerously close. Rusain is pelted with rocks and Earth. He shakes his head and extremities knocking the loose dirt off of him. And continues assessing the map. He glances left looking for the young officer he had just flagged. He finds his arm and weapon had made it to him, but not the other important appendages. Rusain scowls and again turns his attention toward the battle.

As a plan begins to take shape in his mind, Rusain looks up at the enemy's tanks and weapons placements. Satisfied that his assessment of man power to enemy capability is correct and that the heavy weapons are too powerful to overcome with his dwindling force, he picks up the mic. "Command Actual, before we sustain any more vital loss of life and equipment, I recommend and request the release of code name Imperial Protocol. I repeat, I'm calling for Imperial Protocol."

Suddenly, a Sudanese soldier is on top of Rusain. "Shit!" Rusain drops the mic and throws himself backward on his back looking up at his incoming attacker and fires his Scar automatic rifle killing the assassin. His riddled body falls on top of Rusain. The commander rolls right pushing off the Assassin. The attacker moans only a few seconds. Rusain pulls his bayonet and places it through the skull of the assassin granting him the mercy of a quick death. He frees the blade, wipes it on the corpse to clean it and returns it to its sheath.

A Sudanese T54 tank fires its primary cannon from in front of the main entrance to the airport. An Arcanian Humvee with a soldier firing a roof mounted fifty caliber machine gun on Rusain's advancing left is hit and explodes instantly. Pieces of the soldier that was firing the roof mounted weapon is blown to the four winds. An appendage of one of the soldier's lands next to Rusain, he grimaces. What's left of the Humvee's squad has fused to the twisted metal. Watching another Humvee destroyed, Rusain stands and grabs one of a two-man Javelin team that was just happening to be running past him on his right. He pulls him to a knee. The spotter follows and takes a knee as well.

"Sergeant, is that a Javelin on your back?" Rusain asks him in a tone that overtly states why aren't you using the damn thing?

The Sergeant Looking over his shoulder reluctantly replies, "Yes, sir."

"By all means son, you know what the hell our beloved fighting force bean counters purchased them for?

"Yes, Sir."

"Put that damn thing to use son! Take it off your back and go to work and find me a target of the tank variety and make it go away."

The Sergeant unstraps it and takes it off. He goes through the motions of making it safe to fire. He takes extra caution and reads the instructions.

"What the fuck?" Rusain yells.

The Javelin carrying soldier looks at Rusain then drops his eyes to toward the Earth. "It's not mine sir, I took it off Sweet's dead body. I've never fired one of these."

Unable to control his temper, Rusain finds that voice from his drill instructor days that puts fear into souls. "Does that fucking Javelin you're holding work, Sergeant, yes or no?"

"Yes, Sir! It, looks to be in working order, Sir!"

"Then, target the nearest fucking piece of armor and vaporize it!" The sergeant's partner helps loads the Javelin onto his shoulder and taps him on the top of the helmet signifying that he is ready to deploy. From a knee he hears the tone verifying that the Javelin has locked onto a target. He fires the Javelin rocket; it finds its target and hits it square on destroying it. The sergeant pumps his fist and looks at Rusain. His celebration is brief as the young sergeant is instantly struck by a sniper's bullet through the head. The blood spray from the temple artery is warm on Rusain's face and the spotters. The commander blinks to clear his eyes of the arterial spray and chunks of brain matter. The lifeless body of the sergeant slumps over.

Rusain uses his sleeve to wipe his face then points to the spotter that's a private. "You there, private, can you do what he did and make that thing go boom?" The private nods yes. "Then grab that piece of equipment, reload and go to work!"

The mic squawks. Rusain realizes that he's been distracted and haven't been listening. He falls prone and again gives communication with command his full attention. "This is a go for Morning Dawn at Tango Alpha." The explosions deafen Rusain to the transmissions. "I did not copy last. I repeat, I did not copy last." Three explosions in succession takes out more of his men on the right. "Acknowledged command!" Seeing a target of opportunity Rusain drops the mic firing his weapon.

A master sergeant runs up and falls to one knee with a leveled rifle beside Rusain. His barrel is red hot from almost constant non-stop firing of his weapon. The unmistakable *Clack* sounds tells him that his weapon is now an empty one as the master sergeant fires to a lock back. With hardened muscle memory, he reloads his weapon and continues firing without looking at Rusain, but is more than capable to carry a conversation.

"What did actual say Sir? How far out are the inbound reserve forces?"

"Too far to matter. Standby, sergeant, and prepare to witness a weapon like no other. Imperial Protocol has been approved and enacted."

CHAPTER 22

INITIATE BANE

"I know what you're thinking Philistine. Where does such anger and wrath of which the likes have fallen upon you hail from? It hails from the arrow that you placed through the heart of my wife over a prejudice. You took it upon yourself to judge me unworthy. Now, as I have laid waste to your meager infantry purposely, saving you for last. Now, it is I that will judge you. I find you guilty of hatred of your fellow man. I find you guilty of crimes against Elohim which I derive my strength from. Your sentence... will be to watch me lay waste to the entirety of your Kingdom."

Quote ~Samson

Wixom, Michigan – DUSK

Frustrated, Jericho takes his helmet off and whips it with a velocity that carries it into a tree, shattering it.

"Jericho, what the hell?" Gloria yells at him. "I'm not buying you another one. You hear me?"

He looks at the shattered pieces of the helmet that have exploded everywhere. Pieces are even near his foot. The tree that it struck is more than twenty yards. "I didn't mean to, Grandma. This bike is killing me. This thing is hard to get a grasp of."

"Well, you wanted it?

"I know; it was just hard to keep up riding a pedal bike when all my friends have dirt bikes."

With no effort, Jericho pulls the red and white Yamaha dirt bike up from off its side with one hand. He knows that he should have struggled picking the bike up from the ground, but strength has never been a problem for him. It makes him smile at times to think that at only five-foot-five and a hundred-ten pounds, he can play with boys twice his size and measure against them pound for pound and sometimes more. Like picking up a huffy pedal bike to change directions, Jericho picks up the dirt bike and sets it so he doesn't have to turn to get going up the incline.

"Jerry, I told you stop doing that. You turn that bike like any of your friends would. We don't need people asking questions. Why do you think I drove all this way out here for you to learn how to ride this damn thing? Because, I knew that you would do exactly this."

Jericho mimics his grandmother nagging at him by syncing his lips to her voice. Seeing him mock her, she hits him with her purse repeatedly while she tries to keep from laughing.

"Boy, you get on my last nerve. You're gonna find yourself punched in the throat."

Jericho starts to open his mouth.

"And if you say how many more last nerves I got, I'll throttle you." They both know she wouldn't. Gloria's proud of the young man that he's becoming. She remembers the toddler years and the first time she knew there was something special about him.

Detroit, Michigan: 2022, Eight Years after the Birth of Jericho

Watching from her front screen door, Gloria watches as Jericho, Isis, and Jason tear down the street on their bicycles. She starts to call out for him, but realizes it's useless as he sped past not even giving the house a moments glance. If she wants him, she'll have to risk life and limb to stand in front of the trio to slow them down. *Eventually, he'll get hungry. Well maybe thirsty before hungry. I'll catch him then, because that room of his is atrocious.*

As Gloria turns to leave the front door she hears the unmistakable sound that every parent dreads, the screeching of a vehicle coming to an abrupt stop followed by a heart stopping twisting of metal and smashing of glass. As if a torpedo was fired from its launch tube is the swiftness which Gloria exploded from the front door. She took the seven steps from her porch in two strides. On the ground barefooted with her jogging pants and t-shirt on, she was well on her way down the block.

Unsure if she's even breathing, she doesn't stop running. Her stride and speed to check on her grandson would rival the fastest Olympian. *Smoke, not far now, please let my baby be okay, dear God let him be okay, I can't... I just can't! Not her baby. He's all I have of her, he's all I have left.*

Gloria arrives at the end of the block she rounds the corner and her heart sinks even further. She witnesses two twisted bikes in the road. Along with a severely front end damaged black ford explorer that was laying on its side. She slowly walks out into the street toward the wreckage. Her legs feel as if they're turning to mush. Her sight starts to darken out around the edges of her peripheral. She realizes that she's not breathing. She has been holding her breath since she leapt off the porch. She makes sure she inhales, to faint now wouldn't do anyone any good. Tunnel vision has overtaken all of her senses as she searches for the children, searches for Jericho. Sounds of other witnesses and those involved in the accident are muffled. She can't hear them yell for first responders or cries of pain. Without second thought and complete numbness of pain, Gloria walks across the spilled fluids of transmission, gas, and oil not to mention the shattered glass that sits atop all of it. With each step, the tiny pieces of coated glass tear into the bottom flesh of her feet.

The smoldering Explorer that's on its side ignites and catch fire in the engine and interior of the vehicle underneath the dashboard. Gloria still frantically searching for the children walks past the middle-aged woman screaming to be let out of the burning SUV deathtrap. Not seeing the children Gloria looks toward the second involved vehicle. As she turns to approach the vehicle, she instantly recognizes it as the City of Detroit Animal Control recovery truck. Four of the small door flaps are open still swinging back and forth from the sudden impact. Many of the others doors and wounded animals that occupied the small cells are strewn around the collision scene. The rest of the truck is nestled in the side of the Stewart's home which sits on the corner.

Gloria stops, her breathing intensifies so much so that it becomes shallow and laborious. She sees Jericho's bike crushed between the side of the truck and the side of the house where it crushed a path entering the home. She takes off in a full sprint jumping on top of and climbing the side of the truck only to slide down the post into the hole created by the collision and entering into the house herself. Gloria checks the side where she saw the mangled bike and finds nothing. She turns and instantly starts to tear through the debris that was caused from the truck's missile like entry.

"Jericho! Jericho, baby, where are you?" she yells out as she overturns plywood, brick and drywall.

A white light from the Spire's Zero Realm strikes the ground. Gabriel exits from the light appearing invisibly phased next to Gloria hiding her presence. She places her hand on Gloria's shoulder. "Under the truck!" she whispers giving clue as a dangling participle.

Shit! My baby, I'm looking everywhere but under that damn truck. Please, God, don't let him be there. If he is just take me. Gloria shifts her attention toward the truck not believing that isn't the first place she didn't look or maybe didn't want to look. As she reaches the tire, she franticly starts to pull debris away looking under the truck, but stops when she sees the face of her grandson. He's pinned under the tire from the chest down. *He's quiet as a mouse, and so still.* Through the tears, her grandmother maternal instincts have taken over command, she don't remember how or when, but she was under the truck herself grasping for whatever part of Jericho she could get a hold of. Gloria kisses her grandson on the stillness of his face and begins to dig. When she creates enough space to the left side of him she lays prone and see that Isis is down further under the truck and Jason is just to the right of her.

Lord, not the babies. "Jason, Isis, can you two hear me? Ja—" The truck moves and slides to the side slightly. The weight shifts and the bumper traps Gloria halfway underneath as well. The weight pins her against the pile of bricks she was crawling over slowly suffocating her. *I did say take me Lord if you took him. I'm ready.*

Gloria turns her head toward Jericho. She blinks her eyes trying to remain focused on the sweet face of her baby, as darkness starts to creep from the far end of her peripherals inward again overtaking everything that she held dear in this life, she starts the process of letting go. The noise of strangers congregating outside to watch the tragedy unfold are starting to slip away as sound becomes distant. Resigned to give herself over to death she surrenders her last breath.

Suddenly air rushes and fills Gloria's lungs. The smell of motor oil and airbag powder never smelled so great as she takes in a deep breath. Her vision clears almost instantly clears to disbelief. She's startled but not terrified by what she sees. She thinks she's dreaming, but the pain reminds her that she's very much awake. Gloria's eyes stretch as she witnesses Jericho slowly push the tire well upward off of him. The leverage of being flat on his back gives him enough position and power to lift the vehicle far enough that the bumper lifts off of Gloria's chest giving her room to squirm.

Not believing what she witnessing, she suspends all reasoning and just accepts it for the miracle it is. "Push baby, push!" she yells at him.

Jericho continues slowly bench pressing, pushing along the left side of tire well's undercarriage as far as his little arms extend. Gloria takes advantage and slides further under the truck to grab a hold of Jason and Isis. She grabs the children by their clothing and scrunches their collars tight around their nape of the neck for a good grip and pulls while sliding herself out from underneath the vehicle. She continues repeating the pull and slide to extricate them.

Jericho watches Isis closely as she's pulled past him. He breathes a sigh of relief as he watches her chest rise and fall.

"Push, baby! Don't stop hold it just a little longer." As Gloria pulls them out, she backs her foot into debris bringing a halt to her efforts. The dust from the bricks and smoke from the engine has obscured her vision. She can't see a clear path to pull them out. *Damn! Climbed too far underneath.* She swings her legs in and out like making a bottom half snow angel attempting to feel for the exit or another path of least resistance, but she lost her path of entry or it collapsed behind her.

Jericho starting to struggle with bumper reaches deeper and grunts as he pushes harder to keep the truck raised.

"Hold on, Jerry! Hold on, baby!" Gloria, panicking, starts scissoring her feet to look for the end to the debris that blocks her extricating efforts. She feels for it in hopes to use it as a way to guide herself out.

Jericho pushes hard enough to exchange his arms for his legs gaining more leverage. Once he switches, he legs presses the vehicle up further.

"Shit! I can't find it; I can't find the way out." Gloria panics more as the smoke and dust starts to overcome her.

Fire ignites from the engine embers. Small pieces of burning rubber from the vehicle's interior hoses falls on her and the kids. The hot liquid rubber burns her exposed skin on contact. Wincing in pain with each liquid drip that hits her back she tries to calm herself to tend to the task at hand. *One crisis at a time, Gloria.* Metatron suddenly appears over the top of Gloria. He extends his wings to cover them encasing the last remnants of fresh air while Gloria works to free everyone from the burning hot debris falling out of the engine, from the structure that could collapse at any moment.

Seeing her situation and understanding the remedy, Metatron turns his wings vertical and with one flap expels all of the smoke and dust from underneath the truck. He touches Gloria on her hand. "The way is clear, go now!"

Gloria having a clear line of sight pulls with everything she has until herself, Isis and Jason are free. She pulls and slings them towards the front door. They are still unconscious as they slide across the dusted hardwood floor. Not even taking a second, she runs back to Jericho and grabs his hand. "On three, sweetie, and I pull you out." Water from the fire hose of the responding fire department blasts through the opening of the structure dousing the truck. It distracts Gloria for only a second as she never even heard them arrive.

"One, two, three." Gloria pulls Jericho by both arms. As she pulls him he legs presses the truck with all he has clearing room for him to be pulled. Gloria pulls him free and into her arms as the truck slams to ground. Once in her arms Gloria doesn't stop, she beelines right for the front door. As she reaches the front door the children are gone. She starts to look around frantically when a fireman in full turnout gear grabs a hold of her.

"We have them, ma'am, the children, we have them. They're safe. C'mon, let's get you two out." The fireman says as he escorts them outside.

As the fireman escorts them out, Gloria breathes in the fresh air of relief. She sets Jericho down and looks him over. His clothing is a little wear for tear, but otherwise he doesn't carry a mark upon him. She watches as he runs over to his friends that are placed on gurneys of the responding ambulances. They have started to regain consciousness and are up and somewhat alert, although sluggish.

"Your feet, ma'am," the paramedic Dwayne says, drawing Gloria's attention to her feet.

Dwayne helps her lie stomach side down on the gurney and begins to lightly bandage her feet and address the burns on her back.

Gloria just continues to look across the street at Jericho as he talks to Isis and rubs her head. *What I saw him do today was nothing short of impossible. There is something about that boy. Damn! Did anyone else see what he did?* Gloria looks around to see what witnesses were looking at and possibly talking about. *Good, no one seems to be looking at him.* "Jericho!" Gloria yells out. He takes a last look at Isis before he runs to his grandmother.

Gloria pulls him close and whispers to him, "You listen to me. Don't you ever tell anyone what you did here today! You hear me?"

"Why? What I did was freaking awesom—"

"Can never be told again. If people saw what you did you'd be placed in a light that would never turn off. We don't need that kind of attention. Shh! We'll talk about this later." Jericho nods his head as the paramedic comes back from opening the ambulance's double doors.

"Hey there, little man, give me a hand putting your mother in the back?"

Jericho doesn't bother to correct him. His grandmother is his mother in his eyes, and he's never second guessed that fact. She risked all for him today. He simply nods yes and helps to place her in the ambulance. She looks at him and he understands. He plays helpless as they place her in the ambulance. Gloria winks at him. He smiles and climbs into the back with her. Dwayne closes the door and smacks it twice signaling his partner their ready to roll.

Wixom, Michigan – Dusk, 2026

Gloria's thoughts return from the past. The sound of Jericho's laughter brings her back to the present and the reclusive spot she has brought him to while he learns to ride his motor bike.

Jericho laughs and sits on the bike. "I know, I know. Just give me a minute, let me get up this hill and—"

"No way. You just broke your helmet. We're done until you replace it," Gloria says.

"Do you know how many lawns I'd have to cut for that?"

"I don't care now go and pick up your mess. Stay green and all that jazz you kids say."

Giving a reluctant sigh, he gets off his bike and heads into the brush to retrieve the pieces of his helmet which resulted from his momentary lapse in anger management. As he kneels down to pick up the pieces, he turns to see a beautiful woman holding the broken mouth guard section of the mask. Gabriel's materialized for him to see her. Her cloak has been transfigured into a grayish-white trench coat with angelic glyph on the shoulders and gold military strip marks down the left forearm.

"I found this piece over there, handsome," she says, while flashing him a smile.

Mesmerized by her beauty, the preteen trips over his most common word of etiquette. "Th-Thanks."

Gabriel turns to Gloria, who's coming through the brush. When Gloria sees Gabriel, her pace quickens as her over protective nature kicks in.

"Hey, I didn't know anyone else was out here," Gloria says.

"I've been watching you two for quite some time now. The boy's indeed grown powerful at such a young age, stronger than I remember Samson being at his age."

Startled, by her observation and the instant lead in on his strength Gabriel can tell that Gloria's first thought moves toward defensive. Gabriel gets right to the point before Gloria can muster a lie to counter.

"I mean no harm, mother of Rachel. I am here only fulfilling a vow that I once made."

Gabriel listens closely to the sound of Gloria's soul; she hears her heart skips what must have been seven beats. Although her daughter has been dead for years, Gabriel knows the impact she would instantly feel whenever her name is mentioned.

"You knew my daughter?" Confused, Gloria is more apt to listen to the stranger.

Gabriel had thought of playing it safe, but time was not on her side any longer. Progression of the abomination Cyrail had her forego the indirect approach. "I know her even still, Gloria Bane, even in the company of Death."

Gloria's eyes start to well up with tears. "You're lying. She passed some time ago."

"And, yet, I know her still. I was with her when she died passing away from this realm of reality." Gabriel places her hand on Gloria's shoulders. "Look into my eyes and you will find truth. I am the messenger, Gabriel, second in the Order of the Arch of Angels. I've been sent here on behalf of the Lord Iehovah. Fear not, for He is with you even unto the ending of this age. And Gloria that time draws nigh." Gabriel looks into the eyes of Jericho. "He alone has been chosen to help in the coming days."

Gloria in disbelief slowly grabs her grandson by the arm and begins to pull him away from Gabriel. "They say that psychotic people don't know they're psychotic."

Noticing the disbelief on her face. Gabriel's voice echoes in thunder as her wings extend suddenly from underneath her coat. Her visage is nothing less than almighty as her heavenly light displays her gleaming armor. Gabriel's countenance is almost too much for Gloria to look upon. She instantly covers her eyes and falls quickly to her knees looking downward. As his grandmother averts her gaze, Jericho doesn't have to. He's able to look upon her through the blinding light. Gabriel dims her brilliant visage by folding her wings back within her coat. Visibly shaken, Gloria looks up slowly.

"Stand, Gloria Bane. We are sisters in this eschatology. I am simply here to fulfil the covenant that was stricken between Elohim and your daughter, Rachel. I am here to help Jericho along the way to his destiny that was written before his birth. Take pride, mother of Rachel, Jericho will be responsible for saving the lives of millions. *Or to watch as many perish.* Was thought and telepathically sent to Gloria's mind from Gabriel's that she may be the only one to hear. I am here with you to make sure it is the former when that time comes. I am here to make you ready child."

Gabriel tells Gloria and Jericho of his birth and the covenant that was stricken. She goes into detail of how his pact can only be violated if he relinquishes his virginity. She repeats all that she told Rachel in the hospital the night of her passing.

The story of the night of Jericho's birth is at times jagged razors for Gloria to hear, but she listens intently. At the end of Gabriel's tale, Gloria sits down to catch her breath. For the whole of her life, she thought that the bible was collections of myths and fairytales. But the strength that she witnessed firsthand in Jericho and now the manifestation of Gabriel forces her to rethink her entire life and choices about the supernatural order of things. The book may have caught glimpses of the ancient world that were not mysticism, but truth.

Gabriel kneels before Gloria. "You search for truth in this matter when it has been in front of you this whole time. You know I speak truth. When Jericho raised that truck four years ago he changed your lenses on existence and opened your eyes to the possibility of what could be. Times that by one million and divide it by infinity and that is how he will affect the last souls of this world. It is I, mother of Rachel, that will make him ready in the use of his growing and un-harnessed strength. Look at him, as he comes of age he will only become more powerful. Along with my brothers, we will make sure Jericho is the divine force that his mother foresaw, a leader of men." Tuning to Jericho, Gabriel awaits an answer. "What say you, child?"

Gabriel knows Gloria has no say on the matter, but courtesy extended goes a long way.

Standing closer, Gloria looks at Gabriel. "How can you place the weight of possibly the world on his shoulders at twelve? How can he understand a concept as huge as to encompass the works of fate and destiny?"

"Because he must, Gloria Bane." Says Gabriel. *Else, all fall to ruin,* is projected into the mind of Gloria.

Jericho looks at his grandmother. "You say that my mother gave me life to ensure that I would be here to help."

"She did, young one."

"Then, grandma, how can I say no? My mom believed in me enough when I was nothing. She believed that I would be the best that she had to offer. I can't say no. I can do all theses things. You said I would one day know why. This is why.

Gabriel has come to know human emotion over the time she's spent with them. Although she can never experience it as a human does, she feels the intensity as she watches Gloria cup Jericho's face and she listens to the tears and pain in each word his grandmother exhales to his youthful face.

"It's easy, baby, to say no to what she's selling. What she's offering you is a life that's not your own. A life of pain and loss. If the Bible's stories are true, then their God is cruel. Look at the decision your mother had to make. Your life can be what you make it even for what time she says remains. A life of servitude is no life, believe me."

"With the time that you have remaining?" Gabriel interjects. "I assure you that this world is coming to a close on this current system of things. That is without question. Whether it's an according to the planned peaceful resolution or violent malevolent apocalypse is what we're here to fight for. What say you, child Gloria? The boy will need your support."

Gloria turns to Gabriel with a temper unmatched by the heat of the sun's radiation. "Must you speak with talk of calamity? For christ's sake!"

"For Christ sake is why I speak it. What say you Jericho? Gabriel says more determined and resolute.

Jericho looks into his grandmother's eyes; Instantly looking through the windows of her soul he knows what he's being asked to fight for. He's would be learning to protect her and those like her. She is his whole world and so are his friends and the life that they've all made for him. They are all worth it. Jericho kisses his grandmother. "What makes me ready now Gabriel? Why now, why today?"

"You're twelve Jericho, the sins that you commit are now attributed to you. No longer will the red stain of sin mark your elders. You are now responsible for them. If you are man enough to incur sin, then you are ready to make choices that tips the balanced scales of your life."

Jericho stares at Gabriel. "When would we start?"

"It has already begun, child of Rachel. Now, it's only a matter of catching you up."

Gloria tears fall unrelenting. *If the Bible stories are true, then you will not survive this, baby. The heroes I read about never did in the tales of mythical nonsense. I fear your fate will not be unlike theirs.*

Gabriel turns in Gloria's direction having heard her thoughts. Gloria drops her head and acquiesces the battle for the boy's fate.

CHAPTER 23

EVER CLOSER

"We no longer answer to Elohim. This child is mine Rabbi and all of those that I deem to have access to this body. Take your prayers and pitiful human wishes and leave before we see fit to claim another. I am legion here in this child and we are many and what are you but mortal. What power do you think that you possess to say that we should listen?"

Quote ~Crethos

Al Fashir Airport – Night

Within the plane hangar marked 37, Fante Forshay, a Sudanese General overlooks his remaining troops. He walks the ranks inspecting them and their weapons. He makes note of their exhaustion and injuries. Only now seeing his men backed into a last stand position does he think that maybe he was hasty in his decision to wage war against the Arcane Empire.

Well Shit! We're here now and this is the reality of our situation today.

Forshay, proficient in seven languages chooses to address his men in their native tongue, Sudanese Arabic, <"You are the last proud few who will fight this evil. The world leaders may be fooled by this devil

Arcane, but not I, not the men and women of the Sudanese military. We few here understand and know what is at stake. A student of various religious studies this Arcane seems to be. He is the western messianic prophecy foretold of this time, which even I must give admission too. Not even I of Islamic faith can deny it no longer. I have seen our future and it is death whether we were to have chosen the path of war or not. Looking at you all, here and now, I'd rather die fighting before that bastard takes what we've built here on our side of the world and twist it for his own ill gain.">

An unknown voice shakes the air, interrupting the general.

<"So there is no misunderstanding, I will speak your tongue,"> the voice says in Sudanese Arabic. <"What exactly have you all built on this side of the world? Do you think you've built a civilization that can't be toppled? Maybe you think you've built an empire that is above reproach. Shall I tell you what you have built dictator, terrorist, and purveyor of mass genocides? You have built a den of sin solicited by thieves, warmongers, and rapists. Vices that the Arcane regime will no longer tolerate and has attempted to cleanse, but alas you turned away our gift of salvation and repentance. Now, there will be no recompense nor sanctuary for any of you. Prepare… fore I cometh.">

The unknown voice is heard by all the Sudanese troops. They look around confused trying to determine the origin of voice.

The Sudanese general takes his sidearm out and walks to the front of his troops. <"Then come, we await you,"> the general shouts. <"If your troops will permit me to fight alongside of you this night, I will be the one who is truly honored. Many of us have done evil in this uniform. Many of us have disgraced the ideal of soldier. Tonight, we rectify the mistakes of our past. We embrace our karma that has returned one hundred-fold. Tonight, I am no general. This night as my last official act and command, I sentence myself to death for crimes I perpetrated against humanity. My punishment will hopefully not be swift for I don't deserve a quick death.">

The Sudanese general chambers a round into his pistol. <"Pray to whatever god will escort you into the next life. For my god will see me to hell if he's been paying attention!">

The doors to the hanger begin to open. <"But, not before I take as many Arcanians with me as possible."> Flashes of flame and the rage of war blisters outside the hanger bay. <"Push these bastards back to Cainsin!">

The Sudanese commander points outside. <"At the quick step, forward march!">

"You've spoken from a renewed heart and the heavens have heard you, General." The Archangel, Uriel, removes his influential hand off of the Sudanese General's shoulder removing his phased spirited influence. He then stands watch as the general leads the last of his men into what he knows is their final night, their last fight and shot for redemption.

The Sudanese soldiers' jog at the quick step toward their destinies outside onto the tarmac, the last field of battle they will more than likely fight upon in this life in the mobile husks of dust. The Archangel Uriel quick steps alongside the Sudanese general as they emerge onto the field of battle. Without hesitation as they exit the hanger they open fire. Uriel takes out a white hot edged bladed Bo Staff and begins spinning it fast enough that it becomes a shield deflecting enemy fire cascading in his direction. Men fall dead on either side of him.

Commander Rusain watches as the Sudanese pour out onto the Tarmac. He and his Arcanian soldiers continue firing on the enemy's positions. Rusain's radio again squawks, informing him from reconnaissance that another garrison of enemy troops are moving into position to assist the broken flanks of the Sudanese soldiers. Rusain turns towards a group of soldiers to his right and immediately bellows out orders.

"Form a firing line over there. Two columns. Target that third tank from the left. Mortars, dial in and fire for effect! If we can't hold here at this choke point, we'll have to fall back. It is vital that we hold. If Leonidas and his band of three hundred could hold the hot gates against tens of thousands, then we can hold here." Says Rusain.

A deafening boom sound is heard. It's so loud that it can be heard through the theater of war. The sound then turns into a whistle. Men and women on both sides of their respective factions look to the sky. A white streak of light crashes through the roof of the airport. Within seconds of the detonation of the roof, men and women begin to scream inside shortly thereafter.

The sergeant fighting alongside Rusain reloads his rifle. "What the hell was that?"

Rusain stops firing momentarily. "That was the Imperial protocol."

CHAPTER 24

WATCH AND REPORT

"Of all the species across multiple realities, I could not see into the hearts of only a few mortals over the ages since my charge to protect them. This King Xerxes is one of them. For the power that he wrought and the nations of men that he commanded, not once did I hear his soul respond to question. He defies the influence of my ethereal touch. He has autonomy to act with unchecked impunity. Xerxes is dangerous. There was no soothing the soul of that man. It's as if he was disconnected from the universal collective and carries a silent anger for it. This is the third account over the last seven generations that I have encountered such a dark soul. Difference is this dark soul feels familiar. I just can't place it.

Damn! He moves towards the Hot Gates. I have been ordered to stand with Leonidas and keep counsel with him. Pray for me, Metatron. I fear that War himself will descend upon my charge, fore if he does the fall of the Spartan King is assured this day as well as is my own."

Quote ~The Powers Kinkadia

Angel's Spire

Michael gazes from the balcony of the Spire. He focuses on the events in the Sudan with undivided attention. He narrows his eyes to make sure that his vision is in no way deceiving him. His face furrows as he grimaces at the unfolding events.

Uriel? Michael calls out through telepathic line.

Returning communique through the same angelic telepathy Uriel answers back almost immediately. *Awaiting orders Captain. The situation on the ground has changed here immensely in the last few seconds.*

Uriel, do what you can for our mortal brothers and sisters when you can, but I want you to observe and report on that abomination that has just landed. Do not engage it until we know what Lucifer has done to it. Do you hear me? Do not engage! As soon as someone frees up, I will ensure they come to you. If not, I will aid you myself. What I see in that creature is something that we've never dealt with. It's been altered from the ones that plagued the times of Noah. I need to seek counsel. Hold for my next command.

Al Fashir Airport – Night

Uriel's touches a soldier, easing the pain of his passing unto Death. A grenade lands behind Uriel and comes between him and a female soldier that is actively reloading her weapon. Seeing the grenade, she scrambles for it to throw it back before the five second fuse detonates the tightly helical shrapnel core. Nervous and racked with fear as she tries to grab hold of it, it slips through her grasps a couple of times before she finally gets a grip on it. *Damn!* She feels the click of the primer strike the detonator in her palm. *"Fuck!"*

The grenade detonates. The resulting explosion knocks the red soul sphere right out the back of her body into the hands of Death as he runs past her. He grabs the soul, then spins left, grabbing another before spinning right to catch the blue soul of the soldier that Uriel was comforting.

Uriel observes the dead and dying as a rocket propelled mortar shell lands directly next to him. The explosion doesn't even rock Uriel as angels are unaffected by human instruments of destruction when they phase out of our reality into their ethereal forms of another. Hearing ungodly screams originating from the airport, Uriel averts his attention from the battle on the Tarmac toward the direction of the screams. Uriel moves his fingers and taps into the spiritual prayer lines on its way to Elohim. The prayers from inside are almost hard to make out, because they are coming so furiously at one time. *By heavens there are many.*

"The Abomination," Uriel says, before heading off toward the origin of the crisis that had come to Al Fashir.

The Sudanese General, hearing the cries of his men only fights more vigorously. During the course of firing his weapon, he hears a whistling sound, but after years of fighting he doesn't flinch for an incoming shell. He knows that if it's meant for him, then he will be hit. There's no hiding from fate. His surrounding troops find cover by going prone and placing their hands over the back of their heads. Within milliseconds, it detonates. A body of one of his men catches the full force of the blast. The soldier's body, filled full of shrapnel, is blown into the general, knocking him over. He quickly pushes the torn-to-shit body off of him and reclaims his rifle and again continues fighting. He looks to one of his lieutenants.

<"Have them hold the line! Nothing comes through! Nothing! I think we actually have these bastards on the verge of retreat. It looks like they underestimated our forces..."> Straining to see the full view from his limited position, Forshay looks for hire ground. <"I need a better view of the field. Hold here, and wait for my order to advance. If you don't hear back from me in ten minutes, then assume I'm dead

and advance when you see an opportunity."> General Forshay turns and runs back into the airport through the opened hangar bay doors.

Michael claps the last piece of his armor on. He secures the right gauntlet, then knocks them both together to make sure they're fitted and ready to repel attacks. He begins to yell for his number two "Gabrie—" Gabriel is already beside Michael nodding with her fist to her chest saluting.

Michael looks directly at Gabriel's face, deep into her being and places his hand on her shoulder. "It's time; Go!"

Gabriel nods and leaps off the balcony of the Spire. With a spin, she phases and passes through the grounds of Heaven and streaks like a flash of lighting back towards Earth.

General Forshay runs down the hall toward the screams of his soldiers. He comes to the dead-end T of the hallway. A six-man special forces tactical team is being forced to retreat backward across the top of the T in a reverse bounding formation. As they bound back, one fires till empty, then runs to the back of the team while reloading. The next man up continues firing. They repeat the cycle. Seeing his most elite guard in retreat gives him pause. As he draws closer, he slows down to see how many of the enemies have breached the airport and are forcing his most elite warriors to retreat.

Looking at his surrounding and realizing he's compromised where he stands, Forshay lays prone among the dead and those dying. From the looks of them they must have already met the cadre of superior trained soldiers that have infiltrated the airport. Lying among the bodies he pulls a corpse over top of him to blend in. He readies his weapon to attack their flanks once they're in the middle of the T. Looking through the scope of his Scorpion AK47, he holds his breath to stable his weapon. When he finally has eyes on the attacking force, he exhales rapidly. His blood turns cold. The rifle slowly falls from eye level as he has just been the first to witness the final solution, aptly named Imperial and he's awe stricken and terrified all at once.

Imperial stands just over two meters in height accompanied with a muscular stature. Over his black, fitted Arcanian uniform, he's wearing angelic armor complete with generated helmet. The armor has demonic glyphs on the shoulder guards and shins of his metallic boots. The glyphs are written in reverse of angelic. Cyrail has grown into his full hybrid human/angelic form. He is Imperial and he is Nephilim, constructed for a singular purpose.

Imperial's moves lighting fast. Bullets and tracers from the soldier's rifle's ricochet easily off his armor. Planting his feet and crouching, he rockets forward and closes quickly on the retreating men. The advancing malevolent force spins into a scissors kick catching the face of one of the soldiers. From the sheer force his neck breaks as easily as a toothpick as soldier's lifeless body takes to the air.

Next soldier up fires until empty. He drops the rifle and pulls his sidearm to continue firing. The left wing of Imperial switchblades quickly and decapitates him. The soldier's headless body falls, still gripping the sidearm. The remaining four all fire their weapons at once in a concentrated effort. They continue firing expelling shell after shell through the ejection ports of their rifles till empty. With projectile weapon exhausted with no further backup weaponry, one elite special force soldier pulls his knife and charges the muscularly sculpted behemoth. With a flash, the sword of Imperial is pulled and re-sheathed. The advancing soldier's body is sliced into halves. There was no red mist spray. The body was cauterized by the blade. The remaining three turn and run in a terror.

Having witnessed the unbelievable, General Forshay remains prone and deathly still in an attempt not to be detected by what he can only describe as a walking demonic entity. Imperial pauses momentarily and looks down the hall in the direction of Forshay meeting his gaze. Imperial lets him know that he's not gone undetected and turns his attention back to the remaining special forces and leaps into flight down the hall past the cross section of the T in pursuit of them.

A quick expanse of his wings and the two slowest are decapitated easily. The last soldier rolls forward just as Imperial passes over dodging the flight of decapitation. The soldier rolls up to his feet quick drawing a side arm that was on the floor. It must have been dropped by one of the countless bodies lying around. He racks the weapon chambering a round and fires for the back of skull of Imperial. From flight, Imperial flips forward, landing on his feet sliding a few inches forward. His wings shield him from the small arms fire. Without looking back, he fires a red bolt from the palm of his right hand gauntlet blaster. The blast picks the remaining soldier up and throws him backward. The body lands in the middle T of the hallway. General Forshay can only watch as the body slides to a burning halt in front of him. The body is charred and barely recognizable. For the first time in what seems forever, Forshay experiences an emotion he thought long lost: bone-chilling fear.

Uriel appears unseen by mortal eyes kneeling next to Forshay. He lays a hand on the general's back. "Calm yourself! I advise caution, this enemy is beyond your current skill... Now, run!"

The Sudanese general slams both fists on the ground in an act of defiance. He gets to his feet in spite of the fear and runs for his mortal life.

Uriel watches him run down the hall. Once the general has turned the corner, Uriel turns toward the T-split and walks into the middle of it and listens for the screams of men. Hearing the carnage off to right of the T, he walks off in the direction after Imperial. No longer observing he begins to pursue. "Forgive me, Michael."

Michael's eyes turn red with a slight mixture of gray as he hears Uriel disregard for orders while he awaits consultation from Yeshua. "Damn you Uriel! I told you to hold." He whispers under his breath.

Uriel pulls an angelic glyph covered one-foot cylinder from his metal holster nestled underneath his cloak. With a flick of his wrist, it expands into his bladed Bo Staff. As he slowly maneuvers down the hall, he rotates it in a circular motion. As Uriel crosses another T-shaped intersection, he feels the eyes peering into him. He stops and turns left and watches as Imperial walks towards him. As he advances on Uriel, Imperial's blade slowly drags along the ground, leaving a heated scorch mark trail.

"I seeeeee yoooooouuuuu," Imperial sings out in an octave just above whisper.

Surprised slightly the hybrid can see him, He is phased into reality 1814 which overlays the current 2814. Uriel readies himself. This hybrid is something different. "I've heard rumors of you, abomination, in the quiet spaces of the Expanse. Now, I see they are true." Uriel moves into the on-guard position. "I was there when we hunted your kind to extinction before. I will ensure I send you kind there again."

Letting his sword's tip cook the stone tile of the floor, Imperial just stares at Uriel. "I am no abomination or nothing of the kind you knew past. I am the harbinger that will ease your passing from this existence to the next. A place for you in Palengrad has been made available. Have no mistake, angel, I am your superior here. As you face me you will come to understand that this day your God has all but abandon you to me. Today you will bow in subjugation to my father's will on this plain of existence."

Imperial quickly shoots two bolts from his hand. Uriel side steps one, and slides on his knees underneath the second. He comes to his feet spinning to gain more force to cleave Imperial. The hybrid doesn't bother to defend himself. Uriel spins the blade, gathering momentum for his strike. As he rounds the blade from a spin Uriel turns his hips fully into the swing to put Imperial down. Before the weapon connects, the blade stops right before connecting with Imperial's neck. Surprised Uriel instantly backs away and re-engages and does a flurry of blade spins and twirls before pressing the attack a second time. Again, the blade stops short of connecting with Imperial, as if there is an invisible shield protecting him.

Uriel backs away again. "What madness is this, Demon?"

"You call me demon. I am honored to be called such, as that is what my father has been called for centuries and looks how far he's come. From servant to king."

Imperial quickly closes the distance and front kicks Uriel. The blow is so hard it carries him down the hall Impacting and crashing through several walls crossing the adjacent hallways. The archangel only stops when he hits a metal reinforced door in luggage storage. Imperial rockets through the destroyed walls entering into the luggage storage area where Uriel landed.

The stunned angel sluggishly tries gets to his feet. He knew he'd take a hit or two, but wasn't expecting the hit to rock him as hard as it did. Uriel tries to stand, but falls to his knees. A feeling of regurgitation begins in his chest. A fit of violent coughing leads to Uriel spitting blood. angelic blood glows dark red when it runs fresh from the body. When it lands on the ground of Earth, it turns black. Uriel spits the remaining viscous fluid from his mouth and stands to his feet.

Imperial calmly walks toward Uriel. "You're thinking what, I wonder? Why can't I smite thee? It is angelic law the way I understand it, is it not?"

Uriel gets it now, he understands. It comes back to him instantly. Then, his thought is interrupted by a quick sharp pain to the abdomen as Imperial strikes him fast and hard doubling him over and driving him prone. Uriel pushes himself up to one knee.

Imperial takes a knee and uses the tip of his sword to raise the chin of Uriel so they're looking eye to eye. The tip of blade singes

Uriel's chin. "There it is! There's that light. The one which shines on ignorance at the second of enlightenment."

Uriel fires two bolts from his hands point blank into the chest of Imperial. The bolts dissipate just as fast as he fires them.

Imperial smiles and lets Uriel's chin fall. With one flap of a singular wing, the demon spawn is back on his feet. "Angelic law angel. Repeat it after me! No angel is to directly intervene in the affairs of men... Let me repeat this part again as you seem to be slightly distracted. The affairs of men, understand?"

Two Sudanese soldiers run past the hole in the wall leading into luggage storage. One glimpses Imperial and taps his partner signaling an enemy contact. They return in stealth and see only Imperial standing in the luggage storage. On the mortal plain among the soldiers it looks as if he's talking to himself as they can't see Uriel. He's unseen to the eyes of mortals unless he chooses to avail himself. Having Imperial's back toward them and the element of surprise they open fire on him being the described unknown hostile reported over their comms. Bullets pelt and ricochet off the unidentified threat. Surprised when their bullets have no effect, they look in disbelief at Imperial and then each other. They start running.

Imperial looks over his shoulder momentarily at the annoyance and then returns his attention back to Uriel. "I'll kill them momentarily."

"Uriel's eyes turn burning red.

"Does that anger you? Good. Then I will have you know that I will not leave one soul attached to their husks this day. There can be no witnesses."

Uriel tries to stand. "I will—"

"You will what? I am an affair spawned of men and gods. You have no power over me." Imperial elbows Uriel in the face driving him back to both knees.

"I have power over you angel." Imperial swings his sword with precision separating Uriel's wings from his body. In a blinding flash, the angel's armor disappears. He's left wearing only a white tunic and pants. Uriel's blood that was glowing loses its illumination and turns human blood red and remains red as it strikes the ground. His skin loses its ethereal illumination and turns and dark caramel complexion. His eyes, which seconds ago burned an intense red, turn blue.

Uriel pushes off Imperial and falls back on his ass. "What have you done?" Immense paralyzing fear overtakes Uriel. "I- I can't hear their song anymore?"

Imperial turns and walks toward the destroyed wall. "Of course, you can't. You're mortal. Well, at least for now. I just wanted you to witness my father's wrath through me. I will kill every being in this place. When I'm finished, I will then return for you. Pray that I'm distracted."

Uriel draws back overcome by a feeling that he's never felt with such rawness: fear. He backs into a corner of the humongous storage area reeling from effects of being violently cut from the ethereal collective.

Imperial laughs at Uriel with arrogance. "Oh! That feeling that you are experiencing right this very moment—it's fear, in case you were confused." Imperial steps back through the hole and brings his hilt to his face before taking off down the hall to kill more of the Sudanese troops.

Broken, Uriel rolls himself over to all fours. His hands are smearing his blood over the floor. He looks around in disbelief at his wings, which lie beside him. Startled by the sound of air raid sirens, the newly minted mortal backs away under the baggage carrier belt hiding. The sirens in the distance only becomes louder.

Pissed off, Uriel slams both hands to the pavement in anger. The ground does not shake and he feels intense pain from striking it. He pushes himself out from under the conveyor belt. With his weapons and armor having dissipated during his conversion, he slides his hand over a large metal pipe which was ripped from the wall upon his forced rocketed entry into the baggage storage area. His gear has been left in reality 1814. He uses the pipe to right himself, but he's barely able to wield it because of the weight and sheer density of it. His anger subsides slightly as he realizes his predicament. He's no longer ethereal or celestial. His powers have been nullified. His anger and fear turn to despair and sadness. He's broken. Uriel crawls to his wings and holds them as he watches them slowly decay and turn to dust.

Looking up with tears in his eyes. He stares long at hard at nothing. "I can no longer see you, but I know you're there… Captain?"

Michael kneels down next to him making himself visible. Tears streams from Michael's eyes. "I'm sorry this happened to you, brother. I told you not to engage. There's something different about this one. I wanted to know what we were dealing with. I wanted you to only report."

Uriel's face frowns in regret. A feeling that he never comprehended till this very moment. He pushes the feeling away and wipes the tears from his face, and then Michael's "Are you ready for my report, captain?" Uriel says through more falling tears.

Michael takes in a breath and steels his visage. He stands tall as he tries to keep his composure. "Report, Arch Uriel!"

"Yes Captain. This abomination calls itself Imperial. It's stronger than any Nephilim I've encountered in the past. He's faster than what we've ever dealt with. He's intelligent far beyond the agreed collective design of living intelligence. I sense that he's not been long of this Earth, but he stands outside the creation caste collective. He can't be read, nor anticipated. His thoughts are shielded. The ways he spoke is as if he walks two worlds. He was able to identify me by mere glance. I didn't reveal myself. He saw me from onset even though I was phased."

Uriel reaches for Michael to pull Michael closer. "Most important, Michael, he can't be assaulted by us. He carries mortal blood within him. We can't intervene directly with him. He has all of our power with no checks. Only another mortal can lay hands to him. I just saw him wipe out half a battalion of mortal men. It has our strength, but no weakness that will give him pause. However, I witnessed the mortal's weapons strike him. That is my full report, brother."

Michael takes in the full report. Saddened, he attempts to help Uriel to his feet, but can't. He can't directly intervene in the affairs of man. Uriel is now mortal. Michael sobs and takes a knee next to his fallen brother. "Uriel, I can't... I can't help you up."

Uriel grabs a hold of the conveyor belt and pulls himself up to stand on his own. He releases what's left of his disintegrated wings and lets the remaining feathers fall to the ground. He stumbles at first then finds the strength and the coordination to carry himself to the hole where he made earlier entry by crashing through. Michael follows him.

"Uriel?" Michael solemnly calls out. Uriel turns and places both of his hands on either side of Michael's shoulders. He hugs his brother tightly.

"Captain, brother, forgive me for not listening. I could no longer ignore the sound of the King's creations crying out in pain." Uriel releases Michael and backs out through the hole, back into the hallway. He looks in the direction that Imperial was last seen pursuing the soldiers.

"Uriel," Michael yells.

Uriel throws down the pipe that he intended for the use of Imperial and picks up a rifle that one of the soldiers dropped. He fumbles through the mechanics of it at first, but quickly realizes how to use it. He's watched men load and fire weapons the last couple of centuries. Uriel looks around and spots one of the men killed by Imperial. He exchanges his empty weapon for the loaded one. Uriel takes a sigh and looks at Michael through the hole.

"Until that day, captain.... I really would have loved to have met the boy you and Gabriel try to keep secret. No, you weren't careless in your orders. I peeked before they were sealed. Hell! We all know." Uriel smiled. "Oh! And tell Gabriel she was right, will you? She'll know what I'm talking about."

Uriel winks at Michael and then takes off down the hall in pursuit of Imperial. His trail was an easy one to follow as it left behind death and destruction.

Michael can only can stare out the hole into the hallway. "Die well!"

Death passes in front of the hole and looks at Michael. "I assure you Arch, he will die anything but." Says Death. He continues in the direction of Imperial and now Uriel. He collects the souls of the departed as he races on.

Uriel finally reaches the end of the trail where the terminal's hallway dead ends at the main lobby, he sees nothing but a sea of appendages and cauterized bodies of those killed in the final last stand as their barricade had been torn asunder. Uriel looks past the host of broken and decapitated bodies. He witnesses the last of the opposing force die protecting their general. Uriel attempts to sneak up behind Imperial. He witnesses General Forshay firing the remaining rounds from his Glock 22 sidearm into the chest of Imperial.

After his last round is spent, Forshay lets his weapon fall to the ground. Clack! The weapon slides away from Forshay. He raises his chin in defiance as Imperial closes in.

"You are a spawn of Satan come for my soul, eh, Demon?" Says Forshay.

"Easy for you to call me such nomenclature that you think malicious. You are actually giving me great honor by calling me such a being." Imperial walks up to Forshay, towering over him. He revels in the fact that this once feared commander of armies now had to look at something greater than himself.

"You call me Demon? How hypocritical of you, Fante. What of the evils that you've committed? With the hell you've unleashed on your fellow man for the gain of pitiful monetary compensation, you are more a child of my father than I. Because you have lived, a great many others have died in your wake in numbers that far surpass mine." Imperial starts laughing. "And you call me Demon. I am in great company it seems."

Forshay spits on the ground doubling down his defiance. "Kiss my ass Demon. I've killed my share, but I'm here in my time to commit such acts. You, on the other hand, have no place in the world of men. You are an abomination, an outcast. Yes, I know why you're here and I know what that Lucien Arcane is. At least I can tell God before he passes judgment on all that I've done that I confronted you and tried to set right the evil that I've perpetrated. What will you tell him when you see him?"

Imperial Looks down smirking at Forshay "I am forever. I'll never have to answer to him nor have to tell him anything… But, on the off chance that it does happen and I am before him, I'll tell him I was framed."

Suddenly, Imperial's wings encapsulate the both of them secluding himself and Forshay just as Uriel unloads the whole magazine into him from behind.

Imperial nods to Forshay to let the Sudanese general know that his hour is upon him to die. Forshay in the seclusion of Imperial's wings straightens his uniform and stands tall. Imperial grabs him by the neck and raises him off the ground. With ease, he slides his blade into Forshay's torso, slicing his heart in two. When the body goes limp he just lets it fall from his blade. Satisfied that the head of resistance has been eliminated, he turns to face Uriel who's expended his last round.

"Eager to leave this Earth so much so that you couldn't await my return? So be it. Let us deal with this now. With the brief departure of Fante Forshay, you are the last, just as I promised you would be," says Imperial.

From two of the bodies, Uriel grabs their bayonets and unsheathes them. He readies himself in his on-guard stance. As he stands ready for the dual of this hour that was tasked him. Scores of angels materialize behind Uriel in a show of solidarity that they are with him even now when he must stand alone.

"How quaint. They've all come to watch you escorted into the next life. Pity you can't see them. They appear to be rooting for you. Put on a good show will you! And just maybe the heavenly choirs will sing of you in the time they have remaining, that is the time I allow them to have before I tear them asunder just as I did Forshay here."

Soldiers from Arcanian forces that was just recently battling for the vital airport start to make their way inside the lobby to secure it. As they see the two poised for combat, they can't help but marvel at

Imperial. Talks begin to reverberate through the ranks at what they're looking at. Commander Rusain pushes his way to the front of the troops to see what the commotion is about. He steps in front of the troops facing them. "Shut up, you motherless bastards and watch what genetic engineering can accomplish. I know you've heard the rumors. They are no longer that. What we could not do in the last seven and half hours, he did in less than twenty minutes. We are a force that will soon rival those conquers of the old world and we will do it with Arcane leading the way. This man in front of you, is project Imperial Protocol."

Rusain turns and walks towards Imperial, nodding at him. "You have the floor, Sir."

Imperial raises his blade within centimeters of his face saluting in respect of his incoming enemy and then lets it fall into a low guard welcoming Uriel to attack. "When you're ready."

The angels start to harmonize a battle chant for Uriel's victory, but it's lost on him, he can no longer hear their song. He feels that they are there and that is enough for him. The rest of his Elite Archs are there watching him except for Michael who remained in the destroyed luggage area of the hallway, because he simply couldn't bear to watch him die. Also absent was Gabriel who's off on urgent business and Raphael that's recovering from his run in with Agathan.

Without any more hesitation, Uriel presses the attack. This isn't the first time, he's fought a larger foe, although he's never been mortal, either. Uriel feint attacks high, but slides low on his knees hoping to score a strike. Imperial thrust his wings and uses the force to dodge the blade by adding lift jumping the attack while simultaneously using the directed gust of wing generated wind to blow Uriel off balance. The gust attack works and Uriel does slide off balance, but uses the momentum to roll and dodge the descending counter strike by Imperial. He's heavy, slow, dumb footed. Damn the human form and damn gravity!

Uriel is instantly on his feet again, pressing the attack. His movements deliberately slow, but coordinated. Thrust, thrust, slice,

241

spin, slice thrust. With a one-handed rapier blade defense, Imperial parries and counter each strike. The moves continue on for a matter of seconds. The soldiers cheer Imperial on as they watch the exchange for entertainment. After four and half minutes for the first time ever, Uriel is feeling more fatigued then he has ever felt since creation. *Tired, can't breathe. I hurt all over. Soooo tired.*

After the last series of strikes, parries and dodges, Uriel has received more than a few lacerations during their exchange as he could simply not match the pace of Imperial.

"Need a moment of respite, mortal?"

"No, why? You tired? Ready to surrender?" Uriel says as he tries to catch his breath and fight off the shock resulting from the blood loss.

The audacity of the taunt laid down by imperial instantly infuriates Uriel, but not more than the fact that he knows that his adversary is just toying with him. He's being used for entertainment and morale boosting. He knew from the moment that he pursued him up to this point that he was out matched.

Imperial just smirks. "Shall we end this pathetic display?"

"Yes… Let's." Uriel is only able to raise one arm as the tendons had been cut to his other rendering it useless.

"And here I thought you celestials would be more of a problem. I'm a bit disappointed, tell you the truth."

"I made a fatal error in underestimating you. To those that come after me, it won't happen again."

Before Imperial can respond, Uriel seizes the moment and dives in slashing for any piece of him. Imperial uses his right wing to parry the strike upward. Once he does, it exposes the entire torso of Uriel. With no hesitation Imperial spins and thrust his blade downward into the Uriel's chest cavity. The Arcanian soldiers erupts into loud cheers. The angels that witnessed their brother's end, fall silent.

Imperial watches the somber faces of the celestials as they look on unable to do anything. Having their attention, he digs into their emotions by reverse donkey kicking the body of Uriel off his blade.

Uriel's corpse is flung through the air smashing into the wall above the entrance.

"Is there anyone else? No... I thought as much." Imperial walks over to Uriel and uses his tunic to wipe his blade clean. He sheathes his sword and does an about face and walks into his cheering crowd of soldiers that he easily towers over. He walks past them and leaves through the lobby's front door of the damaged but very much intact airport.

Metatron and Azrael along with a few other lower choir angels surround Uriel's body only opening a path for Michael. A path that he dares not walk. From a distance, he looks down the path at the slain body of his brother. His jaws tremble as he holds in his sadness. Of all the injuries over his existence, the passing of Uriel in such a manner stung him almost as much as Lucifer's betrayal.

"Please take care in your handling of him," says Michael as he watches the body never removing his gaze to acknowledge Death.

Death appears and walks from behind Michael down the path that lay open. The angels turn and face each other and pull their weapons creating a tunnel to honor their fallen brother as Death passes to collect his soul. Death stands over Uriel for a moment giving any other angel a chance to say anything before he takes him. When met by silence Death kneels and reaches down into Uriel's body. Death extracts a blue soul sphere from the body and slowly with reverence places the sphere into the inside of his coat. Death turns and slowly begins to walk back through the angelic tunnel of honor. At the end of the tunnel, Death stops and faces Michael.

"I will only carry his soul alone in this instance. Once he's safely installed, I'll return for the others."

Michael nods in acceptance eyes still fixated on Uriel's body that still lays on the floor.

"Whether you believe me or not Captain, I'm sorry for what it's worth. I liked him, he was always still pleasant toward me." Death disappears.

The angels sheath their swords and look to Michael who solemnly returns their gaze.

"Their day is coming... Michael says. "Azrael?"

"Yes, Captain." Azrael turns and places his fist to his chest while bowing his head saluting Michael.

"Burn the body! The rest of you resume your duties. This abomination, this Imperial will be dealt with. I promise you."

Azrael shoots a charged bolt into the body. It erupts into a blue flame that instantly turns the body to ash. With the cremation of Uriel's remains the angels all dematerialize except Michael, he remains for a few minutes looking at the body's outline of ash.

"From your insignia, you're their captain, yes?"

Michael looks up and sees Imperial standing in the door way. "I am their captain. And you are, you are abomination?" Michael starts to walk over toward Imperial. "What was your given name?" Michael asks. "It wasn't recorded. You are nameless as you aren't even to have ever existed.

"And yet, here I am Captain of the Archs." Imperial says as he walks closer to Michael. "You all will come to know my name. They will soon speak it in every nation and on every tongue and every language."

Michael now standing before Imperial face to face. "We will mourn this day, abomination, but know when the days of mourning has concluded we will deal with you in ways that are most unkind."

"I look forward to it, Captain. What was it your angel said? Ah! Yes, I remember. Until that day was it? Until that day, then, Captain."

Imperial turns his back and walks out the vestibule doors. Michael pulls out a scroll that the seal has already been broken. As he watches Imperial leave he crushes the papyrus trying to bottle his rage. Once Imperial has left his line of sight, Michael vanishes into a brilliant white light.

CHAPTER 25

PREPARATION

"I regret no action that has brought me a step closer to finality."

Quote ~Uriel

Void of anywhere

It smells like ozone. If ozone even has a smell to it. No, wait it smells like cookies and rain. Where am I? Jericho is standing in a white void. There is nothing in sight but him. There is no way to determine up, down, north or south.

"Hello. Is anyone there?" His voice only echoes.

The innate fear of the unknown starts to rise within him. His breathing starts to labor under the weight of that crushing fear of when one is alone in an unknown predicament. Jericho starts off in a light trot to escape the fear that slowly overtakes the lost. The more his heart race the faster he runs until he finds himself in a full sprint looking around mercurially. He continues to runs for some time only to realize that after a while his running is taking him nowhere. Out of breath, he stops and assesses his new location. Looking around he's not improved his situation his eyes tell him he's in the same place that he started.

"Peace, be still Jericho Bane," Gabriel says to calm him.

"Where am I? Where's my grandma?"

"Still here, in a sense. I needed time with you alone."

Jericho looks around. "Why can't I see you?"

Gabriel appears behind Jericho touching him lightly on the shoulder. "Because you haven't looked for me."

Jericho turns around and sees Gabriel. She is even more gorgeous to him in her celestial form than her human appearance. *I expected angels to wear dresses and hold trumpets and harpsichords.* To the contrary, she's wearing a white slender trench coat over her white high collard tunic. The coat has three red stripes on the shoulder with angelic glyphs on the forearms of the sleeve and the back, White pants with gold colored stripes down the side, and gold armored metallic boots.

"Y-you're the beautiful woman I've ever seen!" he stutters.

"I'm flattered. Thank you." Gabriel raises her right eyebrow slightly with a smirk. "But, I think you're smitten a little with another aren't you?" She walks up to him. "And I think she's even more beautiful than I." Gabriel nudges him. "Walk with me, will you?"

The two of them start walking in the empty void.

"What is this place? It's so quiet. I mean really quiet." Jericho takes a long pause studying his situation. "I'm dead!"

"Far from it. In fact, you are very much alive. Let's just say you're suspended in sense."

Gabriel points off to the right and small portal appears. Through it, Jericho sees himself laying in the hospital bed. Around him is his grandmother sitting to his right. On the left side is Isis laying partially on the bed with her head resting on his arm.

Jericho walks to the portal peering in for a closer look.

"Is that happening right now?"

"It is. And it isn't. It's one in many realms of possibilities of how this day could have gone had I not intervened indirectly in your affairs today. It's now the past and or the future. Time and space works differently for us Jericho. To us time is an allied accompaniment; to others it's an enemy. We have a great many eons learning of its properties and potential. So much so, we mastered it enough to slave it to our purpose." Your grandmother and your friend Isis are safely in reality 2814. There you are watching the events as they occur in real time. You and I are sitting outside the realm of that reality. We are watching them at a different vibrational scale.

Gabriel swipes her hand across her left gauntlet closing the portal.

"This place is not a place in the manner of which you're thinking. Structure, physics, and rules of reality as you've come to know them does not exist here. We have total autonomy when traversing across plains and universes. Just as you travel in say, an automobile, we've mastered travel within the spectrum of light."

Gabriel nods and points to another opened portal. Inside Jericho witnesses the wooded area where Gabriel is talking to Gloria. Suddenly there's a bright flash and Gabriel vanishes as Jericho falls unconscious into his grandmother's arms. The portal closes, leaving the two again in the endless white void.

"That just happened didn't it? You brought me here and just left my grandmother holding me there? She's has to be terrified out of her mind.

"Actually, Jericho it happened two days ago. As you saw moments ago you're comfortably resting in a hospital surrounded by loved ones while we have this time to ourselves to conversate here in this place."

"That's what I want to know— where is here? What is it called?"

"Here, is what you mortals have come to refer as the third realm of Heaven. A waiting place sort of speak."

Jericho stops in his tracks. "Heaven? Like gods on throne Heaven?"

"Similar to an extent, but not. Heaven is vast, it's infinite to that of mortal thinking. Within Heaven as you've come to know it, there are multiple realms. Unlike the society that you're growing up in there are no joint minds of checks and balances, no democratic ways of thinking. The rule of all is a monarchy. The way you all revere us as gods is even misconstrued. To help with how you process us, let me take a little of the mystification out of it. Think of our species as alien. We have a superior technological advance over your primitive ways of cognitive thinking. To put our existence into comprehension, think of us as a superior technological dominant race that have an infinite number of years head start on you. If you were to return back in time right now to agent Egypt with your current technological advances and knowledge of the pending future, you would be considered a god among men. They would call you prophet. We are no different than modern man versus Neanderthal when put to perspective. You follow me?"

Jericho nods his head yes. The two began walking again.

"My grandmother had always said there is no such place. She said that it's all myths and fairy tales made up for the week minded."

"I've heard that. Yet, I speak to you as real as the grass that you lay in or the air you breathe. She isn't wrong in a sense. Your grandmother is partially right, we are fact that has become myth and fairytale. Years of solitude and moving unseen will do that."

Jericho keeps looking past Gabriel at the void. "Not much to this place."

"Oh! I beg to differ there's plenty!"

The void around them turns from white to a dark gray. The world around them rushes past a break-neck speeds. When it ends, they are in a bedroom watching a little girl play with her doll. The doll is in the little girl's twin sized bed. Jericho's eyes widen as the doll moves as if it was a real person. The little child who owns it is tending to it dressed as a nurse and treats the doll as patient in a hospital. What throws the young man even more is that the little girl is similar in human construction, but is clearly alien. Her skin is an orange hue and she has purple eyes.

"The third realm of Heaven is more than a waiting place. It is a way to communicate with you mortals and other species of living sentients on a subconscious level. Look closely at her. Look at her surroundings"

Jericho takes in the scenery around the room. As he looks closer, he realizes how the doll is animated and moving as he speculates her race does. He further notices that the characters painted on the walls are moving as well. Suddenly it clicks, he gets it, even snapping his finger in the aha moment.

She's dreaming. "She's dreaming, isn't she?" Jericho says.

"She is dreaming. She's on planet called Marwinain in the city of Zanayaa, in the reality of 2634 in her bed right now fast asleep with her doll. You see to her, that doll is made up of all the love and imagination that she can muster. Look at her. Look how natural she is in taking care of her friend that is in reality void of life. It's plastic and sytenillan, but yet she sees it as an embodiment of friendship. A way to extend her caring nature."

Another little girl enters the room. The second girl is dressed as a nurse. She passes a stethoscope to the tending little dreaming practitioner. The little girl nurse backs away. As she does the little nurse transfigures into an angel. The angel watches the little girl play.

Jericho looking astonished "Did you see that?"

"I did. He's nurturing her. Helping her along a path which she is best suited for."

Jericho snaps his fingers again. "A doctor? She's going to be a doctor?"

"A doctor, we hope. We can't make mortals do anything, but we can strongly suggest or give reminders. We have a certain influence on the souls of sentients to help guide."

The world around their reality changes again.

Gabriel and Jericho are sitting in an empty sanctuary side by side in a pew at St. Richard's Cathedral.

"I use to come here when I was in elementary school," says Jericho, recognizing his surroundings.

"I know, I watched you from right over there." Gabriel points toward the confessionals while she places her other arm around Jericho's shoulder.

"I'm also dreaming, aren't I?"

"In a sense. I needed to talk to you, Jericho. You, like the rest of your mortal kind are the most receptive, the more openminded in the dream state of sleep."

"Talk to me? You didn't want my grandma to hear?"

"Away from the ears of your grandmother I will give you full disclosure. I'm going to explain a few things to you. What I tell you is not to be taking lightly."

The world changes again around them. Jericho and Gabriel are sitting on the same pew looking out over the valley beneath the famed biblical mountain of Mount Sinai.

"Do you truly understand what a covenant is? It's a pact, an agreement that is entered into by two or more people. Your mother Rachel entered into a covenant with the most high on your behalf."

"My mother?"

"She is a beautiful sight, Jericho. You look a lot like her, you know."

Jericho looks at a Shepard and his flock that are passing beneath the two in the valley. "My strength was part of the deal, right?"

"Dark days are ahead, Jericho. A figure has already been loosed upon celestials and mortals alike. I'm not going to lie to you. You have been chosen to carry the torch lighting the way for those who are lost and to put down an evil that has not been seen for some time. You've been blessed and given a power that has not been seen since the time of the judges, nor will it ever be seen again after you. The strength that you possess has only been wielded by one such human since your kind's inception. Unlike him, you have a certain amount of invulnerability."

Henry Ford Hospital

Jericho's grandmother sits to the left of his hospital bed keeping watch over him as he lays in a coma. His best friend Isis, there for support sits next to Gloria leaning on her giving her additional emotional support by hugging her. After a few minutes, she breaks the embrace to reach into her backpack and pulls out a familiar furry friend. Isis pulls her and Jericho's shared teddy bear, griddles. She shrugs her shoulders and passes the bear to Gloria. "It helps," says Isis.

Gloria inspects the bear. She runs her fingers over the stitches reminiscing of all the times she's repaired Griddles. She notices a new set of red stitching along the seam of the ear. She runs her fingers of the new thread and looks at Isis.

"The old stitching was starting to give way. The ear was dangling, so I sewed it myself." Said Isis.

Gloria's eyes begin to well up, but she holds back the tears in admiration of what Isis has done for her daughter's bear. She gives the bear back to Isis. "It's a beautiful job you've done sweetie. I appreciate that. Jericho will appreciate that."

Isis places the bear on Jericho's chest. "I brought griddles. You can hold him for a little while, but you have to give him back, okay? That was our deal when we first met. Remember?"

Gloria smiles at Isis and plays in her long hair. Rubbing and calming her. The neurologist specialist walks in the room. "Evening. Mrs. Bane isn't it?" Gloria nods. "I'm Doctor Pitor and you, young lady, you're Jericho's… let me guess… sister? The doctor guesses."

"No friend," Isis replies quickly. But the look in her eyes betrays her.

The doctor just glances at her and lets out a smile at the poorly attempted hiding of puppy love.

"Mrs. Bane, I'm Dr. Pitor. I'm the neurologist on duty here tonight."

The neurologist checks the equipment. Then, he pulls a chair up next to Gloria. "All tests that have been done all say the same thing they said when he first came in yesterday. There is no medical reason that Jericho is in this coma. He's perfectly fine. For all intents and purposes, he's just sleeping. A sleep that he seems unable to wake up from. We'll continue monitoring for any changes, but he could come to anytime now."

"Will he?" Isis says, concerned.

"All my training and expertise says yes he will. We just have to be patient."

Gloria looks at the doctor nodding her head in thanks for the reassurance. "Thank you, Doctor."

"You two need anything before I make my next set of rounds?"

"No, thanks, we're getting ready to leave soon. I have to get her home. I was just so worried when he fainted. I just wanted to know it wasn't anything serious." *Other than that heifer keeping him... I didn't mean that.*

MOUNT SINAI – DAY

Gabriel stands and places her hand on Jericho's shoulder. "I've come to ask you and only you away from the influence of anyone if you will fulfill the covenant that your mother made with Elohim? This pact must be free of outside influence."

"What will I have to do, honestly?"

"You won't understand the sacrifice as of yet, but there will come a time that you will see the ramifications of what you agreed upon. You must abstain from sexual intercourse. If you agree that you can sustain from such and you freely enter the pact, your power will greatly increase and from the moment that you awaken, you will have entered into the covenant fully. You will feel, like you've never felt before. You will be stronger than you've ever been. You will see in a clarity that you've never seen. When you awaken, childish things will be put away. Your knowledge will be increased exponentially as to become mental rival to what you must endure."

The world around them transfigures again.

Jericho is standing in a field that expands as far as the eye can see. He standing in a field that has never recovered from the battle that waged their epochs ago. The ground is pocked with craters, divots and cracks. Swords and other melee weapons still litter the ground of angels that fell in the first recorded battle and those that fought them. Jericho stands petrous as he gazes across the vast field. "What happened here?

Gabriel turns silent for a moment as she hears across the telepathic net that Uriel has been killed by Imperial. Her face turns somber, her eyes begin to well, but she forces the feeling away. She strains to keep her eyes a neutral color and not reflective of her emotions. *Must keep to the task, have to disclose what he's agreeing too.* "The same thing that happened here on the fields of Glayden will happen, is happening to your world, your very fabric of reality. It is for this reason you must learn all that I have to instruct. You must learn to sharpen your mind as a fine edged razor and learn the ways of combat.

"Learn to fight? I've never been in a real fight before." Jericho says as kernel of fear again starts low in the pit of his stomach.

"I will teach you to fight young one. You will learn the art of offensive combat and to move as we do as well as how to fight as a mortal does. When the time is upon you, I will have made you ready."

A flash turns Jericho attention towards Gabriel. As he turns Gabriel is dressed in her battle regalia. He's awed by how awesome and badass she looks. "What am I supposed to do? Who am I even fighting? He says."

"You will know in time. I promise... What say you Jericho, son of Rachel? Of your own volition, will you accept the covenant given as is and fulfil your mothers vow taking it as your own?"

After a few moments of deep thought, it dawns on him the gravity of what Gabriel's asking. "So, what you're saying is that I can't ever have sex at all? You do know that's all we talk about at school, right? I mean, in my head I've built this singular act up as the end all be all."

Gabriel smirking even through the pain of losing Uriel and her not being there. "I do know what you boys talk about. She waves him closer. "I even can hear what you all think." Gabriel shudders to elicit a laugh from Jericho. It works, he smiles, but it's accompanied by a slight embarrassment. "This is a choice tasked you that is not of light accountability. There has to be sacrifice on your side for the gifts that you've been blessed with to show that you are committed… What say you?"

After a long lost in thought pause. "And if I fail?"

Gabriel kneels down and takes his hand. "You won't."

"But if I do?" Jericho turns clasping his hands behind his back. "If I do, what will happen?"

Gabriel takes a long pause judging his maturity of if he can handle truth. She judges him perceptive and worthy. "Then your covenant will be forfeit. You'd lose your strength and be just as any other man. The light of the Lord will have left you. Ultimately you will have failed and the ending will be decimation ending the age of man and possibly all other sentient life across the realms."

Jericho looks around and finds an old helmet planted firmly in the hardened mud of Glayden. He sits on it still looking across the fields and the seemingly endless remnants of a battle long since fought. "I need a few minutes."

Gabriel nods and backs away giving him time and space.

Jericho takes over an hour to ponder what Gabriel had told him. He went into deep painstaking thought of whether he could hold out. He knew of sex from what his friends had more than likely lied about, but he knew for sure that someday he'd want to. He even had a strong idea who he'd like to try it with.

Jericho losses himself in a time when he was walking a neighbor's dog. Isis had seen him and crossed the streets to walk with him. For an hour they talked and laughed at the secrets and inside jokes they've carried. He knew he was in love with her. He smiles at the thought that when they returned the puppy home that she wouldn't surrender the leash back to him unless he gave her what she wanted most, a kiss.

The sun was blazing hot that day, and he'd already been out in it for over an hour. He was willing to negotiate anything at this point to receive the leash. He agreed to hear the terms. She made it simple. She wanted him to be her first kiss. He laughs at the thought of how nervous he was in that moment when she gave the terms for her to surrender the leash.

Hormones in their infancy, he watches the sweat glisten on her neck. As he looks into her face he knows he's attracted to her he fixates on her lips. He wasn't fixated on them before, but she drew his attention to them. When she asked for the kiss something within him awoken which prodded him instantly to agree to her terms.

Isis, leans in and kisses him. Although it was a peck, it was enough to make him take notice of his pubescent erection. Embarrassment seizes him as the crotch area of his shorts begins to bulge. Satisfied she passes him the leash all the while smiling at him. They laugh at each other.

Jericho's thoughts keep him smiling at what has been and what could be with Isis. However, within the same thought, he can't overlook the fact of where he currently is and that a being that has long since passed into myth is talking to him... Telling him of his mother and what she did in her final acts of love. If it was this important that the heavens talked to him what choice did he have? How could he refuse? *I can simply help with whatever Gabriel wants and then be with Isis. I can do both right?*

"If my mother thought I could do it, as well as the heavens, then I should accept, right Gabriel... You hear me?" Jericho pauses for minutes and turns looking to Gabriel. "I accept of my own free will."

Gabriel's voice is disembodied and cracks like soft thunder. "So be it, Jericho. On these fields of Glayden, my kin and I will train your body and your mind. You are to read literature that we provide to sharpen your mind into the most brilliant of edged weapons, become well adept in the biblical scriptures of not just Christianity, but all faiths as they originated from within one and are all interconnected to a time when the earliest man heard us whisper in the night. Arm yourself with knowledge because, that is true key to unlocking potential."

Off in the distance of the fields, a reddish hurricane begins to swirl. It turns from red to Territ, a color that Jericho has never seen in the Earth's color spectrum. He couldn't even begin to describe it. "Amazing!"

The hurricane starts to overtake Jericho on the field he stands letting the tumultuous wind whip dirt, grit and mud at him causing him to squint his eyes and shield them with his hands. Gabriel appears next to him in the midst of the storm. She doesn't bat an eye as it overtakes them. "We'll speak again soon," she says as the high winds swallow them.

Henry Ford Hospital

Jericho's eyes open. He sits up quickly in the hospital room. There is no one in the room with him except his shared Griddles Bear sitting propped up in the chair next to his bed. He grabs the bear and slowly squeezes him tightly. He smells it and realizes it smells of the vanilla scent of Isis' lotion. Smelling her scent confirms a realization that he has had for some time. He knows unequivocally that he doesn't just like Isis as a friend, he's in love with her. Puberty kicks into full swing and emotions churning within him, his only singular thought is what has he done? He's promised an angel he'd never touch her.

ISRAEL, JERUSALEM

A calm wind blows from the east along the sealed eastern gate of Jerusalem. A cylindrical white beam of light strikes the ground. Michael suddenly appears standing in front of the gate. Devastated from the events at the Al Fashir terminal, he's wrapped in his cloak with the hood pulled. He removes the same scroll from underneath his cloak that he accidently crushed while engaging Imperial in conversation. Michael tosses the scroll to the ground. As soon as it contacts the Earth thunder cracks a cacophony across the skies followed by a period of what seems endless lightening.

Michael looks up to the storm-filled sky. His eyes turn gray in the thought of Uriel, but more for what is to come in succession for the world of man that will reverberate through all of reality.

"So, it was written, so let it be done." Michael's wings blade from underneath his cloak. Driving his wings down forcefully, he takes to the skies rocketing toward the heavens foregoing the Zero Realm spot to spot beam transport. It won't take him long to return to the Spire, he just wanted the time to clear his head.

CHAPTER 26

DOMINATION IS KEY

"My countenance has failed. I am more ghoul now then angelic, yet I'm free. A small price to pay to no longer have to heel to any master. Although I sit free, it does not resolve my anger. To ease such, I have vowed to shake the heavens till they fall, until the ethereal caste looks as hellish as I. When Lucifer sets all created ablaze, I shall be there lighting the torch that will ignite it."

Quote ~Verminesk

Arcainaque, Cainsin City, Vespian

Lucifer watches from his balcony as Warsivious has Commander Rusain and his men at attention in the Vespian courtyard of his home. They've haven't long returned from the battle of Al Fashir. Warsivious stands fully erect looking down to Commander Rusain. He gives a close inspection of his choice that he chose to elevate and trust with the truth of his identity and all else that followed. He overlooks his eight-point hat making sure the brim has a high shine. He inspects each side of the Commander's jaw for stubble making sure that he's more than presentable. He then does an about face and looks forward towards the massive courtyard doors that protect the Vespian's Courtyard. Pleased with what he's seen, Lucien leaves the balcony and heads for the courtyard. Within minutes, Lucien Arcane walks through the massive doors leading to where War and his men await. As he enters the courtyard he enters with an arrogant vigor aided by confidence. He slow claps purposefully at the task just completed by his men.

"You men are of stellar performance and superior stock. General Warsivious, you have outdone yourself with these men. I've read the last of the reports just moments ago." Lucien walks up to Warsivious.

"My lord, thanks for the praise, but it is deserved elsewhere this day. I actually had other matters to attend to in the west. I left this critical mission in the capable hands of Commander Rusain who I must say performed exemplary under the conditions presented him."

Lucien steps again to Rusain, this time in front of the troops. "Then a promotion for the commander is long overdue. That was exceptional work Commander. I want you and the general to come with me."

Warsivious and Rusain bow their heads placing their fists to their chest in acknowledgement. Dressed in their Class-A uniforms they fall out and follow Lucien. The three of them head towards the door of the Vespian Lucien's name of his Earthly Spire. Lucien turns around almost forgetting to address the men. His voice amplifies without any assistance from ma conceived tech. "Men of the Arcane forces 3031 Assault battalion, you are at ease until further notice. Fall out for rest and relaxation."

The three continue their walk into the hallways of Vespian. Lucien turns snapping his finger. "Oh! Arcane 3031. For your discreetness in observing an experimental weapon that you've all had privy to witness in action, a raise in pay of what you would consider a monumental proportion will be added to your salary within the next two pay periods. And the families of those that have fallen will be cared for in kind. One more thing, congratulations to all of you for proving your worth and loyalty, not one leak has been captured of what any of you bore witness too. To find trust as such in so many is a rare gem that I will continue to polish. You have all been reassigned to the Imperial Protocol Battalion designation to remain 3031." Cheers erupt across the immense courtyard.

Cainsin, Vespian – Night

As the trio walk down the hall anyone working or walking in their immediate vicinity stops and acknowledges Lucien and salutes the officers.

Lucien moves into the middle of the men as they walk. "You two know what I want to hear... Give me the report that matters."

Warsivious outstretches his hand toward Rusain. "I defer to my commander. It was he that enacted the Imperial Protocol."

Lucien gives Rusain his undivided attention. "Commander?"

Rusain snaps to attention. The metal heels and taps strike in unison on the stone tiled floor creating an echo making the attention sound crisp. "Yes, sir. I enacted the Imperial Protocol. The situation that we were faced with proved challenging with my forces split on two fronts. It proved even more difficult to make leeway without destroying the prized location. Sustaining heavy losses, I thought that the situation became ideal for the protocol. Also, per the orders and instructions given to me by my immediate commanding officer the situation doubled as a perfect opportunity to gage the training and leadership ability of the Protocol Solution.

"Your unbiased assessment, commander?" Lucien asks.

"Sir, his performance was nothing less than legendary. It's a shame Sir that there is only one of him. His attack was relentless and unequal to any I've ever seen. He was a precision instrument amidst blunt weaponry. His actions alone turned the tide of the battle for Al Fashir within minutes." Rusain attempts to hide his excitement at what he witnessed, however it creeps through every time he thought about his place in the Arcane Forces backed by weapons such the likes of Imperial. "My lord, he's not just an entity and an instrument of War. He is a malevolent force. A demigod that could alter the face of the planet. In my expert opinion Sir, he is more than ready and capable of field deployment."

Lucien nods his head in approval. "Hmm! A malevolent force you say?" He looks over to Warsivious. "I've heard that before about a very capable general once. I see I made the right choice in the one who should train Cyrail's physical prowess." Lucien looks back to Rusain. Still, would you continue to follow him into battle, to receive and execute orders from him Commander?"

"After what I saw, sir, I would follow him to hell and back."

Lucien places his hands on the commander's shoulder. "I was thinking more of to Heaven and back. Iayhoten someday to more precise." He then turns and walks down the hall leaving the two men. He stops momentarily and looks back over his shoulder. "Oh! Warsivious, the second seal has been just broken."

Rusain looks puzzled by the comment. Warsivious starts laughing boisterously. "Then I have been truly loosed."

Lucien nods, "so, it appears you have... Now unleash war." Lucien says as he turns back to continue his stride down the hall with his hands clasped behind his back. I expect to have plans completed within the month of how you plan to do it?

CHAPTER 27

GAUGE OF HAPPINESS

"Look at them! They are a marvel of my father's creative skills. In them are his hopes for custodial caretakers that would revel in peace and sing higher praises to him. Not once had I thought anything against such a beautiful tapestry that was in the creation of man and their purpose until, Lucifer. Now, I'm unsure of the architect. There is that kernel of doubt that was sewn by the Morning Star of old. I now question: is it arrogant to create for the soul purpose of subjugation and for those subjected to only sing of your praises? Is that not the way of the Babylonian king who sacked Jerusalem? Is that not the way of the Roman emperors and those that were made to bow and hail Caesar?

Quote ~Yeshua

Year, 2034
Detroit, Michigan

Jericho has grown into a handsome young man. He's slender and slightly muscular but not overdeveloped. He's average height standing at five feet, eleven inches. He just made over the threshold of tall.

Jericho and Isis are partners in a J.R.O.T.C. exercise regimen at McKenzie High School. The last instructor retired unexpectedly, so the school substituted a Phys-ed instructor to take over until the proper militaristic replacement could be sought. The gymnasium is full of their peers with the attitude that they'd all rather be elsewhere as they struggle through the end of the day drills of their physical education requirements. Their Phys-ed instructor is an ex-marine turned physical education teacher. He has all the earmarks of an intimidating man of war. His face is scared from bursting shrapnel. An eye is told to have been pulled from its socket from a close explosion. However, no one has ever seen the coach without his Red eye patch with the: have a nice day smiley face on it.

He stands firm and confident in spite of his right lower prosthetic limb. He makes his class complete sit-ups to the count of an ordered cadence that only his warrior blowhard lungs can bellow. As Jericho completes a sit-up evolution, Isis kisses him on the lips. She continues to hold his feet down as he rocks back to set for another spring of a sit-up. He raises again and she kisses him while keeping count.

The coach yells in his drill-instructor voice, "That is not the motivation that I was speaking of, Miss Rayne. However, your method has seemed to have improved the disposition of your lazy ass partner's pace and repetition. I'm impressed. I don't think I've ever seen him move with such vitality and purpose."

Coach then moves down the line to another set of students. He turns to two others. "Mr. Keys and Mr. Priest, your lazy asses' disposition has not improved at all during this semester. You two are the same unhealthy scrotes that you were when you started. I don't even know how that is possible." He looks at his clipboard of their pre-testing scores of the same set of exercises completed at the beginning of the semester. "You have two have progressed in reverse. By human nature, you should have improved by at least one sit-up... Look to the left for inspiration gentlemen if you need some."

The boys look over at Jericho and Isis. They see them kiss at each evolution of the apex of the sit-up. Still with his hands locked behind his head Priest looks at Keys and then back to Jericho and Isis, finally back to Keys. "Well, I'm not kissing you."

The class bursts into laughter. The coach even smirks a bit, but fixes his demeanor instantly.

Jericho and Isis laugh as he continues his series of sit-ups. As Jericho comes up she kisses him again. With such temptation he rests in the sitting position just looking into her eyes.

"Are you ready for tonight?" she asks. "Please, tell me you picked up your tux."

"You're kidding, right? Of course, I picked it up. Prom is like the only thing I've been thinking about since... Hmm... Ninth grade!"

"What made you think I would let you go to prom with me back in the ninth grade?

"You're kidding, right?" Jericho says sarcastically. "Who else would it have been but me? Remember, how cute I was, how debonair? El'shunte baby and all that other French talk."

Laughing, she shoves him. "All that French talk, you say such the sweetest things to me in the sexiest of languages. And, you were far from debonair. If I think about it, you were sort of stalkerish."

"Persistent," quips Jericho.

Isis laughing. "Can you say that to me in French?"

"Yeah! Pesistnado, but in French." He jokes, shrugging his shoulders and winking at Isis.

She bursts into a gut busting laugh. "Stop, you're killing me. The look on your face when you talk your version of French kills me." She can't stop laughing.

The bell rings signifying the end of class. Jericho falls on his back exhausted. "Thank God, last class for the day." He raises his hand for Isis to help him up. She just walks away smiling leaving him there.

"Jare... Don't be late tonight!"

Jericho looks over to Jason Priest that was next to him during the calisthenics. He raises his hand toward Jason as he walks past.

"Well, I'm not helping you up," jokes Priest.

The Rayne's Home - Later that night

Isis seems to glide down the hardwood stairs into the center of her luxurious living room. Her elegant prom dress is as beautiful as she pictured it when the concept muse took hold of her more than a year ago in preparation for prom. The dress is a strapless dark blue with dark red edged slits up the right leg. She walks with an elegance that could have only been taught by an aristocratic tutor. Her hair flows down to the middle of her back.

Isis' mother is just as beautiful for a forty-year-old. She's in tears of happiness as she watches her daughter walk down the staircase. Katherine Rayne starts to touch her daughter's hair but doesn't. Isis knows that her mother feels like she ought to be doing something, but she made sure that nothing was left to chance for tonight. Isis took the time in the mirror creating perfection. From her makeup to her choice of jewelry, down to her red bottom shoes on her feet, it was all perfectly planned and crafted. This night after all had been long awaited and every detail dreamed out.

"Look at you… You look stunning, baby!" Katherine says.

Isis starts to pose as a model and whips her hair. She smiles. "I know. Marvel, Mother, at a queen. No wait, an empress that you've passed the mantle on to. I promise that I will rule just and with a since of fashion for my kingdom that will never be matched." Isis starts laughing. An unexpected snort works its way into the laughter causing her and her mother to cachinnate uncontrollably for a spell.

"Oh! Well, your highness, pardon us common folk, but if I may be so humble to ask, we need pictures. Your father is going to want to see pictures." Katherine rotates her cell phone horizontally and starts to take video and photo bursts. She can't stop laughing because Isis can't stop laughing at herself.

"You know, sweetie, you looked so great floating down the staircase, I want you to do it again for the camera. Take two and no stumbling or snorting." The two start laughing again.

The doorbell rings twice with a pause then a third chime soon after. Katherine shakes her head. *Why does that boy do that? He knows it bugs me, I swear that's why he does it.* "Stay right there empress, I'll get it." Ms. Rayne opens the door and lets the biggest Cheshire grin run the length of her face. Jericho walks into the living room wearing a white tuxedo with black stripes down the legs. His vest and tie match the red slits of Isis' dress perfectly as they were made from the same material of her handmade beautifully crafted dress.

Kathrine takes a series of photos of Jericho. "Ooh! Look at you, so handsome, so debonair."

Jericho looks at Isis with a grin and winks. "See? Told you I was debonairo, in French."

"Ugh!" Isis just rolls her eyes at him attempting to keep her laugh from exploding all over again. She really doesn't want to cry through her makeup laughing.

Gloria walks in the open front door taking photos of the two as well.

The two women see each other and join together in their gushing of the two love doves. After hugs between Gloria and Katherine, they turn into full on paparazzi.

"Gloria, he looks so handsome."

"And Isis is a doll," replies Gloria. "They are so cute; I don't know what to do."

"Girl, just keep taking pictures." Continuous flashes light up the living room.

Jericho and Isis just stare at each other smiling. They pull close together and look into each other's eyes as the parents continue taking photos. Jericho can barely be heard as he whispers. It becomes more of lip-reading session between the two.

"Bonsoir, and all that jazz."

"You have such a command of the language of love baby," she says, laughing. "Good evening to you as well."

VESPIAN, CAINSIN

Cyrail has matured even more in the last six years. He's third in command of the Arcanian military power answering only to Lucien and Warsivious. After the battle of Sudan, he took on more of a prominent role in the force applied throughout the rest of Africa. The campaign for supremacy of peace is swift. The world stage has been forced to take notice of Lucien and his Camelot ideals for peace.

The cheers of thousands can be heard. All the campaigns that Cyrail has been a part of leaves no witnesses to tell the tale of his divine gifts in battle. The world has, however, heard rumors of a general that Warsivious had been grooming and that the general was a strong enforcement arm of Lucien only called upon to quell the most vicious of engagements.

Lucien is decked out in a black suit with a blue tie as he meets Cyrail in the hallway leading to the balcony of the Vespian Courtyard.

Lucien pats him on the shoulder. "Your progression in combat has truly been impressive. You make me proud with each day that passes and every conflict that you've put down."

"You have to forgive me, Father. I'm not accustomed to hearing such praise from you."

"When you are doing exceptional work, I'm the first to commend. But it's normally your hesitation to dispatch some of your enemies that again has me a little concerned. It makes me think you're conflicted."

"Concerned, how? I won the last set of conflicts damn near single handedly. If there was any hesitation it was, because I was showing restraint off the advice of the newly promoted Colonel Rusain, you know practicing the art of winning hearts and minds for when that time is upon us. Mortals are but ants to me. I would easily kill them as to look at them. What a bore they are."

"Which leads me into our next lesson..." The two prepare to go onto the balcony. Lucien straightens Cyrail's uniform. "Compassion." Lucien gestures for Cyrail to hang back as he's not ready to introduce him to the world as of yet. Cyrail's contempt has been noted. Lucien walks out onto the balcony.

Thousands of troops and civilians fill the courtyard to hear what news Lucien has promised. News outlets from all over the globe has appeared and are patiently at the ready to capture images, salivating for any tidbit of information that would come from the self-proclaimed ruler of Cainsin City or any missteps he may make.

Lucien walks out on the balcony and looks down upon the capacity filled courtyard. He throws his hands in the air, igniting an even louder eruption of cheers. He turns back to Cyrail who's in the shadows of the room just out of the sunlight of the balcony.

"Compassion is a word that I can't remind you enough is useless," he says. "It has no meaning in our house or in our order of things. However, Colonel Rusain is correct that it must be shown. These mortals eat it up. Cyrail, you must understand that we are superior in every way to the world of men that we walk among. As such we have many enemies, that will show us no compassion or mercy. So, we have none. The world is in strife right now. A strong hand is needed to guide it back to peace and order. For more generations that any can remember, I have torn down empires, kingdoms and societies only to rebuild them not in his image, but mine. I did it to show a rule that can never be matched. It is finally ready. Look at them, Cyrail. You will soon be that instrument that I wield to promote and bring peace throughout this reality and all others to follow. We will take them one by one. You are an instrument that will set me high on the throne that was denied me putting me in the place where I could do the most to benefit all."

Lucien nods his head as a signal to Warsivious, who walks to the head of the troops and does a textbook about face.

Shouting loud enough that all can hear him, he cries, "Atten-*hut*! Men of peace, keepers of Lucien's law. Eyes up!"

Upon hearing the command of General Warsivious, the troops stand at attention, perfectly in unison snaps their eyes up toward the balcony.

Lucien faces Cyrail. "Leave compassion to me. It is a tool that I shall wield on our behalf. You will have no compassion. You are Nephilim. A god among men. You have no rival or no equal. You can and will walk both worlds. You've been giving the tools and the insight to do all that you need to conquer."

An assistant walks up to Lucien, attempting to put a small head set microphone on him. He waves it away. Lucien's voice carries supernaturally as if his voice was amplified twenty times. For the first time, he subtlety shows his supernatural abilities to the world.

"You, men, are my top military brass and the best of my non-commissioned. Many of you have been leaders of men for many years. Your amassed wealth of knowledge on the battlefield has echoed the vast experience. You've been training the next and hopefully the last generation to practice war, at least I pray. In four days' time we will expand our world campaign to bring stability, peace and a new quality of life, to not just torn desolated regions of our neighbors here in the east, but the world. We have the backing of over 130 nations, although what could have been our greatest allies have decided to sit this one out saying what I proposed was the impossible, over ambitious, and foolhardy. I say not!"

The troops and civilians erupt into cheers.

"It will be a long campaign. But, if we stay the course within twenty years, time we will have achieved what the men of the west called impossible. I agree, I'm overly ambitious. I agree it's foolhardy. But, don't you agree that it's time for senseless death that comes with war to come to an end? Time for disease to be eradicated, time for the hungry to be fed? Don't you agree, or am I alone?"

The troops and civilians cheer and give thunderous applause.

"Well, I'm glad to hear that I'm not alone. It would have been a pretty embarrassing and a hard-uphill battle if it was just me." Laughter falls on top of the cheering and jeers.

"Commanders, take my vision to your troops, take it to your families, take it to everyone that will listen and even those who won't. Take my vision and make it your own. Make it your troop's vision. Make it the world's vision. I believe that I have been ordained for this mission and that divine providence will help me through this massive undertaking and I will not fail. Nor will I allow you brave men and women to fail. We will all see this unto completion, because this is providence. When I weary, I will be replenished by divine forces so that I may replenish you all... Are you with me? The roar of the cheer is deafening. "Are you with me?"

The courtyard responds with the repeated chant, "Ascension, ascension, ascension."

"It's time to right the ship of the belief in democracy. It has failed and will continue to fail. It's time to return to the monarch society of old. One world, one peace, one king."

Lucien waves to the massive gathered troops, as his son looks on. *Where it's my world, no peace, where I alone am king.*

Rayne's Home – Evening

Gloria waves them off as they walk down the walkway to a waiting red Cobra Mustang.

Kathy rushes out the front door holding a laptop yelling. "Wait! I have your father online." Isis smiles and turns quickly back to the porch. Gloria walks off the porch passing Isis. She leans in and gives her a peck on the cheek. "You two have a wonderful time, baby!"

"We will," Isis continues on toward the porch and happily looks at the lap top with her mom. Isis talks to her father gleefully about prom and her date.

Gloria walks up to Jericho. She can't believe how tall he is or how fast the time has passed from when she held him as a baby. She takes another picture of him standing by himself. Jericho hugs her and smiles. "You have enough prom pictures, old woman?"

"Okay, okay! I'm done. Your mother would've been so proud of you tonight. I'm proud of you."

She hugs him tight while kissing him on the cheek. Unbeknownst to him, she slips a fifty-dollar bill into his blazer pocket. "Okay, you're making me tear up. Don't make me regret renting you this car! You hear me!" Gloria yells at him while patting her eyes dry.

"I hear you, Grandma. The whole neighborhood heard you."

Gloria pinches his cheeks and backs away as Isis walks pass her. She blows Gloria a kiss. Jericho open the passenger door for Isis. Once in he closes it and trots to the driver's side door. The key in his pocket gives him remote keyless entry. He sits in the smooth Corinthian leather seat and starts the push button starter with a smile that would rival the Cheshire cat from Alice in Wonderland. The car starts with a roar that only a V8 can muster and rockets off, only to instantly break and ride off calmly.

Gloria turns and waves bye to Katherine as she walks towards her vehicle. Suddenly, she's startled by what she knows to be a familiar voice.

"Those two are a mighty good-looking couple."

Gloria turns around and sees an old man using a walker. She looks at him as if she should know him. She just can't place his face. It's been years.

"Yes, they do. I pray they beat the odds of high school love and actually make it. They're great for each other. They've been inseparable since childhood."

The old man rests on his walker. "Your son or daughter?"

"My grandson actually," Gloria proudly replies. She opens the door to her newer model Nissan than the jalopy she had previously. The old man is frail and looks exhausted from walking with his cane.

"Are you okay there elder?" she asks.

"Just a little out of breath. It's been a long walk. Hesitant, "may I trouble you for a ride, mother of angels? I would be most appreciative."

Gloria pauses, she remembers the old man now. It's been years. What are the odds that he would still be alive, further alone walking this particular neighborhood block? Curious and nervous, Gloria thinks against the ride. The constant pain in her side has made her irritable. She really had to put on a show for Jericho and Isis as not to give the nagging discomfort in abdomen away.

"No, sorry, I'm afraid not. I don't ride with sweet men that I don't know, even those as charming as you." She closes her door, starts the car, and drives off holding her side.

"I understand mother of angels." Metatron transfigures into his angelic form yet again. "You never know who you may be riding with. God speed, mother of angels." *If you had but accepted my invitation, perhaps things may have been different this night. I was given the authority to safeguard you only had you accepted. The date etched on your forehead this evening is concrete.* "The choices we make."

Gloria starts turning radio channels in her car. She turns to the news station. Where she locates the most trusted newscaster in the radio business. He's quick-witted and entertaining as he delivers the news even when it's heartbreaking or gut-wrenching. His voice puts all at ease.

Gloria slows her vehicle. Déjà vu! She's seen this before. It strikes her that the whole exchange is what she said before to some extent.

The newscaster continues, 'I just don't know why America has not allied with Arcane in this endeavor that he's getting ready to undertake. On the eve of the world's biggest offensive undertaking, America is sitting it out. I just don't understand what—'

Ploom! Gloria's Nissan's right tire blows out. Instinctively, she slams on brakes sending her into a swerve. She swerves right, swerves left counter swerving into a light pole. The force of the strike crumples and spins her around the pole and into a four-way intersection where she's hit by a semi-tractor truck. The force of the collision is so violent that it snaps the fatigued metal anchor point of her seatbelt. She's forcefully ejected through her driver's side window slamming her head into the grill of the tractor trailer. Her skull cracks and shatters, killing her instantly. Her body falls lifeless back into the Nissan slumping over the driver's side door through the shattered window.

There's a quiet calm after the accident. Sound has all but muted except the sound of metal boots on pavement. Death kneels and looks into the vehicle's interior. There's only been a few times over the eons that has given him pause. Gloria has become the eleventh time he's paused. He slowly reaches through the window knowing that her soul was once red, that of a non-believer, red as the purest grape wine. He reaches into the husk that is racked with the cancer, a cancer she hid from her grandson and grabs her soul with reverence. *I hope you accomplished all that you could in the borrowed time that was afforded you, mother of Rachel.* After securing her soul, he pulls a red soul's sphere from her broken and pestilent body. Having her, he slowly turns and walks away from the vehicle as it catches fire. In an instant, he's gone taking with him one of the last Earthly attachments to Jericho.

Jericho is immersed in hearing the roar behind the Stang's motor. He drives as Isis stares adoringly at him. "I can't believe how good you look tonight."

"Yeah, I can't believe how good I look either," says Jericho.

"See? This is why I plan on ditching you as soon as we get to prom." Laughing, she elbows him.

"Wait, what?" Jericho says as the joke finally catches him. He laughs.

"Oh, yeah! You're laughing. I'm serious. I only used you for a ride because my new boyfriend is pretty much a deadbeat and has no car, but he's much cuter than you."

Grinning. "Oh, is that so?" Jericho grins as he takes a turn beating the yellow light.

"It is."

"Well, there seems to be a slight flaw in your plan, if you don't mind me saying."

"I'm open to criticism. As long as it's constructive." Says Isis.

Jericho signals left then overtakes the slower vehicle. "Well, good, because I have some constructive critiques. The flaw seems to be that you've told me your evil plan before we've reached our promised destination."

Isis looks at him with a seductive smirk on her face.

Jericho grinning. "So, what's to stop me from pulling over and putting you out?"

"You'd put me out as sexy as I look tonight?"

Smirking, he shrugs. "Well, yeah. I'd put you out then turn around and pick up my first choice for prom."

"Please! You've never had a first choice but me for prom. You've been in love with me since puberty. If I thought harder about it probably before that."

"You can't prove that."

"I don't have to. It's in the way you look at me. I mean, I think it's cute and all, but it's just time for me to upgrade obviously. Now, that I think about it, I should be searching for a Frenchmen. I love the way they talk.

"Okay… What if I tell you that I'm in love with you and you're one of the best things that has ever happened to me, Isis?" Jericho takes his hands off the stick shift and holds her hand.

Isis looks at him, her eyes welling up and face starting to overflow with emotion. "I'd say that I was thinking very hard about telling the new guy that maybe things aren't going to work out between him and me." Isis voice cracks and she tries to hold back tears of joy.

"Hmm. Okay, then, what if I told you that I wanted to marry you after graduation from the Naval Academy?"

Isis catches a tear before it crosses the barrier of her freshly applied eyeliner. "Don't make me cry. You know how long it took to apply this make up right?" Tears start to stream down her face anyway. "I'd tell the new boyfriend that you and I were able to reconcile our extreme differences and it seems that we are going to continue to be an item."

The two arrive at their destination. After he parks, they look at each other.

"I'm going to miss you over the summer, Ice— right?"

"You say that every summer."

"It's true, though. I be missing you tough."

"That is the only time I get to spend with my father, Jare. It's not intentional. Besides, I'll make sure I come visit you on friends and family day."

Jericho reaches into the glove box and pulls out a purplish white Corsage.

Isis smiles at him. He slowly puts the corsage on her wrist, savoring the feel of her smooth skin. "I forgot to give you this at the house."

"It's beautiful. You tell Gloria she did a great job picking it out."

Jericho laughs. "I will... C'mon, let's go dance into forever!" Jericho slides out the door. He skips around to the passenger door opening it for Isis. He takes her by the hand and leads her up the red carpet toward the hotel only stopping to toss his keys to valet. Jericho then turns and holds his arm in a reverse c for her to slide hers into his interlocking the two and cementing their official prom couple status. They head toward the automated sliding doors and into the hotel where music of their generational music can be heard blaring. Jericho looks up at the sign that is above the automated door. It reads: The Hyatt is the premiere hotel of downtown Detroit.

Jericho and Isis walk into the Prom arm in arm. Isis's girlfriends immediately scream in excitement of seeing her. They swarm her and break the two apart. Like a sandstorm, they whip her away with frivolous girl chatter making her vanish before Jericho's eyes. Jason Priest finds Jericho alone and walks up to him placing his arm around his shoulder passing him a cup of punch.

"Didn't think you'd make it playa have a drink with your boy before Lucien ends the world in eternal fire with his bid to truly be the one to end all wars." Jason throws back the last of his punch.

"A little dramatic in your toast wouldn't you say? And as much as we talked about this night for the last four years, you'd think I'd have missed it?" Jericho sips the punch checking to see if it's been spiked.

Jericho can't take his eyes off of Isis across the room as he half listens to Jason. *She's stunning.* She permeates sexy. He watches her fit, slim body, her thick thighs. He follows the line of her legs up to her roundness of her ass. He knows the cut of her stomach, as he's watched her in cheer practice. Her breasts are supple and firm. Sex is all he can think of. The pact be damned tonight.

Isis, although amongst her friends, can't take her eyes off of him from across the room either. She watches him with anticipation of the apex of nightfall. It's fast approaching.

Jason snapping his fingers in front of Jericho's face. "There you are. You know what? You two give me hope that there really is such a thing as story book love. He says while making a gagging face." Jason looks over and waves to Isis and blows her kiss. Isis waves back and dodges the kiss as she acts repulsed by it, then laughs.

"Ours is not unlike many others." Jericho takes another swig of punch.

"Yeah, keep telling yourself that." Jason downs his whole cup of punch. "You two are like the stories told by the age-old Greeks. I'm sure if those prolific writers had to endure your guy's inseparable bonds as much as I have to, you two would be written into a constellation.

"Well, thanks, but didn't most of those tales end in tragedy?

"Not all of 'em."

"Yeah? Name one!"

Jason's stumped. He becomes hesitant on answering the question. "Ugh, yours."

Jericho, laughs softly. "Priest, I'm just happy that I met her. Life is in just a really good place—I'm having a blast.

Jason smiles, points, and waves past Isis' aiming for her girlfriends, especially Jamie Blount. Jason Looks back Jericho. "I hope you guys make it Playa. She really is beautiful tonight, Jare… And don't tell her I said that! She'd never let me live it down."

Jason reaches into his back pocket. "Need Condoms?"

"No, you dumb ass!" Jericho says as he rushes Jason to put the latex back into his pocket. "Don't let Isis see those!"

Jason Laughing! Why not? It's prom, I'm sure her purse if full of em."

Jericho shaking his head. "No thanks, man. Thanks for thinking of us though. By the way who is your lucky date tonight?"

Jason looks at him with the obvious you know stare. "Funny man, huh?"

The two laughs. "Sorry, preacher."

"It's priest. Or at least I hope to be," Jason corrects. "I was thinking of bringing Evelyn, but then I remembered she didn't like me."

"For the best then perhaps. Besides, when do you start Seminary? You ready?"

"In the fall and no."

Peter Gabriel's "Book of Love" sends couples to the dance floor as its slow rhythmic beat makes it perfect for the students to slow dance and quell the raging hormones by dancing closely placing their chaperones on full duty of keeping the teens apart.

Jericho slides from underneath the shoulder of Priest. "If you'll excuse me, Priest. Which is weird by the way, you becoming a priest with last name of Priest. Just plain damn creepy." Jericho quickly downs the last of his punch and passes the empty cup back to Jason and walks over towards Isis.

Jason takes the cup. "You be careful tonight eh, she looks vicious. Planned Parenthood is a booming profession after prom season— so, I've heard."

Jericho looks back. "I love her to much not to make it special for our first time."

Jericho walks up to Isis who is gesturing to her girlfriends about the blown kiss still flying around the room from Jason. Isis' friends immediately stop laughing and glares at him as if he's crossed into unfriendly territory deep within enemy lines. No lingering gesturing, Isis turns and stares Jericho up and down attempting to hold a straight face free of laughter.

"Hmm! You are a bold one to walk into our conversation," Isis joked. "You've possibly overheard G14 classified talk. We might can never let you leave here."

"Really? I hadn't noticed anyone but you." Jericho winks at her, sure to flash his dimples.

Isis' eyes soften. Jericho nods to her friends. "Hey, ladies."

The friends instantly attack for entering the confines of the lioness pack. "Hey, Jericho." Another adds, "Well, if it isn't the Bane of our existence." The last of the lioness pack isn't as dangerous. "Oh! Be nice ladies, I think he's handsome tonight. He's more of date than ours have been."

Jericho takes Isis by the hands. "Ms. Rayne, may I have this dance?"

With grace, he pulls her to the dance floor. While the song plays, he dances with her to the steps his grandmother was sure to beat into muscle memory. The two of them are graceful in each step they take across the floor, it's as if their gliding. Isis wipes her eyes to keep the tears from rolling.

"What's wrong?" Jericho asks, concerned.

Isis smiles through her tears. "Nothing— nothing at all. Everything is right. Although the world is in turmoil and I don't know if I'll be accepted into University of Michigan in the winter, just for tonight everything is perfect and I don't care. Jare, I'm really gonna miss you over the sum—"

"Shh. Don't think of that right now. Let's just dance for tonight. We'll think of the summer later. We'll just dance the night away, we'll tell jokes, laugh, and watch Jason continuously debate Mr. Aperture on the finer points of faith versus agnosticism. Then continuing dancing the night away intimately."

"And then on till morning," says Isis. The two dance as the song plays into the night.

Isis lays her head on Jericho's chest grinning as they spin and twirl, Isis searches and finds Mr. Verochie still has a number of couples to separate before he makes it to them. She pulls Jericho closer feeling the warmth of his body. His breath on her neck. Her blood starts to rush, pulse increases, the veins in her neck and temple become visible. She's turned on. Her body begs Jericho to set aside the gentlemen for one night and let raging hormones and stupidity over take him. She wants him. *It was fine being abstinent when we were kids, but I'm ready* is all that Isis could think. If my body is screaming for sex, his has to be.

Isis kisses Jericho on the neck hoping to set his passion ablaze. She can already feel him rising to the occasion. She leans in and breathes softly into his ear knowing the gentle heated breeze has to set him off. "I want you, Jare."

From the corner of the room a cloaked and hooded Gabriel watches the two. She pulls her hood off and just watches him dance with a girl he loves. She watches as his first real test of commitment to the covenant is being tested. Gabriel glances around and begins to shift phase through different realities to see if there are any demons in the vicinity pushing this girl's hormones higher than normal, but at cursory glance, no other ethereal appears to be present. This lustful drive of temptation is all human. Satisfied, Gabriel just watches him enjoy his night, because she knows that in mere moments his night will be shattered. The law of the land will soon be here to give notification of a recently deceased. She passed the vehicle on the way to him. Tonight, a piece of his soul will chip when he's heard of what's happened. She'll console him then. For now, he can have these precious few moments. He can enjoy his time with Isis. He can simply dance, because come morning there will only be weeping.

Jericho slowly dips Isis to the last stanza of the song. When he raises her up, he passionately kisses her. His kiss is strong, but not forceful. *As many times as we've kissed, I'm not sure I ever felt tongue. I was always too scared, always holding back trying to observe that damn covenant. A dream of a mother I never knew. No longer. I'm taking Isis tonight. I don't care what the heavens say.*

Jericho goes from kissing her supple lips to licking along the vein of her soft smooth neck. The intensity of her breathing only increases his wants even more. In his mind they are already in the mustang having sex. With the completed thought of intercourse his justification for finishing the act in deed kicks in. *Whelp, I've already done it in my mind, may as well do it for real.*

Jericho, stops making out long enough for him to dip Isis a second time at the conclusion of the song. He looks at her making his intentions known. "I want you so bad right now, let's get these pictures and get the hell out of here."

Isis slowly nods her head yes never losing his eye contact. Jericho raises her back up and hugs her. As he looks across her shoulder while embraced in a hug, he sees Gabriel in the corner she has materialized into reality 2814. At first, he feels ashamed, but Gabriel smiles at him and claps a few times to cheers his waltz. He nods, acknowledging her, and then pulls Isis by her hand off the dance floor.

Isis, feels his moment of un-comfortability. "What is it, baby?"

"Nothing, I just want you so bad right now, I'm ready to get out of here." *Nothing personal, Gabriel, but this is my life. Fuck that covenant!*

Jericho and Isis take their professional prom pictures. Their parental units would kill them if they hadn't. The night must be kept for posterity in digital form is what Gloria would jokingly say.

"C'mon, Ice. Let's go." Jericho says why gently pulling Isis away. She waves to her friends as they begin to make their way to the exit. Jericho nods bye to Jason who's closely watching the dance floor for that right song. Before they exit Mr. Verochi taps Jericho on the shoulder. He turns around and sees that his geometry teacher is in the company of a plain clothes detective which she surely makes known by the badge clipped to her belt.

"Jericho, this detective would like a word with you."

CHAPTER 28

DECISIONS

"Do not weep or mourn for the dead. Their struggles have since passed. If you want to cry or feel pain, then mourn and weep for those who live, because it is they that must endure."

Quote ~Gabriel

Detroit, Michigan

Rain falls on a solemn crowd at the burial services for Gloria Eloise Bane. Jericho is dressed in a black suit along with his uncle, Jerimiah Bane. Jerimiah is a scruffy-looking sixty with a crooked nose that date back to the origin of a 1991 boxing match gone south. His beard is more gray than black. Jericho never really had much to say to his great uncle after a drunken fueled rage thirteen years prior to the day. He never forgave him for whatever subject that was discussed between him and his grandmother that caused his uncle to lash out and strike her. He was all but dead to him. He last heard that he'd sobered up, but that was only after a terminal prognosis of liver disease. *He must be near the final stages, as he resembles a skeletal figure as opposed to the once burly man that I remembered him to be.*

Isis stands to Jericho's right holding his hand tightly. Among the crowd of those in attendance stands Isis' mother Ms. Rayne, Sister Eva,

Jason Priest and his parents, as well as a host of others. The minister speaking the last internment is completely soaked as is all in attendance from the deluge of rain that pours down upon them. The minister holds a bible open, but it's turned to no particular page. The business of death has been prevalent and constant over his long career; so much so, he knows the passages by heart. The opening of the Bible to a random page is for show, the public has come to expect it.

A host of angels stand in anonymity around the worst kept secret in heaven's history. They stand with heads bowed in solidarity with what very well may be their only hope in defeating the rising threat, Imperial. Offset in a parallel reality they watch with great concern as to the reaction of the young mortal in light of today's loss.

Hours later all the attendees have left, ethereal or otherwise. Jericho still sits in the cheap plastic folding chair draped in mourning black cloth and purple chair covers. He stares into the grave unmoved. Isis still by his side, she continues to hold his hand. The grave diggers return for the fifth time and continue to try and wait him out so that they can get on with their task of burying the dead. One tries to be subtle by glancing at the time on his phone as he switches pockets.

Time pauses, freezing everything in its place for all but Jericho. Startled that the rain has paused in its place, Jericho tries to stand but the rain drops hold him captive in his chair as he can't move against time's immobile effect on the rain. He tries to move his arms and push the rain drops aside, but they are hard as concrete and immovable. Gabriel appears sitting next to him able to move as freely as she pleases.

Trying to turn his head up and toward Gabriel, it remains facing the grave. "This is my punishment for wanting to have sex with Isis, isn't it? This is because I was willing to give it all up for her, right? And god forbid I do—we can't have that can we?"

Gabriel stands and looks into the grave. "Do not weep or mourn for the dead. Their struggles have since passed. If you want to cry or feel pain, then mourn and weep for those that live, because it is they that must endure. Like them, you must endure, Jericho. You may see this as punishment. Have you not learned in your studies that accidents are sometimes just that? You all have an appointed time that was decided by Elohim and penned by Fate. The possibility of eluding Death can never be avoided. Delayed maybe, but never avoided. Even under the right circumstances we, my kind are not exempt. He comes for us as he does you mortals, or a Trathis Star or a galaxy."

Jericho tries to stand, but still is forced to remain seated by something as trivial as rain. Jericho no longer able to hold his pain begins to cry, his grief manifesting as anger. "This was no accident. This is a direct result of my choice that was coming. I thought long and hard on the choice that I was willing to make and your Elohim, God, executioner or whatever you want to call him took my grandmother from me to ensure I would remain compliant that night."

"What's coming is beyond your simple thought of compliance. With or without you, Jericho, events will unfold the way that it must. Look, you're right in your option to choose. You can either be the man that your mother knew you would be, or the boy that is ruled by lust and self-gratification. I never said life would be easy nor the choices that you would have to make. In fact, I said just the opposite. I told you the way would be hard and there would be much sacrifice."

"You could have done something, Gabriel. You could have asked for more time on her behalf."

"And how do you know Jericho if she already wasn't on borrowed time?"

Jericho stares at Gabriel. "Let-me-up!"

"No…"

Jericho pushes with all he has. He uses his strength granted by Iehovah and slowly he pushes himself from the chair. Using his strength, he pushes himself through the time frozen rain droplets. As he pushes for each step it feels as if he's pushing through individual brick walls that have combined to create and ocean of blockades. He forces himself beyond what he thinks he's capable of toward the direction of the headstone of his grandmother's grave. The rain frozen in time shreds his suit as he forces himself forward. When he makes it to the apex of the grave, he looks down and reads the final epitaph, the last thing that will forever be written of her on the stone as it lies on its back. He reads the inscription over and over again. The dates that she was born into the world and that of when she died. He reads beyond the inscribed words. He reads within the script the loss of his mother and the gaining of a grandmother, but his eyes focus on the script beyond the obvious rhetoric. The script that reads: The collapsing of the walls of Jericho changed the world once and it will again.

No longer able to bear the weight of time literally on his shoulders, Jericho collapses to one knee exhausted and gasping to inhale breath. Gabriel kneels next to him. You have indeed grown more powerful. Such brawn will mean nothing if your power does not grow to wield emotion as well.

Time returns to normal. Gabriel has vanished. Isis looks a little confused as to how Jericho had gotten up without her seeing him and kneeling before the grave, she just chalks it up to having spaced out. However, she has no explanation of how his suit had been torn either. Over the time they've been friends before teenage lovers, she knew there was something different about him, she just always believed when he was ready, he'd tell her what. This moment was just one that she'd file away among many others.

"Jare, you okay, baby? You ready to go?" Isis says, as she walks to him.

No longer able to hold in his grief and anger, Jericho palms the top of the headstone and picks it up from its prone positioning on the ground with one hand and slams it downward driving it into the rain-soaked Earth. He drives a thousand pounds two feet in. He then looks over to Isis who's looking at him in shock.

"Baby?" Is all Isis can say before she goes speechless.

"I'm fine," Jericho says harshly. He then looks at what he's just done and then he looks to Isis. She's speechless. Jericho softens his tone, "I guess we need to talk."

Isis just nods her head as she stares at the tombstone that he singlehandedly power drove into the Earth.

Talking amongst themselves the grave diggers attention is directed toward Jericho when he signals and then gestures that he's leaving. He takes Isis by the hand and leads her away. As they walk out past the awaiting Limo he waves the driver to just leave. The driver stares at him, confused. Isis nods her head that it's okay for him to leave.

Jericho looks at Isis and studies her reaction as they walk toward the front gates of the cemetery. "The simplest of ways that I can explain me is by referencing to frame you a picture."

Isis has a more than a few questions, but decides to hold them to give him a chance to speak. They just may be answered.

"Do you remember that day when we were all riding our bikes when that accident happened?"

Isis just nods yes.

"I saw that truck coming as we came across the intersection. It was the first time that I think my reflexes moved as fast. I jumped off my bike and braced for the hit just as you two had started to come across the intersection. I slammed my whole body into the front grill of that truck with everything I could muster hoping it would clear you and Jason. I didn't even think of myself until it was over."

"But it didn't clear us, did it?" Isis whispers.

"No, It didn't." He says in a light whisper. "I think I may have sent the cab into the air slightly, but the momentum still carried me into you guys and into that house. You guys must have been just below me when the front cab came down on me. I absorbed the shock for you two, I guess, I don't know, I blacked out for a few. After waking up, I called out for you guys to move, but I don't know if the force of the blow or the fumes had put you guys out."

Isis just stares at him hanging on every word.

"I was given, blessed, cursed or whatever you want call it with a strength that is unmatched by anyone else—supposedly. The only reference that I have that I'm similar too is that of Samson." Jericho shakes his head up and down. "Yes, that Samson from the bible, the story from Sunday school."

As they walk past a mini grocery store Jericho pulls Isis into the parking lot. "C'mon!" Jericho walks to a rear of a green Dodge Caravan. He looks around to see if anyone's paying attention to the two of them. Satisfied that no one is watching he grabs underneath the rear bumper of a black four door Audi and lifts the back of the vehicle suspending it in the air for a few seconds with ease. Isis places her hands to her mouth in disbelief. She turns her gaze from the vehicle towards Jericho. Having her attention, he sets it down.

Isis' eyes widen in amazement, still with a side of disbelief. "That-is-so-effin-awesome! So, you said all that to say that you're who I have to thank for saving my life all those years ago?" She grabs Jericho's face and pulls him close kissing him. "Shhh! Don't say anymore right now, let me just kiss my own personal hero." As the two kiss, Isis starts to smile.

"What?" Jericho questions.

"It's nothing really... I just think it's cool you're like a superhero or something." She starts laughing. "Are you an alien? Tell me you're an alien?"

CHAPTER 29

Greyhound Bus Station - Morning

Isis and Jason talking of various ice-cream flavors of yesteryear yammer on about having to wait for the ice-cream man to make it down the block. Jericho listens to them reminiscing. It's a moment that he's sure to commit to memory, because their life paths are about to separate as everyone gets ready to head out into their own respective lives. As they near the loading platform to the bus that awaits to carry Jericho to Annapolis' Naval Academy, it becomes real that their friendship is about to endure a test of time.

"You can always choose another path, Jare," Jason says as he slaps him on his back.

"I don't think the seminary would welcome me as easily as you, Priest. Besides, that collar has to be uncomfortable that they wear." Jericho laughs again.

"What the hell is so funny?" Jason asks still grinning thinking of ice-cream.

"Nothing. I swear. I just think it's funny still that Priest is your last name and will be your title eventually. How the hell do you distinguish the two?"

Jason shakes his head and pats Jericho on the back. "It will be priest all the time I suppose. Actually, now that I think about it's your two guys fault. That accident all those years ago changed me. It changed all of us, you me Isis and even your Gran-gran Gloria. That truck not killing us was divine providence—at least that's what I took from it."

More Jericho rather than divine providence. Isis thought.

"I keep telling you that Jare, but you don't want to believe it. I keep telling you we're all destined for greater things. Hell, take your girl Isis here. She moved her entire archeological motivation to ancient biblical studies because of that singular incident whether she admits or not. She's going to be that one someday to discover that elusive tangible proof that will cement God's existence."

"Or disprove it," Isis quips.

"Our divine saving was so that we could change the world and you would waste yours fighting in endless wars that Lucien started no doubt? He has thrown the world into chaos and for what? For what? Please somebody explain that asshole's motivations to me."

Isis steps in between the boys. "Jason, for all we know this divine providence you like to speak of and throw around, is what is directing him to the military. Second, Lucien is one of the few leaders of a country that is actually taking the war to evil regimes and fanatical empires that oppress the human spirit, drives slave trade, and murder for the sake of ethnicity. His goal seems one of genuine loftier purposes. Africa is a hot bed of violence and has been for some time. The east has its problems as well and Lucien is the only one attempting to solve them without money motivating ulterior motives."

"That we know of." Jason says. "There is always a motive even in the best of intentions."

"And think, it won't be long before the U.S. backs Lucien's lead in the bid to end all wars." Jericho says as he leans in and kisses Isis for backing him. "I want to be in on that change when America arrives to intervene. I want to be at ground zero when we take the world back."

"Not me, brother. You'd never catch me over there fighting no matter the intentions. Well, I see it's too late for you, you have been sold on Lucien Arcane's war machine propaganda." Jason hugs him. "I love you buddy. I'm gonna miss the hell out of you. Have a blessed and safe trip mi amigo, with a side of traveling mercy." Jason lets his go and gestures the sign of the cross in front of Jericho. "Mind those books, study the ways of war and I'll be sure to see you on friends and family day buddy." Jericho hugs Jason a second time tightly in an embrace that speaks loudly the unsaid words, take care if I never see you again in this life. Having felt like it was the last goodbye Jason backs away and waits for Isis to say her goodbyes. A tear begins to fall, but he captures it quickly and rubs his sleeve across his eyes.

Looking into Isis' eyes Jericho's own start to well up. "The dreaded day we knew would someday come, huh?"

Isis wipes his tears. "The day we knew we'd have to part for just a fraction of our lives... Oh baby! It's only for a little while. Think about it Bae, we have the love no doubt, but it won't pay the bills later on. Unfortunately, we'll have to work for that." Isis wipes more tears as they roll down his cheek. "We have Smartphones and snail mail; we'll survive the distance for a while. Oh! I never did tell you thank you?"

"For?"

"For not laughing at me stumbling in those heels on prom night." They both laugh. Isis leans in closer and whispers so that Jason will not be privy. "And saving my life all those years ago. Jason is right, we were spared for a reason even if it was you that spared us. What you can do, that strength, is for a reason. And you won't be done with this pain of feeling burdened until you do what you're supposed to. We'll have our time, Jare. We just have to take care of our other obligations first. You need to finish whatever it is you feel you have to finish. Matter of fact finish it quickly; my virginity demands it." Isis winks and kisses Jericho again. "Now, go baby, like Jason said, we'll be there on family and friend's day. Isis hugs him tightly one last time and pecks him on the lips. "Can't wait to see you in your cadet dress whites."

Jericho the last to board waves bye to the two and steps into the bus still waving until the doors slide shut.

CHAPTER 30

FIRST CONTACT

"They've been among us since our beginning. They battle for us in the shadows and plains of the ethereal realms to ensure that we are unopposed as we discover our purpose in this system of all things. They stand so that we may fall. And not a question of if, but when we do. If you listen quietly with your spiritual beating heart that lies just below the metaphysical one, you will hear them telling you to rise. Rise, to challenge the mental incapacitating thoroughfares that impair you. Rise above the debilitating inconsistencies of ravaged thoughts and impure notions. Rise past the dark forces that haunt you in the dead of night. Simply, rise."

Quote ~Exorcist Jason Priest

Year, 2044

America is two years into the war for the Congo in Africa. Currently, their operations are in the Republic of Congo backing the Arcanian forces. Ethnic and religious cleansing has reached a disturbing high of two million killed over a span of the southern and middle countries of the continent Africa prior to America's entrance.

The death toll is still rising. The President's waning poll numbers added with the country's building love and support for Lucien Arcane and his privately funded crusade to bring peace has forced the U.S. executive leader to step in and do what is ensuring of re-election over morality. The President succumbing to public pressure and sentiment has placed American troops in harm's way and in league with a man that he feels in his soul is unjust. Power and the want and need to always keep it corrupts even the best of men, even Presidents.

The Destined Sun Militants have been in the region pillaging, murdering, raping, and extorting the citizenry. Their carnage has left so many dead in its wake that the invested nations, corrupt policy makers, and those with eyes toward profit could no longer idly standby and miss out on prime opportunity to land grab real estate racked with the money-making potential of oil fields and diamond mines. With Lucien's intent for peace in the region, interested parties that look to privatize portions of southern Africa secretly fund his crusade and campaign in hopes that his forces can restore order at no cost to those interested nation's own troops. After all, dead troops are never good for any nations elected leaders.

Through a series of explosions of dirt and shrapnel, American Marine forces push through the enemy encampment. They trudge forward in bounding formations in an intense fire fight. The terrain is unforgiving as they press forward through thick underbrush and foliage. Rounds whiz by the men with some finding their targets. A number of advancing troops fall dead instantly as rounds pierce foreheads and severs spines at the base of necks. Others fall and writhe in pain as they are maimed being left too injured to continue fighting.

A mortar shell lands in front of an advancing five-man squad of Marines. Shrapnel tears into their flesh exposing some of the men's innards. The Marine closest to the exploding shell is attempting to shove his intestines back into his body before a stray round ends his suffering as an enemy bullet finds its mark and passes through the Marine's left eye. *Thank God,* he thinks with his final millisecond of life.

The others in the immediate blast radius die within moments of the dispersal of tightly wounded metal cord. Another of the Marine's squad member which was caught in the blast radius's shockwave is blown into the base of a tree trunk. The force with which he's thrown is so forceful that when his body collides into centuries age old trunk it only shatters the bark. The shockwave knocks his helmet and face mask off before his body falls to the ground. As he stirs and stands to his feet, it's clear without the helmet that the Marine is Jericho. Having taken such a blow at close range he has a hard time trying to get his legs working. The explosion discombobulated him briefly. He falls back to one knee in need of a minute to catch his bearings.

Constant battle has given Jericho age in more ways than one since graduation from the Naval Academy. His after-five shadow is screaming, and he's been more than forty-eight hours with no sleep. The last explosion was so close that his ears won't stop ringing with tinnitus and has left him in disarray. Still hazy, he realizes that at some point prior to the blast he was carrying a weapon. He fumbles through the underbrush hoping that he can find it. Of course, he could use one of his fallen subordinates, but his weapon is his and has seen him through many of conflicts on the foreign lands he's visited. He looks past the weapons of the dead in hopes of finding his that was issued to him, besides you never want to use the weapon of a dead man if you can avoid it. It's just plain bad luck.

More affected than he thought by the close proximity blast, perception for Jericho has become fluid. The blast followed by the subsequent tree hit was so hard that it alters the way he perceives reality for a moment. As he shakes the haze away, he momentarily catches a glimpse of the ethereal plane. As he watches his platoon aggressively advance past him, he sees angels fighting fallen demons alongside his troops. Not just alongside his troops, but above them as well. Swords, shields and axes clang in fierce oppositional conflict. Limbs are sliced from the body of one demon as he buries his ax into the chest of the opposing angel. Jericho shakes his head again not believing what he's seeing. He slaps his face and thumps the side of his head with his palm in an attempt to get himself back on track mentally.

As he starts to rise for a second time, Jericho bears witnesses to the ultimate equalizer, although he doesn't quite understand it. Death is in the midst of the human condition of weapon firing conflicts and angelic melee collecting souls.

Having the feeling of being seen Death turns his attention briefly to Jericho making eye contact with him. Shh! Death gestures with his finger to his lips for Jericho to be quiet. He then waves that same finger in a no, no, no, gesture all the while still looking at Jericho. Death ducks as an angel's wildly slung blade just nearly misses his head. After the dodge, he again stares briefly at Jericho then continues on with soul reaping. Harvest this day is bountiful and has been as such since Warsivious was unleashed on the world having all restraints removed from him to wage war by the act of the breaking of the latest seal.

Jericho smacks himself and shakes his head again. *That did it.* Time and reality regain normalcy. Speed and perception return to current reality. "Hell yeah! There it is." He grabs his rifle chambering a new round into it and continues pushing forward. With his quickened pace, his feet happen to damn near out run him. Jericho stumbles falling forward before he's caught and assisted by the platoon's chaplain.

"You need to get those feet working properly, Captain. To die here today over a matter of clumsiness would be very un-warrior like," says Father Jason Priest.

Jericho looks at him. "Yeah, yeah. I'm good. What the hell happened?"

"War, Captain. the theater of war has happened. Now, get going. You can't lead act from back here." Priest pushes him on.

Worried, Jericho turns around trotting backward so that he can face Priest. "What about you?"

Bullets whiz by peppering trees and the ground. A round ping off the side of Priest's helmet, slapping his head to the side as if he was punched.

"Jesus!" Jericho stated at the luck of Priest surviving that strike.

"Indeed, Jesus will look after me Captain. Now go! I have last rights to administer to these men of the dead and dying back here."

Jericho nods and runs off into the fight hesitant of leaving his friend in such hostility, but he's right he has men to lead.

Priest turns and kneels over the destroyed bodies of those that had fallen silent in the most recent of moments. Without hesitation or delay, Jason begins the Catholic Viaticum, Last Rites.

"Oh my God, I am heartily sorry for having offended Thee, and I detest all my sins because of Thy just punishments, but most of all because they offend Thee." Jason looks down at the expiring soul. "In his holy temple there are many mansions. Your room has been prepared for you—"

Further up the battlefield, a militant's armored vehicle with a roof mounted fifty caliber chain gun heads toward the Marines. It stops so abruptly that the rear tires slide for a few inches in the soaked Earth. The chain gunner unleashes the full auto function of the weapon. Fifty caliber rounds mixed with tracers unleash its full fury on the men who have been known as the first to fight and the tip of the spear of all the American militaries.

Marines are cut down mercilessly. Jericho arrives to the front of the carnage and meets it head on. Having only mere seconds, he assesses the situation and devises a plan to defeat the troubling threat of the mechanized behemoth. He looks on as the casualty counts continues to rise. Without giving a second thought, he throws a smoke grenade and heads for the vehicle through the endless hail of bullets. His men follow suit and they too toss smoke canisters hoping to obscure the gunner's vision.

The militant gunner aims his weapon at the last coordinates that he seen the tip of spear titled men that clad themselves in dress blues to recruit unsuspecting children from high school. As the smoke fills his vision, he pulls down his helmet's visor with H.U.D. display that identifies friend or foe through various spectrums. He moves his eye over the infrared icon and blinks twice switching his view from day to infrared vision. The Marines again become crystal clear to the gunner through the smoke. Again, he lets loose another barrage of fire tearing into the troops.

Jericho takes off into a full sprint in the direction of the chain gun. The soldiers next to him just stare in amazement and bewilderment as Jericho disappears into the smoke. "Cover fire for the captain. Adjust fire to the right on my tracers," a Marine yell out. He fires in sporadic bursts. Within seconds the rest of the men that were in earshot adjusts their fire to give Jericho cover as well time to succeed in whatever he's planning.

Running into the smoke as rounds pock the ground and trees, Jericho advances on the armored vehicle. A few rounds hit him square in the chest. It knocks the wind out of him but he continues. One of the fifty caliber rounds strike his left leg. It doesn't pierce, but it causes a hell of a lot of pain and throws him into a summersault. Without breaking momentum, he returns to his feet continuing his run. Serpentining, not making himself an easy target, Jericho runs wide and flanks the vehicle hitting it from its side with his shoulder and a great deal of force. The vehicle rocks up onto two wheels. Jericho backs up for momentum and shoulders it again, this time flipping the vehicle on its side. The militant in the chain gun capsule curse a paragraph of expletives in his native tongue trying to figure out what happened, what hit them with such force. Below the chain gunner, the occupant militants of the vehicle instantly start scrambling for their side arms and looking for a quick exit to deal with the coming Marine threat.

The chain gunners' protected pod is suddenly torn from the roof of the vehicle exposing the gunner. Jericho pulls him out and throws him into the smoke in the direction of his advancing Marines. The militant lands with a loud thud and crackle of breaking twigs and branches of the underbrush. It takes him a few seconds to get his bearing. When he does, he quickly grabs for his Beretta M9, however before he can bring it to sights an advancing Marine puts a round through the militant's shoulder and stab the militant with his bayonet. He screams in pain, but it also a scream that conjures up adrenalin. The militant grabs the bayonet to hold in place while he pulls a serrated knife from his boot. Three more Marines as they run past stop and use their bayonets as well impaling the militant until he goes silent. They extract their blades and continue the hard charge. Death runs past and collects his blue soul sphere.

The rest of militant soldiers inside the vehicle looks at Jericho as he pulls a grenade from off his dragon scale manufactured body armor and tosses it into the armored vehicle. Jericho turns and runs as it explodes. The force carries him forward and into another tree. Knowing the blast was coming, he guards his head this time by crossing his forearms in front of him protecting his face and head. He strikes the small tree hard enough that it gives under his forced weight and breaks. He falls to the ground dazed, but functional. Within seconds, more opposing militant troops are on top of him. Unbeknownst to him, they were in the tree line behind the armored vehicle. Without hesitation, they begin kicking stomping and punching him. A few of them spear Jericho with their bayonets, and others fire rounds into him.

Feeling much discomfort, but very little to no extreme pain, Jericho gets to his feet and fights through the melee of enemy combatants. Militants look at their bayonets and see that their blades are either bent or broken. There's no blood on them. Before they can take stock of what was happening, Jericho turns on them. As he punches and kicks the enemy militants he can hear bone breakage with each of his strikes. Jericho's punches carry such force as he strikes the enemy, they fly off in different directions. His strikes are astounding and grimily devastating. He grabs two of the militants by their necks, raising them off their feet and breaks their necks simultaneously with only the smallest effort of applying pressure.

In the ethereal realm overlaying the reality 2814, angels battle demonic forces simultaneously alongside Jericho and his Marines. The Angelic forces are led by the Archangel Raziel who quickly dispatches three Demons above Jericho. He then lands behind the mortal captain, taking on two more fallen demons that are moving past Samsonic mortal. Raziel's weapons skills easily removes demonic heads from their bodies. With only a few seconds of respite, he observes and notes Jericho's progression in his hand to hand combat. The respite and brief connotation are quickly assessed as he hears an inhuman growl. Raziel squints his eyes narrowing where the growl originated.

"Possession." Raziel says.

Jericho tries to catch his breath when he hears the growl of what sounds like an animal. He turns, but before he can react he's shoulder checked by a huge burly militant. The sheer force of the shoulder check knocks him through two tree trunks and into shrubby and thick underbrush.

Raziel witnesses the blow and instantly knows the attacker's body may be that of a mortal, but its soul is not of human origin any longer, nor of this Earth. The Arch takes to the skies and studies the militant. Through ethereal vision, he can instantly tell that a fallen demon has possibly stepped through reality3814 to inhabit the husk of the mortal. 3814 overlays the current reality at a higher vibrational rate. He'd have to match frequency to give chase except there is not enough time. The ethereal battle that is currently ongoing could end for him disastrously if he takes the time and his mind off the present. He looks to Jericho and realizes this will be a test of his metal to handle this until he and his angelic knights can dwindle the numbers to a manageable size where he can pursue.

Raziel turns to address another wave of incoming when he hears a faint voice. He turns back and focuses his vision again. He adjusts his gaze and, in an instant, can see that the human host souls intertwined with that of the demon. His soul should register as red, blue or in rare cases white, this one appears gray and ashen. It's devoid of color meaning his soul has in fact been over taken and blackened by the possession. Raziel has to rethink his approach the second he has another moment of respite. Because the mortal still inhabits the body he cannot directly intervene.

In possession form the demon looks like a winding smoking gray mist snake wrapping around and intertwining through the body. The Arch takes a deep sigh at the turn of events for Jericho. Raziel turns and takes on another attacker. After dodging a series of blows and blades, the Arch moves with ferocity and grace as he repels and parries the attacks until he finds an opening. Once the defense of demon lapses Raziel quickly puts him down. Finding a moment in between the continuous melee, he assesses the battlefield. His angelic force is gaining no ground. They seem to be stagnated. He knows he needs an edge. Looking down at Jericho's new foe, he knows the captain needs one too. Raziel tightens his fist and pulls downward quickly. A torrential downpour of rain begins to fall.

Jericho absorbs the hit that he wasn't ready for. He's slow to get to his feet as the possessed militant is quickly on him.

"What is that odor? It's a familiar stench that I haven't come across in sometime mortal. I smell a familiar stink all over you," the militant states as he approaches a dazed Jericho. The militant kicks him through a ruined burned mud and stone structure that was once a meeting hall of the indigenous tribal leaders that once claimed this now hotly contested land.

"It's a pungent odor that I had long since forgotten. No matter, I will quell that insufferable smell by removing it from the confines of your soft clay shell."

Jericho watches as the militant pulls a machete from its sheath. "You will try," Jericho quips.

The militant approaches Jericho with the serrated long blade in hand. As he begins to raise the blade, Jericho nods his head, warning the militant to look behind him. Not wanting to fall for such a simplistic juvenile trick, he can't help but to; in a battle with multiple adversaries how couldn't he. The militant turns around and sees a priest half submerged in shrubbery holding an M-4 battle rifle. Before the militant can react, bullets tear into the chest of the possessed being. Priest emerges from the shrubbery as a squad of Marines follows him, also shooting and pushing forward. Having been struck multiple times damn near point blank range, the possessed militant falls to the ground dead.

As the Marines push forward past the recently deceased militant, they again come under heavy fire from more militants of the Destined Suns. The opposing troops continue firing on the Marines from a distance. Many in the Marine advancing force fall, but the hard chargers keep pushing through in one large advancing firing line. They advance through the trees and foliage under heavy rain just as the colonial troops did in the old theater of the Civil War. The force is focused and gives the illusion of being overwhelming with superior numbers when in fact they aren't. The Marines pass through the ruins of the burned-out village continuing their attack forward repelling the militants. The sheer overwhelming firepower sends them into a tactical retreat. Having been saved, Jericho takes a knee to catch his breath. One of his passing lieutenants gives him a nod, letting him know take a minute to compose himself while he heads up the charge and pursues the fleeing militants. Jericho nods back in acceptance of the break.

Priest halts his advance and falls out of the line advancement to tend to those that had fallen during the push and to make sure Jericho was okay. Priest screams, "Medic!" in hopes that one would appear to start treating the wounds of the injured. He throws down his empty weapon and runs towards Jericho.

"Saving your ass, again, has caused me to violate my rule to never fire a weapon in angst of taking a life. Now get your ass up, Jare," he says.

Jericho sighs and gets back on his feet. "That guy kicked my ass. Did you see that?"

Priest helps him up. "I know, I saw." Priest looks around and picks a weapon up and places a rifle in his captain's hand then pushes Jericho off in the direction of the fighting. "Go on!" Jericho starts to trot off but is quickly stopped by Priest. He grabs Jericho by the arm and spins him in the opposite direction. "That way, Captain. The fight is that way."

"Damn!" is Jericho's only reply.

"What?" Priest states as he gets ready to administer more last rites.

Checking his cargo pockets, Jericho acknowledges a painful fact. "My radio's gone. I need to call in a sit rep. If we're hitting this much resistance, we're not going to make the rendezvous with the Arcanian forces... Damnit!" Jericho starts trotting off but pauses briefly looking back to the Chaplin. "You good, Priest?"

Priest waves him off. "Keep going. I'll catch up. There's enough bodies lying around that I'll be tied up for a few. I have to give rites to these men... I'll grab their tags for you when I'm done. Now go, will you? Your men need you in the front." Jericho nods and runs off in a full sprint to catch up.

"If you find my rifle, hold on to it for me," Jericho says as he takes off in a full-on sprint.

"How am I supposed to know which one is your rifle?" states Jason as he looks around at the numerous caches of weapons. He spots one with the name Isis. "Oh! Must be the one with Isis etched on it."

Priest turns around and gets to the business of checking for survivors and those who dog tags would need to be collected. While taking stock of the tags, he references them to decide what denomination they were for the purposes of receiving last rites.

One of the Marines that was shot during the charge grabs Priest by his ankle. When Priest turns to acknowledge him, the wounded Marine tries to speak through his severely lacerated neck wound.

"Damn! No wonder the medic never came! You are the medic." Priest already recognizes that his condition is grave. "Shh! don't talk

Lance Corporal." Priest moves the Marine's hand from his neck to look at the severity of the trauma. Instantly, blood squirts from the carotid artery with each beat of his heart. Priest holds his neck to slow the loss of blood "Aww buddy! Shit! You're a mess." Priest looks at his dog tag. "You're Jewish huh? I'm Catholic by denomination, but does that really matter today?"

The Marine looks up at Priest, but his eyes looks past him into the dark hooded face of Death who's standing behind Priest. The Marine shakes his head no in fear of Death and what's to come, but Priest reads the no as, it doesn't matter today if you give me last rites.

"I don't think it ever has mattered, tell you the truth," Jason prattles on. "In the end, I believe we all go to the same place to be judged." He leans in close to the Marine. "Look, when you get there, if it's any consolation, you can tell them you died Jewish. I promise I won't tell, it'll be our little secret, huh?" Using his free hand, Priest uses his thumb to makes the sign of the cross on the Marine's forehead in blood. Priest begins… "In his—" Before he can say another word the militant that he thought he'd killed, grabs him by the pull strap on the back of his level-three body armor and throws him backward up and over his right shoulder.

Unable to control his descent, Priest lands in underbrush and red clay mud. Pain tears through Priest's back, but he manages to roll onto all fours and get to his feet quickly to look for his attacker. *God be merciful and keep me from doing harm to another,* he prays to himself.

The possessed militant just looks over his shoulder at the Chaplin. "There is no God, here today, Priest. Only me."

The possessed militant without any remorse steps on the head of the wounded soldier and slowly crushes his skull under boot hill. With speed that's unnatural, he's suddenly in front of Priest giving him a boot to the chest. Priest is on his back sliding through the mud. His vest took a large brunt of the impact redirecting it. Having the advantage militant jumps in an attempt to land on Priest breaking him. Before he can, Arch Raziel lands next to their exchange. Seeing Priest outmatched, Raziel checks his forehead. His date of expiration is not this day. Raziel nods gets around the direct intervention rule by kicking a felled tree in Priest's direction. The tree slides across the mud and into Priest knocking him clear of the militant before he lands. That brief reprieve was all the time needed for Priest to get to his feet again. Raziel nods at Priest and takes to the skies readying himself to encounter another demon.

Priest trying to regain his breath pulls a knife from the sheath on the inside of his boot. "I am a man of the cloth. I have no quarrel with you personally, outside the fact that if you try to kill me, I will defend myself. Do you understand me?"

The militant stretches his arms wide so that Priest can see his deity in his bullet riddled body. "No quarrel, Priest? Was it not you that riddled this husk with holes?"

Observing the militant, Priest realizes that his body is all tore up and should not be standing, let alone talking. Something that has taken a hold of Jason in his youth begins to rear its head. Not the fear compared to the thought of what's in the dark or the fear of public speech, but fear of the supernatural. The fear that echoes from childhood and never quite can be vanquished or made silent even in adulthood, the fear of monsters. Monsters like the one that entered his bedroom many nights in his youth.

"You... You should be dead. You should be dead," is all that Jason can muster.

The possessed militant moves inhumanly fast again and grabs Priest by his neck and raises him off the ground. He pulls Jason close so that he can look into his eyes, and even further than that, he wants to see the color of his soul.

"You say I should be dead? You'd have to have been alive first. Isn't that right, little Jason Priest?"

Jason struggles to talk through the increased pressure of the vice like grip around his neck. He can't speak. The expression on his face tells the militant that he now clearly understands what it is that is strangling the life out of him, a monster from another time, another plain. The one that stalked him in childhood after the Earthly monster left his room.

Militant releases the pressure slightly. "Quiet, be still. I don't want you passing away just yet. With you, I feel there is no need for introductions. You know me, do you not? I am that which watched you play as a child. I haunted your nightmares well into your adulthood. I haunt you even now boy. I'm the reason you called yourself picking up the cloth. You are but a mere con-man, a charlatan who wanted a free ride in life and protection. Protection from the nightmares, protection from the guilt of your deplorable desires, protection from me. The irony is, there is no protection for you, little Jason Priest. Nowhere you can hide. I've borne witness to your past and have decided that you will make a fine addition. You will be honored as a saint in the halls of Lucifer's coming kingdom. I will personally make sure you have a seat at our table— worthy to eat my scraps."

The militant releases the neck of Priest. Near unconscious, Jason falls to his knees, terrified and grasping for the sweetness of the oil and gun powder laced air. Although terrified, he's relieved that he can simply breathe again.

The possessed militant looks down at Priest. "Yes, there it is, on your knees. It's where you belong. It is there that you do your best graveling and whimpering, always begging for it to stop and realizing that it never will. How does it feel when you stand where I am; when you pass that same fear?"

Priest clasps his hands together interlocking his fingers and starting to pray. The possessed militant closes within to millimeters of Priest's bowed head, the rain drenching every inch of their being, water cascading down the bridge of their noses. Militant speaks in his archaic tongue. <"It will never stop. Your false God cannot hear your fabricated prayers. He can't hear the mind of those that are far from his purpose. Charlatan, flimflam, muurrrddderrrrr! How far you've fallen from the sanctity of your mother's protective embrace. Still the scared little boy that I remember.">

Priest slowly and purposely looks up straight into the dead dark eyes of the militant. He looks past the flesh of them. He looks into the depths of what has replaced the soul of his onetime Earthly enemy combatant. He looks into the cavern's void and the chains that binds the soul of the helpless man caught between this mortal plain and the ethereal. Fear no longer drives the soul of Jason. Compassion begins to take root. A renewed sense of strength and purpose invigorates the Chaplin.

The Archangel Raziel had returned and placed his hand on the shoulder of Jason. Although Raziel is bound by the rule of no direct intervention into the affairs of men, he can encourage a stout and resilient heart. Unknown to Priest, the Arch has granted him a strength to formulate a reply for the dark one who was removed from the holiest of holies. As Raziel speaks, the words pass through Priest. <"But, how can I not believe when you're very presence and verbal outcry dictate to me in a language that has long since been dead? If you are real Demon, then so is God.">

Priest once again finds possession of his tongue. "You see, Demon, it is because of you that I cry, 'oh, Lord save me!' It is you that single handily reaffirmed my faith. With my faith restored, I now know that I go to him—"

"–To burn," Militant says as he raises Priest's chin slightly. "You go to no God Priest. You come to me."

Militant pulls a knife slowly from the chest sheath of his bloodied and torn tactical vest. The militant's demon-possessed hand slowly raises the knife to bury it deep into the chest of the Chaplin. Priest closes his eyes and excepts this is the price for his sins. The bill has come due on the rot that he's allowed to fester and decay in his soul. The worst of what he believes himself to be... put aside; he thinks of all the things in life that he would not accomplish, all the tasks that would be left undone. He knew that war could possibly be the death of him, but he did not think that this would be the way that it ended. Flashes of his mother dance through his waning moments. Never knowing the touch of a woman intimately, only knowing the touch of monsters could not be suppressed in his fleeting moments. At that precise second, he knows his death is imminent and that the love for God that he claimed to have had, had taken a backseat to desires of the flesh. After all, that's why he was even here in the Congo to begin with. The Bishop thought to hide him here from unkind allegations. With his last breath all he could think is, *I'm damned!*

Jericho shoulder-checks the militant as hard as he can, returning to him the same blow he was given earlier. The force with the added momentum of Jericho's person carries them both through the air and back into the soft dirt and clay of the jungle's floor. The two continue sliding through the mud until enough of it builds into a mound which slows them to a stop.

Raziel nods his head in a sigh of relief of Jericho's intervention. For as long as the human soul was held captive by the demon, he could not intervene. Satisfied that Jericho should be able to handle this, he takes flight to continue battling the demonic horde that are fueling the hatred that fuels the battle for the Congo.

The possessed militant appears to rise from his back to his feet with no use of limbs. Unseen to Jericho is the phased interdimensional reality where the demon pulls the husk of the militant back to its feet before re-entering it. Jericho scrambles to his feet readying himself for the one on one conflict that he knows is surely coming. Militant flicks his hand, conjuring a gust of wind that is lightly-laced with hot embers of brimstone. Jericho places his forearms in a cross-guard block and takes the heat laced blast of wind. The hit is hard and unexpected. Jericho howls at the intensity of the burn. The force causes him to slides inches backward in the mud. The sleeves of his uniform burns away, leaving his forearms exposed, but no skin damaged.

The possessed militant's eyes squint as he realizes that there are no burns or any signs of injury to Jericho's arms. Having that moment of surprise on the enemy, Jericho charges the confused militant. Recovering from the shock quickly, the militant charges Jericho. The two collide, initiating a small shockwave of wind that shakes the water from the surrounding smaller trees.

Priest looks on as the two combatants exchange a series of blows and kicks. Jericho throws a furious combination of punches; which militant is able to interrupt. The demon blocks a blow from the right and uses Jericho's body against him to hip toss and sling him left into the side wall of a wood shack structure that recently caught fire during one of the resulting explosions from an earlier grenade. The shack was more than likely a home of one of the families that were cleansed by the Distant Suns.

Raziel again takes pause from his battle and lands behind Priest briefly. He touches Jason on his shoulder. Jason immediately has an idea. He digs deep into his rain-soaked cargo pants pocket and pulls his Bible out, opening it. Without a moment's hesitation, he flips through the pages which becomes increasingly hard as the rain continuously pelts the thin pages making them soggy and easy to tear.

Priest gestures the sign of the cross, and speaks to himself under his breath, "In the name of the Father, the Son, and the Holy Spirit." He then speaks loud enough in a boisterous voice to defy the demon within the man. "And in the synagogue, there was a man which had a spirit of an unclean devil, and cried out with a loud voice..."

An instant burning sensation ignites the ears of the possessed militant. "Damn you, Priest!" is all that the militant is able to utter before Jericho takes advantage of the distraction. Springing from the ruined hut, he lands a solid hit across the jaw of the demon-possessed husk, sending him cascading through a manmade stoned enclave's outer wall.

Jericho looks back to Priest and gestures by rolling his hands around each other quickly like a rolling tire. "Keep going! It's pissing him off and keeps him off balance. I need you to keep him off balance."

Jericho runs and dives through the hole. Priest follow him stopping short of entering into the enclave.

Raziel's irritation rises as he can only watch; for as long as the demon is within the human body, he's still bound by rules and can't take ethereal action and the fighting has been to continuous for him to pursue. The Raziel ducks a slash meant to separate his head from body.

He sends his right wing up quickly upper cutting his attacker. Dazed from the wing strike and his head at maximum apex, Raziel turns and cleaves the head of his attacker in clean strike. He then takes to the air again.

Priest continues reading scripture, "Saying, let us alone; what have we to do with thee, thou Jesus of Nazareth? Art thou come to destroy us? I know thee who thou art; the Holy One of God."

CHAPTER 31

It's dark with only little crevices of light entering inside. Jericho decides against switching on his L-shaped LED flashlight that's attached to his vest to illuminate the darkness. Turning it on would be giving away his position and practically be committing suicide. Instead, he slowly and methodically looks for the militant careful of each step, listening for any sound that would betray his foe. The demon, however, has no problem seeing in darkness. He uses the darkness for concealment. He watches and stalks Jericho from the shadows. Militant observes Jericho quietly trying to determine what makes him unique. He delves into the centuries of memories to recall where he's felt this presence, smelled the familiar scent. He attempts to look into the soul of his mortal pursuer, but finds it difficult.

He continues studying Jericho quietly as he looks from his position of concealment. He smirks at how careful the mortal is not to make too much noise that would betray him. *How idiotic this mortal is to pursue me here knowing that he's met a superior foe.* His observation of Jericho keeps him silent and in thought. *Odd this one is, but unique somehow,* was all that militant kept thinking. Unique enough that he knows he should retreat from this encounter to alert Lucifer of this gifted mortal, but to give in and retreat from a human was something he couldn't stomach. Execute the anomaly and take the corpse to Lucifer would be best he decided.

Twigs from the trees and vegetation litters the floor of the cavern. Each step for Jericho is trying as he hunts his prey in the dark. Or is he foolish in thinking that he isn't the prey? As he listens for any change in the stillness, he can't help but think of what a disadvantage he's put himself in by following an enemy into an unknown location. *Damn! This was idiotic. Isis would resurrect me just to kill me again if I get myself killed.*

"Who are you mortal?" the militant asks, his voice echoing through the darkness of the cave.

Jericho doesn't answer right away. He attempts to pinpoint the origin of the voice, but with the horrible acoustics and the echoing off the walls of the cavern he knows he won't locate it. He has to bait him. "Me? I'm no one."

"But you are... No mortal save one comes to mind that had strength like you and he's long since been departed this reality. Again, who are you?"

Jericho remains still. He knows he's being watched. "The question of the day is what are you? Angel, fallen, or some other being? Your wounds are beyond fatal. It's impossible that you are even moving around."

Footsteps shift in the cavern. Jericho head moves rapidly as he tries to anticipate the coming attack.

"I don't want to kill you just yet. You have spawned curiosity. First, I want to know what you are. I want to know what specimen I'd be taken back to my Lord." The militant moves again, rustling the interior to instill fear and ignite anticipation keeping his enemy off balance.

"I find it interesting you know archaic tongue of names that you shouldn't know. Impressive as well is that you know of our song? I truly believe that my Lord will be interested in the likes of you alive, but to be safe I'd think I'd just better bring you back vacated of life. Especially, if you're of the same blood that I believe you are."

The militant's annoying burn, which started in his ears now starts to spread across his entire body as Priests faint words still reach him. It's not the words that illicit the pain. It's key phrases and their construction that causes him to writhe in pain. The very edges of his demonic nerve endings went from an uncomfortable annoyance, to a simmer, eventually culminating in a full sensation of being on set ablaze, and only intensifies. "Shut him the fuck up!" He cries out in attempt to quell the intensifying burn.

From outside the cavern, Priest continues to recite scripture, he continues reciting biblical passages. He raises his voice to command authority; it affects the possessed militant a great deal more as Priest's confidence is firmly interjected.

The writhing pain becomes so unbearable and intense for Militant that he inadvertently gives himself away. Without hesitation, Jericho presses the attack. His punches are fast and fierce. The militant does his best defend and counter, but Priest's biblical call to action makes it impossible for the demon to concentrate. During a series of blocks, the militant gets lucky and catches Jericho's hand. He bends it in an unrelenting game of mercy, bending Jericho's arm with incredible unholy force in an attempt to break and mutilate it, but it doesn't break. Jericho in turn flows with the arm bar takedown. He flips forward to alleviate the pressure of the vice grip of the arm bar. He then rights himself, planting his feet firmly before stepping back for leverage. Once he has all the leverage he needs, Jericho pulls hard and slings the militant back out the enclave through the already-crumbling stone wall masonry. Militant lands hard onto the muddy soft African jungles of the Congo.

Priest continues reading and reciting the passages. He doesn't let up, not even for a second. He remembers his brief training during seminary of confronting demonic spirits and the art of spiritual combat. His instructor Father Omei had become gravely ill. A substitute that took over for the remainder of the semester was an exorcist that happened to be in town for a case that month named Father Dugan. Dugan had agreed to teach the class for the last few weeks. Dugan was far from an affable man, matter of fact, he was quite the opposite, but he knew his shit when it came to battling entities. At least that's what Jason believed. The man was missing an eye for cripes sake. Dugan is the reason, that Jason even gave thought to studying exorcism. It sure wasn't Father Omei.

Trying to wrap his head around the last few minutes, Jason deals with his sanity that he's now confronting an entity that can be explained away. A man that should be clinically dead is attacking him and his friend Jericho. Having to confront what he can only describe for lack of a better term as a demon, recalls Dugan stating an important tad bit of knowledge: to gain the name of the demon was paramount to have control and authority over it. With that thought renewed vigor and authority, Priest continues reading and reciting, "And Jesus rebuked him, saying, 'Hold thy peace, and come out of him.' And when the devil had thrown him in the midst, he came out of him, and hurt him not."

The possessed militant tries to stand and focus through the pain, but it keeps him wincing in terrible burning agony. "Stop, you fuck! I'll have your soul you keep—"

Priest stops reading and reciting the passage. "No, no! I won't stop, you most unclean foul thing." Priest gestures the sign of the cross.

The demon turns his full attention toward Priest. "I'll tear the soul right out of—"

Jericho grabs Militant from behind in a crushing bear hug.

Wiping the rain from his brow and eyes Priest continues, "And they were all amazed, and spake among themselves, saying, what a word is this! For with authority and power he commandeth the unclean spirits, and they come out."

The burn starts manifest becoming tangible. It emanates from the militant. Jericho can feel the heat himself. His nose hairs begin to singe at the odor of brimstone and burning flesh. "Let go of me, you bastard mortal!" The militant looks at Jason with enraged dead bulbus eyes. "I'll kill you, Priest. It is your death will be most unclean." He yells.

The Chaplin continues reading. "With authority and power he commandeth the unclean spirits, and they come out."

Jericho struggles to hold the militant. The heat becomes even more intense. In a last-ditch effort to escape, the militant throws his head back smashing Jericho's face. The blow is blinding as the bridge of

Jericho's nose take the full brunt. The nose doesn't break, but it draws a trickle of blood. His eyes instantly water up. The pain flashes right to the core of his nerve's pain receptors. He sees the blue flash that occurs when struck in the face and still Jericho holds.

Priest doesn't stop, he can't stop. "With authority and power he commandeth the unclean spirits, and they come out." Priest walks up to the militant and traces a cross on his forehead. "Tell me your name, monster!" he yells again with authority. "Tell me your name!"

Arch Raziel hovering has caught a moment of respite. He finds Jericho among the forest battleground and continues to look on as Jericho and the priest battle the ethereal. He watches in admiration of the boy who is destined to set the path correct if he doesn't succumb. *A lot rides on you mortal.* More than he personally thought should, but to question the will of Elohim was something that could have had him easily ending up where that demonic being was at this moment. *It's best to leave those matters to superiors far greater than I.*

A charging scream catches the Arch's immediate attention. *Damn!* Raziel thinks to himself as he dodges an incoming blow. *I've got to keep my wits about me.* Without looking, he shoots a heated plasma blast infused with and electrical charge giving beam and lava lightening effect from his hand. He briefly incapacitates another Demonic foe before dispatching him. The ethereal battle continues to rage on around him. However, he notices the bulk of demons retreating along with the retreating militants.

Motivated to get away from the Priest's reciting of biblical text, the militant gathers all of his strength and breaks free of Jericho hold. He turns and exchanges a series of blows and kicks. Jericho repels most, but is struck by a few. With each blow that lands, he can't remember if he's ever been hit so hard. Seeing the Demon break free, every fiber for self-preservation tells Priest to run. He doesn't. He holds fast. The militant looks to Priest and flips his fingers upward. The Bible that the Chaplin is holding bursts into flames. Priest continues from memory. "With authority and power he commandeth the unclean spirits, and they come out. Now, tell me your name Demon!"

Wanting the pain to stop, the demon possessing the militant husk finally submits. He yells "Crethos!" to the heavens, begging for the pain to cease.

Priest, exhausted, falls to his knees knowing that this spiritual battle is almost to conclusion. With his name, he can now command the unclean spirit to leave. He just can't find the strength to seal the deal.

With the pain diminishing, Crethos knows he has to end Priest immediately. As he starts to head his way, Jericho strikes Crethos hard enough that on the this plain of reality, the demon's grasp to the mortal husk detaches slightly exposing ethereal flesh just enough from the militant's possessed body that it's visible around the nape of the husk's neck.

Raziel seeing just that much of the demon detached and exposed from the body is all he needs. Without delay, he flies into a dive. He's precise when he phases his hand as he grabs hold and yanks the fallen demon by the nape of its phased neck and pulls it out of the mortal's body. The tattered remains of the militant husk fall dead as Raziel takes to the skies with Crethos. Raziel spins midair, slinging the demon like a slingshot into a tree. With a spinning whirl, the Arch quickly separates Crethos head from body. Satisfied that he is dead, Raziel continues to lead his reaming angelic knights in pushing the remaining Demonic horde into retreat.

Exhausted, Jericho falls to his knees to catch his breath as well. His hands embed in the muddy Earth creating impressions similar to those on the stoic Hollywood walk of fame. Jericho looks and finds Priest just staring at the body of the dead militant for a moment. He looks for any sign of life; satisfied there is none, he sluggishly gets to his feet and trots over to Jericho.

Priest falls to his knees next to Jericho. "Thanks for coming back, Captain. You good?"

Jericho still breathing heavily nods that he's okay. He takes a few more minutes to catch his breath. "When I didn't see you catch up, I figured something had happened to you. It was as if someone told me to come back and check on you to be more exact."

Jason hugs Jericho. "Thanks for coming back bro." Priest says as he gets to his feet and while helping Jericho to his. The two just stare at each other for a few seconds. They place their hands on each other's shoulders in camaraderie.

Having a moment to reflect on the past improbable few moments, Priest looks at Jericho as if he's ashamed of what Jericho might have heard about his past from Crethos. "You know, what he was saying—"

Jericho quickly cuts him off. "Was none of my business, Chaplin. I didn't hear a thing. When you're ready, if you're ever ready, you'll tell me. I've always known you weren't here of your own volition. C'mon, you fighting in the Arcanian Wars? Not hardly a choice you'd make on your own. Something brought you here. If you ever tell me, fine, if not... well that's fine too."

Jason continues to stare at Jericho before letting a smile through and nodding in a thank you gesture.

Jericho nods back. "Save it. If we survive the day, we'll have to compare notes of what happened here, Priest... But for now, c'mon, we've got a battle to fight."

Priest watches as Jericho takes off. "What the hell do you call what we just did?"

Raziel watches the last of his ethereal forces finish off the demonic. His toll was costly as he takes in those of his force that's been injured or sent to Palengrad. He glances at Jericho thinking, you *don't know how right you are. You still have many battles remaining to bring this all to conclusion.*

Jason waves Jericho on again. "Go! I still have a job to finish here and you have a war to tend to, Captain."

Priest turns and kneels over the body of the militant that just tried to kill him. "May this vessel that housed pain be cleansed and acceptable to you, oh Lord"

Jericho nods his head and begins to trot off. Raziel lands behind Jason and touches the Chaplin for support. "You have no idea how right you are mortal Jason Priest... He does have War to tend too. Your part in this tale has not been concluded either."

"Shit! This one isn't mine either." Jericho picks up a rifle, checks it for ammo and starts to jog along to catch up to the rest of his Marines. "When you're done, Priest, there's more ahead. Collect the tags of ours and find my rifle!" he calls out before disappearing over a hill.

CHAPTER 32

Angel's Spire - Day

Raziel's boots clack across the pure white marble stoned floors as he enters into the Spire. His chest plate and gauntlets are covered in splotches of dried demonic blood, battle-damage from parrying blows and taking more than few hits that he was unable to dodge and mud. Raziel is part of the third caste of the Angelic Celestial Order, but his skills are on par with those of his seconded-casted older brothers. As he walks through the Spire, the regular citizenry of Heaven's Golden City center pay acknowledgement to him as he's one known order of the Archangels.

Raziel battle helmet retracts from his face repacking itself into his collar line of his armor. He uses his forearm to wipe away the sweat and blood from the minor scratches that were incurred during his most recent campaign in the Congo. As Raziel approaches the Arch-emblem-crested door it retracts in on itself allowing him passage into the Arch's portion of the Spire.

At the back of the Spire are a series of white beams of light. They seem to extend into forever as they go up and down as far as the eyes can see. Raziel steps into one of the lights. Just as passing through a waterfall, Raziel emerges on the other side instantly and has been teleported to the Tactician War Hall of the Archs.

Michael through time and experience has become master tactician of the Archs. It's not a position that he ever wanted or thought necessary in the beginning, but he's excelled since his inception. Far removed from the conflicts as of late, he watches for breaches of Apollyonic Tunnels which demons travel to Earth' surface. The tunnels also serve as a backdoor to the vast realities. He hopes that he can cut off those backdoor routes as he spots them. Michael is wearing his traditional tunic that has his rank and caste in angelic glyph. It's their version of relaxed casual wear. As Michael studies the 4D holographic table constructed of the bluest of flowing water he's letting his wings stretch and retract. He's intensely studying Earth through the water and mist of the 4D constructs, but the view is that of the entire Milky Way Galaxy.

Raziel enters and salutes Michael with his fist across his chest. Michael nods and signals that protocols aren't needed. Raziel walks closer to the map and begins his debrief.

"The battle over the Congo was fierce. The battalion that I led has just about taking the west end. The East was silenced by men under Jericho. The fighting was heavy to loosen what control the fallen demonic had on the mortals. Under War's persuasion and the assisted suggestion of the demons they were killing innocents on a scale that was unacceptable."

Michael moves his arm and spins the holograph's construct. "Did the abomination show himself?"

Raziel nods his head. "He did, my captain. Jericho was unaware of his presence. The abomination, as you call him, was involved in a more distant battle from where we were. He was not so much worried of us; he knew we were no threat to him. And he still remains oblivious to Jericho. Although there was a breach of a soul enemy. Crethos was dealt with. He made an attempt on the boy not fully knowing what he was or his purpose."

Michael pulls his hands apart increasing the magnification of the water and mist construct. "Let's assume that Lucifer already knows of Jericho shall we? Have you heard from Raphael? He's not been able to report as of yet. His platoon was in a smaller operation in the same region."

Raziel nods yes. "Arch Raphael and I did meet briefly in the south. As reported from lips of Raphael who currently fights in the north. He reported if a force cannot be swayed or turned for Arcanian purposes then they are vanquished completely. Those who do submit are only an addition that will someday have to be rivaled by human forces... From what I've personally seen with my own eyes, his domination of forces are gaining ten times that of Persia's during the rule of Xerex. And like Xerex forces, those of military might that witness his strength wish to make it their own and they bend their knees in allegiance."

Michael looks up from the tactician's map. "I saw that intrusion of Crethos. I sent a team to seal the breach after he made himself known. With War fueling the prophecy as the seals are broken, they have become more powerful and emboldened. With the power that the fallen generate, I can track their movement, but this... this abomination that Lucifer's created, I can't track his movements. He exists just out of our line of sight." Michael turns and walks out to the balcony and looks down into the galaxies from Heaven with his own eyes.

Raziel walks up aside of Michael and peers over the balcony as well. "They are becoming more emboldened behind Imperial, Captain. Without the removal of the head..."

"I know!" Michael cuts Raziel off. He looks into the eyes of the young Arch. "You dare utter that name within these walls? Here of all places? It's sacrilege! It's blasphemy—"

"Or it's respect for an enemy that has garnered our attention. He is a force that commands respect. He dropped Uriel before our eyes. You were there— Brother, we've never had to engage an enemy of his like. Our Lord ordered his ancestors wiped from existence never to return. A king ordered a genocide. How powerful was that command? Now, Lucifer brought the long extinct lineage back and altered it somehow. It is not with a reverent tone that I speak his name. I speak the name Imperial for the enemy that he is." A single tear streams from Raziel's eye as his iris turns gray. "He bested Uriel. That not only commanded my attention, it garnered respect and made me observe him for the clear and present threat he is."

"And I have given him one as well and it is abomination," Michael shouts back.

Michael sees the hurt in Raziel at the loss of their brother no longer being among them. It still hurts, the feeling of loss and he feels as equally if not more than Raziel. Uriel was Michael's caste mate. Michael relents softening his demeanor a little and pulls Raziel close and hugs him. "In due time, brother… Imperial shall he be dealt with. Till that day, utter what you would like of him. Classify him as you see fit and I will follow. The threat of— Imperial is one that is real and present. Even I must concur the fact."

Michael releases Raziel and looks back down into the galaxies. "Help the rest of our brothers secure what remains of the Congo! Then, get yourself cleaned up, relax a bit then take these orders to Gabriel!" Michael passes a sealed scroll to Raziel.

Raziel nods and again places his fist across his chest, saluting Michael. "So, let your will be done, my captain."

As Raziel turns to leave, he notices that Michael is really focusing on something in the galaxy's midst. "Captain, what troubles command your attention?"

Michael leaves the display table and walks to the balcony overlooking the galaxies with his own eyes. He leans a bit closer over the railing focusing on a specific point in reality. "In the land of Moab, a notable concern long thought exiled to Palengrad just materialized into this system. It is someone that even I have not seen since before the time paradox had begun and has been absent long after."

Raziel walks to the balcony to see what has Michael concerned. "I see nothing out of the ordinary, captain. Should I investigate this new found concern of yours?"

Michael's wings stretch wide then retracts. "I assure you, he's there, just east of Jordan. He's of the first caste of the angelic order. His creation even predates my own."

Raziel looks harder, but is still unable to see anything.

"His light is one that you've never seen, but I assure you it is distinct and undeniable." Michael studies it a while longer. "I need to see the Prince."

Michael turns to Raziel placing his hands on his shoulders looking a bit worried. "Take leave, Raz. You have your orders. We all will convene soon." Michael gives Raziel a comforting pat on the arm before taking leave. He walks with purpose into the white beam of light at the center of the Spire and vanishes.

Raziel peers over the balcony again. Seeing nothing, he shrugs his shoulders and follows Michael into one of the many white beams of light, vanishing himself.

CHAPTER 33

NO DESTINY, JUST FATE

"Purpose has been assigned to us all. If you're not performing your purpose, then a piece of you will wither away each day ensuring your death from malcontent. If you find your purpose and take command of it, then celebrate for you will have a sense of self and happiness. You will be fulfilled in knowing that you are doing what you were meant for."

Isis Rayne

Jordan, Mount Ramm

In the blazing heat of the east, northwest of the East African Rift System an archeological dig is preparing for entry into an archaic chamber to get underway once the approved funds have been confirmed transferred and proper paper work stamped with the Jordanian seal of approval. The excavation is a privately funded artifact search and recovery by the independent board members of Eastern Michigan University's Archeology Department. The board was convinced to invest after a two-hour long presentation by their leading archeologist, Nathan Asher. He and his team were approved more than six months prior to the imminent recon of a discovered cavern that is ready for breaching.

The collective board of regents officially denied the excavation of the site in Ramm. Of course, that was officially, because they could not justify the expenditures to the already agreed upon year's budget and the fact of how much guess work was involved in the hypothesis and not enough substantiated by fact. However, that didn't stop individual members from having a personal curiosity of great religious interest. Those members of the board wishing to remain anonymous met in secret outside the purview of the university and agreed as an unofficial whole to back Asher. His presentation was compelling enough to spark great interest, enough that not only did the regents donate, they had no problem convincing their respective religious institutions to do the same as well. All parties across multi-denomination of faiths involved wanted to know if in fact a biblical relic that is of divine origin could truly be located where Asher and his team predict. And this was not just any artifact, but one that could prove the Bible to be a true inspired word of God. Asher would get his money to fund the small dig. However, to truly believe he was committed, the unofficial board members concluded that Asher himself would have to put up any expenses for equipment... to be reimbursed of course in full upon discovery of evidentiary proof of biblical relics that were described in the ancient texts of the Torah.

Dr. Nathan Asher was more than excited to pick his team. He knew for sure that his number one prodigy in antiquities and biblical history would be his first pick. Without a second thought, Dr. Asher picked his best pupil, Isis Rayne. He groomed her from freshman undergrad to be a shining doctoral candidate. Through much pain and strife and sleepless nights she was finally at the threshold of obtaining her Ph.D.

The sun reaches its zenith making the heat damn near unbearable. Each breath is an inhalation akin to opening the oven door to check on your roast and gulping a full breath of super-heated air. After gaining approval it took 24 days for Perseus Drilling to hit its mark of a depth of 4,500 meters starting from Jordan's surface. Within that depth, Asher made the call that the drilling had gone far enough once his geologist Zoe, a bright girl with a slightly crooked nose whose left nostril is observably larger than the other discovered rock and sediment from the period which she believed to be around the 1500 B.C. Within the sediment, though, she found traces of rock that was peculiar. Because the trace was minimal, she didn't think it noteworthy enough to make a deal out of and report it to Asher. She could not confirm out there in the field with her limited testing equipment, but she was sixty percent sure the pieces within the historical sediment could have been from the somewhat fabled Antediluvian period, the time between the supposed fall of man and Noah's flood.

The pointed serrated teeth and claws of the drill slows in reverse gear as the constant running water cools, it. The drill is retracted from the perfectly smoothed freshly bored hole. The drill clears from the hole completely so that the Zoe and structural inspector can begin the arduous task of checking the stability of the site after the immense manipulation of the ground. The women are quick but thorough, the inspection check last just over two hours. Having completed her task, the inspection agent looks over towards Dr. Asher and nods her head yes giving the professor permission that to repel is a safe as can be under the current conditions.

Having been given the green light, Isis happily smacks Dr. Asher on his back. "Welp, that's a go Doc." She's more excited than he is. Isis can see the adventure in the dark descent and the accolades to follow with a successful discovery. Asher on the other hand sees the injuries, lawsuits, and personal financial ruin if the dig turns up shit. Taking the slap on his back he reaches over and rubs his shoulder of the arm that is broken and strapped close to his body with a sling. Asher face turns up in slight discontent at the pain.

"Sorry, sorry." Isis apologizes letting a slight smirk show.

Asher just nods his head at her and waves her on to get ready for descent. Once the pain evens out he finds a slight smirk himself. Worried as he is, there is a tinge of excitement that he can't dispel at the prospect of six years culminating in this dig.

Isis was already partially geared, but now she could don all of it, even the self-contained breathing apparatus. She had started to gear up more than two hours prior to being given the okay. As soon as the ultrasound and sonar mapped the sight particularly the side tunnel which slid into a side cavern which branched off the main hole at about a 35-degree angle, she knew she found something big. Anticipation of being the first into a possible Israelite chamber in over two thousand years based off her research and countless scans, is almost more excitement then she could bear. The realization of the cavern being archaic and having been buried for centuries, to her feels equivalent to the first lunar moon landing and she would be the first footsteps.

Isis adjusts the mounted camera on her helmet and double checks her riggings. Satisfied that she won't fall to her death embarrassing herself or her profession, she pulls out her smart phone and taps the letter icon. A smile crosses her face as she scrolls through her e-mails between Jericho and herself. It's been days since their last correspondence, but she was aware that he was heading into the field and would make contact when he could. There isn't a day that doesn't go by where she doesn't long to be with him. The fact that they still haven't had sex is far from her thoughts in the mist of the dangers that he's been faced with, but still ever present frustrating her. Keep busy has become her mantra. In fact, keeping busy is what has brought her to this day.

With blazing speed, her fingers and thumbs dance across the face of the phones screen. She types: My time is now. Today's the day that I make momentous history… if only in the field of academia. LOL! I'm going in. Love you, baby. Will tell you all about it when I'm topside. Isis sends the e-mail, then places her phone in her cargo pant leg pocket. The structural inspector, an elderly bronze woman with an orange hardhat walks up to Isis and checks her riggings. She smiles and slaps her helmet signifying that she's a go to repel. Dr. Asher walks up to her next. He checks her harness a third time.

"You mind if I take pic?" Dr. Asher jokes as he pulls his smart phone from out his sling. "Give to the camera! Your best triumphant pose, nothing less." He laughs, making her laugh as he takes the picture of Isis strong woman pose. Laughing, she makes a serious face and does a couple of different poses before finally capturing one that would lament the front of her doctoral phot album. She holds her harness and looks into the depths of the hole. Dr. Asher seeing the perfect shot clicks the camera icon and freezes Isis' image for all of time. A moment that will never move further than that second. The pics you don't prepare for are the best. "Your rigs look great. We don't need you falling and becoming a part of any dead artifacts or relics that may rest down there." Asher points the camera for a selfie with him and her. Click and shutter sound paired with a flash and it's done. One for the media.

Isis reaches into a nearby orange plastic container box marked "illumination" and pulls two handfuls of glow sticks. She passes a few to Asher. They both revel in the immediate joy of cracking them just to give it a quick shake to intensify their glow. A little problematic that Asher has to step on his and pull it to crack it with his one good arm, but you learn to get along when disabled. At max illumination they drop them into the hole. They watch as they fall into darkness glowing all the way till they disappear into the far deep darkness. As they hit the floor in mass, there is a dot of light that gives Dr. Asher an estimation to branch off of the cavern entry tunnel that their most interested in.

"Isis, if there's any problem, Mel over there is geared up and ready to retrieve you," Dr. Asher says, as he points to Mel Mcquaren, their Jordanian rescue specialist.

Isis gives a half nod that can be seen is mixed with excitement and fear as time to descend draws nigh. She's the most nervous that she can recall in sometime. Her stomach starts to turn at the gravity of the undertaking she's venturing into feet first, literally. Finally, she pushes through the butterflies and catches Asher's joke about becoming a relic that he cracked to ease her own nerves and tension. "No, professor, we don't need that. However, if I were to become a relic, I know I'd be in great hands."

"The best, my dear," Asher replies. "Okay, now, stay calm. You've done this a hundred times already across other sites. Only difference is this time you're setting the trail for all of us to follow. Now, I have you on live video feed. We're all monitoring you. If you feel confined, short of breath…"

"Professor, I've got this. I promise to only step on the most important of artifacts and drop the most ancient of pottery as I stumble through the untouched graves." Isis smiles, trying to hold back from the loudest of laughs.

Dr. Asher's face becomes solemn quickly.

"I know, professor. This is a simple snatch and grab. I'm just messing with you. C'mon!" She punches him in the shoulder. He winces in pain again. "Per protocol, one set of feet inside to observe, document, record, and return. I will take shots before I even step down, professor. I have this, trust me. I think we should worry more about the glow sticks we dropped. We just polluted."

Dr. Asher cracks a half smile still believing she may be telling the truth in a perverse sense of humor. "I feel bad that it's not me going first. To ask you to take the risk for me is a bit much. Those that put their faith and money on the line expected me to do it. Now in a bind and short of funds I'm asking you to do this."

Isis attaches her line into the carabineer. "It's okay, professor, really just go easy on the arm. After all, you broke it repelling when I told you, you shouldn't do it in the rain. Your fault. My gain. Now pay attention to that screen." She laughs. "And walk me through any hard spots if you see that I'm stuck."

Dr. Asher gestures a look at me now modeling pose with his arm in a sling. Now you're giving me orders. What has this world come to? A paradoxical shift?"

Isis sits and swings her legs over into the opening. "Just remember how I took the bull by the horns in this instance when you confer that doctoral on me next month."

"I assure you, Miss Rayne, if I confer you next month— if? It will be received by the most gracious and humble student I see now before me possessing not a hint of arrogance, right?"

Isis smiles nodding and scoots up to the hole's opening before sliding down feet first descending into the subterranean levels of Mount Ramm.

Isis places on her goggles and descends into darkness cutting on her helmet lamp for increased visibility. She slowly repels into the manmade abyss, careful not to descend to fast in an attempt to avoid the harsh and painful sensation of rope burn. It takes her thirty-two minutes stopping for rest and hydration before she reaches the depth of the branching tunnel leading to a side cavern. Once there she kicks backward off the smooth drilled wall to gather momentum swinging forward entering into the creviced tunnel that slides at a steep angle into a larger open cavern. It takes time, a great deal of patience and maneuvering to defeat many of the natural barriers. Finally, she hits a smooth portion that has been carved out by water over the centuries.

Her radio crackles to life in her ear of Asher checking on her progress. "We see you slowed considerably. Is that fatigue?

"You wish!" Isis says. "It's become extremely tight down here. I had gotten hung up a few times, but I'm through. Do me a favor would ya? Could you take the slack out the rope? I have a natural slide formation down here that I don't want to necessarily take a ride on."

"Understood. Ropes being drawn taut as we speak. Just take it slow and easy," said Asher.

Scooting on her posterior, she slides down the incline. "Aww! You worried about me Profess—" Isis heel catches a bit of gravel sending her foot into a slight slip. The slippage shifts her weight bringing her whole body into the slide. Before she can control her descent, she takes off down the slick smooth rock loosening more gravel as she goes. The excess flowing gravel aids her bid in gaining more momentum. Isis rides the flowing loose gravel until it launches her off the end of the smooth surface into a short freefall into darkness. Her two safety lines draw taut leaving her dangling and breathing fast and shallow. Funny, how fear increases and enacts the body autonomous responses. She inhales a deep breath to even her breathing out then exhales. Calm, Isis rotates herself around while dangling from the rope take in a full recorded view from her helmet mounted camera before disturbing the cavern any further. Once recorded she gently lets herself down.

"Isis, the ropes went tight. Your view was bit obscured by the lighting down there but it looks like you were in trouble. You good, you alright?" A frantic Asher crackled over the comm.

"No problem boss, everything is fine. I'm peachy," Said Isis as her feet find footing on soft sanded ground. She had a bit of scare, but no need to worry the professor anymore than he already is. Isis looks around slowly taking in the scenery when suddenly, reality hits her, she's walking on ground that has not been walked on in centuries. Her first initial gaze focuses only on the illuminated glow stick pack that slipped from her belt during the slide in. She's careful to observe that they didn't break anything vital upon striking surface. Careful of where she steps Isis walks over and picks up the glow sticks and tosses them carefully further into the cavern where she can only guess empty pockets of sand and rocks are. She looks in all directions before tossing the remaining glow sticks to illuminate the rest of the buried ruins. *It's a risk throwing them around somewhat blindly, but then again falling into crevice or breaking an ankle is no good to the excavation either.* She thought.

Isis keys the mic on her Motorola X27J radio. "I've touched down, professor. The caverns are bit more expansive then we originally guessed."

"How expansive?"

"Without proper lighting I can't truly gauge it, but I'd say a few city blocks at cursory glance. The cave looks to span on forever."

"Isis, dear, I was only able to copy half your transmission. I need you to repeat. I think that all I copied was that the specs aren't too far of—" Radio goes out.

"Dr. Asher, come in again! I didn't copy the last transmission. Is the camera transmitting?"

Dr. Asher standing topside studies his tablet. The night vision camera that Isis is wearing isn't working properly. It's full of static with no visual at all. As much as he delves into the interworking of the system that he helped design, Asher is clueless to the instant malfunction. He can't figure why the equipment is not synching or connecting.

"Isis, if you can hear me, transmissions have apparently gone dark. I have no eyes on you, nor ears to copy your transmissions. It's no longer the ideal of conditions. Asher looks around at his rescue tech and the geologist Zoe. He makes a judgement call. "I'm going to permit this a little while longer why we try to re-establish communications." Specifically looking at the rescue tech Iserit Asher says, "Get connected on that line! Start your descent when I give the word." Asher turns back to the radio. "Isis, did you acknowledge, communication has gone dark? If you can hear me you have five minutes then we're pulling you up and starting Iserit down?"

Dr. Asher Immediately retrieves his cell phone and begins dialing a number for technical support to sync his gear.

Isis still steps carefully as not ruin the integrity of the recent discovery. Although her communication equipment has taken a dump and isn't working, her repel line hasn't been yanked yet. She knows that Asher is more than likely working the problem permitting her to look around as much as she can before he has to call it and pull her up. She looks carefully around the cavern, making a mental note of the layout of her first official find that she'll receive partial credit for.

While looking around Isis reaches down into her cargo pants pocket and takes out a pencil and mini notepad. Immediately she tries to draw a sketch, not knowing how much time she has before Asher grows too worried and pulls her up. Every few steps could be her last for the day, so she purposely moves the rope to the right slightly to signal that she's moving and is okay. It's a signal she previously worked out with the team. She's just unsure if the signal will be read correctly with the line intertwined between stalagmites. She remains methodical in her movements; anything that moves the rope beyond deliberate could result in a misinterpretation of a perceived danger resulting in a bailout notification to the safety team above rendering her actions concluded, which would have her pulled out immediately.

Moving through the cavern she reaches an abundance of ancient pottery. She notes where it's positioned. She squints her eyes and looks for natural signs of decay of the materials, she looks for the years of accumulated dust and sand that should be covering the artifacts, but there's nothing. The cavern although untouched for centuries looks as if it was abandoned yesterday. Looking at the pottery outside of the normal that it appears new, it's just that ancient pottery. Museums are full of them. There nice, but expected. What Isis is in search for is the unexpected, so she isn't so enthralled with the clay of the ancient Israelites.

What the doctoral candidate archeologist is really seeking is a possible fact that has become fiction. Her intensive three-year investigation that she conducted in secret alongside Dr. Asher's search for holy artifacts tells her that her find and claim to publication is in this cavern. She's looking not for a relic, but a body. A set of remains that could turn religion itself on its head. Sure, she'd have to share credit with Asher, but her name being associated with finding the first sound proof of a biblical character thought mythical nonsense would lead to astounding fame in academia and possibly beyond. The thought of re-writing religion itself now drove her passion; passion that didn't really ignite until she saw Jericho pickup and slam that tombstone years ago. She knows what he told her wasn't the whole truth, so, she'll find it the answers wherever she can till he does.

Not knowing if she is recording, Isis continues speaking anyway. "Professor, I have one indigenous to the cavern." She uses her high powered Streamlight Flashlight to illuminate a particular section of the cavern. The stone formation is different from all the others. Within the formation is a linen wrapped remains. Before entering, she pays particular attention to the archway. As she runs her gloved fingers across the archway of the smooth rock, she knows instantly that it's marble. Her fingers slide over the grooves of the glyphs that cover the way. Isis takes a knee and retrieves her camera and begins to take a series of digital photographs. After a series of shots, she checks her photographic work only to realize that all the shots are black and void.

Shaking her head in a mix of confusion and frustration, Isis just continues investigating with her remaining time. She again pulls out her notepad and pencil to start a sketch only to realize her previous sketch she had completed upon entry has vanished. *What the fuck!?*

A tinge of fear sends her neck hairs up at seeing her sketches dissolved, but more confusion than fear starts to well up in her. *Calm down, maybe I just thought I drew a sketch in all the excitement of coming down here. I'm lying to myself but it's working,* she thought.

Putting pencil to paper, Isis again starts drawing, but this time it would be of the magnificent archway and the mummified remains of a lone singular person that rests among the pottery. As she roughs out the edges, the sketch takes form and starts to resemble what she knows to be the inside of the old King Solomon Jewish Temple that was destroyed in seventy A.D. It was a smaller scale and very ceremonious.

Without manipulating the remains, she looks carefully at the wrappings to see if she recognizes any pattern in the garment. Just off of a glance she knows it's Hebrew in origin. Her breathing becomes more intense as she starts to get excited. Knowing that Asher will have her ass, she can't help but examine the skeletal remains. The body looks as if it was sacrificed upon a pyre on the alter. The body is blackened and scorched, but the garments are untouched of any ignition point of flame. Only age has desecrated the garments and that was only slightly.

Again, she speaks, hoping her log is recording. "At best guess, a male, possibly elderly when he died is what my assumption is looking at his teeth. The pottery and the garment tell me that this male was more than likely Hebrew, maybe even an elder or someone of prominence." She looks at the pottery. *It's all intact. The eerie thing is again it looks as if it was only buried yesterday. Age has taken no effect on the clay.*

Isis whispers to herself the mantra that Asher always tell his students. "Follow the evidence of time. If it happened there will always be a reaction."

A piece of wood catches Isis's eye. It's a carved staff. The detail on the polished wood was more than intricate. Embedded deep into the wood are the same glyphs that were on the archway. *Proof, the Hebrews were in fact this far during the supposed exodus. This doesn't explain why there is no evidential proof they were ever in Egypt. This is most curious, what are you doing out this far from home Hebrew?*

A booming baritone voice erupts in the darkness. "Incredible that a creature such as yourself have found your way down to such depths. A wondrous species, indeed, you are. Now close up the book Daniel until the time that has been appointed."

"My name is not Daniel," said Isis.

"That remains to be seen Flightless Bird." The voice replied.

CHAPTER 34

Ardenne, France

An elevator opens on floor thirty-seven in the Echelon building in Champagne Ardenne, France. A bald Nubian man in his mid-thirties wearing a fitted three-piece black suit, black shirt and a white skinny tie with a red cross on it emerges from the elevator holding a black binder with a raised silver metal cross on the cover. He places on his black rimmed eyeglasses as he straightens the same miniature designed red cross pin on his lapel. Konado Addi scratches his silver goatee as he passes others in the hall who are dressed as similar as he. Exception if it could be called one is that the women, however, wear black skirts, but otherwise appear similar in fashion down to the same white tie with the red designed cross and lapel pins. As the Nubian approaches a dead-end at the end of a hallway, an access panel opens in the wall about chest level. A retinal scan slowly emerges requesting identification. He bends down and places his eyes to the retinal scan. After a series of tones, the wall that was a dead end becomes visible frosted glass and slides open. The Nubian walks in on a meeting in progress and sees he's the last to arrive.

"Apologies for my tardiness, Grand Master Brashear," Konado says while bowing as a sign of respect and further apology.

The members of the meeting were all facing a 77 inch razor thin television. The subject of the program had just ended when Konado made his late appearance. The Grand Master's chair spins around, revealing a woman in her mid-fifties. Her hair has become more silver than auburn. Her glasses are black and thick rimmed and a suit tailored to her still athletic curves of her body.

Konado Addi finds his place at the massive wooden black table with an equally massive red Knight Templar cross logo painted across the massive table's top.

"Apology accepted, Knight Commander Addi... We know you have a lot to monitor and assess in your particular region, which has been most busy as of late. Speaking of your region, what news from the Congo?"

Addi stands and opens his binder to reference. "At most recent check in, the Knight Commander of the region reports that the Arcanian forces as well as the United States Marines are making a final push to bring the Destined Suns to heel. Casualties have been mounting on all sides of their uneasy alliance. I'm also sad and inclined to report that a few of our embedded operatives have been killed in the most recent conflicts on either side. The most notable was our Knight Lieutenant who was embedded under the newly promoted Colonial Rusain."

Grand Master pulls her glasses off and sets them on the table. "That is troubling... Do we have any other operative high enough to keep tabs on the Nephilim?"

"Grand Master, we do not that I'm currently aware of."

The Grand Master nods, giving Addi permission to be seated. She looks around the massive table that has capacity to sit up to more than a hundred of the highest ranking of the Templar Order. "Was it coincidence that our covert operatives were killed in action or were they discovered then assassinated?

Brashear stands. "All signs of the investigation points to the former. Just bad luck in a very intense battle. However, the investigation is still preliminary and the findings could change.

Brashear just gives a dismissive nod that all operatives just happened to have been K.I.A. Brashear leans forward in her chair placing both elbows on the conference table, "The Church has charged us with the most sacred of duties by keeping tabs on this Nephilim.

We are all no strangers to what happens in the unforeseen shadows of this world. We each have seen a portion of it and even in some instances directly dealt with what we can only classify as existential spiritual threat for a lack of a better term, otherwise we would not be here in this division. However, with the orders that have been coming down the pipeline lately our intelligence suggest we can assume the Vatican has been compromised and heavily influenced by the Arcanian Empire. Where we once found support there is only push back now and extreme cutting of funds. Lest history repeats itself, it may be time to take certain… precautions. We all have studied history of the events leading to Friday the 13th, we are no strangers to the Vatican's history of betrayal."

The forty-seven in attendance of the meeting all start to whisper and talk amongst themselves. Those not in attendance in the brick and mortar room, attend via electronic mounted tablets that raise from the table, allowing those in distant lands to attend digitally.

"The Vatican infiltrated, surely not, because If that is the case then the hour is later than we estimated and the seals have already been broken," Addi says as he stands. "If the Vatican is compromised, what hope have we to defend against this threat if not backed by the resources of the church?" Addi sits.

"Knight Commander Windsell of the Queens Army, ma'am."

Grand Master presses a button in front of her, which lights a green light in front of Windsell which signifies to all he has the mic and the floor to speak. "We recognize Knight Commander Windsell, what do you have to add?"

Windsell stands. "Thank you, Grand Master. All that are in attendance today have known since inception of this countdown of biblical prophecy that we'd play a part. Each of our sects have been aware over ages that we were counting down to this inevitability. We knew when the antichrist first touchdown that the end of days was not far off. As of 0837 hours todays date, a secret fund was turned over to the Order in excess of one hundred million dollars. That was without the Raptu initiative being initiated. If your contact on the inside believes the Vatican is in danger of falling under the sway of this Lucien Arcane, I suggest... No, request that we crack open the Raptu Ragnarök scenario."

Addi stands and raises his hand. "I second it." Then, he sits and waits for the vote.

Grand Master stands. "In this zero hour we put it to a vote. All in favor signify by saying—"

All the members in attendance raise their hands unanimously saying "Aye."

"The ayes have it. Ragnarök has been passed. I will immediately initiate Save Chance and contact the Grand Prior of that region so that she may begin her planning. Understand once the Grand Prior executes the will of the Knights, we will be revealed and the conflict that has been brewing for centuries will once again come for us."

Addi again lights his response and stands. "Let Lucien come and he will find the Knights Templars ready. We will not go silently as we did when the king of old betrayed the order. The world may not be aware of this Imperial, but we are well aware and have started contingencies to deal with him. Lucien is not all powerful, there is only one that is and we must have faith that he will see it through to the end that was foretold."

Isis still startled by the voice is on her feet in an instant whipping her flashlight in every direction. "Who are you?"

The voice address Isis again. "Daniel, I command you to keep the message of this book secret until the end of time, even though many people will go everywhere, searching for the knowledge to be found in it." The disembodied voice echoed through the cavern.

It's behind her. No, it's in front of her. *Damn! The voice sounds as if it's everywhere.* Isis keeps frantically searching for the source that keeps calling her Daniel, but she sees nothing in the illuminated interior. She turns slowly counterclockwise finally catching a glimpse of a silhouette of what resembles a tall silhouetted man.

The unknown man walks into the light beam of Isis' flashlight. Like Michael and the rest, the angelic ethereal order, his boots are knee high and resembles white polished marble. His pants are white with an even brighter white strip down the sides of each leg. His coat is a modern slender cut white slim fitted trench coat where the length stops just below his knees. The trench's collar is cut in a Marine Class A uniform's high neck with a hood. He has dark skin and wears the white hood pulled over his head.

Isis is taken back in a brief instant of fear. "Who the hell are you?"

The unknown celestial walks up closely to Isis and slightly bends at the waist to peer into her eyes looking deep into her soul. The celestial is almost two meters in height. Looking through her husk at the real Isis, he smiles at what he finds and repeats. "Daniel, I command you to keep the message of this book secret until the end of time, even though many people will go everywhere, searching for the knowledge to be found in it." He winks at her.

Isis returns his glare right back at him as her mind races a thousand miles a minute. "Daniel, close up the book?" She repeats to herself under her breath. "What the hell are you saying?" Isis, slows her thoughts, controls her breathing. *The man isn't attacking or acting dangerous, he's talking as if I should know what he's yammering about. Think, slow down, think… He's testing me. This is a test.*

He continues to slowly walk around her and observe her mannerisms.

I get it. It's a verse. She answers. "Daniel twelve, four, old testament," Isis answers.

"So, it is. So, it is… Daniel twelve, four… Impressive. I see that you study scripture closely. So, you will understand and are not able to claim ignorance. Just one scripture source or are there many you pull resources from?"

"Many." She answers. Although managing her fear, she yanks on the rope and pulls it left to clue topside that she's in distress. She does it subtly behind her back. *Professor, get me out here now.*

Fear rises throughout her body, but she does well hiding it. She watches the stranger and notices the hilt of his blade. Isis, finally succumbing to fear, loses decorum and starts yanking on the rope like a crazy woman and alas it doesn't move. The only portion of the rope that is able to move is the portion that she's holding in her hands. The rest of the line that heads topside is frozen.

"Professor, get me out of here! Please, help me!" she screams at the top of her lungs.

"Calm yourself, flightless bird. I'm sorry that your name escapes me, which rarely happens, but all the shouting is of no use. The professor can't hear you, nor anyone else for that matter. For the moment you and I are sitting outside of your system of reality. Time has all but stopped, save you and I." He again draws in close and reads her forehead. "Remarkable... Child of the creator, I simply would like to, ugh! How do you say? Ahh, yes! Have words with you. Forgive me for delay in syntax, it has been some time since I've spoken to anything or anyone." The celestial being gestures for Isis to sit on a nearby boulder. "No need for you to waste the energy life of that object you hold there in your hand any longer is it?" The celestial points to Isis' flashlight. He adjust something under his sash and then begins to illuminate himself brightly. The cavern looks as if it's twelve o'clock in the afternoon.

Isis squints her eyes trying to see past his bright aurora. *Impossible.*

"And, yet, it is so. And still here we are," quips the anonymous host. "It seems that after Jericho revealed himself and his purpose to you that impossible would no longer thrive in your vocabulary, still you think impossible. I would attest improbable, but not impossible."

Isis thinks for what seems an eternity on her current predicament. *The rope is suspended in midair and can't be moved. A possible celestial being that shouldn't exist is talking to me which validates all that Jericho revealed to her of where his strength more than likely came from. She* concedes following his gesture and sits on a smoothed rounded large boulder. As she sits, she can't help but think that she didn't notice the boulder before sitting.

"Comfortable? Good. We may exchange words and ideas yes? Again, forgive me if my vocabulary seems a bit delayed." The celestial waves his hand and a boulder that has been positioned since the formation of the planet loosens and breaks free of its confines and slides over to him as if someone slid him a folding chair.

Seeing the rock bend to the will of the being's thought should continue to scare her more, but she tells herself that he hasn't hurt her yet so, she must be safe for the time being.

"I must admit that I'm surprised at the tenacity of mortals over the centuries. Once your kind puts mind to a task, you all are a persistent lot which reaps great benefits. All because of that tenacity… Incredible. All of you always in search of knowledge. Then there are those of you that don't except the written narrative. No… you few are constantly looking for evidence that there is more then what you've been told. That is why you're here today yes? Proof of something greater?"

The being digs both of his hands into the dirt and grabs two handfuls of Earth and transfigures them into stone cups with water. He passes one to Isis.

"You have no idea of the gravitas of the situation which you have upended this day do you?"

Isis accepts the cup and eyes it before taking a sip. "First I'd have to know what I've done that is so upending?"

The celestial again moves his hand in a come hither gesture. Isis' boulder slides closer to him with her on it. He carefully looks her over. "I normally keep a distance from such matters as trivial as human and celestial interaction, but I was curious of the being that would have me alter the course of my best laid plans which I have not been called on to rectify since Lucifer went rouge."

Isis just stares at amazement at the being talking to her. The name he just stated sends an unfamiliar shock through her soul. She then looks over to the centuries old human remains under the archway.

Suddenly, all that is happening starts to make sense to her. *"That body, that has to be why he's here."*

He leans in closer to her. "Now you're beginning to understand. Wasn't such a linear exhaustive pace was it? The body is why I'm here." The being takes a sip of the water. "I can't taste this liquid. There is an abundance of it, across this particular planet, but yet I can't taste it and it is odorless to me in this reality. Turning his attention back to Isis. "Come now, let me hear the scripture… You know the ones I speak of which pertains to this intrusion on this most sacred holy ground. At least sacred to your kind."

Isis turns back and looks the being in his light gray eyes. She just holds his gaze.

"The scripture?" she repeats at a loss.

"Yes, go on, let me hear it!"

Isis tries to remember a scripture, but for the life of her she doesn't recall one at the moment that would fit this situation. Then if she does recall, how the hell does she recite the exact one he's looking for? The situation is all too excitable and surreal for her to concentrate. She can't remember any sort of scripture. Suddenly, there it is, like a lightning bolt flash it comes to her.

"I have one."

"You have my complete attention, dazzle me."

"It goes, so 'Moses the servant of the Lord died there in the land of Moab, according to the word of the Lord. And He buried him in the valley in the land of Moab, opposite Beth-peor; but no man knows his burial place to this day.'"

Isis looks around and realizes that she is in the former land of Moab.

The being in white nods in acceptance. "Until this day flightless bird, no one knew his where about… Until this day."

Isis keeps reciting. "Although Moses was one-hundred-and-twenty years old when he died, his eyes was not dim, nor his vigor abated. So, the sons of—"

"—Israel wept for Moses in the plains of Moab thirty days; then the days of weeping and mourning for Moses came to an end." The celestial being finished. Having closed his eyes listening to Isis recite what he believed to be poetry he asks her, "And where's Moab young one?"

Isis, realizing the point that the stranger is making, answers, "Jordan. Where we are now."

The being reaches out and touches her hand. He instantly knows her whole life.

"Isis, what a pretty name. The Isis you are named after was the first daughter of Geb in ancient Egyptian mythology or was it Kemet mythology? Not so sure anymore, the days of man all seem to run together after a while; couple that with the penchant you all have to rename cities, it becomes quite bothersome. I digress. A beautiful soul she had though, the real Isis I speak of. I met her once when she was newly created and exited the well of souls. So bright, so powerful."

The being stands and as soon as he does the boulder that he was resting on slides back to its original settled position. He opens his eyes and raises his index finger to his lips. "Daniel, I command you to keep the message of this book secret until the end of time, even though many people will go everywhere, searching for the knowledge to be found in it."

He walks over and touches Isis' face.

"The command of Daniel, which has been in play and repeating in constant, has been silenced this hour. All things appear in the matter of eschatology will be laid bare. The book has been opened by you this day. The convergence of gods and mortals is now inevitable. It is just the matter of will the road to conflict be expedient."

The unknown being turns and begins to walk away.

Isis stands quickly. She doesn't know why for a second, but then she realizes that she has been one to always seek answers. This moment was no different. She has to talk to him.

"Are you not going to try and stop me? It's why you're here right? To stop me. If this discovery will—"

"—Will only expedite the coming Armageddon if you lay claim to those bones. If you make others aware, you will only increase to the already overburdened woes of man. Look at your world. I think you've all been taxed enough would you not agree?" The celestial says cutting her off.

Isis needs to understand, she has to keep him talking "How? Men are already fucked, in case you haven't noticed. This discovery here will pro—"

"—Will prove nothing." The celestial turns around toward Isis. "God through Moses parted a sea and mortal men did not believe. Elohim then sent his son to reconcile all. In his span of three years, he defied all laws of your physics and reasoning and still men did not believe. What you call God has given you all insight into your destruction and yet, no one believes. If you leave here with those bones in tow flightless bird and make your discovery known, the ideals of the many religions will collide in an unending holy war to disprove what you claim. Man cannot exist without the lies and dogma of man-created religion. So much so, that man's inability to reconcile the destruction of that most basic belief will lay waste to a third of the Earth. If that happens, pestilence will ride and he will not be merciful. Mortals created boundaries of the mind to understand and put things in perspective that is far beyond them. They are irrevocably small thinkers, boxing themselves in an endless conundrum never thinking past the reality they perceive. It's laughable that you look to superior advanced beings and call them gods. Gods would have mercy."

Isis face betrays her thoughts to the being. She hears and knows that what he says rings true.

"Whatever is not destroyed quickly will waste away in disease and famine." The being squints his eyes at Isis as if looking deep into her soul. "But then you already knew this even if you don't want to admit it."

Isis looks down toward her feet in a semi defeat. She knows he's right. "Who are you?"

"Who am I? I am inconsequential this late in the hour. I am now merely a spectator watching the Shakespearian play of men in the final act. Nothing more. I've written the way long ago. I'm just here to ensure it comes to pass and that the most fact changing and relevant participants are on the board and in play in this most mercurial game." The nameless being turns and walks away and as he does so, he starts to vanish as he shifts realities. "I am called Fatetanen in my native tongue. I have been given the name, Fate in your tongue. And it seems Isis Rayne, your part in all of this is still yet to be played." Fate completely vanishes.

Isis looks around the ruins. The rope near her hand once again moves, and she realizes time has begun again. She then looks upon the remains that have been identified as Moses and can't get past the fact that what she has worked so hard for to define herself esteemed in academia has just been met with celestial force that has forewarned her of a possible calamitous outcome that would be less than favorable if she pursues her discovery. Her name added to the greats would have been a stellar achievement. This is that gut check moment that everyone experiences in their lifetime. Her thoughts are interrupted when her comms crackle to life.

"Say again, Isis? Your transmission went garbled after you said you've touched down." Dr. Asher could be heard saying over the transmission.

Could she be so cold as to bring about the woes that Fate just prophesied about? *If that is who that truly was.*

"So be it Fate… Help me close the book," Isis yells out, hoping that he heard her.

Fate's voice again disembodied, "consider this matter reprieved after you conceal the remains of the one they once called Moses. Lucifer must not learn where they are for that is the very reason they were hidden. However, I can no longer assist in closing the book. You may delay this chapter to a later period, but you have already arrived at the appointed time and set in motion a path that cannot be undone."

It's fate as you mortals are fond of saying and no one knows it better than me... I inked it."

Isis keys her mic Taking a breath before speaking. She then releases the Mic. "So, no matter what choice I make today, what will be will be? That is not free will Fate."

"What made you believe that there was such a notion? He says. You have opened the book by stepping in a place you did not belong. The discovery has been made. The secret has been broken open and laid bare for the world to claim. If it is not you to make the discovery known, then Asher will find it later. Your tenacity has seen to this. Your hubris has carved a name that will rival and surpass Julius Oppenheimer. You have unwittingly become destroyer of worlds."

Isis feels like her heart has sunk to the bottom of her stomach. She starts to breathe rapidly and shallow again. "I... I can say there's nothing noteworthy here." Isis depresses her mic, "I only see pottery, doctor. It appears we've went bust." Isis takes off her helmet with the camera affixed to it. She places it on a rock shelf about her height facing the pottery. She then turns to the remains that she now knows are that of Moses. *The legends are true. The angel, Michael, hid the remains from Satan.*

Isis stares at the remains of Moses for a minute deciding on the best course of action. She walks over and picks up the remains. With a heavy and weighted heart, she walks to the edge of a fissure to the left of the marbled archway. She pauses for a minute and throws the remains into the abyss of the fissure.

"Isis, do you copy? The video feed has cleared, but the camera is stationary. You okay? Do you copy? Isis? I'm sending down..."

"No need, professor. I'm coming up. And I have taken a few of the clay pots. When you are ready, I'm ready."

Isis knows she has to sell the professor and the small contingent of student interns on her less than stellar find. It hurts her pride tremendously to feign defeat, but then again, her thoughts reconcile in that, *there was a freaking angel talking to you Isis, a being telling you that spiritual Armageddon could decimate a planet. It's okay to take the L on this one.*

"Very good, then. I'll see you top side in a few. No matter our loss today. Your safety is paramount. Great job. We'll savage what we can and tag it. It's a win if we have actual proof of Hebrews this far in region. It lends credence that we are on the right track."

Isis can hear the heart break that Asher is trying to conceal by not blaming her. She can even feel his sickness of him regretting that it was not him to descend down into the tunnel. Before her ascension topside, Isis looks around one last time at the cavern and then just stares at the place where Fate vanished. As she is starting to be hoisted up, she hears his voice as a whisper in the wind.

"Nobility has no meaning here in this reality. In this system, the prince is just as equal as the pauper. Woe to the realm of men for that great and terrible day is almost upon us all, ethereal and mortal alike."

The ground and cavern around Isis begin to shake. Rocks begin to crack and slide. Stalagmites and stalactites crumble into a vivid picture of teeth consuming prey as the mountainous underground terrain collapses.

Her radio keys up with Dr. Asher's voice.

"Earthquake! We're pulling you out. Don't panic, we got you."

Ascending quickly, Isis reaches top side in just under 20 minutes. As the rescue specialist and interns pull Isis clear, projectile of rocks and dust expel from the collapsing hole signifying cave in. The once smooth bore hole quickly fills up with dirt and debris. The shaking intensifies. The land that once stood cover atop the recent find begins to collapses in on itself causing a small circumference of Earth to sink two feet as it erases and bars access to the find from existence for a time longer in hope that it will buy time.

Dr. Asher rushes and escorts Isis away from the shooting debris. He looks her over to make sure she's okay, but his attention quickly returns to the site as he watches his funded work fold in on itself. He can't even look at her as he's consumed by the destruction. He just stares at his life's investment gone bust. "You okay?" He asks her without even making eye contact with her.

Isis attempting to catch her breath. "I'm fine doctor... I'm fine." She looks at Asher and knows she can never really tell him what happened down there. In keeping him in the dark about what happened in the cavern, she realizes that Jericho probably keeps her in the dark about certain aspects of his life probably for the same reasons. *Damn Him!* Isis, consoles Asher, as he's lost everything. Someday she may even tell him why.

Asher looks at the filled in hole and thinks of a rhyme he use to sing to himself when he was a child playing on the beach with his mother, *Play in the sand filling it in, when it falls apart, start over again.* His mind repeats it over and over again as tears fall from his eyes. *Play in the sand filling it in, when it falls apart, start over again. Play in the sand filling it in, when it falls apart, start over again.*

"Play in the sand filling it in, when it falls apart, start over again," Pestilence whispers into Asher's ear holding the mortal's shoulder tightly.

Fate watches the exchange between Asher and the demon. "Human tenacity is an incredulous thing." He whispers to himself. Fate disappears into a blinding white column of light.

CHAPTER 35

"SITUATIONAL REPORT"

"Prayer changes things. That is the oldest lie I think that I have been told. Prayer is what I spoke in the hours before the Destined Sun's befell my village. I don't think that no one on this Earth gave a more faith filled and purposeful prayer than I, my family, and kinsmen. We prayed as the Catholic Church taught us. We prayed for Jesus and his angels to intervene and stop you vile men that would come and ravage our wives and daughter's bodies. Yet, you are here and not only did your men ravage them, but mutilated them as well, separating breast from body so our women could not feed our starving children. We prayed that our children would be spared and yet your soldiers castrated our boys before hanging them. That is the power of prayer in a God it appears is no longer listening. We should have been instructed to pray for God to save you, but fight as if he will not.

I have learned a great personal cost that prayer is for the weak and those that are afraid to take matters into their own hands for fear of angering the gods Jesus and Jehovah. Believing in prayer, I have failed my people. When I was believing in the power of prayer, I should have been believing in the power of violence of action to save my tribe. I, Alexis Tokomen, tribal king of the

Whodanti will pray no longer. My last breath to you General and your devilish army will not be spent on my knees in prayer of intervention fore I understand more than anyone that there is no divine coming to save me."

Quote ~Alexis Tokomen

REPUBLIC OF CONGO, BRAZZAVILLE

The headquarters of the Destined Suns Militants located in the City of Brazzaville has been decimated by the Arcanian half of the coalition force. In their destructive wake, a series of burned out buildings have been left in ruination. Stone, glass, brick and cement are strewn all about the once powerful warmongering nerve center complex of men that committed unspeakable acts of genocide. Fires still burn hot in pockets throughout the compound. The once pinnacle of their power has been laid waste.

Colonel Rusain walks among the destruction and countless recently deceased bodies of the bloodied and charred Congo Militants. Even the Colonel himself has not walked away unscathed by the events of the day. He is bloodied, battle weary and beaten from the long battle that him and his men began fighting from the east of the Republic. Exhausted, but proud of his fighting force and all they've accomplished in the days most recent campaign, Rusain sits and rests on the tracks of a destroyed enemy's tank. Rusain wipes the sweat, small lacerations and scratches of blood and mud from his brow and face before reaching into his tactical vest's pocket and retrieving a protein bar. Hands still shaking with adrenaline, he tears open the package and bites into the bar.

The Colonel closes his eyes finding peace and sighs reflecting on the day's events. His calming technique is short lived, his attention is pulled to the west corridor of the complex where a commotion is starting to arise. He rolls his eyes and continues peeling the wrapper to open his protein bar knowing he's going to have to hear some blowback from the American force that he was supposed to have connected with before taking the militant's headquarters. He had spoken with the captain whose name escapes him at the moment numerous times down to the exact minute of how the attack was to be executed, but all that went to shit after the first round fired.

Jericho enters the complex with the Marines who survived the onslaught of enemy flanking maneuvers and their constant barrage of fighting militants from the west. Exhausted and tired as Jericho and his battle-weary Marines are, they have arrived at the gates. Once they enter and see the stronghold has been taken they gain a renewed vigor because they made it to their goal, realizing that they didn't have to fight for it, the Arcanian forces had already done that. Jubilant that bloodshed was over for the day. Marines cheer the men of the Arcanian forces from sparing them another battle.

Arcanian forces quartermasters and logistics officer assist Jericho and his men in finding water and food. One of the Arcanian lieutenants points a detachment of his men to help with the wounded and those that were killed and in need of recovery. Jericho nods at the lieutenant in recognition of his war bonding brotherly gesture and care of his wounded and respected dead. He raises his freshly-acquired water bottle that he was given in thanks. The lieutenant nods back in kind. Jericho turns and whispers to one of his surviving lieutenants, "tell the men to eat rest and clean their wounds." Jericho makes the cross sign as well letting the lieutenant know to locate Priest. The corporal salutes and starts to gather some of the remaining able-bodied Marines to locate the Chaplin.

Jericho takes a long gulp of water to quench his cotton mouth and parched chapped lips while he walks over to an Arcanian soldier.

"Corporal rank isn't it?" The Arcanian soldier nods yes. "Where can I find your commanding officer?" The soldier points toward Rusain. With a nod of thanks, he dismisses the corporal and walks over to Rusain, who's still sitting on the treads of the blown-out tank. The walk is a bit sluggish as the mud is thick and enriched with spilled blood of the enemy and Arcanian troops as they fought to secure the compound. Jericho makes his way toward the Colonel. For courtesy, he surrenders a salute and then begins to lay into him. "Colonel Rusain! Let's not get caught in pleasantries shall we. I'm far from in a pleasant mood. Are you hard of fucking hearing or what Colonel?"

"I am just as hard as hearing as you are mute Captain." Rusain says looking Jericho up and down.

Jericho gives a smug smirk, the one that says I'm really not for your shit and there's no way I'm playing nice. "I know damn well who you are, Colonel, the world knows who you are and your accomplishments. What I don't know is why you're here. I thought that we were to join forces before taking the stronghold."

Rusain takes another bite from his protein bar. "Have we not joined forces, Captain?" Rusain gives Jericho a smug look right back that said you walked into that one smartass.

Jericho looks at the complete destruction of the headquarters and the ruination of the vehicles and supplies. He pauses for a moment as he watches the Arcanian forces gathering the bodies of the enemy for burial. Many of the enemy's bodies have been severed, but there was little to no blood on the bodies that were cleaved. At his assessment any soldier that was hacked it was clean, no blood, they were cauterized after the slice.

"Losses appears to be complete. There were no prisoners, huh? Not one, Colonel?" Jericho says.

Rusain takes another bite from his protein bar. "You've fought these bastards from the west. I heard your situational reports as you progressed. You know firsthand of the ferocity of these bastards. They fought to the last of them probably, because this was their stronghold. Believe me when I say that we made every attempt to capture one alive," he says condescendingly. "However, it seems that it wasn't to be." Rusain smirks and takes another bite of his bar.

Jericho just stares at Rusain, contempt for the man seethes off him. He could kill the man with a look Rusain would have burst into flames. "It's good that you were monitoring our situational reports, Colonel, because you're going to be the topic of my next one to the

Joint Chiefs. We are not the animals that those men were. If you're anything of a representation of what Arcane seems to be at face value, then you'd have understood that. But seeing what shit you're capable of here cements my belief in who and what Arcane is and stands for."

Rusain, now pissed, leaps off the tread of the destroyed tank. He takes the last swig from his water bottle and throws it to the ground. He stands damn near toe-to-toe with Jericho.

"Tell you what, Captain. I really don't give a shit what you tell the Chiefs. I stand outside of your democratic farce of a government and your weak demoralizing morals. Now, while you and your men were engaged in the west we moved almost unopposed from the east until we hit heavy contact at our intended rendezvous point. We fought and repelled their forces. Having the advantage, initiative, and seemingly the surprise we pursued. You being a captain here of some known renown, I'm sure you would have too. I've read exploits of some of your engaged conflicts."

"You pressed the attack when—" Is all Jericho could say before being interrupted.

"—You damn right I pressed the attack. I ordered the pursuit which led here. I then decimated them at the source… at great fucking cost of men and equipment mind you. My actions here cut reinforcements drastically that was hammering you and your men further west." Rusain steps closer to Jericho. "Think, captain, those that were meant to engage and finish you subsequently had to split their forces to deal with my advance. With that divide, the majority of them returned here to reinforce their base which made them instantly my problem. My men rendered the enemy incapable of fighting, thus saving you and your men's lives Cap-pi-ton!"

Rusain continues to stare Jericho in the eyes. Jericho knows he's looking for a sign of weakness. He's looking to see if there is a blink or shirk away. Jericho stands his ground and doesn't give one iota of weakness. Rusain smiles and backs away slightly giving in on the pissing match.

"Quiet as kept Captain, your forces in the west are fledgling. America has become a fallen empire that can barely sustain itself on the world stage amidst the global unrest. You all have taken the low path of Rome believing in the goodness of charity and false sense of security. You sacrificed morals for a nature of feel good public opinion of not wanting to offend the good sensibilities of the next-door neighbor; your political leaders are whores that will jump for the least offered illegal monetary gain. It won't be long before you're all marching to a different beat of another government; possibly China's, who will come to collect their eighty percent of debt your country owes them, maybe Russia who constantly test your borders taxing and exhausting you paper money that is backed by nothing." Rusain smirks hard to drive the next point. Who knows Captain what the future holds? It may even be the beat of the Arcanian force's cadences that the American troops step too."

Jericho now in a little show of power walks up to the face of Rusain taking his personal space and ground. "Not likely you bunch of murdering sons of bitches. America will never concede to the likes of Arcane, hell would have come first before that ever happens."

The moral high ground of this feeble-minded kid makes Rusain burst into laughter. He backs away again giving the competition to Jericho. "Hell is exactly what your country will have, you've shown a warrior spirit," he says as he glances at his name tag. "Bane, J. I'll make sure you retain your rank when we acquire your forces. Anything else, Captain, before you bitch to your Joint Chiefs?"

"I know of your tactics, Rusain. You and that fucking general of yours, Warsivious. When we settle this conflict here on this great continent, you better be sure we'll look to the Arcanian forces next. The atrocities that you've all committed will come to light... I promise you that. A reckoning is on the horizon; in time it'll be us Marines that come to settle the debts of all those you killed unjustly."

Rusain's laughter dies. "You make it sounds as if we've murdered in cold blood to delegitimize countries, collect monetary gain, or set the way for profiteering. We conquered... understand? Conquered for an everlasting peace putting an end to ideals which fuel wars as well as the atrocities you accuse us of. We win this together Captain and we all go home. Now, off with you, go and perform your perfunctory task of reporting to your Chiefs you automaton." Rusain turns to walk away then stops after remembering something. He digs in his pocket and retrieves a gold chain. He looks at it then turns tossing the chain to Jericho. "Catch!"

Jericho catches the chain and looks at it. "What the hell is this?"

"That is the chain of the tribal king, Alexis Tokomen. One that the Destined Suns more than likely killed as he hasn't been seen in weeks after the militants over ran his village. I will say that he would beg to differ your point of view that we are murdering sons of bitches. If he were here to tell it, I'm sure he'd call us avenging saviors followed by a gratuitous thank you."

Rusain turns away slowly and begins to give orders to his men.

Jericho clutches the chain and slowly backs away, watching Rusain. He turns his attention and quiet rage away from Rusain when his gunnery sergeant tells him that a lieutenant colonel is online awaiting his report to relay up the chain of command to the Chiefs. Jericho does an about face and heads to one of the last buildings standing in the compound that will soon be his command communication center when his men finish erecting the equipment.

CHAPTER 36

Sanstraghten Realm of Heaven

All the saints that have lived in the world at one time or another resides in the Sanstraghten. Over the centuries it's been aptly renamed by men as Purgatory and a host of other names. The saints are a breed apart from all others who have been claimed by Death within the course of the time of mankind. The saints have their own portion of Hades that is dedicated solely for them and their training in the ethics of ruling and judgments of a promised new rule to unite all the realms and coalesce them as one. Within the confines of the Sanstraghten they are tasked with someday becoming regents in not only the new world of men, but the new all-encompassing realms of galaxies that all species will reside in under the custodial caretakers of Elohim. They intensely study the laws of Zero Realm that will one day be applied to all inhabited planets.

All of the Regents are taught within the structured confines of monarch rule. Training of course comes easier to those who already had lived under the rule of a king or queen in their prior life. Those that have already understand how they are to assist in ruling. They accrue the current knowledge as second nature compared to those that died under a tribunal, communistic or democratic society. The others will take time in adhering, learning, and applying the new rule of law.

The saints can be easily identified by the soft blue and orange scripted glowing numbers upon their foreheads. They dress in gray tunics and loose slacks with darker gray hooded robes. They each where a sash with Heaven's glyphic writing seared into them. The sashes are a multitude of colors, which represent how the saints died on their respective planets and what rewards are due them according to their works of remaining faithful. There are a 144,000 from each species represented.

Purple sash was that of a Majestic. That particular saint died in the name of Prince Yeshua. An honor that was the highest, only a few could receive. A gold sash was that of the evangelicals that spread the word throughout their respective worlds. A red sash was worn by those that died in battle, but a battle that was ordained by God. And the blue sash was just worn by those that were blessed to be considered saints and teachers of men spreading the gospel of the coming rule.

Rachel is a regent in training that falls on the latter end of other than monarch. She lived her entire life under democratic rule. Taking a break from the Regent's studies she leaves the Sanstraghten for some time in the beauty of Hades. She finds a quiet spot next to a river that flows in opposite directions at the same time but doesn't clash. She removes her sandals and swipes her blue sash to the side and places her feet into the river. Sitting contently, she runs her hands through the plush bluish-purple grass and fixates her eyes on the vast black sparkling diamond mountains that are off in the distance. As the cool breeze starts to overtake her she lies back in the grass and lifts her chin to the skies feeling every bit of the breeze as it blows across her face. It's as if nature was constantly giving her gentle blown kisses. She closes her eyes and contemplates rest in the climate that is always perfect, never for a moment is it too hot nor to cold. She's so in the moment that she temporarily spaces out not hearing when her mentor, John of Patmos has found her and is awaiting a response from her.

John playfully splashes a sprinkle of water in Rachel's face. Her mind is instantly teleported back to the mundane of the Regency. "You with me, Rachel? Glad I found you, I see you moved the studies outside today. I'm comfortable with that as well. I have just learned that section one-forty-three will be your regency." John is met with a sigh, then silence. "Understand? That will be where those with disputes will have them resolved. It will fall to you to set the matter to track."

She slides up and rests on her elbows while still swirling her feet in the water. She looks at John to let him know he has her full attention. "And if I can't set it to track?"

"If you can't set it track then a tribunal of three will be called. You may utilize any two regents to help you settle the matter. Now if the tribunal of regents fail then it is taken before the king. Understand?" Said John.

"I do. So, only those sealed by God will complete the role of regents, I got it."

John smiles at her. "Progress at last, dear. Now, it seems you understand."

Rachel smiles back. "I'm sorry, it's just hard to concentrate with all this beauty that surrounds us. How can one ever not get use to this?"

Rachel lays back in the grass again. Suddenly, a shadow slowly covers her. Startled, her eyes widen with surprise as Diplodocus' head passes over her and drinks from the river that she's sitting by. She rolls away from the side of the river and looks at the yellowish tinted aurora of the behemoth.

John walks up to the neck of the thunderous reptile and rubs it. "I was just as shocked when I first saw one of its kind. If you think about it, they are not unlike us. They, too, were alive and lived an entire life. They had families and friends I'm sure as well. They lived under the same sun as us for eons, the way they tell it."

Rachel looks as John curiously. "The way they tell it?"

"Sure, the way they tell it. Touch the animal to establish a connection, then listen closely and you will hear them as plainly as I talk to you."

Slowly and apprehensively, she approaches the lumbering anachronism she has only read about in books. With awe-inspired wonder she gently rubs the neck of the long passed into extinction dinosaur. A smile stretches from ear to ear. *This can't be happening.*

It's surreal. She begins to laugh at the thought that she's touching a dinosaur. Then it happens… she hears the thoughts as formed words of the prehistoric behemoth as it greets her and introduces itself.

"I am called Foot That Was Slow."

Laughing! "It's nice to make your acquaintance, Foot That Was Slow. You have the most interesting of names that I've heard yet," Rachel says aloud. "May I ask you another question, John?" Rachel continues to rub the Lizard of old.

"Feel free, that's what I'm here for," John replies.

"Did you have any inkling that you were one of the sealed and the responsibility that you would be asked to carry?"

"Not for sure, not until Death came for me in my sleep. I had an inkling, but there are others who are here that knew well before Death took them. When, I talked to Martin he said that he knew. It was revealed to him in a dream. For me it was different. I was greeted by Yeshua son of Elohim and told by the Prince himself that this would be my task. It confirmed it for me when he spoke this to me. He mentioned it when I knew him in the flesh, but I did not understand his meaning until my arrival into this realm.

Looking remorseful, John bows his head. "But how lowly am I? For I actually saw and talked with him that I believed. I saw him perform wondrous miracles. But you and the saints that followed the first of us, you all hold more power as a regent than I, for you believed and had never seen nor spoken with him. Blessed are you, Rachel, and those that came before you and the one still come."

Rachel smiles and leans in closer to John. "What was he like?"

John reaches a hand to pull Rachel up. "Walk with me while we talk. I have another appointment."

Rachel grabs her sandals and bids Foot That Was Slow, adieu.

"Yeshua" John says, "Hmmmm! What was he like? He was… he was my friend. He was always smiling. I mean just happy to be alive. It was as if he reveled in each breath that he took. He made you believe that there was nothing like it. He was excited about the smallest of things. He was committed to save not this one or that one, but everyone. He burned with the zeal of the sun that warmed us. He was special. You knew it just to talk with him."

Rachel was simply captivated to be hearing a firsthand account.

"And he was funny." John said while starting to chuckle. "He was incredibly funny. Between him and Judas, I couldn't tell you who was the best at eliciting laughter."

As they walk, Rachel pets a lion that passes by her. With his furry main he turns and walks past her again rubbing against her leg as the most docile kitten would when shown affection. She smiles and laughs with John as he remembers his time fondly with the prince. Suddenly, his laughter slowly dies out as he looks over Rachel's shoulder. He nods to signify that someone is behind her. "It seems you have a visitor who wishes for some of your time as well."

Rachel turns around and sees Death staring at her from a distance. She looks back to John, who backs slowly away, hands raised.

"We're done for now anyhow dear. Go on! I'll catch up with you later."

Rachel winks at him and shines a smile his way. "Later today I'll catch up with you. I would love to hear more."

"And I will love to tell it. Remember, any questions are permitted. You know where to find me." John walks off, waving bye.

As Rachel turns and walks toward the direction of Death, souls that she passes nod their heads in constant respect to the sealed saint as she passes them. Inquisitively, she approaches Death, who standing among the beginning of a forest of trees that reaches far into the skies of Hades. The leaves are shades of reddish orange and bluish purple. Death watches her approach as he leans on his staff for resting support. Rachel's the first to speak.

"Watching over me, huh?"

"Watching you becoming adjusted is more like it. This way of being seems to fit well with you, Honorable Regent."

Rachel turns and gazes at unending beauty and the entirety of Hades. She looks even beyond the walls of the secluded Sanstraghten where she resides most of the time. She takes in the people of all walks of life that have literally died to be here. It's not often she gets to walk outside the walls of the Sanstraghten. That is why she tries to enjoy every minute of it when she does.

Rachel looks at Death and then looks over Hades again beckoning Death to look as well. "Do you know everyone here by name?" she says as if wanting to play a game.

"Yes," Death replies stern and matter-of-factly.

She looks at Death studying him. She can't see into the darkness of his completely shadowed face, but it always draws her attention.

"So, you can find anyone anytime you want?

"I can when needed."

"Then you were purposely looking for me?"

"Y-Yes," Death says, mildly hesitant.

A long while goes by with nothing being said as the two stares out into Hades. Rachel taps Death on the arm and then pulls him slightly.

"Walk with me, will you? It's not often that I get out to walk through the lushness and beauty. This place is something else; it's a wonder to the senses."

Death straightens himself and allows her to pull him. He walks with her without protest. "You speak to the beauty of it, yes? How we of the ethereal see things so differently from you mortals. You of flesh see beauty that is magnanimous and unending. The conversations that I've had with you saints individually have more than convinced me of this. Your beauty is fleeting. You all tend to forget that, Sheol is but a stop along the way to finality that can't be undone. Although some do try in vain to avoid what's coming."

Death no longer gazes out into the third realm of Heaven. He looks almost longingly at Rachel. "I really don't take the time to admire such views for it is not permitted. Time as you perceive is the one thing I will never have. There is never enough… time for me."

As they walk along the tree line of the forest again Rachel witnesses Death off in the distance ushering in a child's soul. When she glances a bit further to the right, she witnesses him walking in another species soul from some distant galaxy or plain of existence. Her face saddens a bit at the site of the distant soul. Rachel can't help but think did other species see her and her kind as the distant souls.

"Did all worlds fail to measure up?" she asks as she turns to face Death. "Or was it only us that seemed to have fail miserably?"

"Would you like honesty, Saint?" Death asks?

"Please," Rachel replies.

Death stops walking and faces her. Even looking into his face, she still can't see him. "When I say this, it is not to pull a rise nor expound on your ignorance or insinuate that you are anyway narcissistic, fore those ways of thought have since passed away for you. Saint, your race, the race of humanity, is an arrogant lot. Before the majority of you that are here, now, presently or are soon to arrive have not once given real thought to the possibility of life other than that of your own having been created under one authority. Such hubris I find with you and your kind. Unfortunately, hubris is not a sin that is truly owned by just your people."

Rachel quarter turns and looks at the galaxy far flung species. She recognizes the humanistic features in their appearance. "They are not that much unlike us in appearance. Guess that speaks bounds to the phrase that we were all created in his image."

Death nods. "With the fall of the first Seraphim, on the eve of man's destruction, his actions caused an Archelliac reaction that reverberated through all of creation where other species became self-aware and soon after met with folly. The path of humanities follies is nothing new, it is but an echo of a reverberation that started before the concept of thought. It is just that it happened on humanity's watch that the schism was cemented, sides chosen, and the pull of the string that could unravel all realities. You think us gods? Your constant need for the greater blinds you all to a fact that your addled minds overlook, that just maybe at one time we were you, just vintage."

A little broken with Death's assessment of the arrogance of man, Rachel looks down for a few seconds. Death begins walking again. This time Rachel is in tow as she deals with the slight that he dealt her on a sarcastic playing field.

Suddenly, Rachel stops, which caused Death to pause. "Why are you here? Like right now talking with me?"

Death faces her. "I'm am here, because unlike most, you have a knowledge that I long to possess. It beckons to me and I fear it will call to me until I'm cast away for all time. Even then I fear it will haunt me, taunt me. You have what I've forgotten and wish to remember."

Looking confused, Rachel shrugs her shoulders. "What could that possibly be? What could I have besides God's grace?

Death turns to Rachel and tells her what he wants that makes him so enamored with her. He leans in close to whisper and tells her that he wants—

Rachel's eyes widen as she steps back in disbelief.

CHAPTER 37

PAST AND FUTURE COLLIDE

"I won't just tear one god from his throne. I will tear them all from their place on high and set the Heavens ablaze. I will conquer the Palace on High just as I have conquered and bent the knees of men, here below on Earth."

Quote ~Gilgamesh, The Legendary Sumerian

Republic of Congo, Brazzaville

Jericho is on his off time relaxing on the rooftop of the seven-story building that Marine forces are occupying as a makeshift command center. It's the nerve center of coming American-led joint operations in the immediate region. Having just received orders for rest and relaxation, he's laying back resting on his rucksack looking up at the starlit night skies. The air smells sweet in this part world, this supposed cradle of life. Taking in the night air, he reads enough e-mails from Isis equivalent to construction of a novella. As much as he loves it, the pain of not being with her eats at him, not being able to watch as the sun makes her skin glisten causing her hair to stick to her face and long smooth neck. He often finds jealousy creeping into the nether regions of his mind. She's beautiful, and it's a constant thought to him that men will be drawn to her, men that are less chivalrous than him.

Albeit, under forced contract chivalry. What could he do if she was tempted and drawn toward lust and sensual temptation? He's worlds away from her and asks her to accept his abstinence.

"Penny for your thoughts as you mortals say." Gabriel says suddenly appearing beside Jericho.

Seeing Gabriel is no longer is a pleasant surprise to him. In fact, it has become a stark reminder of what he can only equate to betrayal. He takes a swig from his can of Belgium imported beer. "Penny for my thoughts?" he echoes back sarcastically. "Okay, I'll bite, I'm thinking how peaceful the night appears. Key word being, appears." He takes another swig. "Until you tell me there is a world upending calamity down stairs. Jericho says while starting to laugh. "Or… No wait, until you tell me that God has fallen from his throne and its impact is imminent. You know you're good for calamity inducing apocalyptic conversation and all.

Gabriel adjusts her hooded cloak and sits next to him.

Jericho continuing looking into the night sky. "These last few years have been so hectic with the endless campaigns of war. I realize that I don't really get a chance to admire her vastness and beauty much. Look up there, Gabriel… Look at the stillness of the night." Jericho faces Gabriel. "Why are you here? You don't answer when I call, you show when I don't need you. Why have you come tonight?"

"To help put your mind at ease of what you experienced the other day out in the jungle."

Jericho looks at her. "Oh! You're here to help me debrief. Make sure that P.T.S.D. has not overtaken my feeble mind after trading blows with a demon-possessed man." He laughs to himself, feeling mildly intoxicated.

Gabriel grabs one of his beers and examines the can closely. She holds the contents to her nose in a faint hope that she would be receptive to an odor through the aluminum.

"Does this beverage taste of wine, ale, or mead as it was called a time ago?" She asks.

"Nothing of the former or latter. It's an acquired taste of rubbing alcohol and painkillers." Jericho takes another swig. "You know Gabe, in the beginning, I was naive to war. I bought into the hype of those damn commercials of the military and the shit show you sold me. I bought into that whole save the world and I'm special crap. What I've seen—Oh! The things I've seen in the shadow of war—"

"—Is what all men of wars have seen," she interrupts. "No one is exempt from the horrors of it that participates. No one." Gabriel sets the can down. "Not even my brothers and I were spared from conflict, and there was much conflict."

"Men died! My men; more than I could count that day or even cared to. Men under my command." Jericho takes a longer swig. He passes his open can to Gabriel. She waves it away. He shrugs and takes another swig.

"Thanks for the offer, but I wouldn't be able to taste your beverage. At least not in the way you can. We don't eat or drink of realms like Earth. We can, but it's pointless because we can't taste or feel the way you do. Just like within our reality you cannot eat or drink from ours."

"So, what do you drink, or even eat for that matter?" Said Jericho, swirling the last remnants of the can.

"We eat and drink manna that Elohim provides." Gabriel smiles, "however, there are times that curiosity gets the better of us to experience what it must be like for your species to live your existence, but it's futile as our taste cannot align with any other reality than Zero's."

"Your loss, I suppose." Jericho finishes the can and opens another. It's close to ten minutes before he utters another word. He takes a sigh, looks at Gabriel studying her. He wanted to be angry at her, but just the character of her overflowed with altruism. He felt he had to mentally unload. "I've never seen such pervasive evil as I've seen in those jungles the other day. Not just what the enemy did, but us as well. Even the now world famed Arcane Forces, they killed men I'm sure surrendered... The fucking animals! I've seen the old footages of war that the academy continuously have you pour over and study. I've listened intently to the talks that you and I've had concerning conflict, but these wars of late are something different... darker, far more reaching, more violent."

Gabriel, now finds herself looking into the night sky. Far beyond that of Jericho's mortal eyes, she looks through the vastness of the ever-expanding universe all the way through to its end. She sees that the infinite void no longer expands as it had since its creation. No, it's cooling, slowly retracting in a naturalistic countdown signaling that the stewardship of men and their tenuous at best rule is close to an end, an end not even their juvenile scientific ignorance are unaware of.

"You call men animals, Jericho? You think them animals? Do you see them differently than you or any other species for that matter which populate this very Earth?

Jericho guzzles the next whole can in one go. "We Marines don't kill women and children... at least not intentionally. We don't cut off their tits so that babies can't drink their mother's milk. We don't crush the skulls of infants with our boots because of a bloodline born across town. Men that practice in such are the very definition of an animal which I speak. A blood-lust ravenous beast that is—"

"The sum of men, Jericho. The same type of men that I have borne witness to for the entire length of your species existence," Gabriel said interrupting him again.

Upset, Jericho looks at Gabriel, while reaching for another can. "There was something else too in that jungle. It was powerful. More than anything I've seen. It was unyielding. It was—"

"A demon by the name of Crethos that I thought long since imprisoned. He's a lowcaste fallen demon."

Psst! Air escapes Jericho's can as he flips the tab. "Lowcaste? What the hell is that?"

Gabriel removes her hood. The beauty of her caramel complexion never ceases to enamor Jericho. Her beauty is unmatched to that of any woman he's ever seen, save one, his Isis.

"Lowcaste, meaning he was never Angel, Fallen or otherwise. He was a citizen of the realm before the divide. He bought into Lucifer's lie as well as scores of others."

"Well, damn, if that was a lowcaste, I'd sure hate to see high caste." Jericho crushes the can.

"Raziel reported that you handled him."

"Just barely." Jericho says as he tosses the can casually behind him. The aluminum smacks the floor next to others.

"What of your friend, Priest?" Gabriel says.

"We haven't had a chance to talk much about what happened out there. He's been in prayer since we've returned. Well, that the lie he's telling me anyways. But I must admit, his faith held firm... more than mine, I think. Hell, he's lucky I didn't cut and run. If I think about in hindsight, I'm luckier that I didn't shit myself. Men is one thing; other reality is another."

Jericho watches as Gabriel stands up and walks to the edge of the roof and look over the Congo. "I see the uncertainty in you Jericho, the doubt of whether you feel you have what it takes to deal with the surmounting storm on the cosmic horizon. This feeling of yours is quite natural and will even reside with you when the threat you were warned of one day enters onto the world's stage."

Still looking into the distance, Gabriel begins a cautionary tale. "You spoke to the evil of men; shall I tell you a story? Shall I tell you a segment of your history that reverberates even to this very day? I will tell you of evil, but there is a lesson that you must find within it. It starts a little over one hundred thousand years ago in what was known in your tongue as Mesopotamia."

Gabriel turns and walks back to Jericho placing her hands over his eyes. He instantly sees the past through her eyes; an army of enraged bloodthirsty ragged men are in position poised for battle. Their armor is pieced together bronze and wood, laced by bounded leather from the carcasses of creatures long since extinct. While assembled they are far from a disciplined ordered set of rank that would be associated with modern combat. Within their ranks all types of debauchery happen.

The soldiers if they could be called such, drink to excess, fight with each other, fuck women that are just as wild and blood lusting as the men. All the of the undisciplined acts of mutinous nature takes place while awaiting their commander to lead them to their next victory where they may conquer and attain more spoils for looting, women for slavery and raping. Children were not overlooked or spared the wrath of the dog soldiers. If they were found to be of strength, they would be conscripted into service. If found wanting, they were held for Demitrode be and decimated.

Off in the distance standing on the shore is their young leading commander. He stands looking into the blue skies of the heavens except he's not looking out past the universe, he's looking to defile God and those associated with him. Not for glory or ascension such as Lucifer, but because just the for the sake of having been born.

The young commander takes a deep breath and fills his lungs with fresh, crisp air. He breathes it in, knowing that soon it will be filled with smoke and the odor of burning flesh, the finer points of war to him. He reaches into his large satchel and pulls out a smaller wolfskin satchel. He puts it to his lips and downs the whole of its fermented honey contents. He turns and looks to his men that await him. He gently removes his tattered cloak and leaves it on the beach. Satisfied that he's made whatever peace he can with himself, he leaves the beaches shore and wades into the sea of savagery and debauchery where he maneuvers through until he attains his place at the head of his army.

Jericho looks closely at the leader; his face is marred in serious scarring and mud. If there were a time that his face had smooth curves, it was long ago, before it was covered by the thickest bush beard that obscured his facial features, concealing what madness he's truly seen. Jericho watches as he takes his place at the head of the depraved bunch with his war-scarred face and a missing left eye. He observes him as he reaches into the mud and grabs a handful of Earth, smearing it across his face. In wet moist clay he paints the outline of a black skull on his face. He uses another handful of mud to slick his long dark hair to the back as not to stifle his one good eye in the heat of battle.

Being able to see Gabriel's view point, he now hears her voice whispering in the inner regions of his mind. *"Lost to your history was a man named Jazekial. He was a force that was unmatched in the world before this system as you now know it. Through carnage and death, he rose to power. He arose quickly from within the ranks of those he conquered. In time he raised a mighty army that he thought might one day challenge the Heavens. Within his ranks were men and creatures that were never meant to walk this Earth, but because of my brother Lucifer, foul things were created and others invited to this reality to aid in his conflict against life."*

Jericho's attention is held by the vision that he sees of men upon thousands of men walking. His eyes widen as he observes what also walks in the ranks of men. Within their ranks are giant cyclopes, Nephilims, wolves that looked to have human traits mixed within them. Jericho also saw men that had been turned dark and demonic looking. *"Those breeds of men were called Nosforotos. They were from where you call the Andromeda system in today tongue. That name had been lost to history, but when spoken of through tale and song they became the mythical creatures that were plagued by vampirism, the Nosferatu."* Jericho further saw other creatures that had fallen to myth and legend as clear as the day's sunshine. He continues watching in amazement as all the dark men and creatures march on what looks to be a settlement of humans living in the last bastion of a civilized people.

"The village that you are looking at is the last house of the remaining semi righteous men, women and children. Beyond that in the not too distant background is Noah's ark, just after completion."

As if a bird in flight, Jericho's view changes to where he's looking directly at Noah and his famed ark.

From the top of the highest roof of the ark, Noah can see the approaching horde in the distance. Just as Noah and his family can see the coming horde of carnage, so can the people of his village below. The last bastion's villagers are experiencing a range of emotions as they watch and await the dark ravenous men and monsters descend upon them.

Some villagers pray to the god who they feel has turned a blind eye to the coming carnage; others are petrified with overwhelming fear to even attempt to flee or call for any unearthly savior. Then, there are those few that will not cry or dare contemplate fleeing, they are the ones that grab whatever weapons they have or can fashion into one so that they can stand their ground and fight.

Gabriel's voice cuts into his vision again. *"I heard the prayers of a few faithful, but they fell on death ears in the high court. The thoughts of the many that believed Iehovah had turned away were right... he had. He did not hear the pleas of those that had fallen from him all save one... Noah. Still, I heard those of the last mortal bastion as they prayed for the lives of their children to be spared if not themselves. The bargains they were willing to make were of the sadness that breaks hearts. I along with many of my brothers stood obedient and watched powerless as they prayed for deliverance. It was denied them."*

"God seems unjust to let this occur." Said Jericho. "Then again, to hear cries and do nothing is a trait that humans have mastered as well."

"Indeed." Gabriel says.

Gabriel glances at Jericho. "Our prince told us that we were not to intervene in the destruction of Bastion. We were to protect only one family of hardened faith in abundance."

Sarin, The Name of The Last Bastion

Noah lowers the massive ramp that also doubles as the front main hull door to the recently constructed ark. He hurriedly exits the gargantuan boat and into his family's makeshift camp, where he quickly runs about making last minute eyeball assessments of provisions that he would need for his family to survive the coming journey. As he moves about the camp, his wife is moving as fast as he is getting their sons ready for the journey. Believing that his family isn't moving with enough haste, Noah quickens their pace by shoving them along reminding them of their assigned responsibilities. As Noah moves them along toward the ark, he realizes that he's short one son, his boy, Shem. Noah runs into the camp again this time to find his son Shem. After nervously searching, he sees his son in the distance heading toward Sarin.

Without any hesitation, he runs after his son. Adrenaline moves him faster than he knows should be possible. As he reaches his son, he tackles him and pins him to the ground.

"What are you doing, boy? Time is short, preparations have been made. God has given us a window which to complete our task. That hour of closure draws nigh."

Shem pushes his father off. "How can we leave our people when they need us the most? Father, that bastard, whore-loving tyrant is coming for Sarin. If you will not help them defend our home, then I will. Death comes from the east horizon. We must band with our kin and together, fight."

Noah strikes his son across the face. For the briefest instance, Shem sees the blue flash of error. The flash that represents a brief disconnect in the brains ability to communicate. Blood trickles from Shem's nose at first and then starts to pour as if a faucet has slowly been turned on. Noah shakes Shem. "Death comes for them all the same. You think me not in my right mind, because all that I have done these past years. Far from it. I was told what is to come. No one is to survive the coming storm, no one. Bastion is already lost to the dead, they just don't realize it yet. We can only pray that tyrant Jazekial grants them a quick merciful death. Now get to your feet and live!"

Noah slings his son in front of him and pushes him to run. "Don't look back, lest it be at your own peril."

"I choose peril then," shrugging Noah off Shem runs back toward Sarin.

Noah stares as his son runs toward a decided fate of his own making. Having to acquiesce, he returns to the Ark with the morose and somber look of defeat having to leave his son behind to his own folly. Not hesitating a moment longer, he pushes his other son up the ramp toward salvation.

"Boy, move with haste! They will be upon us soon. We mustn't let this vessel fall to them, else all is lost."

"What of Shem Father?

"He is lost to us." Said Noah as he grabs a crate of provisions.

"No... Wait Father, maybe not. Look there!"

Noah, follows his second oldest son's finger to see Shem running with all he can muster toward them. As he draws closer, Noah begins to make preparations to receive his son and prep for departure. His happiness at his son's change of mind and subsequent return is short lived as he watches Shem stop in place during his frantic run.

Shem is frozen in the midst of a full sprint. It's as if he's become a life size statue. Taken back in confusion, Noah leaves the Ark trots at first. He then runs at full sprint up to his son and attempts to move him. Not even with the strength of twenty men could he had moved his son. Scared, he turns and looks toward Sarin only to realize that everything is frozen, everything but him. Time has simply stopped. As he turns back to tend to his son, a silhouetted prince of Heaven, Zero Realm emerges from a white column of light before him. The prince levitates just above the ground as his time has not yet been given to him to lay foot upon Earth.

Noah instantly bows at the sight of Yeshua, a force that he knows is greater than he. Yeshua begins to speak to Noah. And tells him that the prophesied day is upon them. And to prepare to receive the chosen creatures of the Earth that have been given a reprieve and admission into the next system of life on Earth.

"My brothers and I were split into three battalions," Gabriel says. "The first would gather the creatures of the Earth that Elohim had chosen worthy."

Seventh Ocean - Pre-Flood

A white beam of light shoots from the heavens all the way into the deep depths of the Seventh Ocean. That singular beam is then followed by thousands of other beams of lights which shoots into the depths of lakes and rivers across the planet.

From within one of the beams of light Uriel emerges deep in the depths of the ocean. As Uriel leaves the beam, it retracts back up from the depths. Like moving through space and being subjected to weightlessness, the water slowly moves Uriel's tunic about that is exposed from underneath his armor. Uriel smirks at the wondrous beasts that are swimming along in the ocean. There are creatures that even in the singular are larger than twenty sperm whales combined. Their majesty is unmatched in the tranquil sea of Seven. Uriel takes a scroll from underneath his breast plate. Although he's under water and at extreme depths, the parchment remains dry. Uriel breaks the seal and lets the scroll go leaving it to float. Once released from his hand it dissipates into the underwater current. Within seconds chosen life such as that gargantuan wondrous beast begins to convulse, writhing in pain in its final death throws. Then it falls eerily still. The deed is done.

Various other species of marine life in the oceans, lakes, rivers, springs and ponds all die in the same manner. Not just in the Seventh Sea, but across the world. Uriel nods his head in satisfaction that his task is completed. Like a rocket, Uriel shoots through the water toward the surface where he erupts from the depths of the ocean. Once clear of the Seventh Sea, Uriel hovers, making sure the scroll's orders are fulfilled and that all the named creatures were destroyed. As he awaits confirmation Death explodes from underneath the surface as well with the souls of all the creatures that were named in the sealed heavenly order. Satisfied, Arch Uriel and the choiretics under his command that awaits him above and below the surface of water all take to the skies.

LANDS OF THE EARTH

The Arch Cassiel and his choiretic soldiers under him soar through the skies among hundreds of thousands of avian species. His speed is seemingly without cap or exhaustive as he moves through the atmosphere of the planet. His choir are unable to keep his pace and fall back slightly. As he flies among the avian, he travels through them above them, below them and down below tree lines. Uriel engages his helmet comm system which puts out an amplified echo of a static sound that emanates from his vocal chords by speeding the vibrations within his throat. His sound waves added with those of his choir that tails him over the entirety of the Earth, calls and wake every species of the avian clans forcing them to take to the skies and be seen and accounted for.

Metatron hovering just above the stratosphere watches the all the avian species take flight in numbers so great and astonishing they appear as a singular swath of cloud that covers continents and darkens the skies. Metatron's iris turn gray knowing the fate of those avian that have been chosen for dismissal causes him not only grief, but intense emotional pain. His mind wanders as he awaits command. He's been caretaker of the avian for only a short while, but he has come to love them as any other creation that he tends over all the realms of realties. The end of this day would see the end of many of the avian species. This day, more than a third would be forever wiped from existence.

Unlike the other Archs, Metatron is the true empathetic, sympathetic heart of the Corp of Archs. He's close to every living being that exists on the Earth just for nothing more than the shear love of them. It hurts him to his core that he himself doesn't know which are bound for extinction until the breaking of the seal. To lose even one species feels too much. Hearing the command blow across the wind, Metatron breaks the seal on his scroll and lets the wind take it to fulfillment. As soon as the scroll leaves his hand, it too dissipates. Those avian species named in the scroll are not meant for succession into the next age of men and fall dead to the Earth in droves.

Back at the City of Sarin every human and non-human eye look toward the skies as the land darken under the mountainous cloud of birds. Jazekial never looks up to the Heavens, not once. He just fixates ahead on those that he wants destroyed. Dead carcasses of the numerous species of avian begin to fall and pelt those that are underneath them. Bodies of birds fall to Earth everywhere except on the camp of Noah. As the birds fall a path is created of illustrious greenery as the birds fall to either side of a grass path creating a road of pure green. This lush green path leads to the building camp of Noah and the Ark that will soon sail into biblical recorded history.

Jungle Lands – Day

Arch Samael appears out of a stream of light from Heaven that ends high above the Jungle lands of Panthea, what in modern tongue would be called Africa. He lands in the dense jungles of Panthea. Among the trees and lush underbrush, he sees and hears all living creatures. He doesn't just hear those in his vicinity of responsibility, but over the entirety of the Earth. Samael looks to the heavens. He nods his head in submission to the given command and breaks the seal on his scroll and throws it on the ground. The scroll touches the land and dissipates just as the others. Animals not chosen for succession and named in the scroll begins to keel over and die where they stand. One such animal that is stricken from the record of existence is that of the now-fabled Unicorn which too has been lost to myth. The fabled creature was created outside of God's purview by a set of citizenries from the City of Gratenan called, the Muses. They were a pack of witches that were granted power by Lucifer to mix breeds of existing animals.

A Unicorn was a really beautiful creature whose blood had healing properties. The animal was no longer deemed necessary for the coming system of things. Satisfied that the scroll contents had been fulfilled, Samael takes to the skies. *Shame, really. They were truly a beautiful creature. Metatron won't take this lightly. Then again, I'm sure he already knows.*

Still watching through Gabriel's eyes Jericho continues to hear her mentally. *"Just as the first were ordered to begin the systematic destruction of living beast, amphibian, and foul, the second battalion would keep Jazekial of Casmontage at bay just long enough for Noah to complete his task and usher in a set of those chosen for succession and enough food for provision and sacrifice into the Ark. I stood poised with my brothers, never had I seen evil more personified than I did in that man, Jazekial. I often wonder if he could even be classified as man. Others would follow in the coming history; sure, but to me, he was the first. He marched on the last bastion Sarin without cause, care or mercy. He marched on Sarin simply for the hate of being given life.*

"Jazekial lead his men and creature alike into the city. They killed the faithless and righteous with impunity. He spared the unrighteous and wicked only to bolster his ranks. As he marched through Sarin, he used his sword to cut the heads from men, women, and children alike. He even slayed their beasts and pets. He did not discriminate."

Sadness takes Gabriel's voice. She pays particular attention to the human and angelic hybrids, the Nephilims. Through her eyes she makes sure that Jericho gets a good look at them. He watched as Nephilims of various sizes crushed and swatted Sarin's opposing warriors out of their way with such force that men's bodies would explode. *"With lines of defense broken on all sides, Jazekial's men and creatures of such an unholy alliance delve further into human city. Nosferatu's quickly found their prey in the beds of archaic hospices. Those that were too helpless to fight back quickly found themselves feasted upon by godless creatures that were never meant for existence. The greed and improprieties of Lucifer's fallen army were center blame for the godless monsters. Never should the two species of ethereal and mortal have mixed in any reality. The pale carnivorous species from Andromeda found the hospices and nurseries unguarded except for a few caretakers that remained behind. Without any regard for life they tore the heads off of sleeping infants and toddlers so that the arterial carotid arteries would spray forth blood. They drunk from them not only to quench their hunger, but for the sheer joy of the terror that onlookers displayed.*

The battle for Sarin was over in less than an hour. The village was completely overtaken in three. Those that were captured and had put up any resistance or refusing to bow was held for the Demitrode."

"What is the Demitrode?" Jericho asked.

"It was a name given to a destroyer of flesh. It was a furnace that was constructed from a metal that was once plentiful on this Earth. This metal was an ore that fell to this planet after crossing a singularity early in the galaxy's construction. One of the powers dropped it accidently letting it fall and seed this planet. It is an ore that our weapons were partially created from. It was of such temperament that only the celestials were to be able to manipulate it and wield it."

"Then how did this Jazekial manipulate it?"

"Lucifer's General Verminesk assisted Jazekial in the forging of it." Said Gabriel.

Gabriel continues her story giving Jericho full disclosure of the events. He watches Jazekial, enjoyment of being covered in blood. He watches and studies the hate filled leader revel in the utter devastation that he wrought.

Satisfied there were no more threats uprising from Sarin, Jazekial turns and points to two Nephilim awaiting at the city gates. They nod while reaching to the ground to retrieve two massive chains. They pick up the chains and enter Sarin with a huge black burning furnace in tow, the Demitrode.

"Those that were not killed in the initial onslaught were held as sacrifice to Lucifer. The Demitrode is archaic tongue for the Forsaken

Furnace. Jazekial laid waste to those people that defied him by burning them alive."

A blood-soaked soldier runs up to Jazekial and points out Noah's ark in the distance. Jazekial wipes the sweat and blood from his brow. He licks his lips at the thought of more to conquer and spoils to plunder, women to rape and children to make servants out of or eat, it made no difference to him. Jazekial points toward the ark.

"If they fight, destroy them! If they pray to the god of that old man Lamech, save them for me and I will serve them to Demitrode."

Jazekial, still pointing toward the Ark, closes his fist signaling his forces to begin their assault. Half of his forces begin to head for the Ark in a heated sprint. The bloodlust and hardwired penchant for evil guide their battle cries as they converge on the wooden behemoth.

Gabriel makes her voice audible to Jericho. "The second battalion of Archs is where I stood with my brother Archs Michael and Azrael," Gabriel says. "We were backed by seventy-five of the fiercest fighting choiretic angels to stand against that coming onslaught of personified evil. Michael stood and pointed his sword and told us to hold the line unto whatever end. We stood ready and engaged men, creature, nephilim, demon, and cross realm aggressors alike. We were not barred from intervening in the affairs of men in those days because of the unholy alliances made with men."

Jericho watches as waves of Jazekial's forces crash against the sturdy barrier of Archs and Choiretic Angels. Michael's movements are swift as he separates heads from shoulders and impales his blades deep into chest cavities. After spinning free of two blades meant to hack his midsection, Michael catches a blade of a Nephilim with the hilt of his sword. The pure power exerted by the hybrid drives Michael to one knee. From behind Michael a short red bolt of lightning from Azrael drives the hybrid back. Gabriel launches over Michael and takes the head off the shoulders of the Nephilim. Michael recovers turns to the left and drives his blade through the thigh of an approaching human soldier. As the Jazekial soldier falls to a knee, Gabriel runs by and takes his head.

Because the forces are many, a few manage pass the Archs. Once behind them, they are left to the tier one choiretic angels. They quickly dispatch those that look for confrontation and those that turn back to flee from it once witnessing the ferocity of the choiretic. Without warning, the demon general Verminesk falls within their midst. The fallen demon is merciless as he instantly cuts into the choir forces. His speed and precision are unmatched by the lower class of angel.

"Farriat of the angelic choir breathes heavy as he witnesses his brothers falling to the blade of Vermin. He's heard stories of the fallen angel, but never knew him personally. He was off expanding the vastness of space when the battle for Heaven's throne city was under siege by Lucifer. He's never had much experience with fear, but he wonders if it's what gives him pause or is it the slaying of a kin. Witnessing the brutality of Vermin, Farriat realizes how grateful that he was to have missed the battle that day when the Heaven's burned.

Two more of Farriat brothers fall to Vermin. Jericho feels the pain of loss watching the angel lose his brothers. Like Farriat, he knows the kindred sense of solidarity with those that are fighting with you, the bond that battle creates because you all fight for something greater than the one, you fight for each other. He can't turn away from what Gabriel shows him. He continues to watch as bodies continuously fall at the feet of Vermin.

Jericho pays extra close attention to the one that Gabriel named Farriat. He knows the look on his face all too well, because he's often had it, that the look of fear coveted by vengeance as you witness mates fall one by one, the look that Farriat carries now after losing his mates.

It's evident with which the ferocity Vermin kills that Farriat knows that he will soon be upon him. He grips his spear tighter in anticipation of the coming conflict. He grips so tightly that his knuckles turn white.

His helmet suddenly makes him feel claustrophobic. That manna that he received and ate earlier is churning in his stomach. *Maybe I should have skipped that extra ration this morning,* is all but thought consuming.

Vermin falls the right flank from behind with that surprise attack from appearing deep within the choir's ranks. In fear the remaining angels back away from him, but remain ready for his next attack. They have their orders. They hear their captain yell it clearly, "Hold the line!"

Vermin covered in arterial spray of angelic blood looks to his next victims. "Let me pass!" He hisses.

The remaining choir just stare at him giving up no more ground. Farriat looks at his brothers and feels that he can't witness one more fall without him having done anything. The bond that ties siblings makes him do what he thought was impossible. He walks from behind his brothers and stands in front of Vermin. He briefly looks past Verminesk in the direction of the Archs. They are battling repelling waves of men and monster on the frontlines.

"Vermin takes a moment and kneels on the field. He uses the white tunics of his victim's clothing to wipe his blade clean. He does so calmly only to strike more psychological blows to his opponents. He stands and waves the young choiretic angel forward. "Step to my blade or let me pass, little one. Your choice."

Why is he such a dominating force on the field? Farriat wonders. The speed with which he moves is nothing, but fatal. *I can't breathe.* Farriat's bio mechanical mask and helmet retracts below his armors neck line. He reaches to the side and with a quick unlatch his chest and back plate falls to the ground. He knows he needs to move faster than his armor will allow. His opponent is able to move as swift, because there is nothing to encumber him. He picks his staff up from the dirt that belonged to one of his felled brothers in addition to his spear and gives a series of intimidating twirls and spins hoping his prowess with the spear and staff will have a fear inducing effect on Vermin.

"Perhaps a blade, little one will suit you best, yes?" Vermin says to him.

Farriat twirls comes to a dramatic finish as he poses ready for Vermin. "No blade is needed, Demon. Let's go!"

Farriat begins to press the attack, but stops suddenly. His eyes widen in shock. His glare is one of disbelief. He looks down and sees a blade protruding from his chest. He looks back up and witnesses Vermin laughing at him.

Farriat's eyes then looks to the hands of Vermin. *He still retains his blade. How is this? How am I undone?* Suddenly, the Demon Painell emerges alongside Farriat's profile.

Laughing along with Vermin, Painell twists the blade, making a gaping hole in the rear of Farriat's back will not close.

My back was protected is the thought just above the pain he's experiencing of being impaled. He turns his head just over his right shoulder and sees the trial of headless bodies behind him that the demon celestial created.

"You are undone by the blade of Pain." Painell places his armored boot on the back of Farriat and pushes him off his blade while simultaneously pulling it clear.

Jericho's anger rises as he watches what happened to the angel, but then again, it's war and all is fair even if it appears that it isn't. He can only look on as blood flows heavily from the wound, as Farriat falls to his knees. Vermin walks up to him and looks him over. Farriat looks up into Vermin's eyes. He could continue to fight, but fear he thinks stifles him yet again. Then, it happens. Farriat finds peace. He feels a need to no longer feel the incapacitating effects of what fear does. He can't explain it at first then it becomes clear why he feels at peace, Death has arrived for Farriat. He looks past Vermin and sees the unmistakable black attire of the great equalizing force in the universe. As he stares into the shadow of Death's face, he finds a tranquil peace. *If this is what death is then it's not so bad, he isn't as bad as I've been led to believe.* Death gestures for Farriat to look into the blackness of his hood and remain there until it is done.

After observing the brave angel for a few seconds in hopes that he would beg him for a few more minutes of life, Vermin severs his head.

Having vanquished another, he looks to the remaining few that block his path to the Ark.

"Did you not see him, Gabriel?" Jericho asked.

"I saw, but like you, I had orders to hold the sea of villainy at bay."

Painell turns and backs up next to Vermin. They loosen their necks by slowly and deliberately moving them from side to side releasing tension and pressure causing a crackling sound. They stretch their wings out and then retract them. They know they've angered the remaining choir that was battling in perimeters. *Good, they'll attack with reckless fervor and we'll kill them all for it.* The pair's eyes turn red as flame. An in an instant, they press the attack.

CHAPTER 38

Jazekial watches as half the masses of his military might crashes against the wall of angels. He breathes heavily as he becomes upset with the progress.

"This is not what you promised me Demon. It seems the god of Lamech has come to Sarin. You spoke these lands were forsaken and the people cursed did you not?"

Lucifer walks up alongside of Jazekial. The lands are forsaken. They belong to me and is ripe for the taking mortal. You question me again and you shall be forsaken more than you already are. Don't forget, it is I that granted you power. Only by my will did thou come far as Sarin unopposed."

Lucifer pulls off his hood and drops his cloak. Warsivious places a hand on Lucifer's shoulder. "My liege, you should not enter into direct combat."

Lucifer side glances Warsivious' hand and War quickly retracts same.

"It has been some time since I've engaged with my brothers of old. Maybe this is the day, they listen to reason in the midst of clashing blades. Anyway War, the day feels ripe to stretch my wings. Sarin has already fallen, now to finish this by killing the seed of Lamech," Lucifer says, as he takes to skies heading for the line of Archs.

Gabriel runs her sword through two men at once. Her white hot edged blade cauterizes the men's wounds as soon as the blade enters them. She lifts and throws the dead men over head with the blade and then ducks low just as Azrael wing flies over her decapitating the heads of three more incoming soldiers.

Azrael lands and blocks an incoming blow by a Nephilim and then spins to his flank, grabbing him by the neck. He squeezes mercilessly until the Nephilim's neck breaks under the pressure. Only then does he see the choir of angels in the rear of formation struggling with the two fallen demons, Pain and Vermin. Azrael's wings strike the ground causing a hurricane force wind that blows every advancing enemy tumbling backward creating space. Azrael glances briefly at Michael, who gives him the go ahead. In a flash Azrael heads for the terror of Pain and Vermin.

Before Pain can strike another angel dead, Arch Azrael lands between the two demons and his brothers of the choiretic. Azrael catches Pain's blade with his and pushes him backward. Azrael's helmet disengages and falls below his armor's neck line. Azrael's face shows faint signs of battle scarring which he's incurred over the many centuries, but unlike the others, he allows facial hair to grow on his chin. "This is where I find you, Vermin. Haven't seen you since the holocaust on Aspear. Now, I find you here on Earth, besting those beneath you. You're a coward."

Pain and Vermin look at each other. A smirk crosses their face as their eyes flare a deeper red. The two engage Azrael promptly in a flurry of wild swings solely meant for decapitation and midriff separation. In a series of coordinated attacks, the demons swing for Azrael high and low simultaneously. Azrael retract his wings and parkour somersault between the blades. After clearing the blades, Azrael lands and steps backward onto the spear of Farriat's kicking it upward into his left hand. With a quarter turn he catches both of the demon's counter strikes and holds their sabers in a lock.

After dispatching two more humans, Gabriel looks back briefly and sees Azrael out the corner of her eye outnumbered two to one.

"Michael?" Gabriel shouts.

Michael glances back and briefly at the situation that occupies Azrael.

"Go!" Michael shouts at her and returns his attention toward the last of the incoming horde of the first wave.

Gabriel takes flight to even the odds with Painell and Verminesk. She lands next to Azrael and the two instantly begin coordinated two prong attacks.

"To the captain!" Gabriel yells out to the remaining choiretics.

Relieved to be free of the superior attacking demons, the remaining choir leap, run and fly to assist Michael. As the remaining choir reaches their captain, they rush head long into the fray as the second wave descends on them.

Michael, having a moment of respite, falls back. He gives his sword a thrusting shake to fling the blood from his collapsed Celliance Star ore's blade. In an instant, Michael kicks the nearest choiretic angel away from his flank to save him. Michael holds his blade at the high guard. Lucifer lands where the choiretic angel would have been. As he lands, his blade strikes Michael's guard. Michael barely just able to raise his blade in time before taking the strike. He wasn't quite fast and solid enough. The power and momentum behind the strike was intense. It sends Michael, wheeling feet over head backward, skipping across the ground creating shallow craters. As he rights himself and gets to his feet, Michael prepares his guard, he knows Lucifer will be instantly on him throwing a series of strikes.

Ready this time, his guard and parrying techniques are at peak form as he deflects and counter Lucifer blows. Lucifer stabs for the chest Michael turns profile, letting Lucifer's blade slide across his. Michael rolls and turns left and catches the face of Lucifer with a strong elbow strike. It staggers the former Morning Star slightly, but not enough for Michael to have an advantage. However, it gives their battle a moment of respite.

Lucifer smiling. "Is my reprieve up so soon? Have you come to collect?"

Glaring through the eye slits of his helmet, Michael's red eyes, burns. He growls, "Your reprieve should have been revoked when judgment was nigh at Chasm.

"Perhaps, but it wasn't. Instead, I was given rule of this realm, keeper of this reality. I'm merely setting the foundation that all of peace will be set upon... Even still, you can't see my vision."

"I cannot, brother." Michael says shaking his head. "The blind hatred and wanton destruction that you've wrought must have blinded me to your truest intentions."

Lucifer raises his sword in preparation of another flurry of attacks. Michael raises his blade in kind.

"Michael, I never wanted to end you. I never did, but I have a destiny outside that of Fate's script. I will do what I must to see it fulfilled. I must, for you, for us, for everything."

"And I will do what I must, Morning Star to make sure that his will is enforced and that you never ascend. I will see your schemes and machinations to an end."

"You can't beat me, Michael. We've been down this road before you and I."

Lucifer starts to edge toward Michael. "You couldn't beat me then on the Fields of Glayden. You couldn't beat me on the steps of the Most High's Palace, and you can't best me now."

Michael edges toward Lucifer. "And still you were bound, chained and brought before the Almighty Elohim."

"Why can't you see brother that your king is the enemy here, not I. Just ask yourself why would I lie? What do I have to gain?"

"Everything," says Michael.

"I suppose so." Lucifer voice softens for a second.

Lucifer charges in, and Michael falls back and to the right, causing Lucifer to move past him. Michael kicks out his foot tripping Lucifer throwing him off balance. A cheap move, but it works. Lucifer stumbles forward, Michael takes a swing for his neck— Clank! His attack is blocked by another's blade. Michael quickly looks left, he sees the owner of that blade glaring furiously at him. Warsivious holds Michael's blade at bay from taking the head of Lucifer.

"War!" Michael scowls.

"Is ever looming," says Lucifer.

Michael takes a step back and readies to engage both Warsivious and Lucifer. The two demons ready themselves as well. Michael pauses, then takes to the air. He nods at the two of them, then whisks backwards toward the Ark. He gives a telepathic order blast to his remaining forces, who also takes to the air in a tactical retreat toward the Ark.

Gabriel rolls and ducks a dual attack from Pain and Vermin. Having taking a blow to the face with the hilt of Vermin's blade, Azrael is slow to get on his feet, but he does before Pain's blades does a three sixty spin and downward slash towards him. As anticipated, Azrael finds himself ready for Pain. Their blades connect in fury and Azrael instantly goes offensive with a flurry attack. Pain parries and blocks his way through, but he's left reeling, which gives Gabriel the chance she needs to score a strike across the abdomen of Pain dropping him to a knee. As Azrael brings his blade down for the finishing strike, a red bolt flies with intentions of piercing Azrael's chest.

Gabriel stands in front of her brother and slings her left forearm up, igniting her collapsible circular shield from her left gauntlet. The shield locks into place and hardens just before it takes the full impact of the bolt originating from Vermin. The force, however, knocks her backward into Azrael and sends them both hurling through the fray of plasma bolts, clashing of blades, lightning, and spears of battle.

As Gabriel and Azrael stand, they dispatch two men, three nosferatu's and one nephilim before hearing the fall back to the Ark summons by Michael. From across the bloody streets of Sarin they stare at Pain and Vermin. They hate to disengage, but they are there for a purpose other than those two. A time will come when they will answer for all they've done this day and the many others that were like it. The two Archs take to the skies heading for the ark.

Just on the outskirts of the Ark, the Archs and Choiretics regroup with Michael at the head. Michael looks over to an exhausted Azrael and Gabriel that just landed. Azrael, reading the eyes of his captain, breaks rank and heads off toward the west. Michael turns and looks at the rest of his remaining force.

"This is it… We hold them here. Press on and don't stop until the last chosen creature and mortal is aboard. We hold for them, we hold because it is our task, we hold for the crown at all cost," Michael shouts before turning and pointing his blade toward Lucifer and his subjugated minions born of exacting sin.

The angelic choir spearheaded by the Archs engage men, demonic, nephilim and creatures of abhorred reality crossing led by their leader, Jazekial.

Jericho had no questions as he was witnessing an event long thought mythical by man, even by those that claim the devout clarity of Christianity, Judaism, and Islamic, would claim what has happened never did. Jericho just continues listening, making note of the enemy Jazekial to look for any meaning and understanding that he could find in what drives such a deadly opponent. He sees what Gabriel was telling him in that what he's experienced in his brief time of war has nothing on what past men that engaged in art of battle saw. The only difference was that the weaponry had changed, not the nature of men or the lot of the soldier. He understands what Gabriel wanted him to learn. She said it was an old adage and it was. Evil cannot persist if the righteous rose to meet it. However, he believes Edmund Burke said it best. "The only thing necessary for the triumph of evil, is for good men to do nothing."

"While we fought," Gabriel says, "Azrael escorted the pairs of chosen animals to the Ark. It took more time than we had prepared for under the threat of attack. It was a meticulous event as Azrael had to make sure each reality that he was spreading the creatures across would not place them in danger from that specific realm's apex predators. Once made safe, he placed each paired animal into stalls that we equipped to phase reality to place the chosen survivors of the liquid purge in pocket dimensions. Finally, when the last of the chosen were loaded, we held the line until Lucifer's forces disengaged, leaving only Jazekial."

Jericho was still watching the events unfold, but if could have seen Gabriel's face, he'd have sworn she was crying. He continued to listen to saddened voice of Gabriel.

"Death had claimed more than half of our angelic forces that held the line for Noah, son of Lamech. As we fell back into a holding pattern awaiting any other counter attack, it happened, Michael retrieved a scroll from under his armor and released the already broken sealed scroll. The destruction of that system of Earth had found finality. Rain began to fall with droplets large enough to crush mortal and celestial alike. Arch Cassiel who was assigned to the protection of the protected family gave the signal that Noah's task was at last complete. Michael ordered the full disengagement, clearing the way for the third battalion of Archs that saw to the total annihilation of all living things on Earth. The caste of the Powers tier of angels were mighty that day. They brought Lucifer's first unholy campaign to a resounding close. Jazekial's evil was thwarted, but the destruction, the loss of life that he left in his wake would have made the modern day tyrants pale in comparison."

Gabriel removes her hand from Jericho's eyes. "You see... the evil of men has always been. What you experienced is nothing new. The only difference now is that you and those in existence, currently may be the last that has to endure instances of personified evil of the demonic fallen and those they possess."

Jericho sits up. He's a little sluggish after having seen all that she's shown. "Haven't I endured enough, Gabriel? I've fought across more than enough continents in campaigns that were world altering. I've seen enough blood to last me two lifetimes. More than that, I really want to feel Isis. I want to touch her face, run her hair through my fingers, talk to her. Remember her? I want to be with her. I want to have a family someday amidst this madness in our own piece of the world. Haven't I done enough, yet? Haven't I sacrificed enough over the past eight years?

"Have you?" Gabriel says staring at him.

"I for one think I have. I feel that I've fought my share for God and country. No more sacrifices messenger, no more! If I Haven't put down this threat you keep alluding to over the past eight years, then fuck it is what I say. I'm tired of waiting for this challenge that you swear is coming? Well, Gabriel where is it? Where is this threat? I've followed your advice and path up to this damn meeting on this roof and have yet to see what I'm preparing for."

Jericho watches Gabriel's reaction. As much attitude as he just gave her he feels a bit guilty, because she doesn't respond in kind. She just looks at him with a compassion that only the purplish gray colored eyes of an angel can cast.

Gabriel's heart breaks a little as she forms her next set of words. "Unfortunately, more shall be required of you before the end of this system of things."

Jericho looks to the ground a bit defeated, but he knows that deep down in the nether regions of his soul that it was never going to be that easy as just up and saying I'm done. There was no way that he would simply join a militaristic cause and that be the end. He just wants it to be done. Whatever challenge he's waiting for to just come already. "Then, understand Gabriel, I need to take a break for myself. I need to see Isis. I need to know what I'm even still fighting for worlds away from home. I need this, Gabe. Unless you want to tell me why I'm really here and what threat is coming."

Gabriel just looks at him in silence.

"Yeah, I thought not. What good is a messenger that has no message?" Jericho says, as he lies back, finishing another beer. "Thanks for the horrors that you've shown me to prove your point. I'm sure I'll sleep less than I do now., but I got your question and know the answer. Oh! And I'll be forwarding you my therapy bills."

Gabriel breaks her silence now that she's deemed he done bitiching. "A lesser man that have not experienced what you have up to this point might have broken. You did not. You want to know what's coming Jericho? No need to ponder such things any longer, because it's no longer coming."

Jericho sits up and tosses the can aside.

"It's already here." Gabriel says.

Gabriel looks at Jericho and then off into the distant horizon. "This doubt of self-worth and impatience reared its head from what Rusain said to you, yes?"

Hearing that name sends heat throughout his body. Jericho's jaws clench. His heart rate accelerates just a bit faster. The name Rusain turns on the biological body's response to anger. "Fuck that guy! But, damn if he's not right to degree." *That's what pisses me off, why he gets under my skin so damn much. The writing is on the wall, no matter the faith I have in America. Look at the world's opinion of Lucien and his dominating regime. He's the next savior in the making as far as the nations are concerned. He's a gotdamned hero. As much as I hate to admit or even give that guy credit for, Rusain was right. It won't be long before we're allied with him as a singular force. I can't be around for that.*

Jericho looks around and finds one last can of the Germanic brew. Shrugging his shoulders, he picks up the can and pops the top. *Pssh!* He raises it in toast toward Gabriel and takes another swig from his freshly opened can of beer.

"I'm done here, Gabe! I've decided I'll be resigning my commission. I'm done with this fight. I'm done waiting for this challenge. What I see is you all playing an infinite game of right to rule. Count me out of the next hand that's dealt. I'm going home."

Jericho takes a swig from his can, remembering suddenly the figure that he saw that day in the jungle. The mysterious figure wearing all black with the shadowed hooded face. Jericho's no stranger to the mind-altering effects of war's carnage. He's been having flashbacks from his campaigns across continents, but none more than of the other day's battle. Incredible shit happened in those intense hours of fighting, but that figure, the dark hooded man that requested silence of him is oddly what stands out. Who was he? Jericho could ask Gabriel, but he's had enough of prophecy and angels for today. Some other time perhaps.

Gabriel starts to speak when her attention is drawn upward suddenly. She becomes distracted instantly. Looking skyward she finally speaks, "If you are done in this man's military might, so be it. May God speed your journey home to a well-deserved time of respite, but know, Jericho, that it will only be but for a moment. For he comes quickly." Gabriel steps on the ledge of the roof.

Jericho finishes and throws the last can over the ledge now that its contents are empty. "Just like that, huh? I can go home?"

Gabriel looks back at him. "It was not I that said you should serve in this man's militaristic might… Take your respite, you will need your mind and physical strength preserved for what's to come."

Jericho walks closer to the ledge. "You know you can appear more often… right? There are days when I actually need to talk to you," Jericho says sensing her near departure.

Gabriel turns and winks at him. "When you need me, Jericho I'm never far. I can always hear you, but this is your odyssey that was tasked you. Speak and I'll hear, but summon me at will, you simply can't."

Jericho nods his head, expressing his disdain for the cryptic speech of the heavens.

"Gabriel, you know… you never told me if you were there when she died."

"You never asked." Gabriel takes off rocketing into the night sky.

CHAPTER 39

BEST LAID PLANS

"There is nothing wrong with taking pleasure in your work even if it displeases the gods."

Quote ~#27 of Legion

Arcainaque, Cainsin City, Vespian Spire

Lucien is having lunch in his personal restaurant that revolves at the top of his celestial home inspired Spire tower of operations in his Sovereign City. Warsivious, Cyrail and Rusain walk into the restaurant and find him already having dinner. They walk to the table each standing by a respective chair awaiting permission to join him. After savoring a bite of a medium well-cooked steak, he invites them to finally have a seat. They each pull out their chair and sit.

Lucien Looks at Warsivious. "We don't need to eat, but having overtaken this body it requires sustenance. I must admit, I don't understand the repeated ritual having to do this so often, but this vessel slows and reduces to a weakened state if I do not. Maybe this would not be such a mundane task if I were able to taste and enjoy the said meal."

The trio of top command adjust themselves behind their placements. Only Rusain and Cyrail look at the menu to order.

Lucien eyes Cyrail. "I have a task for you. It is to be carried out by you expeditiously." Lucien points his carving knife at Cyrail. "So, put down that menu and listen closely! As always you know your number one objective is?"

"To not be seen." Cyrail answers.

"Not to be seen," Lucien repeats. So, you know what the mandate is?

"Yes Sir." Said Cyrail.

Lucien returns back to his meal. "You were seen. China has procured a witness from your cleansing of the Destined Suns. It appears that Rusain's perimeter was compromised before your arrival."

Rusain's eyes instantly avert from the menu. He places it back on table. *Guess I'm not eating this evening.*

Lucien continues. "There was a witness that fled into the thick underbrush of the Jungle. Chinese Military Operators that were quietly inserted for observational purpose of reporting on our coalition captured a target of opportunity. The bastard all of you missed. He takes another bite of steak. "Your stepping into the light will be done on our terms at a time of my choosing. This witness has become a situational problem that could upset my best laid plans. We don't need that. Would you all agree?

The commanders all nod their heads speaking in unison, "No Sir."

After sipping his wine Lucien places the Glass on the table as well as his utensil. He wipes his mouth then leans in close toward the table. "However, this incident gives us a win on two fronts. China has sat outside of these past conflicts and United Nations talks for long enough. They are a formidable force that must be dealt with sooner rather than later or at least occupied. America is just the ones for that." Lucien turns to Cyrail. "Go to Germany and finish your job that was not completed in the Congo! That witness is under lock and key and will be for some time before a window of opportunity opens. When it does you must strike fast and leave no trace of Arcanian involvement. When you have him, turn the witness over to Death and make sure you leave some form of evidence, no matter how miniscule of United States involvement."

Lucien leans back grabbing his utensils again and places another bite of steak into his mouth and gives a second look toward Cyrail. "You still here?" Lucien then turns his attention to Rusain and Warsivious. "We need to expediate a plan to introduce Cyrail to the world. I need him to step from the shadows and become a more active force. Suggestions?"

Cyrail throws his napkin to the table, signifying he's done with a meal that he never started. He stands politely dismissing himself from the table.

Warsivious watches Cyrail leave then places his eight-point military hat down on the seat that was just vacated. "It just so happens Sir, I do have a suggestion. Intel has given us information on a pending attack. Rusain and I have thought long and hard on how to turn in into an advantage. We believe we have."

Rusain clears his throat. "Sir, we absorb the attack and make it work for us." Rusain reaches beside his chair into a briefcase he brought with him. He pulls a folder from its contents and passes it to Lucien. "These are the details that will solidify your place as king. So much so that you've been chosen to have divine protection. Billions will fall to your feet in worship if everything goes to plan."

Lucien stares at the folder for a second then places another bite into his mouth. "Explain it to me!"

"Rusain leans in closer. "We wait for your speech in front of the United Nations and then—"

Angelic Spire, Zero Realm

Michael walks into the center of the Sparrows Chamber in the Angelic Spire already filled with his Archs. He walks alongside a long gold and white marbled table with matching white marbled chairs on all sides save the head seat for royalty. Michael walks until he takes his place to the right of the head seat of the table. Once there, he nods an acknowledgement to the other Archs, who all stand and salute him.

In preparation for their meeting, in the iconic chamber Michael makes sure to explain protocol again if the prince or king should decide to show. A Meeting of all the Archs has not happened in a millennium, they are dressed in their best white angelic regalia minus the armor. Their ranks and caste, which are normally illuminated brightly on their shoulder patches, have been made white. When at the Table of Doves all patches are white to signify an even playing field where all of the Archs are permitted to speak on a matter regardless of rank or caste.

Gabriel enters the room dressed in her finest regalia as well and finds her seat that is positioned to the left of Michael. With all surviving members accounted for the Archs place their respective weapons on the table in front of them and takes their seat. There are three chairs that are empty which belongs to the Archs that have died over the eons since the rift. The most recent chair being that of Uriel. Like the other three, his chair remains empty as a sign of respect for the fallen Arch. His helmet and weapon are placed on the table in front of his chair. The battle regalia has been cleaned and preserved as a testament to what he's done in and for the protection of the Heavenly realm.

Seeing that everyone has arrived, Michael begins, "I find that we are all here and accounted for, yes?"

Azrael stands. "I have taken count Captain, we are all accounted for and present. We stand at fifteen brothers and one sister of the Archcaste. Azrael sits. "It has been sometime since we've had conclave called. Why now Captain?"

Michael looks to Azrael and then all of the Archs. "It was not I who called this meeting, but another. Movements behind the scenes veiled in darkness have brought about a new enemy that reminds us of darker times. Those of us that were at Sarin, the last bastion remembers. However, the veil which has worked to blind us to all else that moves has brought about forgotten and recluse allies."

The Archs all look at Michael, confused.

"It was I that called this meeting of the Angelic Arch Order." Fate walks into the chamber looking at the grandeur of the place. "Astonishing what you've all done with the Spire since my long self-imposed exile. It looks incredible."

Gabriel and a few of the others Archs that know of his existence, stand and bow in acknowledgement of the ethereal being that supersedes even their own existence.

Fate gestures for them to sit. "No, please, brothers—" He pays special attention to Gabriel staring at her a second longer than others. "—and sister, be seated!"

Those that stood again find their seats. The Archs that did not stand was not intended to show any disrespect, they simply didn't know of the existence of Fate.

Fate stands at the head of the table with his arm resting on the back of the adorned chair. He pays reverence to the adorned chair. His facial expressions betray him just a bit as they all can see that he must wonder the magnitude of the problems that must rest on the troubled brow of the one that sits there at the head of the Archs. "Oh! To be king."

Fate shakes the thought and looks to the faces of those seated. "It is a welcomed pleasure to see a few faces that I remember and it is even a greater pleasure to meet those that I have not met officially. Allow me to introduce myself to those that do not know me. I am Seraphim Fatetanen. You all may simply call me Fate."

Whispers start to erupt in the room.

Angry, Raphael stands. "You are of the broken Seraphim caste, Lucifer's caste!"

Not shying away, Fate takes the charge head on. "That is correct. I was created the same time as Lucifer. We are the first of all the Angelic Orders and Choiretic Caste, Including yours Archs."

Raziel tugs Raphael on his arm pulling him back down to his seat before standing himself to address Fate, "We've heard mention of you and seen your names inscribed around the realm. We thought you were long destroyed in the Battle for Glayden. Your name has fallen to myth and legend to not only mortals, but all things ethereal as well."

Fate smirks. "Legend, you say? Have I been absent so long that I've fallen into shadow? Are not all legends built off of a one-time truth?"

Gabriel interjects. "Why now? Of all the times you could have appeared and made yourself known, why now, why this particular moment in linear time?

"Because he wrote us here. Right Fate? That is what you do isn't it? You write, it happens? Cassiel says.

Fate's white metallic boots clack against the polished marble that moves like translucent fluid. He steps from the head of the table and moves slowly till he's behind Gabriel. He gives Cassiel a long hard side glance and ignores him turning his attention back to Gabriel. "Yes, why now? Straight to the point, Lilith. I've always liked that about you."

At the name of Lilith, whispers rip through the chamber from the conclave of seated Archs. What resonated softly in the beginning as whispers becomes boisterous. Michael glances down for a moment at the calling of the name; His face contorts into a look that says we could have done without this tidbit of knowledge slip. Then again, Michael remembers Fate to never pull his punches verbally.

Gabriel looks uneasy and her irises turn gray. She wants to turn away from the table at the mere sound of the name, Lilith, and what it implies. Resolute and poised she keeps her head straight and looks all her brothers in the eye.

Fate places his hands on the shoulders of Gabriel and squeezes them gently. "Or as you have been so aptly renamed, Gabriel."

Fate releases her and continues his revolution around the table looking at each Arch up close.

"I have returned because my best-laid plans have been upended. Everything that I have written from the alpha of the rift to the omega of mortals has been put in jeopardy of falling to complete chaos and upheaval from which there is no correction."

The faces of the Archs are lost in confusion.

"Bear with me a breath, will you? Let an old Seraphim prattle on for a few. You may just be enlightened at what an elder has to say. In my self-imposed exile, I've witnessed the uprising of the demonic fallen ones. I've seen them attack the souls and ideals of the ethereal as well as mortals with impunity. They have been busy not only in this plain, but throughout the multirealms of realities. I've witnessed you few lead many and risk much to thwart their plans ensuring my written words are adhered to in the name of the king. I am here to personally commend you and encourage you to fight on, because the alternative if you lose is the unraveling of the Heavens and all of creation."

Metatron Stands commanding the floor to speak. "I'm not listening to this Seraphim any longer. His caste is broken and speak nothing but falsity."

Azrael stands and places a hand on Metatron to calm him. He eases his brother to sit back into his seat. "Let's hear him out. I want him to clarify this submitted plan he speaks on."

Azrael nods at Fate, gesturing him to continue. "Your submitted plan? What are you saying? What is the meaning of it?" Azrael asks.

Fate walks the length of the table till he's behind Metatron and Azrael. He places his hands on Metatron's shoulders. "I know you, Metatron. I know that you have a soft heart for the small mortals. The ones they labeled... Ahh! Children, there is the word. Escaped me for a moment. I know for instance that you sit with them in the cancer wards, hoping to ease their passing as they await Death's arrival. I also know that you take joy when they're born in telling them life's secret before you purse their lips to secrecy by indenting them there, in the upper lip." Fate points to the divit above Metatron's lip. "I know that Elohim, the Prince nor even Michael for that matter, will find none more loyal than in your service."

Metatron looks forward across the table at his brother, Zaphkiel who starts speaking. "You say you know me. I find this impossible as we've never personally met. Like many others, even a few here, I knew of you, but we've never had words."

Gabriel looks down the table at Fate. Her irises turning a bright shade of red. "Because he wrote the plans for your path in this linear existence. He wrote them for everyone. From winged foul to swimming amphibian and, yes, even the mortals. Get it Zaph?" Gabriel says.

Michael interjects, "He's a term best defined as the master builder to the true architect's plans."

Fate smirks with modesty. "I am simply Fate, Elohim's master builder of all that moves."

Zaphkiel stands and looks Fate in the eyes. He points at Fate, as if ready to release a bolt of energy from his gauntlet had he'd been wearing it. Anger over takes him. "He's one that our Lord despises. One that never chose a side. You... Lukewarm bastard! You walk in here as an affront to us all and a coward. Where were you when Jacelyn burned? Where were you when the fields of Glayden ran with celestial blood?"

Challenged, Fate releases the shoulders of Metatron turning his attention to Zaphkiel. "It's not so simple, choosing sides. Nonetheless a side was chosen in the days of the fall. Otherwise, I'd not be here now educating you. And, yet again, it appears that a side was chosen for me when Apollyon let Warsivious walk away with the remains of a Nephilim. I did not write that alternate linear event which if comes to fruition, all is lost. I would not build so that all could be undone with but a pull of a single strand."

The two stares at each other before Fate smiles and returns to his pleasant and respectful regal self. "I'm not here for sparring of words among the likes of, Zaphkiel."

Raziel stands. He motions for Zaphkiel to sit. He then looks to Fate. "Then, if what you write is law, your pen can set the record straight for all time, yes?"

Azrael interjects, "Except that Lucifer is of his caste, and being of his caste, he can alter Fate's linear plan just as he originally did with Adam. He altered your plans sending us all down this transformed path of events to begin with... Isn't that right? It's what you meant by submitted and best laid plans, right?"

Fate starts to slowly clap his hands at Azrael. "You get it. The scale of the task was immense and it had never been constructed to such a scale. Elohim had given allotments to us Seraphim's due to the sheer immenseness of the arduous task undertaken. However, we were not made aware of them till after the fall. Simply put, we received one correction that we were unaware of until Morning Star had caused havoc across all of creation. I altered the course once when Lucifer fell correcting for the addition of sin. That was my one adjustment and it has been expended."

Raphael stands to speak. The others give him the floor and sit. "If that is the case, then Lucifer has used his for the fall. He shouldn't have been able to course correct to find and use the Nephilim remains."

"That would be true except that Lucifer never course corrected. Lucifer's fall was not a correction. It was an unforeseen event driven by emotion and rage in an already perfect existence. It was an anomaly in the system similar to a Human's A.I. becoming self-aware. He did not alter the plan purposely. He did what all living things do, he evolved. The problem was that he was the first celestial intelligent species to do so. He never purposefully altered the course until the creation of this Imperial. That was his course correction, that event is what defies a god and proves him fallible"

Azrael stands. "From what I'm understanding then, he never should have known he had the power to correct, which leads to a bigger question that is starting to take shape here." Azrael looks to Michael. "Because Lucifer was not around the realm when it was decreed their line of governed rules dictating course correction until after man had already fallen—"

"—Then how would Lucifer have known that he could alter the course of man any further than he'd already had?" Samael says taking the floor.

Fate slow claps his hand and points to Samael. "That there is the question, isn't it?"

Metatron stands as Samael sits. "And you can't course correct any further?"

"I cannot," Fate admits. "This task will fall to you all. You, the remaining Archs that saved Jacinto, Jacelyn, and Cortanian, and all the other heavenly provinces. You all will have to fight again to alter this equation which will ultimately decide the course of Zero Realm and all the others, including 2814, Earth. You however, are not alone in this task I see. It will also fall heavily on the mortal that has been named Jericho. It will be his bane that may very well set the record straight and on track for all time, at least the time that remains... The clock is inevitably and almost literally four minutes to midnight on the human's doomsday clock for the omega of everything."

Fate begins to walk the room again. He stops in front of Uriel's empty chair. "I look at all you Archs of the remaining castes. I tell you as the master builder, I no longer know how this will play out nor does Elohim in my opinion. Again, we are all in uncharted territory, just as when Elohim had never been challenged in his authority on such a level until Lucifer."

Michael now stands. "Then what good are you, Fate? What is your claim in all of this if you have no power to correct?"

Fate walks to Michael and stands toe to toe with the captain. "My claim warrior, is that I was instructed to create an infallible series of plans for the Lord's approval. My work has been compromised with the possibility of being laid waste. I, as the master builder cannot fail the architect, nor his hammer, Yeshua. I will see my work fulfilled. My claim in all of this is to correct the linear path and bring this system to a close as written. My reputation is on the line."

Michael stands closer almost nose to nose with Fate. "You just said you can't course correct; how will you correct the path?"

"By means of force, the only mean left to us as an option. I will help you, Arch of Angels set right all that has gone wrong. I cannot offer you my ink and quill no longer to change a thing, but I may offer you my friendship, brotherhood, my unwavering loyalty to the throne and house of Elohim and, most importantly, my sword." From underneath his white trench coat, he pulls out his beautiful glyph-scripted Rapier blade and walks down to Uriel's chair and sets it next to Uriel's blade. "Let us put right the words I struck long ago with my burning quill, Michael... Let us correct what Lucifer set asunder. Now! What say you Captain?" Fate looks to the table as a whole, "What say you, Archs? What say you all?"

The Archs all look down the table to Michael.

Gabriel can't say if she agrees or even like Fate for outing her, but he seems sincere and it sure can't hurt to have a powerhouse the likes of a Seraphim at their table. Gabriel starts pounding her fist on the table in a steady beat. Metatron then joins her and pounds his fist to her beat. The remaining Archs then all join in one beat. Michael looks at them and then towards Fate.

"What say you, Captain?" Fate asks.

Michael nods his head in acknowledgement of his fellow Archs decision. He slams his fist to the table, silencing the room. He then takes a long look at Fate. "We put this right. If all are in agreement, we welcome you Seraphim Fatetanen, to the Archs. Michael hugs him. The remaining Archs cheer in one voice.

Fate sheaths his sword and begins to walk toward the door. "With your permission. Captain, I would like to appeal to Lucifer's sensibilities in one last attempt to change his stance. Diplomacy, if you please. It has been some time since we've had words."

Michael nods. "May your diplomacy be a success where I have failed. Your sit down is granted."

Fate turns walking close on Michael so that he may be the only one to hear his words. "Another thing Michael, there was one in the garden of Gethsemane the night when the prince was betrayed to Death all those years ago on Earth. I believe there is another here now. You need to seek out the betrayer among this current celestial order. Lucifer learned of this governed rule after he was cast out only because someone told him of it." Fate stands back and pounds his fist against his chest in salute to his new captain and leaves the chamber.

"Fate!" Michael calls out. Shouldn't it be I that takes orders from you?"

Fate walks back to Michael and kneels before him. "It is I, of the house Seraphim that takes orders from you. You have proven yourself a most capable leader, more than you think of yourself. You are Michael, Captain of Heaven's armies. You were chosen and consecrated by Elohim himself. If the ultimate creator believes he's chosen correctly, it's time you put aside the doubt in yourself and be the leader we all know you are." Fate stands and nods approval at Michael then takes his leave.

Cassiel walks up to Michael. "He's what you were worried about on the balcony of the Spire that day?"

"Aye! I had no idea which way his loyalties would fall," says Michael.

"Is he really that powerful?"

Michael doesn't say anything. He just looks at Cassiel, his eyes tell the Arch the answer. Michael then looks toward Gabriel.

"How many total were in the Seraphim caste Captain?" Raphael says joining the conversation.

Michael looks back at Raph and puts up three fingers. "There were three."

Raphael surprised at the low number can't help but repeat, "Only three? Well, who's the third?"

Michael again remains silent. Raphael knows he'll never get the answer out him. Either he was sworn to secrecy or he just truly doesn't know. Raphael satisfied for the information he was able to retrieve, turns and looks in Gabriel's direction and whispers lowly for only Michael to hear. "What is this Lilith matter that Fate spoke of?"

Michael also looking across the chamber at Gabriel. "That is for her to say."

Michael walks away from Raph, leaving the chamber as well. The third caste angel just keeps staring at Gabriel from across the room as she talks to the remaining Archs that have not yet departed. Gabriel returns Raph's gaze briefly catching eyes with him and then returns back to her conversation.

Raphael sighs! *This matter here requires further investigation.*

CHAPTER 40

ADVERSARIAL

"I have always been slow to conflict. I've often thought of more ways to resolve arbitration that has gone awry than on the end of sword and shield. This conflict that the creator and subject find themselves in is like no other, the rift is more than a son seeking father's approval. This divide is that which has been welcomed by the nature of dueling classes of aristocrats and pauper, automatons and free thinkers.

I have always been a voice of reason to those that look to strike the killing blow. I have been that glint in the eye of victims that beckon to their persecutor and slayer saying, give me one more breath for the sake of a world that would mourn my abrupt departure at the hands of violence. Now in this fifth age, I have fallen into obscurity as so many of my brothers. The hearts of men have waxed cold under the suggestion of Lucifer and his vast armies leaving me little recourse in ending conflicts. Take heed, I have not completely withdrawn from the world of men. If called upon I will answer. Ask and I will make myself known."

Quote ~Mercy

Ramstein Air Force Base, Germany – 2 Months Later

Jericho looks at the many degrees conferred upon the one-star general's wall in whose office he finds himself in. He adjusts the high collar of his class a uniform to compete with the rising heat of the non-air-conditioned room as he reads the names of those professors and educators that conferred the doctorates. When hearing the office door open he turns and faces the general coming to attention.

"At ease Captain! Please be seated," General Kovac says as he extends his arms toward one of two seats in front of his desk.

"Don't let dem papers on that wall der fool you son, I'm the same southern uneducated sum of bitch jarhead that enlisted twenty-eight years ago. I may be a little less surly though. Politics has a way of doing dat."

Jericho eases from attention and smiles a bit at the generals attempt to illicit an ease of tension to the room. Jericho removes his hat from underneath his left arm and sits in the chair closes to him. General Kovac follows suit and ensconces himself behind his desk.

"Captain Bane, I've reviewed your stella record. I've had a chance to read the reports of your superiors and subordinates and find that you are of rare breed in this modern arm of the military. Looking here you have successfully led over thirty combat missions all over dis glorious rock of a planet that we inhabit. The most current being hunting down the Destined Suns. You have made quite a career for yourself that appears to have much progression and promotion in line for you, which is why I have to ask son, why have you requested to resign your commission?

Jericho places his white Marine dress hat into the center of his lap. "Sir, I have fulfilled my commitment to the Corps. I have paid for my education ten times over with blood, sweat and more mental anguish then I sought after. I just believe that it's time for me to step aside."

Kovac leans back in his Corinthian leather chair and tosses Jericho's files on the desk in front of him. He studies the young captain. "It was that der Congo mission, wasn't it, son?"

"Sir, I completed each task that was given to me over there without fail or compromise." Said Jericho

"Well, I see dat Captain, but it was the last mission that brings you before me today right? I read your report that went to the Joint Chiefs. You and that Rusain feller had a few words, straight Georgia dust up?"

"We did, sir. I'm not going to lie general, having to work with the Arcanian Forces was taxing. They are an army that I believe have no solid core morals, no soul like that of our beloved Corps. And as I look into the coming days, let's be honest Sir, we'll be working more and more joint operations with them as they become a prominent force on the world stage. Rusain said that one day we'd work under their banner. I didn't want to admit that at first, but I can't deny Lucien's growing world power. It's no longer farfetched that we could possibly end up taking orders from him in the not too distant future. That Marine Corps, sir, is one that I refuse to be a part of."

Kovac still leaning back in his chair begins to gently rock back and forth.

"Denied Captain Bane!"

Jericho's hands clench his hat crushing the shaped cloth material in his palms. His Adam's Apple elevates up and falls back into place. "Can the captain ask why, sir?"

"The captain may, indeed. I'm gonna deny you on the pretense that you have not thought this decision through. And the fact that you still have three more years on your reenlistment in a time of war."

Kovac continues staring at Jericho looking for a reaction. "However, son, I'll tell you what I'm gonna do. You seem to have a lucky charm up your ass. You've been in over thirty hostile combat missions with just about as many engagements and have not so much split a hair from what your medical records have to say on the matter. You take on one more mission for me, you complete it successfully I'll honor your request and separate you from my illustrious Corps. Seeing how much time you have remaining, I don't think you'd find a better deal."

Jericho doesn't hesitate. "The mission?"

"Prisoner escort," Kovac says as he leans forward on his desk, clasping his hands at first then steepling them.

"Prisoner escort?" Jericho says suspiciously.

"That it, just escort Captain. You take a simple spin over to the Chinese Consulate with three or four special forces fellers and return the prisoner."

"When, sir?"

"Just as soon as I have the lieutenant colonel draw up the transfer orders."

"May the captain know the identity of the prisoner?"

Kovac stands which prompts Jericho to stand to his feet placing his hat back underneath his left arm.

Kovac walks in front of his desk and sits on it. "When Rusain took the Destined Sun's compound he missed one of the militants. One escaped and in his extreme cowardice and terror he happened upon covert Chinese operatives working the area for intelligence on Arcane's forces. They took him into custody and back to their consulate before Rusain was the wiser. From the way I understand it during interrogation they learned something of extreme urgency and have reached out to us. Concern of transmission interception via radio or cyber was deemed too high to pass the learned intel. Dem boys said only face to face was acceptable."

"I want it in writing, Sir. I do this and I'm out," says Jericho.

"Agreed, son. I'll have papers drawn immediately." Said Kovac.

"You could have just ordered me Sir, why didn't you?"

"Son, I've seen men over duh course of almost three decades that known when it was time for dem to retire. They ignored that proclivity for mental self-preservation. Eventually, they lost their shit and men and women died unnecessarily. If you say you've just about done reached your end of mental strength Captain and with your record of combat as proof, well I'm incline to believe you may be close and have that keen presence of mind dem other fellers didn't have to know when to quit... Do we understand each other? Have the general's intentions of forgoing orders clarified the fogginess of the Captains visions?

"Yes Sir!" Jericho said snapping to attention.

"Dismissed." Said Kovac surrendering a return salute.

Within three hours, Jericho is in his battle dress uniform standing next to a black GMC Suburban with all tinted windows. With his rifle slung around his chest, he does a last-minute spot check for provisions and ammo. Minutes later the sound of rotary blades slicing the afternoon sky draws his attention skyward at an approaching Blackhawk helicopter. He shields his eyes as the chopper lands kicking up debris.

Once on the ground, three Navy Seal operatives from Seal Team Four exits the chopper in full battle dress as well. They instantly notice Jericho and starts to trot towards him. When they approach they render the customary salute. Jericho salutes back.

"Sir, Master Chief Nelson, Seamen Riley, and Seamen Griffin of Seal Team Four reporting for duty." Said Nelson pointing the other two under his command.

Jericho looks them over inspecting them quickly. "Seal team? Are we expecting some cataclysmic event boys?"

The seals don't smile.

"Right!" Jericho continues. "It's a pretty straight forward mission. We take this here Suburban, to the Consulate, pick up the prisoner, some high-ranking Chinese spook and their escort convoy and return to base. The escort breaks off upon our entry through the gates. The spook remains with us." Jericho walks around them. "Easy enough mission. Can't understand why any airmen or soldier couldn't have done this so, we're going to assume that command knows more than they're telling us. You Seals normally role more deep than this. I can only imagine that since I only have you three, that any more of you would have raised some eyes that Marines don't want to have raised."

"That would be a fair assessment Captain," said Nelson.

"Mmmmhmmm!" Jericho growls for show. "Well that means our escort must be a high priority. Mount up, Seals! Let's get this over with... Master Chief, you take the wheel. I'm shotgun."

"Yes, sir."

Jericho and the men jump into the running air-conditioned vehicle. As Jericho readies to close the door he sees Gabriel by the helicopter as it takes to the skies. She grabs the hilt of her sheathed blade and nods at Jericho. He nods back tightening the grip on the pistol portion of his M4 Rifle. Acknowledging that if she's sending him off, it's confirmation that what he's in for is more than an escort. *Gabriel's never seen me off on a mission before.* Jericho closes the door and gets his rifle in position to fire out the window if necessary. "Stay frosty, boys. Things may not be as easy as it appears."

All three of the Seals signify in unison, "Aye, captain!"

Jericho grabs his ear piece and listens closely. He then depresses his throat mic. "Confirmed... Master Chief new heading. We are going to the Embassy instead.

Chinese Embassy Berlin, Germany – Day

The massive four block compound of the Chinese Embassy is in full lockdown. Windows and doors have all been secured in the most extreme of preparation to house and protect their high priority captive.

Senior Colonel Kirito waits just outside the steel door to the makeshift prisoner cell. In full battledress he scans the perimeter awaiting the Americans arrival. The Senior Colonel grabs his ear piece and bangs on the door behind him. The door opens slowly with the muzzle of a rifle peeking out first.

< Ten minutes to American's arrival,"> says the senior colonel. The door closes back.

Six identical black GMC Suburban's wait in a row one behind the other. They all look identical to the American's GMC, even down to the

411

tinted windows as they prepare to launch an elaborate mobilized shell game once the U.S. forces join the convoy to transport the prisoner.

Verminesk, Painell, Hazazel, Pestilence and AAmon hover above the Chinese Embassy. Vermin looks down into the compound and observes the People's Army tactics. He smiles at how frail a thing their bodies are. "No one is to leave here alive," says Vermin. "We are to ensure that Death walks away with all the two hundred and twenty-seven soul. Pain, Hazazel, cut their communications! No one calls out or in. AAmon you and I will watch for celestials. With the arrival of Imperial, they have no power here, but all the same we will ensure the success of the protocol… Ascension!"

The demons yell, "Ascension," giving confirmation that the order was received. They move towards the task given.

Second Lieutenant Konomae watches the camera footage throughout the building from the Embassy's nerve center. As she scrolls from screen to screen they all go dark simultaneously. She tries to reboot the power a few times to no avail. She flicks the comms system to alert the director, but comms doesn't kick in. Before she says another word the comms crackle to life, but the traffic that fills the air is not native in dialect, but speaks Chinese fluently.

<"I have come to silence your tongues from speaking on matters that are not yet ready to be made public. As you are an honorable people who believe in a sanctity of pure armed combat, I give you forewarning that my expedient arrival is nigh. I have not come to negotiate, barter, or lay terms. I have come to lay waist to your bricks and mortar and claim what should have been mine in the mist of the Congo. Prepare yourselves. I am coming.">

Civilians and soldiers alike throughout the compound hear what the voice has told them. Over open mics and P.A. systems. The surprise is momentary when the secured reinforced doors and windows activate trapping everyone inside. A few laughs follow thinking a sadistic joke is being played until the civilians see the military soldiers start moving with purpose. Military stationed at the Embassy begin to mobilize destroying any doubt of the authenticity that the drill should be considered anything else but an actual threat. Orders roll down from the top brass to start evacuation of the building. From the nerve center the Second Lieutenant tries to raise the gated doors, but the system is still unresponsive.

With unresponsive secured gated doors not opening, the soldiers quickly go to plan B which is shelter all the civilians in place in the auditorium.

Outside, Senior Colonel attempts to speak through his comms, but there is nothing but silence in return. He again pounds on the metal door. It creaks as it slowly opens again. The muzzle meets the senior Colonel.

<"Come, we go!">

The door opens all the way this time. A five-man team meets the Colonel making it the full six for the detailed protection. As they emerge from the building they quickly run for the Suburban's. As they make their way one of the soldiers yells out, <"Eyes up!"> The team looks up just in time to see a projectile strike the roof of the Embassy. The impact shakes the compound breaking glass behind the reinforced steel shutters and, knocking dust and debris off the building. They don't stop running, they enter into the vehicle with weapons at the ready. The three that didn't fit in the first transport vehicle runs to the next Suburban behind it.

Senior Colonel pumps his fist giving the signal for the driver to punch it. The driver turns to the colonel and replies by gesturing the ridge of his hand across his neck telling the colonel that the vehicle's power has been cut, it's dead. Without a second hesitation the senior colonel opens the door and exits quickly from the vehicle grabbing the prisoner from the back. He looks to the other vehicles in the column; their drivers also signal that their vehicles are dead. The colonel places one finger in the air and swirls it. The six-man team exits from the stalled vehicles and again reform around the prisoner in an off circle.

<"Diamond up! We egress on foot out into the population and procure another vehicle."> says the Senior Colonel.

The team form a diamond formation around the prisoner and begins moving toward the reinforced compound garage door. As the team moves in formation quickly screams erupt from inside the building followed by immense rounds of gunfire from automatics and semi-automatic weapons.

CHAPTER 41

The Seal's Master Chief slams on the breaks. All four doors of the suburban open as the team exits with guns at the ready all pointed toward the Embassy. Civilians that were outside at the time of the lockdown are running in all directions fleeing from in front of the Embassy as gun fire and screams of terror can be heard from within. They public seeing the Seals only become more erratic at the sight of armed U.S. soldiers exiting from a tinted Suburban with rifles.

Jericho scans from left to right seeing only civilians that are non-hostile. He watches them through his 4x scope until they all clear out from in front of the Embassy looking for cover.

"Master Chief get our new friends up on comms and find out what's going on and how we can be of assistance!"

"Yes Sir." Master Chief quickly delegates. "Riley, you heard the Captain."

Riley slides back into the vehicle for cover as he attempts to establish comms with the Embassy.

Windows on the fifth and sixth floor shatter and are blown out from the east side of the building from what sounds like a grenade. The upper floor windows have less protection due to the height and risk threat assessment.

"Was that a grenade inside the Embassy?" Said Seamen Griffin. He starts to rock and bounce in anticipation of combat. "We going in, Master Chief?"

Chief looks over to Jericho. Jericho nods yes.

"You bet your sweet ass were going in. We have a prisoner to secure," Master Chief answers.

Riley gets out the vehicle and back into a defensive position behind his rear driver side passenger door. "No comms with our Chinese comrades. There is no radio or landline. It's all dark.

Jericho studies the building. He closes his eyes and listens to the gunfire. *It's sporadic, then it falls silent before more shots are fired from a different section of the building. It doesn't make sense. If it was multiple hostiles there would be constant bouts of gunfire.*

"We move!" Jericho leaves the safety of his bullet resistant door and heads for the entrance of the building. The rest of the team stacks up behind him. He turns his hand gesturing turning a key. "Keys to the vehicle, Master Chief?" Says Jericho.

"In my pocket, sir."

Seamen Griffin continues scanning the streets and the building. "Funny thing is I don't even see police. Why aren't they here or at least on the way?"

"I noticed that as well. If comms are down, who's calling?" says Jericho.

The team stacks up to the left of the front entrance. Jericho pulls out his cell phone and tosses it back to Seamen Riley. Make the call!"

Riley depresses the on button to wake the phone. It never turns on. "Dead sir." Riley takes a knee and slings his rifle over the shoulder giving Jericho's phone his complete attention. Again, he depresses the button and nothing happens. He tosses Jericho his phone back and pulls his out. "Mine is dead as well, sir. Whatever has knocked out their comms affected us, too.

Jericho and the Seals advance on the main solid mass of steel protecting the front entrance. He hits with the underside of his fist to test the strength. *Damn! It solid. I can take it, but not with them watching. Last thing I need is questions.*

"On me!" Jericho takes off swiftly towards the east side of the building where the windows had blown out on the upper floors. The broken glass crunching under their feet tells them they reached the possible sweet spot for entry.

Jericho looks up. *The reinforced windows are only the first couple of floors. If they are anything like a normal military they spend the least amount of money the higher the building. The windows blew out on five from what it looks like so we know those aren't secure. Level three is our way in; two if we're lucky.* "Grapple?" Jericho yells out.

Seamen Riley snaps his fingers. "In the vehicle." He takes off to retrieve the equipment.

Verminesk watches as Jericho and his team looks to make entry. He softly lands next to them and touches Semen Griffin and whispers, "Such a shame you are here on this side of the world while your brother fucks your wife. Deep down you know that you're raising his child."

Seamen Griffin starts to shake his head believing that if he shakes quickly and briefly enough he'd dislodge the thought from his head.

Vermin moves on to the Master Chief and touches his shoulder. "You are a Navy Seal. The elite of warriors, why are you following this simpleton. He's had nowhere near the training you've had. These are your men, are you going to let him lead them into combat? What training has he done with them? If you don't take over, you and your men will die. With you dead, your military will cease benefits for your boy's cancer treatment, wife will be set out the house. Everything will be lost."

Master Chief moves his heightened alert roving and scanning eyes towards Jericho. He briefly lasers him with his weapon, but hearing the footsteps of the returning Seamen he moves it back to scanning the area.

Vermin smiles and moves to lay his hand on Jericho. Just as he nears placing his hand on Jericho's shoulder Gabriel grabs a hold of his wrist.

"That will be enough that." Gabriel slams her fist hard into the side of Vermin's face sending him sailing across the street and into the side of café shop. The resulting destruction draws the attention of Jericho and his team.

Gabriel touches the two Seals simultaneously. "Set your mind to task and be of your work… Focus, your captain will not lead you astray."

Master Chief and Griffin slide back into their focused mind.

Gabriel grabs the hilt of her sword and waits while she watches for Vermin. It doesn't take long as bricks, mortar, and wood start to move. Vermin pushes the debris aside emerging from the ruins of the cafe. He slowly brushes the dust from himself and begins a slow methodic walk toward Gabriel. She walks out to meet him, pulling her sword.

As Seamen Riley runs back, he turns and drops to one knee with his rifle raised in the direction of the café. After a few seconds of scanning without contact he keeps running back to his team. "Sir, there was no grapple equipment in the vehicle," Riley says. "It just wasn't anticipated that we'd need to scale a building today for prisoner transport."

Jericho looks past him toward the café. "What the hell was that all about over there?"

"No movement from the shop, sir. I only caught a glimpse while I was running, but it looked as if lighting struck it," answers Riley.

The men all briefly look up at the clear and sun filled day before looking back to their perspective fields of view.

I have no other choice here. We have to make entry "Master Chief," Jericho calls out.

"Sir."

"I'm going back to check the entrance again. Who knows, maybe that strike disabled the locks. Keep your fields of fire."

Jericho runs back west to the front of the Embassy and looks to see if anyone's paying attention to him. If anyone were, they'd be too far to see what he was doing or how he did it. He grabs the bottom of the steel shutter and grips hard crushing his hand print into the door. With one arm, he yanks hard throwing the reinforced door up into its pre-fall position. It starts to fall again. He moves just underneath it catching it again. This time he forcefully slams it upward pushing it beyond its locking mechanism and into the ceiling. It stays this time.

Jericho runs back and retrieves the rest of his team.

No words are exchanged as Gabriel walks up to Vermin and swings her blade for the soul purpose of cleaving his torso in equal halves. He parries the blade and starts in with a flurry of his own. Gabriel fights with an intensity that she hasn't in some time. She fights to keep Vermin's hands off of Jericho. He must go undetected for as long as possible. If the demons find out about him, the attacks toward him would be unending, spiritually and physically. The drain on him would be immense.

I must keep them blind to all else that moves. Thought Gabriel.

As she whirls about in a deadly dance with her fallen brother of the rift, she constantly keeps her eyes moving for more demons. She suspects that at the minimum Painell is also around. She presses the attack harder in an attempt to get Vermin to call out to him. She needs all eyes on her and away from Jericho.

Jericho and his team enter the Embassy in diamond formation covering three hundred and sixty-degree field of view. Once through the door they follow the sound of erupting gunfire. The team moves swiftly, but methodically as they clear each hallway and room they cross. Jericho motions his fingers at his eyes and then toward the double doors ahead of the team at the end of the hallway. As they approach the team doesn't stop, Jericho kicks the door and they single file in and spread out in line formation.

The team stops in their tracks at the carnage. The smell of blood mixed with iron, gunpowder and burnt flesh fills their nostrils. Master Chief grimaces at the carnage.

Jericho releases his off hand from his weapon and repeats the gesture of moving forward. The team forms up in their diamond and move towards the gunfire coming from the east of the Embassy. As they move they step over countless bodies that have hacked into clean pieces. There's little blood to none at all of those hacked, as the wounds that were inflicted were all cauterized.

Jericho puts his fist in the air halting their advance. "I've seen this before," he whispers. "the bodies, I've seen this."

Master Chief still grimacing at the carnage. "I've seen a lot shit before, but nothing to compare to this. Master Chief bends down and examines one the bodies. "The young woman looks to be secretary or something. She has three entry bullet wounds; they don't look fatal. What killed her was the severing of her body. There's barley any blood though, what the hell weapon does this and leaves no blood?—"

"And have been seared on contact?" Jericho finishing the sentence.

Seamen Griffin picks up one the shells and examines the round. "She was shot by friendly fire first from the looks of it."

"Because the soldiers that were here were firing wildly and indiscriminately," Jericho says before pointing forward.

The team reforms and keeps following the gunfire.

Senior Colonel and the last of his men of the protection detail fire at Imperial as soon as he emerges from out the Embassy into the daylight of the parking lot. Expecting incoming rounds, Imperial sides step them and uses his wings to deflect the remaining. As Imperial closes the distance he passes the third from last Suburban. The vehicle's door opens and the driver exits firing his sidearm at Imperial. With a combination of wing and blade he deflects the rounds. The one that does make it through ricochets off his armor harmlessly. An ostentatiously designed firing pin clicks flipping into the center of Imperials palm from underneath his gauntlet. The pin glows red charge as it charges a plasma bolt. He lets it erupt. The red focused bolt destroys the suburban completely engulfing the People's Army soldier in flames. One quick slice and the head is separated from neck of the burning soldier. Imperial turns his attention to the remaining threats. If they can be called threats.

From behind the cover of the last Suburban in the convoy Senior Colonel fires to a lock back and falls behind cover while his men continue firing. He looks over at the prisoner whose crouching with his hands cuffed to the rear and a pillowcase covering his head.

<"What the hell did you do to have a Shinigami come for you? What the hell did you do!"> the senior Colonel yells why grasping the prisoner by his collar and shaking him.

The prisoner just continues to yell in a muffled voice as he's been gagged by duct tape underneath the hood The Senior Colonel throws him to the ground and then looks for more rounds on his person. He pats all of his pockets and double checks his ammo pouches. He realizes that he's completely out. His loadout was not intended for a sustained fight in the streets of Germany. He remains in cover listening till the last of his men fire their last round.

Imperial stops short at the second from last Suburban. <"It sounds as if you have expended the last of your projectiles warriors… Not to worry, I will give you a fighting chance just as I have given the others within the Embassy. You Chinese are a people of honor are you not? You believe in single combat and warrior deaths, etcetera, etcetera."> Imperial waits. <"Or, I can always slaughter you where you cower. I'll give you a moment.">

Senior Colonel resigns himself to the fact that he has no chance against a Shinigami that has come for his soul. He looks at his remaining team and completely understands the fear that in their eyes. He's still trying to wrap his head around what he's seeing currently. A Shinigami that stands two meters and is impervious to attack.

Looking at his men, the senior colonel nods in respect of having gone the distance with them in what he knows will more than likely be there final moments. Excepting the fact that he will not live to see the fate of his team, because he's going to except the challenge offered in hopes his remaining men use the time to evade and escape. These are his men, he has a duty to protect them for as long as he can. Taking a breath, he pulls his bayonet from its sheath. The Colonel stands walking from behind cover of the vehicle. He looks back and gestures for the last of his men to free the prisoner. *No man deserves to die on his knees cuffed and blind.* The colonel removes his helmet and unbuckles his reinforced ceramic plated tactical vest.

Imperial studies his collar insignias. <"Your rank is that of Senior Colonel is it not?"> Imperial says as he twirls his blade.

The colonel takes a good look at Imperial and nods yes and then points at Imperial's uniform. <"I see you wear the colors of Arcane, Shinigami.">

Imperial bows in respect of the colonel's bravery. <"It will be the last thing you see unfortunately… when you're ready, warrior?">

Senior Colonel bows to Imperial to show his respect and then takes a low fighting stance.

Jericho and his team quietly and slowly slide through the open metal door leading into the garage compound where only moments earlier the senior colonel and his protection detail were awaiting their arrival. As Jericho and his men enter the exterior garage, they are met by burning fuel and hot flames from the row of Suburban's that have been left ablaze. Jericho again places his fist in the air bringing his team to halt. They all take a knee. Jericho moves his arm in the direction of Imperial. His eyes widen at the sight of seeing a two-meter winged man carrying a blade that glows white hot on its edges.

The team is frozen as they also lock eyes on the hybrid. They don't make so much as a whisper, they just continue to stare in an attempt to have their eyes reconcile with their logic as to not question the concept of reality of what they were witnessing.

Master Chief is the first to whisper, "What the fuck is that?"

"That is what killed everyone we passed... the angel of death personified, Master Chief," Griffin says answering the chief as he gesticulates the sign of the cross, touching his forehead and both shoulders for God's mercy.

"Captain, you thinking first contact?" said Master Chief.

Jericho unflinching and fixated on the entity. "I don't know what the fuck to think. I can go with first contact."

Riley speaks up whispering an octave higher to make to the ears of the captain. "I wouldn't expect first contact to wear the clothing of Arcane."

"Point." Jericho says.

Phasing through the Seals, Death comes from behind Griffin turns and kneels down facing him still unseen to the human eye. "He is no angel mortal nor is he I." Death walks out into the center of the exterior garage compound and outstretches his hand collecting the souls of those imperial have killed.

Jericho can't take his eyes off of Imperial, he's frozen, he only wishes it was because Gabriel altered time, but this is fear that runs him statuesque.

Master Chief slowly scoots up to the side of him. "Sir, orders?"

"Are comms still out?" asked Jericho.

The Master Chief clicks his mic on the back molar twice. Nothing replies. He shakes his head side to side indicating, the comms are dead.

Jericho sighs, "We wait. I want to see what this thing is and what it can do." *Whatever it is, it is wearing the uniform of an Arcanian officer. I bet that thing was in the Congo. That's how that asshole Rusain defeated the instillation.*

"What?" Master Chief says seeing the captain in thought.

Jericho nods his head toward the entity. "That thing was at the Destined Suns camp in the Congo. I'm willing to bet my life on it."

"I'm not willing to take that bet," said Master Chief Nelson. "I recommend we retreat to relay possible first contact to Navalcomm—"
Jericho holds his fist up silencing the Chief.

CHAPTER 42

azazel, AAmon and Pestilence look on in entertainment at Imperial challenging the remaining soldiers. Pestilence looks around and realizes that Verminesk is nowhere to be seen. "Where is Verminesk? It's not like him to miss this." Pestilence studies his surroundings for a few moments. He looks at his left gauntlet and begins tapping on it. The celestials must be here, fan out, find them!"

Each of the Demons fly out toward each corner of the building setting a perimeter. Hazazel is the first to find Vermin and Gabriel engaged in combat. He shoots down towards them pulling his ball and whip chain weapon. AAmon and Pestilence watches as Hazazel disappears underneath the horizon of the west side of the Embassy.

Vermin and Gabriel are engaged in a saber lock. She looks back over her shoulder, out of the corner of her eye and sees Hazazel approaching just before he reaches her she yells, "Now!"

The trap is sprung. Arch Cassiel comes down hard placing his blade through the back of Hazazel pinning him to the pavement behind Gabriel. He pulls his blade from the Demon's back and swiftly slings his blade down in a sweeping motion and removes Hazazel's head rendering him lifeless. He then kicks his body up and over the Embassy.

Seeing Hazazel's body treated with such disrespect AAmon and Pestilence howl as they fly over the Embassy heading for the Archs. Gabriel smiles knowing that she's more than likely pulled the remaining Demons that were in the immediate vicinity her way. At least she hopes she has. She breaks the saber lock with Vermin stepping back over the weapon Hazazel dropped. She kicks Hazazel's ball and chain at Vermin, he ducks it which was all the time Cassiel needed to tackle the demon. The momentum of Cassiel's force carries them both back into the café shop destroying more of it second time through.

Gabriel does an about face with her blade ready to challenge the two on approach.

The senior colonel steps in closer to Imperial with his knife at the low ready, his left hand ready to block any incoming attack. Imperial doesn't move, his eyes just follows the colonel. Quick lead in then a step back, the colonel feigns an attack distracting Imperial. Two of his men that were behind the last suburban did not use the time wisely to flee, they used it to assist with a superior foe. They close in with bayonets and are quickly eviscerated in one parry and two swipes of Imperial's sword. Their bodies fall in cauterized pieces.

<"Four left,"> Imperial says.

Shocked by the swiftness of the Shinigami, Senior Colonel moves in with a side kick which Imperial easily swats away spinning him around off balance leaving the Colonel open, an opening that Imperial takes advantage of by grabbing him by his LBE straps, slinging and slamming him through the front windshield of the last Suburban.

The remaining Chinese soldier's walk from behind the S.U.V. with the prisoner. As they walk out they show Imperial that they have no weapons.

Imperial gestures for them to step toward him. He inverts his sword and places the tip of his blade into the concrete. <"So, it appears that surrender is indeed within the vocabulary of your people..." He looks at them with a slight disgust. <"Fine... Now, bring him to me!">

The lead soldier starts to move toward the hybrid. He suddenly stops and crack a smile before running back behind cover taking the prisoner with them. Imperial's calm facade is replaced by instant irritation. He sighs and again takes up his sword when rounds start suddenly ripping into him.

Jericho and his team fire as they advance on Imperial. They send round after round down range striking his back and legs. Surprise and violence of action are there closet friends. Taken by surprise, the first few ricochet off of Imperial's armor and exposed skin. The stream of rounds has no damaging effects, but are an annoyance.

The team advances in a firing line formation with stagnated fire, allowing for one to reload without a break in the suppression.

Imperial turns and faces his incoming adversaries. He raises his arm to deflect some of the rounds as if swatting flies away.

Jericho and his team stop advancing when they've expended the last of their rounds. Jericho and Chief Nelson throws their rifles down slinging around their waists quickly pulling their side arms from holsters up to eye level. The two Seamen grabs their side arms as well and fall in stacked behind the Chief and Jericho. They remain in a standoff, weapons trained at the seven-foot threat.

Imperial's smile turns Cheshire behind his mask. He starts to clap slowly. "I don't believe that I've ever had someone surprise me in such a fashion." Imperial looks around for his demonic compatriots, but doesn't see them. "It seems my eyes and ears have failed me in this instance... Oh! Excuse me a moment, will you?" Imperial turns his palm toward the Suburban and fires a red bolt through the front windshield of the vehicle igniting the Senior Colonel, the vehicle, the soldiers and prisoner that were taking refuge behind it. The vehicle explodes, leaving only cinders of human remains.

"Not a very noble end, I know, but they had their time to die as true warriors, and I grew bored."

"Sir?" Master Chief says as he finds himself backing up. Fear had him moving in reverse without him even realizing it.

Assessing the situation was done after the first shot made contact with the unknown entity. The target is bullet resistant to conventional weapons, it is seven feet tall with probably strength to match, it has wings that appear impervious and duals as blades, its sword burns white hot with razor edges that cauterize on contact, and has an energy-based weaponry, decades beyond our current capabilities. "Run!" Jericho whispers.

In an instant, Imperial grabs his blade and is behind the Seals. Jericho turns and fires his weapon expelling round after round again until lock back of his handgun. Imperial raises his wing and deflects the rounds. Jericho dumps his empty magazine and slides in another. He pats Master Chief on the shoulder. "I said run, dammit!" From the corner of his eye he watches as Master Chief Nelson stops retreating and stand his ground. "I said run, Chief, that's an ord—" Jericho loses breath when the Chief's head rolls past his feet. Confused, Jericho does a double take and again glances at Chief, coming to a realization that the Chief's body is headless as the corner stone of his visage is no longer sitting atop its neck. Startled by the revelation he looks to the remaining two Seals, an finds Griffin without his head, body falling to its knees then toppling over. Riley had tuck rolled the incoming swing and was rolling up from the ground firing his .45 caliber Colt 1911 at the superior target.

Imperial throws his blade at Riley. Jericho holsters his side arm and grabs his rifle jumping into the path of the blade using his M4 to shield Riley. Jericho collides with it giving it a glancing blow. The blade slices the M4, but it was enough strength and momentum to push the blade slightly off target. The sword slides into the brick wall of the Embassy left of Riley.

Riley pulls his serrated blade from his LBE right holster strap and slowly walks to engage Imperial. He stops long enough to pull the Master Chiefs blade from the holster of the headless corpse. Jericho pulls his bayonet and takes the left flanking route.

Imperial feigns an attack towards Jericho. The captain prepares himself for the attack, but Imperial uses the ruse to head fake Jericho. He spins his right arm under the left armpit firing a blast bolt at Riley. The shot is wild and blows a hole in the wall behind the Seal. The concussive force carries Riley off his feet toward Imperial. The Seal crosses his arms and blades readying himself to turn his disadvantage into an advantage. He yells his battle cry as he descends toward his proposed first contact. Jericho decides and commits to rush in and is given a side kick for his trouble that launches him across the garage lot bouncing off the roof of the fourth burning Suburban falling to the opposite side of it.

Riley comes in hot and screaming. Imperial side steps letting him pass by. Riley hits the ground and rolls up to his feet. He instantly swings the right arm back to use his blade to impale Imperial. The first swing is a miss, but he follows it up with the second blade that Imperial deflects with his metal gauntlet. Now facing Imperial, Riley deploys his close quarter knife combat training for real world application. The two engage in a deadly game of who will strike whom first. Riley continues to scream singing his death song to the heavens with each attack. Imperial draws him close as he falls back. After a dozen swings and slashes Riley stops to catch his breath. At least that is what he wanted Imperial to believe. He spins low grabbing a handful of dirt and throws it in the eyes of Imperial. Through the dust cloud he charges with both knives at the ready. He jumps into the cloud disappearing into it finally making lethal contact with the being.

Jericho finally able to catch his breath after the midriff kick and subsequent launch, finds his feet and emerges from the thick black smoke of the burning Suburban's. There is a handgun on the ground matching his. He picks it up and dumps the magazine. He tosses the slightly singed firearm off to the side. He pulls his 1911 and dumps the empty magazine. Checking his newly acquired magazine, he gives a slight frown to the four remaining rounds in it. Jericho slaps the magazine in place and brings the weapon up eye level waiting for his target in the dissipating dirt smoke screen. When it clears, Imperial has Riley by the neck slowly sliding his sword through his chest. Imperial looks at Jericho as a visor slides back up into his helmet. He pretended to be in retreat to get close enough to pull his sword from the stone wall. When Riley threw the dirt, the visor engaged protecting his vision. Riley goes limp dropping both knives. Imperial releases his neck and lets his body slide effortlessly down the blade leaving Riley's body in a cauterized Y.

"You are alone, Captain," Imperial says as his mask and helmet disengages and falls below his armor's neckline.

"Impressive that you and your team were able to sneak up on me. Oh! And the ferocity with which this one fought." Kicking Riley's body. "I will assume that your leadership skill is what made that possible. Which is why I spared you for last. I will give you the chance I give most that prove a bit exceptional or survived my initial onslaught through skill." Imperial watches Jericho's face for weakness. He finds only confusion. "What I'm saying is, it's simply a chance to best me in single combat. You best me and you are free to leave."

He's human or so he looks it. Jericho tosses his side arm off to the side. *It'll only probably piss him off anyways.* He takes a second to himself and stares into the blue afternoon sky thinking, *that, this is it, my day has come.* As he watches the blue stillness of the sky and the clouds that move at a nominal speed, he quiets his breathing and calms his mind. It's then that he hears another battle out front the Embassy. No time to hope that its reinforcements pushing their way through to him, only enough time to ready the body for a fight to deal with an enemy that he now understands that Gabriel was preparing him for. She knew what she was doing when she took him through time to observe the battle for Sarin.

"Well, Captain?" Imperial says.

Jericho's wandering thoughts returns forthwith. His attention, his eyes now focused solely on Imperial. "What manner of creature are you?"

"Now that is a question I rarely get to hear. I don't hear it much mostly, because before anyone can ask, I've beheaded or gutted them. You are not cowering or running, that means you have heart and will to survive. For that very reason, I will indulge you and answer your question. By most I'm called whatever their tongue decree as angel. The Senior Colonel that was alive mere moments ago referred to me as a Shinigami… It many ways, I suppose he was right, but in reality, I'm far from some idiom of a dogma trained automaton."

"Are you going to answer my question or talk around it?" Said Jericho. *He's cocky, overconfident, how can I use that?* He thought.

Imperial smirks. "I am the inevitability of lies that have spurned the universe. Lies that even you yourself in the deep-seated pockets of your consciousness believe. I am the answer to that question if there is someone in the heavens always watching and silently in judgment of you. That Captain, is who I am."

Jericho looks at his comrade's lifeless bodies on the ground. Although he didn't know them long they were brothers in arms. They had families, they had plans, they had dreams when they eventually discharge from the service, and now hopefully, they have a god of whatever sort they were raised to believe in to return home too.

Jericho stares at their dog tags that rest next to their bodies as they no longer had heads to old them proper. Jericho slowly walks and collects the tags by kneeling down and picking them each up with reverence. Imperial allows him without conflict or taunt to do so. Jericho picks them up palming the metal in his hand, feeling the raised script of their names. He slowly wraps the chains that the tags are affixed to tightly around his hand and knuckles. He then faces Imperial and stands. "I take it that no one has ever bested you?"

"You would be the first," Imperial says daring him to engage, he waves and beckons him come.

Rolling his neck and loosening his shoulders Jericho approaches Imperial in a steady calmed confident approach. Imperial slams his blade again into the concrete and approaches Jericho. When they meet face to face Jericho has to crane his neck upward to look up at him, to find focal point of his face where he plans to strike. His heart rushes, adrenaline dumps throughout his body, his focus has caused his vision to become narrow and singular. His body is telling him this is the fight literally of your life.

I don't pray much Lord, but I pray now. Strengthen me, help me put this thing down. Help me fulfill the purpose of what I believe I was given birth for.

Iayhoten's Palace, Elohim's Throne Room

Elohim sits on his throne listening to Jericho. He sits with his fingers laced resting just below his nose. He is in thought as he watches the events unfold. He says nothing. He remains silent. He's done all he can. This must play out with no more help than he's already given at the onset of his word allowing for the creation of Jericho. To change something now would be him bending the rules. If he bends his own rules, he'd be no better than Lucifer. He awaits just as the rest of the Heavens for the outcome.

Chinese Embassy Berlin, Germany

Imperial having watched the captain pick up the metal tag remnants of his men tells him that he has gotten to him, that he's placed his mind in a state of vengeance. In such a state of mind, one becomes carless and prone to mistakes. Still he did surprise him. That deserves a reward. Imperial bends down and places his chin out to Jericho. "I'll give you the first shot, Captain, strike true." Arrogance causes Imperial to cackle slightly. "Because, you will not get another."

Angel's Spire – Day

Michael peers down from the balcony of the Spire. His knuckles have all but drained of blood as he grips the railing watching the events unfold inside the garage of Chinese Embassy. He looks away only briefly to monitor Gabriel and Cassiel. *She's held them long enough.* Michael lifts his arm signaling Archs Metatron, Raziel, and Samael, to ready themselves. Fully armored, their masks generate from the neckline of their chest armor encompassing their heads. Michael drops his arm. The Archs run past Michael leaping over the side of the balcony. They fall headfirst drawing their arms in close turning their bodies into missiles for the first few miles of free fall. When they've achieved terminal velocity, their wings switchblade out. They thrust in unison and rocket towards Earth.

Chinese Embassy Berlin, Germany

Exhausted and bloody, Gabriel and Cassiel stand side by side. Pestilence, Verminesk and AAmon closes in on them. Three beams of light touch down and the odds instantly shift in the celestials favor as Metatron, Raziel and Samael enter the fray battle ready. The demons realizing they're outnumbered and have already lost one to the warden Apollyon, they disengage and vanish phasing out of 2814's reality. Gabriel and Cassiel fall to their knees in exhaustion.

With the dissipation of the demons leaving the area the ethereal influenced blackout ends, communication are restored.

With communications restored, the radios of the soldiers and Embassy personal starts to squawk. Imperial attention is diverted briefly to the crackling sound of the radio. As celestial and all powerful as he is, his human side makes it second nature to turns one's attention to a sudden noise. He takes his eyes off of Jericho for the briefest of seconds in distraction. Jericho takes advantage of his opponent's divided attention and the fact that the pompous asshole gave him his chin. Jericho plants his left foot and turns his hips into his right cross with all the power he could muster. The strike finds its target and slams the left side of Imperials face lifting the two-meter behemoth off of his feet sending the angelic hybrid goliath tumbling and flipping through the brick steel reinforced wall of the Embassy. He hits the pavement outside rolling and skidding to a stop once he slams into a row of parked cars.

Angel's Spire – Day

Michael pumps his fist in quick celebration. *Knock his damn head off!* He thought. Other celestials are whooping and celebrating at the fact that pain was inflicted on an enemy they themselves had no power, one who's caused such untold devastation.

Chinese Embassy Berlin, Germany

Jericho attempts to jump through the hole to pursue the monstrosity, but he's met by a flying crumpled green Caravan. Just as he makes it through the hole he's struck and sent flying backward himself, back through the hole and across the Embassy's garage lot. He strikes a wall opposite side of the lot. The blow hurt, but it wasn't unexpected. He knew he would take few hard hits from this guy. Jericho finds his footing and pushes himself to stand. Imperial crashes through the Caravan and hole with a fierce shoulder check that finds its target. Jericho barley gets his forearms up in time to block the check. The transferred force of momentum sends him smashing into another one of the burning Suburban's causing the heated metal to wedge in on him trapping him.

Imperial, pissed off walks over and tears the metal Suburban in half before Jericho could free himself. Imperial claps both ends of the burning wreckage together smashing the captain in between them. Jericho places both arms up curling them into biceps interlocking his fingers behind his head. He takes the smash but was sure to protect his head and leverage himself a position to push the metal off of him. Jericho forces both sides of the wreckage away from him by forcing his elbows outward. Once Imperial is opened enough, he puts all his strength into pushing the two pieces apart in an explosive effort gaining room. Jericho immediately jumps and lands a solid front kick to Imperial's face sending him cascading backward into a one of the Embassy's metal reinforced windows. Jericho falls to knee, catches his breath then pursues his enemy. He sprints and launches himself at Imperial delivering another solid right cross. The force of the blow makes a thunderous boom and drives Imperial through the reinforced window and down the hall of the Embassy, taking chunks of brick and other debris with him. Having moment of respite, Jericho decides to run for reinforcements to help deal with the N.H.E.

Metatron helps Gabriel to her feet as Raziel assist Cassiel. The punch on the other side of the Embassy's wall being so fast and impactful breaks the sound barrier causing the never mistaken sound of the sonic boom. Metatron's attention turns toward the destructive sound. He looks back to Gabriel smiling. "Come, sister, we don't want to miss this. Listen! Do you hear them cheering?" Metatron says. He takes to the sky with Gabriel. "Your adopted progeny has to do away with him quickly before they return in mass with Warsivious."

"Let War come, and I will end him." Gabriel says sternly.

Metatron shakes his head. "I believe you will, sister. I believe you will."

Jericho doesn't wait for what the military would designate as, N.H.E. Non-human entity to recover. *I just thought non-human-entity. When did I ever think that I would use that acronym?* He turns to run toward the gate only to stop short. *This is what Gabriel was preparing me for. This is the moment. I win, I go home to Isis.* Jericho looks back toward the hole leading into the Embassy. *I win, I go home to Isis.* He sighs, takes a breath and runs back to the Embassy and follows the entity back inside.

As Jericho enters, he scans the destruction and the collapsed debris, nothing. No, wait! A shadow catches his eye walking past a doorway. Jericho runs into the room to press the attack. When he enters there is no N.H.E., just the surprise of seeing someone concealed in shadow standing to the left of the doorway. The same doorway that he and his team traversed earlier before finding the garage. That doorway leads down the hall toward the conference rooms. At first glance the silhouetted character looked like the man in black from the Congo, but upon closer inspection there's nothing.

Death watches Jericho closely as he enters into the room. Jericho blinks and double takes giving the shadow his full attention. Just as fast as it takes the eye to blink three hundred milliseconds, nothing is there. Death phased from reality when he realized he could be seen. Jericho continues to scan the room. Finding nothing his mind returns to threat at hand.

Red soul spheres glide and float past Jericho unseen in the mortal realm. The spheres collect in the same corner that his attention was just focused on seconds ago. Death continues watching Jericho with great intrigue as he collects the souls of the dead from the bullet riddled and cauterized bodies.

Jericho again slowly and methodically turning looks for his opponent, his breathing remains quickened as adrenaline continues to dump drastically into his body, his hands tremble, but it's not all fear. It's a mixture of nerves and anticipation. As he creeps through the hallway it reminds him of how still he was when he was hunting the possessed militant in jungles of the Congo. He seems to constantly put himself at a disadvantage. He should have pressed the attack when he had the momentum.

A wing punctures through the drywall of the hallway. Like cutting through the butter it slices down through the wall in the direction of Jericho. The edged bladed portion of the wing catches Jericho's face flush dead center just above the nose and sends him to the ground sliding down the hall of the polished floor. The pain is blinding, he instantly grabs his nose and mouth as his eyes well up with water. He slides into a set of double wooden doors. As Jericho senses start to return he removes his hands from his nose and sees that the palm of his hands and the dog tags are covered in blood. *My bl---My blood?* He stunned as he's never seen his own blood spill profusely. As he tries to get himself together he can hear the approaching footsteps of his would-be murder.

Imperial tears through the drywall. "What are you... I wonder?" Says Imperial as he marches down the hall with purpose of violent intent.

Jericho climbs to his feet still dazed a bit. He places one finger over a nostril and blows dislodging a wet clump of blood and mucus from the other. He smiles showing blood stained teeth. "I am the inevitably that there is some form of god up there watching. I am the poof that at the end of long silent judgment comes punishment for those that offend." Jericho laughs defiantly spitting more blood form his mouth in hopes to clear his speech. It's hard speaking through a warm viscous liquid such as blood.

Imperial stretches out both arms touching each side of the wall. He sends constant red charges into the building. As the charge streams through the building, security cameras, audio recording systems, and computers short out. A building such as this would have to be close feed as to withstand cyber-attacks from outside.

Imperial, although angered smiles at the quip. "You have done something that has never happened before. You have given me cause to rise to anger. Let's keep this quarrel between us, shall we? We don't need any more prying eyes seeing how I handle business just yet."

Imperial stops advancing and places a finger in the air calling for a moment of time out. He too spits a wad of blood from his mouth into his hand. "I was never really sure I could bleed Captain. How unfortunate for you to have been the first to draw it." He continues advancing slowly again. His boots methodically striking the pavement to instill fear in his opposition. "I can only assume that since I've not gained knowledge of you that you must have lived your life away from prying eyes concealed by the celestials. What great lengths they must have gone through."

Using his sleeve, Jericho wipes the blood away from his nose and mouth. It's already starting to heal. "You going to tal—"

Imperial with lightning speed is upon Jericho in an instant kicking him in his chest. The kick forces Jericho through the wooden doors that had just stopped his momentum only moments before. The doors splinter into pieces. The momentum of the kick carries Jericho through the doors, but he latches onto Imperial's ankle with vice like grip and pulls him through with him. They both hit the ground with Jericho catapulting Imperial over his head slinging him forward with the added force of his strength, he slings Imperial completing the 180-degree arc slamming the Nephilim face first into the ground smashing the twelve-inch ceramic tile covered concrete to pieces. Jericho flips up off his back to his feet and jumps shoulder first into Imperial's back. He comes down with such force that it carries the both of them down through the floor into the subbasement.

Gabriel holds her breath as she watches the culmination of years of training and carrying for the boy comes to fruition. The rest of the Archs are silent as they continue to watch and see if Fate's plan can be corrected.

Angel's Spire

Yeshua enters the chamber. Scores of angels begin to kneel before him. He raises his hands and beckons them to carry on. He walks toward the front of the Spire and takes position next to his captain. Michael makes eye contact with the prince nods then returns his attention back toward the fight.

"For the king," Yeshua yells out in solidarity with his Archs.

The rest of the angles look at each other in amazement and then, they too return to cheering and hoping that in these next few moments the fate of prophecy will be settled for all time with the removal of Imperial.

CHAPTER 43

New York, Waldorf Astoria Hotel – Night

Awaiting the United Nations peace summit, Lucien is in his suite sipping on a hot sauce spiked vodka as he looks out over New York's evening skyline. A hard knock at the door doesn't disturb Lucien he simply keeps drinking. "Enter." Warsivious enters the room urgently.

"My king, there has been a complication in Germany. Imper—"

Lucien raises his hand silencing him. "I'm well aware of the situation in Germany. It was not unexpected that another would have been created. Cyrail will deal with him." Lucien smiles. "Have faith... In me."

"My lord, I would recommend that we send Legion and—"

"No, I want everyone where they are. Prophecy is still in play. These next moments are critical. More seals will soon be broken and I will be given a wider berth. Imperial can handle the situation in Germany. As a matter of fact, I want him to handle it, if only to break the celestial's confidence." Lucien takes a sip of his vodka. "Damn, this is a great drink."

Warsivious nods and accepts his decision. "Your car to the U.N. awaits you Sir."

Chinese Embassy Berlin, Germany

Jericho pushes a heavy slab of masonry off of himself. He gets up begrudgingly and begins to scan around looking for his adversary. Imperial's hand suddenly explodes from underneath debris and grabs Jericho by his ankle and pulls him to the floor. Imperial bursts from the remaining rubble hovering holding Jericho dangling inverted by his right ankle. Imperial fires a red bolt charge into Jericho while simultaneously slamming him from drywall to cement column, back again to drywall. Imperial finally releasing Jericho slings him all the way through one of damaged drywalls. The particular wall chosen happened to be hiding treated reinforced solid Oak underneath.

Once through the wall, Jericho hits the floor as pieces of his uniform cinders in certain places and is torn in others. The trauma of the repeated slams was so instant he didn't even have the chance to yell out in pain. Unable to make his brain fire synapses giving commands to his muscles, he just lies on the floor motionless. Coughing is his first autonomous action as he startles awake. As he searches for a full breath upon gaining consciousness, he notices a sign lying next to him. It reads "弹药," munitions, in Chinese.

Body is on fire, feels like my skin is burning. Feels like I'm dying. Can't catch my breath, hard to breathe. I think he's coming. God, I have to get up. Get up! Get up! Get the fuck up, dammit!

Pushing with everything he has, Jericho manages to get to all fours. Imperial tearing through the wall seeing him in a compromising position attempts to gives him a metal boot across the face. Jericho falls backward causing Imperial to miss his intended target. Jericho's up in an instant and grabs Imperial by the divot in his armor near the neck. With his right hand he drives repeated strikes into the Nephilim's face. His punches are fast, fierce and furious. Imperial reaches in and pulls Jericho close head-butting him. The blinding pain shoots straight through to the brain dropping Jericho off of Imperial to the ground where he again lands on all fours. This time, Imperial doesn't miss and connects the kick to Jericho's face spinning him wildly into the door of a massive vault. For Jericho everything goes dark.

Imperial walks over to Jericho kicking him again and again up against the door of the massive vault. He repeatedly kicks for the slight of laying hands on him, making him bleed. he kicks him for the punishment that he promised would be dished out when they first exchanged words in the garage, finally he kicks to hear the breakage of bone. When he feels enough pain has been inflicted, he grips Jericho by his neck and begins to slowly squeeze. He can feel the pulse of blood flowing through his carotid arteries. He squeezes harder and finds it a bit difficult to constrict his artery.

"He built you tough, didn't he? All the same you're still simply a man." Imperial lifts and slams him back to the floor and walks out leaving him broken in front of the vault.

Gabriel makes herself visible to Jericho. With tears in her eyes she attempts to hold him more than her allowed light suggestive touch, but she can't. It is forbidden. The tears in her eyes tell the story of her emotions more than the color of her ever-changing iris could. She wants nothing more than to cradle him and pat him up. Metatron and Cassiel appears lightly touching her on her shoulders for support.

"I'm so sorry, Jericho. This was a fight that should have been left to us. This creature was never meant to exist and let alone be your problem," says Gabriel as she rubs him across his head like when he was a child. Again, each of her touches are a gentle breeze that lightly blows his sweaty and blood matted hair. Gabriel's voice then turns stern. "As much as this fight should have been ours, it is not, it's yours. It's not fair, but it is as it was meant to be. You have to get up baby. You have to get up now! Complete you task! Get your ass up and in gear Marine!"

"Why should he? To only endure more punishment," Imperial says as he reenters the vault with his sword.

Gabriel stands and grabs the hilt of her blade as she turns to face Imperial. "You will not touch him again, abomination!"

"Oh! Understand, I am going to do much worse than just touch him again. And when I begin, what are you going to do? When I decide to bend him in ways that will reinvent pain, what can you do to stop me?" Imperial walks towards Jericho with his blade's tip dragging slicing and burning into the concrete.

Metatron and Cassiel unsheathe their blades and hold them at the ready, but they don't step to Gabriel's side, a tinge of fear gives them pause. How does one fight an enemy when he can't be scathed? Gabriel holds her ground and pulls her blade from its sheathe standing in front of Jericho guarding his recovery.

Imperial smirks at her. "Now where have I seen this before? Oh yeah! Al-Fashir, when I killed Muriel was it? No, it was Oreo or something like that right?" Laughing.

"His name was Uriel," Gabriel says.

"Right... that was it, Uriel. Well, whose name am I to remember today when I send you to meet him."

"Gabriel... You will remember me," she says.

Gabriel Looks down at Jericho. She remembers the look in his mother Rachel's eyes when she tasked her to protect her son. Gabriel looks at Imperial and then gives her brothers an I'm sorry glance that tells them, I'm sorry that I won't live to see these dark days to an end, I'm sorry that one more place at the table will be left empty, I'm sorry that I've made you witness my rendezvous with Death. Gabriel attacks.

Metatron reaches for her in an attempt to stop her. "Gabe, no wait!"

Metatron's reach is too slow and much too late. Gabriel holds nothing back as she strikes down with enough force to cleave Imperial in half. Sure, and smug he doesn't even bother to defend himself, he just watches as her blade falls stopping a millimeter short of making contact with even a single strand of his hair. She tries with all the celestial might she can summon to push pass Elohim's law that binds her. She pushes with the force that has in the distant past moved planets, but it moves no further pass the millimeter close to his hair.

Imperial slams her head with the hilt of his blade stunning her. In her blunt trauma second of confusion he grabs her by her hair and slams her head twice into the vault's door before slamming her to the ground and stepping on her neck pinning her in place.

Metatron and Cassiel are joined by Raziel and Samael. It took them a min to catch up, it was a bit more work setting the evils correct that Vermin and Pain had caused outside the Embassy. The two ready their blades. Once they take notice of who their opponent is, they hesitate, because in this instant, they can only watch they are powerless against him.

Imperial looks over to Metatron and the rest of the celestials while twirling his blade building up the suspense and fear in them of what he is going to do. When he feels that they are at their max of nervous anticipation he swipes the blade fast and forceful to alleviate Gabriel of her head. With a loud clank Imperial's blade strikes celestial metal instead of flesh as Jericho slams one end of Gabriel's blade into the metal vault door while he holds the other creating a bridge over top of her. Stunned by the reflecting blow of his own blade, Imperial is forced to take a step backward.

While Jericho grips her blade, he can clearly see Metatron, Cassiel, Raziel and Samael. They look as astonishing to him as Gabriel in their battle armament. No time to be awe stricken, he pushes past the beauty of the celestials and turns his attention back to Imperial, realizing that he must put him down, now for his own sake, but for all their sakes. Seeing them only able to watch, he understands the dilemma they face first hand. He saw the hesitation of the others and the strike that was ineffective by Gabriel. *They can't hurt him.* Jericho instantly recalls the battle for Sarin that Gabriel showed him. He remembers what she said. 'We could never intervene directly in the affairs of men again.' It dawns on him. *He's one of the hybrids. He's half human, they can't hurt him.* Jericho hears Gabriel in his mind whispering, "and if he's human? "He bleeds Jericho answers out loud.

"Whatever bleeds—" Gabriel yells.

"—Can be killed." Jericho finishes.

Seizing the moment, Jericho tackles Imperial who was already stumbling backward to the ground further straddling him. Again, he takes a hold of Imperial armor divot at the neck as a counter balance fulcrum lever. He pulls Imperial up with violent force towards his fast approaching dominate hand punch. He connects fist to face of the Nephilim strike after repeated strike. Imperial's mask and helmet generates covering his face quickly before Jericho rains down anymore punishing hits.

The punches are hard and furious denting in the metal of the mask protecting Imperials face. Jericho punches to exhaustion. When his punches slow enough, Imperial grabs a hold of Jericho's incoming fist and sends another bolt into him causing him to writhe backward in pain screaming. Imperial keeps the charge steady and unending. Flames again begin to spark up on Jericho's uniform. Having a clear shot Imperial lets go of Jericho's fist breaking the charge. Before Jericho can recover in the slightest, Imperial sends another bolt into the chest of Jericho blasting him back into the vault's door with such force that the masonry around the hinges crumble. Jericho falls to the floor unconscious.

Imperial staggers to his feet grabbing his blade to steady himself. He's never had to steady himself. Pain has been inflicted upon him. Intense burning pain around his face where his helmet was dented in. He looks to finish what he started by ending Gabriel first and then the human.

When he looks to finish Gabriel at the spot she was just laying, she's no longer there. He finds her standing with her brothers away from the Nephilim. Imperial degenerates his mask, but it's taken such a pounding and is so massively dented, it sticks. With one hand he rips the helmet and mask from his head taking a deep breath. He smiles and gestures for Gabriel. "Come, dear, shall you and I dance again?"

Gabriel just stares at him, but doesn't move.

"No! I understand." Imperial slices the mag lock to the vault before charging a bolt only to hold it within his fist. He punches his charged fist into the vault's door creating a grip. He then pulls the door from its foundation. The hinges easily give way as they were destroyed moments ago in the confrontation when Jericho slammed against it.

The vault door falls over on top of Jericho, but doesn't crush him as it ramps against the adjoined wall leaving space for Jericho underneath.

The door having being ripped from its foundation reveals a destructive cadre of explosives. Imperial smiles at the arsenal stored away in the Embassy's weapon and arsenal munitions vault. The shelves are stocked with small arms. The walls are covered in rifles and shoulder fire rocket weaponry. The back of the room has crates marked high explosives, claymores, and grenades. There's even a rack that contains well forged Katana Samurai blades. Forgetting the celestials for a moment as they are of no real concern to him, Imperial walks to the back and tears the lid off of the high plastique explosives. He sheaths his sword.

Jericho bruised and bloodied slams into Imperial from behind shoving him into the weapons rack. The N.H.E. designate trips over a stack of weapons crate when he tries to find footing. Falling to his knees, his head strikes the wall of the now broken weapons rack. Jericho grabs a palm full of the back of his skull and rams Imperial's head countless times into the wall till his head breaks through metal and cement. Out of breath, but full of fight, Jericho backs away and looks for a weapon. He nods his head at seeing the stack of Katana blades and reaches for one. He pulls it from the rack flicking his thumb across the blade. Hearing a groan coming from N.H.E. he doesn't hesitate. He screams a battle cry and runs to put his momentum behind his jump lunging thrust. He's off center, but his aim is as true as his blurry vision will allow. The blade strikes its tip just beneath the armor of Imperials back. Jericho strikes meat and draws blood but only a scratch. The weapon shatters into small shards of steel.

Feeling pain, Imperial senses returns. Dazed, he pulls his head from the wall. His left eye is swollen shut and he has a mean laceration over the right eye and a split lip. He throws himself backward with a huge backhanded right swing targeting Jericho. The Marine drops to his ass dodging the haymaker attempt. His eyes lock onto the hilt of Imperials sword. Jericho grabs the hilt with both hands and pulls. The blade is immensely heavy. His muscles cry in agony wielding a weapon of gods just as they did when he used Gabriel's to shield her. Jericho's veins spiders and muscles ripple holding the blade level. Jericho lets the tip fall to the ground. He gets to a knee and pushes forward pole vaulting the hilt of the blade into Imperials face. There is a decent amount of blood splatter and a broken canine tooth. Imperials hands rises to his face before another strike can be vaulted. Jericho changes tactics and pulls the celestial blade's tip up from the floor and arches it around spinning his body for momentum till his back is facing Imperial. Still giving his battle cry, Jericho completes the blade attacking maneuver by slamming the blade backward in a stabbing motion under his left armpit past himself and into the front chest of the N.H.E. The blade finds purchase sliding through metal, flesh, bone, then cement. It cauterizes the flesh around it. Imperial for the first time ever lets out a maddening howl.

Jericho releases the weapon. He turns and falls to his knees face to face with Imperial. He looks him in the eyes and sees that the N.H.E. does not harbor fear there. He does not show the realization that he may be about to die. Jericho only observes resolve. He immediately pushes away seeing the unnatural reaction to a fatal wound, but it's too late. Imperial grabs him by the neck. His helmet regenerates from below the armors neckline damaged. There's no face plate protection, just helmet. Imperial slams helmeted head four times into Jericho's face rendering him unconscious again. He attempts to crush his neck, but again finds it difficult. It doesn't snap as easy as other mortals. Jericho comes around when he's unable to catch his breath. He knees the hilt of the blade buried in Imperials chest. The pain is enough to break his vice like grip. Jericho falls to his knees then onto his ass taking in a full gasp of air. He places his hands on his neck rubbing it.

Knowing he can't let the N.H.E. recover, Jericho pushes himself to his feet to continue pressing the attack. He's seen blood. He can kill the N.H.E. That was his purpose wasn't it? He was literally born to meet his thing head on in battle. Oops! His attention slightly deviated off the enemy while he pondered the answer of his birth. It wasn't much time, but it was enough that he never saw Imperial disengage the pin from a yellow painted high explosive grenade that was rolling around on the floor amongst others that must have been knocked over during the fight. Imperial had tossed it between the two when Jericho was slightly distracted. Imperial draws his body in tight. Jericho reaches for the small arms shelf and pulls it from its bolted mounts using it as a shield. The blast ignites other small explosive devices causing a chain reaction into a moderate sized explosion.

The generated heat and energy concussive wave blows Imperial and the wall he's nailed too into a collapse setting him free. Jericho is blown clear from the munitions vault and into the wall outside of it in the hallway. He slides down the wall unto the top of the vault's steel door. Another reactionary blast explodes from inside the vault. A second powerful concussive wave engulfs the hallway flipping the metal vault door up like a coin. Jericho rolls off the door landing on the floor. The vault door soon crashes down half embedding itself into the wall with the other half piercing the floor, trapping Jericho.

Smoke expels from the vault. The plastique explosives did not ignite. Imperial's blade was blown free from his body. He emerges from the room holding his blade in his right hand and cradling his chest with the left. His helmet disengages below the armor neckline. He walks over to take Jericho's head, but he's buried under the thick steel vault door. Sirens can be heard in the distance drawing nigh. He mouths "Shit!" under his breath. He turns and with his one eye not swollen, he sees his DNA everywhere. He sheaths his blade and returns into the munitions vault.

The room being covered in debris, it takes him a few seconds before he's able to find the Det Cord. He pulls the detonation cord off of a half-broken shelf and jams it into one brick of plastique contained within the five-foot-high container of plastique individually wrapped bricks. There is sixty in total. Imperial walks out of the vault leaving Jericho to burn. He passes Gabriel and the rest of the celestials. He nods his head at them, "not such a bad attempt." Says Imperial before lifting off through the ceiling that he and Jericho only moments earlier had come crashing through leaving only a trail of Det Cord in his wake.

Gabriel watches him leave with the cord in tow. "He's going to detonate and level the place," she says.

Gabriel runs over to Jericho and crawls into the space where he is and touches his back. "He's still breathing. Metatron he's hurt bad. Jericho get up! Get up! C'mon get up baby." Gabriel starts to frantically look around for anything that could wake him. "There's no way to wake him." She places her hand on his forehead and closes her eyes. "Nothing… He's out. In a coma I suspect. His brain has massive swelling."

Metatron places his hand on Gabriel's back garnering her attention. "Then we will stay with him until the end. He gave one hell of a valiant effort."

Cassiel paces looking at the debris where Jericho is wedged under. "He made a believer out me today Gabe. I thought he was actually going to do it for a minute. That abomination isn't natural. He placed that blade true. It was a fatal injury that he should not have walked away from."

Michael's voice emits from the neckline of the Archs armor. "Get moving. That abomination isn't waiting to detonate."

Cassiel takes a quick glance around at the support structures for the building. He plays the blast output in his mind and witnesses' tons of brick and mortar currently overhead collapsing after a few tons super-heated flame incinerates everything where they now stand. "We will not be able to move him. Can he survive such a blast?" asks Cassiel.

Gabriel shakes her head. "I don't know… Samson didn't survive the fall of that coliseum.

"Gabriel, tell me; no bullshit assessment! Can this mortal stop him?" Cassiel asks.

"What do you want me to tell you Cassiel, we're working on faith here. No one knows how this will end. We're off script Damnit!"

Cassiel calms himself and whispers, "do you believe he can put things right? I'm asking you… Yes or no right now! Can Jericho set the balance?"

"She doesn't know." Metatron says. "From what I've seen of this mortal, he won't stop. Did you see him. He knew he was bested and he didn't quit. That attitude of his was Davidic. He almost toppled that giant. The odds were shifted somehow when the fatal blow was ineffective, but sheer will and an unrelenting determination had him place that blade into a demigod. That has to count for something."

Gabriel looks at Jericho then back to Cassiel. "Yes…yes Cassiel, I believe he can set the scales."

Cassiel stands to his feet and unsheathes his blade and throws it to Raziel who up until then remained quiet. "Cut them off!" Cassiel extends both his wings straight back giving Raziel a clean target.

"Wh—what? No! No, I'm not cutting off your wings."

"There's no time. He detonates that brick in that crate and all is lost." Cassiel looks deep into Raziel eyes. "Cut them off." Cassiel lowers his voice again to a whisper. "It's okay."

Gabriel shakes her head no and looks to Raziel "Don't you do it!"

Cassiel grabs Raziel's jaw and forces him to look into his eyes. "Brother, look at me. I can't do it myself, I'd lose the nerve. It has to be you. I won't hold this against you. If this man dies here, we all perish, all realms, all realities. We can't intervene directly in the state we're in. Do it!" Cassiel voice falls to a whisper. "Do it!" Cassiel yells, "DO IT!"

"Arrrrgggghhhh!" Raziel screams. He grabs his brother with his free arm hugging him tightly. He lets go and swirls the blade twice for momentum and slings it behind Cassiel's back separating his wings from his torso.

Cassiel screams out from a pain that he's never felt. The song of heaven is instantly lost to him forever. He watches as Gabriel, Metatron, Samael and Raziel vanish before his eyes. As a mortal his connection is forever severed. He falls to his knees discombobulated as he's never walked as a mortal. *So heavy.* Is his singular thought.

Gabriel screams, "Raziel why? Why did you do it?"

"To give existence it's best chance, Raziel says.

Angel's Spire

Yeshua, Michael and the rest of the angelic choir falls silent. Michael slowly shakes his head, no. Seeing and feeling his pain, Yeshua places a comforting hand, on his captain's shoulder. Another Arch has fallen.

Chinese Embassy Berlin, Germany

There's no time, we have to move. Cassiel grabs Jericho by the strap on the back of his body armor. The strap that is there for just a situation when a comrade needs to be pulled out of danger if wounded or incapacitated. Cassiel grabs a hold and pulls with all the strength that he can gather. His new mortal body screams in pain, but it's fleeting as adrenaline kicks in powering him through the ache of muscles and the breathing of the heavy oxygen-enriched air. He continues dragging Jericho to the fastest yet furthest means of safety.

CHAPTER 44

O nce through the ceiling Imperial lands and begins walking through the halls making sure the Det Cord doesn't touch anything incendiary or electrical until he's clear. Doesn't want to set the cord off to soon.

He retraces his steps through the destruction that was caused when Jericho sent him through the wall. When he steps through the wall back to the outside garage Fate is awaiting him. Imperial releases the Det Cord and pulls his sword form its sheath out of habit more than fear of an angel.

Fate places his empty hands on display. "Whoa, I'm not here to quarrel. I'm just curious as to what has the heavens realms in such upheaval."

"Then stand aside, angel, lest I send you to Apollyon like the others."

"Apollyon? He's on my list of brothers that I plan on speaking with anyhow. However, I'd much rather meet him under my own power. No need for threats, I just wanted to see this nephilim that I've heard so much about up close."

Imperial picks up the Det Cord with his off hand and slowly walks past Fate. The angel makes sure to stay clear of Imperial's blade.

"I'm intrigued that a creature that I wrote out of existence so long ago still lingers and draws breath thinking that he has a future."

"You believe I have no future?" Imperial says.

Cassiel pulls Jericho inside an elevator. He picks any floor at random, because he can't read the Chinese characters. When his ties to the accessing of realities severed, it was like an insane round of musical chairs. The celestials revert to the reality they currently find themselves in at the time of separation. Had this battle been decided in reality 1513, he could have easily been a microbe. When Cassiel became human unfortunately his race and tongue fell to that of Swahili.

Gabriel makes herself seen to Cassiel. <"What have you done?"> She says speaking to Cassiel in Swahili.

<"I don't know. Didn't have time to think about it."> Cassiel said as he feels the sensation of the upward moving cube. <"In hindsight, I may have been a bit brash."> He chuckles to himself.

The elevator doors open on three. Cassiel pulls Jericho to the south side of the Embassy where there are large plate glass windows. Once he gets Jericho there, he collapses under the new-found weight of flesh and blood, also because he's run out of breath.

Cassiel pulls himself up and starts pulling office furniture and whatever else he can find to place in front of Jericho. Making a bunker.

Metatron relays to Gabriel that Fate is stalling Imperial for time, and that minutia of time that he purchased is about up.

Gabriel eyes Cassiel as he tries holding back his tears.

Cassiel sighs pulling in all the air he can to reenergize himself. <"Gabriel, what am I worth to the whole of existence? Nothing... My eyes have beheld wonders sister that beings of lesser creation will never experience. I've scaled to the top of Elohim's Palace. I've slid across the event horizon of the Hedeaus Anomaly. My time has not been wasted in service of one greater than I. It seems that I will now experience what only you have. I will experience a piece of a mortal's life no matter how brief...">

Gabriel stares at Cassiel, her lips quiver at his remark.

<"I know who you are sister; who you really are. I figured it out not long after Fate let it slide when he called you by a name that has long since been stricken from memory, damn near even record."> Cassiel winks at her. <"I can keep a secret. I'll keep this one until death."> He

then looks down at Jericho. <"You believe in this mortal sister and I believe in you."> Tears begin to stream from Cassiel's eyes. <"I don't believe that I've ever been as terrified as I am now… Stay with me, will you?">

<"Until whatever end,"> Gabriel says.

Cassiel sits Indian style with Jericho's unconscious body facing the glass window. He pulls Jericho close to his chest and holds onto him tightly to cushion him. Cassiel then buries his head in between the Jericho's shoulder blades, their backs facing the door.

Angel's Spire - Day

The Spire is quiet as all the angels, powers, choiretic and citizenry watch the events unfold.

Chinese Embassy Berlin, Germany

Imperial stares at Fate. "Before I'm done, you will see my future burn brighter than the sun. In a time that will soon be upon us, you will either kneel to my sword or fall before it just as your mortal hope did. Only the hand of a god could ever bring me to heel and haven't you heard? He's stepped away from the world of men. It's as if he wills this event.

Sirens of the first responders are starting to arrive on the scene. With communications restored the authorities phone lines were instantly flooded with emergency calls. Hearing them draw near, Imperial's wings expand striking the ground lifting him into the air. "Let what I've done today be a reminder to your kind to stay out my father's affairs and by extension mine. You celestials cross me again and I will not wait for permission. I will take it upon myself to become the angelic omega."

Imperial ignites a bolt through his hand and sends a charge into Det Cord to detonate the high explosives. Once ignited he lifts off into the stratosphere with precipitous speed "Boom!" he whispers.

The high explosives detonate destroying the foundation of the Embassy. The building explodes first sending a massive concussive wave that shatters every window in the structure before the violent flow of hot air, flames and debris follow.

Cassiel grips Jericho tighter as the concussive wave blows through the office door and into the makeshift wall of furniture that Cassiel managed to pull together. The blast carries the debris, Cassiel, and Jericho out of the third-floor window. As they are blown out through the window, flames and building material follow. The blast not only engulfs the building, but reaches far out beyond the structure engulfing the first responders and more than three blocks before the building implodes and collapses in on itself.

Cassiel holds tightly to Jericho in spite of the blast tossing them about wildly. When they hit the ground, it's marked with a massive blood smear from Cassiel as his body strikes first. The two bodies separate as they tumble down Märkisches Ufer 54 street. Jericho comes to rest when he strikes the side of a bus. Cassiel's body comes to a stop when he collides into a light pole.

Gabriel appears next to Cassiel to comfort him, but he's already gone. His body is void of its soul. Metatron and the rest of the celestials appear as well and bow their head at the lifeless husk.

"I have him, messenger," Death says. "I assure you he felt little pain. I took his soul at the moment of impact." Death nods to the rest of the celestials and throws liquid from a vial onto the remains of Cassiel. The body ignites and instantaneously burns to ash. Witnessing all trace of the celestial body made flesh turn to ash, Death turns and walks into the dust ploom from the collapsed Embassy disappearing from the celestials' sight.

Gabriel watches as Death disappear into the smoke, ash, and flames. *I've never seen him like this.* Her wings switch blade out and she levitates and hovers over to Jericho. At first appearance he looked to be void of life, but, he's alive; unresponsive, but alive. Death would have made mention otherwise and claimed him.

Fate appears. "Be sure your love for the boy Lilith, does not overcast your judgment. He was not ready and it cost not only the unnecessary lives of mortals, but of Cassiel. This day has exacted a heavy toll for your ignorance and over indulgence."

Gabriel looks up at Fate. "We all know this is a dangerous game we play. The fact still remains, if we don't bring Imperial to heel then we have no chance." She stares into Fate's eyes. "None of us. All of Fate will be undone."

Sighing! "Touché, Lilith." Fate adjust the dial on his gauntlet phasing into another reality. He turns and starts walking down the street as more first responders arrive on scene. The vehicles phase through him as he walks with his hands clasped behind his back pondering on all the events that Lucifer has set into motion.

An officer running toward the Embassy notices Jericho clinging to life. He stops and kneels to check his vitals. Finding a pulse, he stands and looks around for a medic. An ambulance racing to the seen slows when the driver sees the officer flailing his arms for them to stop. The medic driver exits and watches the officer point to a live victim. The officer gesticulates that victim has a heartbeat. The medic nods and runs to the back of the ambulance to retrieve the gurney. The second medic exits the passenger side and opens a utility door on the side compartment of the medical cab. He grabs a blue medic go-bag and rushes toward Jericho to begin giving him critical care treatment. The medic gives him a cursory look over and notices a few possible fractures, second and third degree burns and lacerations. Jericho's uniform for the most part had been burned or torn away. With his uniform in tatters, it obfuscated anything identifying him as a United States Marine. Once the second medic appears with the Gurney, they lock him in to immobilize him. The medics roll him to the rear of the ambulance where they further load him into the back of the medic, stabilize his injuries, and guns it to the nearest trauma unit lights blaring and siren wailing.

CHAPTER 45

"ENTER UNTO THE WORLD THAT IS NOTHING BUT A STAGE"

"I patiently await Apollyon. When the locks turn on this cell releasing me there is but one I will hound until desecration. I will not sojourn, nor give chance to bargain, barter, or negotiate. I will simply end Fate and undo all."

Quote ~Wrath

New York: United Nations—Two Days Later

The evening hour newscast comes across the jumbo monitor in Time Square, New York. Reputable national CNN anchor Richard Sullivan gives the daily news in his famed low baritone smooth voice.

"Scientist are still anxiously awaiting the arrival of Wormwood. It's been more than two decades that the world has been following this story. They are saying that this will be the closet asteroid to ever skim the Earth. Get your telescopes ready America. If you don't have one not to worry as its arrival is years away. You have plenty of time."

Richard moves his attention to camera two. "It has been a tense week as strained China and U.S. relations over events in Germany more than two weeks ago have poured out unto the world stage with fierce accusations of America's involvement. What exactly happened is still unclear, but outlaying governments are calling the tragedy more than an incident, but a provocation to war on a stage that is already full of conflict. Penn State University has released a study that has said as the world currently stands we are experiencing more conflicts then ever recorded in the history of the modern world. Wait!"

Richard grabs his ear piece and takes a few seconds to listen. "… Sorry, we have breaking news. Reports are just coming in on an attack at the United Nations in New York. We go live to Ellen Nichols who's on the ground for the world's resolution peace summit. Ellen?"

Ellen Nichols has been in the killing fields of Iraq. She has reported from the wars of the Sudan deeply embedded with the Arcane forces. Her investigative skills have taken her to Aswan, Egypt in search of a supposed excavation site and missing workers. Now the forty-eight-year-old reporter is standing outside the United Nations behind police and fire barricades. Covered in soot and with small lacerations to her face and hands from shards of glass. Ellen again has waded into a situation where war has possibly found her. She faces the camera with a stern face that hides her second thoughts of maybe she should be running.

As an explosion ignites on the seventeenth floor of the United Nations, surrounding citizens and first responders run for cover from the falling debris. Ellen covers her face and turns away quickly from the explosion, but she doesn't run for cover.

"This is Ellen Nichols, live from what was supposed to have been the Active Peace Summit in New York. Richard, it's utter devastation here at the United Nations. There is more than a dozen fires on various floors of the building behind me. It's not just any building, it's the

United Nations. Moments ago, my partner Steven Brice, was inside covering the conference. It's all unclear at the moment in the aftermath of the blast, but it appears that it may have been an intentional incendiary device that has gone off."

Ellen trying to listen to what Richard is saying back in the studio holds her hand to her ear pressing it closer to hear his questions among the loud and very hostile environment. "Yeah Richard we do have footage of the conference. It was streamed to our backup systems here on the street in our mobile van. As we piece it together we should have an idea of what transpired just before the blast."

Ellen nods to a person off camera. "Okay, it seems we have the footage of the conference just before things went utterly insane. For those viewers at home if there are small children in the room you may want them to leave out, this will be unedited." Ellen gestures to roll the footage.

A conference of world leaders is underway. Men of power from respective countries sit patiently awaiting the man of the hour. They listen intently to the speaker at the podium. News reporters and cameramen have their microphones, boom sticks, and cameras pointed in the direction of the podium where the current speaker has the floor. Each reporter tries to slide in just a bit closer among the plethora of microphones looking for any edge that would give them an upper hand in obtaining the best spot to see and ask questions. To miss one word of this conference could spell disaster for any news crew that miss a vital sentence or phrase.

"As you viewers can see at home," Ellen continues, "our cameraman Jamie is recording the conference. That is William Braddox at the podium talking. Let's listen in. I remind you Richard this is uncut so viewers at home be mindful. Let's listen."

Braddox is a burly man who represents Nova Scotia. With honor, he accepted the invite to introduce the speaker of the hour who all the world is waiting to hear from. Already in the middle of his speech, the microphone activates and he can be instantly heard around the world in multiple languages.

A cut in the footage takes the viewers into session that is already underway. Braddox's mic cues up mid speech. "He has been associated with controversy. He's been called dictator, tyrant, and new world order made flesh. He's also been called, last hope, peacemaker, and savior. He stepped from the shadows into public service to help those that were overlooked and for his hard work an unending dedication he created a utopia for the disenfranchised, the lonely and forgotten. He's given those shunned by society a purpose and has promoted peace not just locally, but throughout the world. We are honored to have this alumnus of United Nations back with us tonight to speak on the condition of his campaign to tame the violence in the Congo and his expectations of how he will amplify that peace for a world which has seem to have gone mad. I give you all Lucien Arcane." Applause erupt followed by standing ovations.

Seated just behind Braddox off to the right, Lucien stands and accepts the applause as he takes the podium. Once there, he continues to bask in the admiration. He waves and nods his head in appreciation gleefully taking all of it in. He stops long enough to arrange his prepared speech which reflects in the teleprompter. Braddox after clapping finds his seat giving Lucien the stage.

Lucien raises his hands and gestures for quiet to the auditorium. As the applause dies down, his charismatic and iconic laughter can be heard. "He was being nice. I'm sure I've been called a lot worse. Probably by many of you here."

The audience starts laughing at his quip.

"Damn right, we've called you worse," shouts Rebecca Sands, the representative of Norway.

The crowd and delegates laugh more unsure if she is joking or serious.

Braddox stands and slightly moves Lucien aside to address Sands. "The chair does not recognize Norway at this time Ms. Sands. There will be order throughout these proceedings here today where you will be able to voice concern."

Hearing Rebecca set straight by Braddox, the laughter dies in an uncomfortable silence. Persistent, Rebecca steps into the aisle way slowly still clapping her hands. "I must admit you had me fooled. It took some time to see past that charismatic smile of yours. You are a slander and trickster who has indeed been called many names. You, who stands up there and mocks the world with your very existence are no doubt the bringer of death on wings of silver. You are no ambassador of peace. If anything at all you are harbinger of doom. The world can't see who you are through all the glitter you blind them with, but there are those of us who can. We see you through the facade that you wear, the fake face you show the world for fear your other will be recognized. And it is on their behalf the ones you have bedazzled, that I've taken it upon myself to rid the world of you just as the heavens did. With my hand un-stayed, by the laws which govern man, we will end you."

The news camera follows Rebecca as she starts to run down the aisle. It's a slow trot at first as her legs barely want to move under her own power, because of fear. In spite of it, she finally catches her stride building the running momentum toward the podium. Rebecca looks about the chambers to make sure the cameras are following her. The footage not only picks up Rebecca, it widens out to catch the expression of the members of the delegation. They are stricken with the momentary confusion of her interruption, but they all continue to watch and see the coming climax if she makes it to the podium.

From the moment she made her presence known, security had already started tracking her on foot as well placing themselves between her and Lucien to cut her off. Not wanting to be intercepted before she reaches her goal, she takes off into a full sprint.

Damn this fear, that slowed my feet to run from the beginning its cost me the precious seconds that I may have needed, she thought.

As she draws closer to the podium, Braddox loses his professionalism and yells obscenities at her along with orders to cease her disruptive action. Braddox starts to push Lucien away from the lectern, but Lucien wanting to see the representative who would dare interrupt what could be one of his most important speeches on peace stands firm. He squints his eyes at his incoming attacker. He's quickly trying to process whether she's a real threat or not.

Having clearly identified her as a threat, Warsivious runs in front of the podium. As she closes in she realizes she was right in her early assessment, that her initial trot mere seconds ago was precious seconds that she would not recover from. Security forces tackle her before she makes it to Lucien. The U.N. undercover plain-clothes operative detail is quickly on top of her. Warsivious stands ready as they try to gain control of the unruly representative.

Sands struggles with the internal security of the U.N. to get free if only for a second more to complete her ultimate endeavor. Security trying to cuff her continuously proves difficult as she rolls over during the struggle to lie prostrate on her stomach interlocking her arms underneath her belly. As the security detail try to loosen her arms to complete the restraining, they stop mid-action. The security forces back down leaving Rebecca unattended lying in the middle of the aisle before Lucien. Confused, she gets up to her knees and looks up toward the podium.

Lucien holds his hands in the air and signals for calm. He then looks to the commotion that is at his feet just a meter below the lectern. "Stop this madness! Release her! Let's hear what Norway has to say. It seems to be of the utmost importance. So much so, that she had to come down and tell me personally... Besides we can't get Norway to talk any other time."

The delegates laugh again, this time some have the nervous tinge of apprehension.

"She is, after all, a representative of her people. She speaks on behalf of nation whom I have much respect for. I for one am interested in what she has to say. Please, delegate Sands, you may have the floor."

Lucien stands aside and pulls Braddox with him clearing the path to the podium. Another delegate from China enters the aisle and assist Rebecca to her feet. He then stands aside bowing giving her the right of way to the podium. Rebecca straightens her blazer and attempts to tame her messed hair. She walks past the remaining partially seated rows of delegates and uniformed and undercover security to take the podium. Warsivious watches her closely. He strains to keep his eye color neutral even through the facade of his human disguise.

Rebecca looks out over the delegates and world leaders. Tears begin to roll down her cheeks. Her breathing becomes laborious. "I know that many in the days to come will look on what happened here today. They will say that when peace came, that I was an enemy against it. That couldn't be further from the truth. I know of a coming peace that will outlast any semblance this man has to offer. With the voice of my people, we declare united and in one voice that Lucien is not a man of peace, not truly. I wish you all could see that… Maybe someday you will."

Rebecca's voice starts to jump and in some instances crack as she realizes her time is at hand. "There is but one God of all of us and it is not Lucien Arcane, although he may want to be."

Rebecca looks over to Lucien. He smiles at her and gestures toward the mike for her to continue. She smiles back at him sarcastically through her tears. She stares at him, searching his eyes for the humanity that she was told was not there. As she looks at him doubt starts to creep into her mind. *He genuinely looks to be a man of peace. He looks as if he is who he says he is. Then again, so did Christ and he changed the world. If he as one man could do that, then so can this one. If he is a man.*

"For all that is holy in this world and for those which I've pledged my allegiance. What I do now is for them."

Rebecca raises her shirt, revealing a slim intricately devised suicide vest. At the briefest first glance it's different from others that had been publicized. This vest was black with blue liquid running through the clear small plastic tubing. The intertwined tubes culminated in the back of the vest in small bulge of a metal disc. Looking at Lucien she wipes the tears from her eyes.

"I know what you did in Aswan. I don't know how, but my brother didn't deserve to just be wiped from existence. This is for my brother, Aaron." Rebecca says.

Rebecca gives Lucien a small pin. He flips it over for closer examination and inspection. In doing so his eyes widen at the symbol of the red cross over the shield design. "Templar, Lucien says surprised." Rebecca leaps from the lectern and grabs a hold of Lucien and whispers, "For the Templars. For my brother Aaron."

She depresses the switch. The explosion ignites the entire podium area. Within a split second after the first detonation, multiple bombs in the auditorium explode which sets another series of explosions throughout the entirety of United Nations building.

The camera that was recording goes dark.

The camera finds Ellen looking back at the devastation that is unfolding in the background. She places her hand to her Bluetooth and turns facing the camera. "We can't be sure how many are injured or have been killed in an apparent suicide bomber's attack. As the story continues to develop, I will remain here on the ground."

Ellen again holds her left ear. "Wait, Richard! It appears that we are getting confirmation that survivors may have possibly survived the assassination attempt that appears to have been meant for Lucien. It's sketchy, but reports from within the chamber of delegates has been overheard possibly talking of survivors."

Ellen looks relieved at the prospect that people may have incredibly survived. She prays that her partner is one of them. Heavily armed Arcanian forces move toward the building at a double time pace.

"I say, again, Richard they possibly have survivors of the attack. Conditions however, are unknown. May the world hold a vigil for those that were lost here tonight and may all say a prayer that Lucien Arcane may have survived although it is doubtful from what we just witnessed only moments ago."

Hundreds of small explosions suddenly erupt from across the street of the U.N. Almost simultaneously in a coordinated effort as hundreds of smoke canisters create an impenetrable wall of smoke. Vehicle's engines can be heard within the smoke. The sound of screeching tires skidding to an abrupt stop pierce the thick veil.

As Ellen and others try to peer into the impenetrable cloud muzzle flashes and the sound of immense gunfire erupts from the smoke. Medical workers and first responders that were on the scene as standby precautions are struck by the rounds as well as civilians that are standing witness. It's clear almost instantly that civilians aren't the key marks, but police, soldiers and U.N. security forces are the intended targets that are intermingled within the civilian population.

Ellen's microphone shatters in her hand as a 7.62 round cuts through it. She screams and turns to her cameraman "Shit! Paul, get down!"

Ellen ducks and runs for cover sliding behind the engine block of a nearby ambulance. Her heart races and adrenalin pushes her so fast she didn't notice the pain of scraping her knees tearing her skin to the white meat. Through immense fear, Ellen pushes herself to peer around the corner of the ambulance to see where the rounds were originating. As she does, her breath leaves her as she sees her cameraman's Paul's lifeless body in the street face down with bone and brain fragments pouring from a hole where his face was only mere seconds ago. From the looks of him, he's been hit multiple times. A few more rounds riddle his lifeless body as she watches.

From the smoke emerges soldiers in black full tactical gear including gas masks and helmets. They advance toward the U.N. building. The only identifying marks about them is their bullet resistant tactical vests which bare reflective red Knights Templar crosses sewn into the entire length and width of the front of their vests. The soldiers advance from across the street in a firing line formation in three rows. The immense expenditure of rounds and extreme violence of action makes them appear numerous as an army when actually It's just under fifty of them. They walk in a line formation in columns of ten firing one row at a time. As one row fires to empty they fall to the back of the ever forward moving columns in unison to reload. The next row steps forward and continues the firing until empty. The knights repeat the advancing system until they advance to the front of the U.N. building, felling anyone that obstructs their path.

Police and Arcanian forces are in disarray as explosions continue going off. But even in the confusion they turn toward the threat adhering to muscle memory. They engage the unidentified forces. During the exchange of fire Ellen gets up and runs for another point of cover away from the advancing force as she's in their direct path. She runs toward another vehicle, but her attempt is short-lived when a bullet rips through her knee cap. Unable to bear her own weight, she falls to the ground uncontrolled. As she lands, she hears the unmistakable snap that her wrist has broken. Determined to live and survive this ordeal, she crawls, scratching and clawing her way to cover. No longer seeing her as any viable threat, the soldiers advance past her, attempting to only shoot at presently armed threats. One of the black clad knights looks down at her briefly making eye contact with her never slowing his march.

As the last of the soldiers' bypass Ellen, she rolls over on to her back looking into the night sky thankful that the men didn't kill her. As she lays on the street, blood continues to pool around her knee. While gazing at the night sky Ellen watches a rocket streak past. Her vision follows it all the way to detonation against the United Nations which has already been severely damaged rocking the structure. Ellen sits up on her rear and scoots backward to prop herself against the cemented entrance gate, she follows the smoke trail of trajectory of the rocket back to its origin which is a fast-moving Apache attack helicopter.

Pilot and the navigator of the attack helicopter are masked behind the darkened shades of their helmets H.U.D. display visors. The pilot wearing his communicator/oxygen mask looks for the next target of opportunity provided by ground troop's lasering the intended mark.

The pilot depresses his radio mic to communicate with the ground. "I understand, that was a negative hit on the superstructure... Roger, understood— structural integrity was not compromised. Five seconds to target. I'm going to need you guys to light up those lasers at the weak points for my payload to effect."

The all matted black copter is all but invisible against the night sky as it whips from around a nearby skyscraper. As the pilot completes the hard right it brings the U.N. building into full view for him. He slows his aerial advance to a hover so he can take in the chaotic scene of the embattled building and the resistance that few are still attempting to mount. Waiting for targets to light up, the copter descends a hundred and thirty-two feet. As he descends the rotator blades and the whining of the engines can be heard by law enforcement and civilian alike. As eyes avert upward the copters only tell sign beyond the noise is the red Knights Templar cross painted on either side of it.

Trying to maintain airlift, the chopper turns from side to side as not create a dead air pocket which could consume the craft and cause it to crash. As it rotates to the left, Death is standing on the landing rail of the copter looking down at the carnage. His trench coat furiously flaps from the generated wind of the blades. Death leaps from the helicopter diving head first with his staff in hand. His coat blows in the force of the wind revealing his sheathed blade's hilt.

"This is Red Blade One. I have a confirmed lock on painted targets. Stand by! Fox trot tango three." The pilot says giving warning before firing. He depresses the trigger and lets a volley of missiles fly weapons free.

As Death dives from the chopper a cadre of missiles from either side of the copter's Gatling style rocket launchers erupt in a chamber by chamber volley. Rocketing at just below the speed of sound, the missiles strike the building creating a ploom of fire and added devastation of uranium depleted shells.

Pulling back on the stick and pushing forward on the throttle, the attack helicopter ascends up and backward. "Confirmed hit... I hear you, say again... Confirmed hit... That's a ten-four. We are Oscar Mic. Red Blade is ghost, see you back at home."

The helicopter breaks off and flies off into the night sky disappearing into the darkness.

The red-crossed soldiers of the Knights Templar order continue firing at the Arcanian and United nation's soldiers as cover fire to keep their heads down. Few are struck mortally as they continue to raise from behind cover and return fire. An untold number of casualties litter the front of the U.N. building. Death runs through the carnage and gunfire amidst the chaos and fallen bodies collecting red and blue soul orbs. As he does, he takes pause long enough to see what's motivating the force behind the Templars. The Fallen Demon Painell; Verminesk, Pestilence and a host of others such as the likes of Legion can be seen touching the black clad soldiers on their back whispering to them in their ears applying subtle commands, swaying and suggesting false pretenses, corrupting their cognitions, all having the Templars believing that they are ensuring the will of God when they are in fact ensuring the will of Lucifer. They play on the knight's religious zeal that burns within them, twisting their minds to believe this task was ordained by the lord himself giving them justification. They rule the spiritually lost fanatics with ease. An ease that didn't just start tonight, but has been slowly ingrained since they turned from their quest centuries ago from the path of spiritual enlightenment to one of forced conversion under the sting of death.

As Verminesk walks past each Templar, he touches their shoulders and says, "For the glory of the true god of this Earth and his righteousness you must fight on and kill in his name. Leave none alive for it is what he commands. Lucifer will reward you for your acts of faith. You all will have a place at his table and revel in his mighty company."

Verminesk moves on to another. He stops, speaks and repeat the aforementioned phrase, then moves on again and again repeating to another continuously stopping, speaking and repeating himself into the ears of the faithlessly lost and confused. Painell does the same working from the opposite end. They only stop when a trumpet from heaven sounds.

A series of white brilliant beams of light strike the ground from Heaven. The lights land directly in front of the United Nation's soldiers, New York Officers, Arcanian Forces, and Marines that are engaged in battle with the Templars returning fire. Out of the beams of light Archangels emerge swords drawn at the ready. Raphael steps out of the lead beam followed by Raziel who steps out of the following beam carrying not only his sword, but now that of Cassiel's. A dozen more beams strike the ground with Archs emerging along with Choiretic angels.

Raziel notices a U.N. officer is huddled behind debris as rounds ricochet all about him. Each round that veers past him strike either metal, glass or concrete. He knows that he needs to return fire if he's to survive. He's just too petrified with fear to move.

A round from one of the Templar's scar rifle leaves the muzzle igniting a colorful display of blue and reddish flame. The round travels through the remnants of the dissipating smoke and flames from the severely structurally-damaged building. The round on its path to target, explodes through brick and further through a windshield of a New York City police cruiser. With nothing else impeding its path of trajectory, it darts for the head of the U.N. soldier when suddenly a brick deflects it.

Raziel accidently repels the incoming fatal round with the rubble from him striking the debris as means of attack toward the demonic. He winks at the soldier. He didn't directly intervene to save his life, but if the act happens in a third-party coincidence, then oh well. Having bought the soldier a few moments he kneels down and places his hands on the soldier's shoulder, "Your family awaits you at home, son of Elohim. If fear takes you now they will be lost to you. Hold steady in your faith that you are exactly where you are supposed to be this moment and no other. Rise, soldier of peace. Rise through the fear and doubt. Rise for those that look to you. Rise with the protection of Archs that fight with you. By all that is holy RISE!"

His heart pumps faster than it ever has in life. He feels the fear falling away to the back of his mind. The thought of his kids never seeing him again overwhelms him with a courage and vigor to fight on like he's never experienced. He charges a round into his rifle and rises to return fire. With a clarity never known to him he pulls the trigger. Three Templars find themselves grabbing their necks, arms and legs falling to the ground lifeless or soon on their way to be.

Raziel smiles at the officer. Then stands and looks to Verminesk who is watching him. "It is you and I, Vermin. You and I."

Verminesk smiles and pulls his weapon. "So, it is."

Raziel takes off as a white streak toward Verminesk. Verminesk takes off toward Raziel in a red and black streak of light. The two, angel and demon collide in the middle of the street and begin to clash swords and dodge bolts of energy and swing with the intension to cleave with the purpose of decapitation in every spin and decisive twirl.

Column three of the attacking Templars unsling their Javelin rocket launchers in practiced unison from their shoulders. Only every other solider of that particular column have the Javelin. They all fall to one knee. Once cleared by their side partner they fire simultaneously at the failing building structure. The lock on self-guided missiles strike causes more added devastation. The Javelin attack was thorough enough so that the left side of building partially collapses. Column three recovers while other columns advance pass them.

The Templars hold their fire, taking one step to the side causing a spilt down the middle of their battalion. A lone Templar in off white battle dress to include cape that falls to the knees walks to the front of the battalion. The leader makes sure that the red cross stitched to the front of the body armor is visible when arriving to the head of the Templar force. The battalion then recovers behind the white clad red crossed, Knight Templar, Grand Prior.

With the Templars holding their fire, so does the U.N defending forces. They hold their weapons level ready to engage if forced. However, they take the moment of respite as a needed break to gather themselves and quickly check the wounded for severity of injuries. Those that are given attention are fallen and wounded soldiers, officers, news crewmen and civilian spectators. The remaining networks of reporters and cameramen that haven't been wounded or killed focus on the white crossed Knight Templar.

The lead Templar speaks in an audio-distorted voice, "It is a shame that our re-emergence onto the world stage had to be under such inhospitable circumstances, but you all have given us no other choice as the reaches of Lucien has intertwined through the heights of governments far into its upper echelons. Please, although tonight's militaristic tactics were harsh and seemingly unforgiving, don't think us savages, we implored diplomacy over the past centuries in the shade out of sight of the public's eye, but in that avenue, you failed to heed out warnings of the coming danger that is Arcane. So, instead of words of wisdom you have elected to receive the stick. Many will say what we have done today is deplorable and shocking. We will be labeled and branded terrorist for our necessary action. Understand that we are regretful and deeply sorry for the unnecessary loss of life here, but there was no better time to end his reign than in its infancy while protection was minimal."

The white-crossed Templar turns flaring the cape and nods to the battalion. "We're done here. Move!"

Just as the Templars advanced, they retreat in the same tactical manner with superior fire power suppression. The remaining defenders return fire while only taking cover to reload. The Templars bound back across the decimated block. Once back across the destruction filled street, soldiers in row three again throws smoke canisters creating a thick smoke screen to block their escape. The Grand Prior takes a look back at the destruction. The Prior's eyes are filled with welled tears behind the mask, but they hold firm and fail to run a stream of sorrow. The Prior turns and disappears into the smoke. As the smoke starts to dissipate the Templars have all vanished even the ones that were wounded or killed.

CHAPTER 46

Raziel and Vermin beat the living hell out of each other. As they continue their one-on-one battle, the rest of the ethereal forces are engaged as well. Angels and demons on both side have been wounded and killed.

Painell and Raphael both parry and block each other's attacks. Pain goes for the winning strike, betting it all that he'd land it. Raphael side steps and spins around Pain. Raph's hand is low and charged waiting to complete the spin to place the charge into Pain. As he completes the move Pain has had the same thought. Each lets their bolts fly. They strike each other in the chest plates simultaneously sending each other hurtling in opposite directions. Painell is sent crashing through the third-floor window of an apartment building. Raphael gains altitude then falls back to the pavement tumbling and skidding across the asphalt.

Painell is the first to his feet. Blood leaks from his abdomen, where a partial bolt deflected after hitting his chest plate. As the melee continues around him, he slowly advances through the smoke and flames toward Raphael. As he closes in on him, He finds the Arch waiting for him.

"I was sure you would have run by the time I made it to you," Pain says.

Raphael says nothing he just waits holding his blade with the tip touching the pavement.

"Nothing to say, little Arch?" Taunts Pain.

Hearing the sound barrier broken Raphael looks toward the sky and then returns his attention back to Pain. "There will come a day when you won't be able to hide behind him Demon. When that day comes, it'll be reckoning of which the likes you've never seen. Glayden will fail in comparison."

"Until that day, Arch. Now... Fly home before you see Imperial's might just as Uriel did."

Metatron emerges from the flames and black thick smoke from behind Raphael.

"Come, brother. Leave this night to Pain. The captain has sounded the general retreat. Imperial has been seen...

"No, brother, he's already here." Says Raph

Metatron pulls Raphael by his arm. As Raph is pulled he continues to stare into the eyes of Pain.

"Come, brother," Metatron says as he pulls him into the flames to cover their retreat.

The choiretic angels disengage and back into the beams of light that returns them to the heavenly realm. Raziel backs into the white beam of light pointing Cassiel's blade at Vermin.

Verminesk mask degenerates. He smiles at the threat of Raziel as he walks up next to Painell.

"The Arch fled before I could take his head. Did you kill yours?" Verminesk asked.

"No. I will remedy that next time we meet. He gave me a wound that I shall not forget. I will remember this night and the Arch Raphael." Pain turns and walks away grabbing his injured side of his abdomen. As he walks ne notices that Verminesk still stands in place looking where the angels had departed from. "What it is it?"

Verminesk turns and joins his brother. "I heard the trumpet of heaven blow but noticed no signs of Gabriel."

A piece of papyrus blows past the foot of Vermin. Seeing it, he picks it up to read. He notices that it is in fact a scroll from heaven. He runs his thumb over the broken seal. He opens it to read its contents which read: "When the Lamb opened the third seal, I heard the third living creature say, 'Come!' I looked, and there before me was a black horse! Its rider was holding a pair of scales in his hand. Then I heard what sounded like a voice among the four living creatures, saying, 'Two pounds of wheat for a day's wages, and six pounds of barley for a day's wages and do not damage the oil and the wine!'"

Verminesk lets the scroll fall to the ground a second time, it dissapates. "It appears the third seal has been broken."

"And will find Pestilence ready," adds Pain. "Come, brother. We don't want to miss the coming event."

Vermin places Pain's arm over his shoulder and helps him walk toward the collapsing remains of the U.N.

"It has been far too long since we have seen our kind take form without aid. Verminesk says.

In the aftermath of the attack, Death continues collecting souls from the bodies strewn throughout the anarchy. As he collects the last soul outside the collapsing building he runs inside amongst the flames, smoke and exiting dignitaries and staff. While inside the entirety of the building begins to shake. The entire left side fully collapses.

Ellen pulls and drags herself through the street. Her fingertips bleed as she grasps at the pock-marked asphalt. Seeing the body of her cameraman she angles herself in his direction and pulls herself towards him. As she inches ever closer to him she looks around at the wanton destruction and all the devastation. Feeling tired and cold, she knows she's starting to go into shock. She knows she needs to stop exerting herself, but she's almost to Paul. *Just a little closer.*

After what seems forever, Ellen crawls over to her longtime cameraman, co-worker and friend. His lifeless body that has been stripped of its soul instantly causes tears to well up in Ellen's eyes as she cradles him. Lost in thought of his now orphaned daughter's existence without him, she rubs his blood-soaked hair.

While stroking Paul's hair, Ellen only looks up when she notices that people are running past her in droves. At first, Ellen barely registered the first few sums of people that ran past her, but when that sum of New Yorkers turned into hordes, she dared a glance at what they were running from now. As she looked in the direction of which they all were running she saw nothing. *So, it's not from but to then*, Ellen thought. She slowly turns her head averting her eyes to what was more engaging then the sea of those that are now counted among the dead that were alive only mere moments before. Through her grief and early onset of shock, Ellen's gently releases Paul and pulls herself up. It takes all she has to get to her feet but, it was worth the taxing of her remaining strength. Ellen's eyes widen in amazement and wonder.

From the flame engulfed front entrance of the U.N., a figure silhouetted by the flames begins to emerge. As her eyes continues their fixation on the silhouette her breath suddenly escapes her. She can't breathe. Not from the worsening injuries, but from utter amazement and disbelief. As she watches the entrance along with other witnesses and news crews an angelic being emerges from the flames with its wings enclosed encasing himself from the fire. As it emerges, cameras are recording.

As the onlookers watch the event closely they can't move, they find themselves frozen by what they are beholding. A small minority of the people are fearful while the majority of others are filled with hope. The angelic being walks from the U.N. entrance into the middle of the street where Ellen is less than twenty feet away. The crowd parts and let him move unobstructed. The entity then slowly opens its wings revealing it's Imperial in full angelic battle regalia minus the sword. His mask is activated, to hide his very real scars that are healing from his battle with Jericho.

As Imperial completely opens and retracts his wings, it's clear to all those that are watching live or across the news feed that Lucien Arcane is alive as Imperial holds him in his arms, cradled. Lucien has a head wound that is bleeding profusely. His body has been impaled with shrapnel. By all accounts he looks to be dead.

The spectacle that the world is observing commands nothing but silence from all that bear witness. Although oxymoronic the silence is so deafening that heavens take notice. Raphael and the rest of the Archs as well as the citizenry of the ethereal realm watch as Imperial reveals himself to the world of men.

Imperial, ignoring everything around him, walks over to an ambulance that has an awaiting gurney. The medics that had just pulled it out back away. Imperial gently places Lucien on the gurney and looks at the surrounding people. "For the Lord called him wonderful, he has sent me. Lucien has been chosen to lead this world into an era as which has never before witnessed. He has not passed into eternal sleep, but has been made new. This is the decree which was given, so sayeth the heavens, so sayeth man, so say we all in one voice. I, Imperial, have become known to the world. There will soon be no more woes to the world of men for I have been sent to see them end. Through Lucien's guiding hand the world without doubt shall be saved."

The masses that witness the miracle all fall to their knees in reverence of Imperial.

CHAPTER 47

"I have witnessed wonders that you would not even begin to comprehend. I have witnessed the birth of all universe's times the span of forever, divided by infinite eternities. I have danced in the midst of black holes as they engulfed suns adjacent to planets four billion years old. I exist now and have existed then. I drew breath before the creation of existence and will exhale after it has ended. My kind was the first citizens of Elohim as you all will certainly be the last. Just as I bore witness to your kind's alpha, so have I witnessed the wrath of your first omega in the days of Noah and the second will be unlike unto it.

The time of the old world have passed into darkness with untold numbers decimated for their transgressions. As deplorable as it was in those days of perdition, you must steel yourselves for there will be a time that fails in comparison. The end of the age cometh quickly. It will be a time of annihilation that the Earth has never witnessed on such a measure and nor shall it ever again. We are not instruments of your destruction, but brothers in guiding you toward salvation. You will not know we are there, you will think us silent. Our names cannot be spoken by the tongues of mortal men. You cannot see us, but take comfort for we are always there, always guardians, always the Arch of Angels."

Quote ~Archangel Michael

Kaiserslautern, Germany:
St. Joseph Krankenhaus *Medical Center*

L eaning pass the bed rails, Isis kisses Jericho on the forehead. She brushes aside the hair that falls to the front of her face revealing a mess. Her eyes are sunken with bags underneath. Tears constantly runs along both sides of her cheeks. The wrinkles on her clothes betrays her less than publicly acceptable style of grooming, as it's easy to tell she's been in the same outfit for more than a couple of days. She rubs Jericho's hair and softly kisses his forehead again before backing away. As she moves from off the bed next to him, she straightens Griddles the Teddy Bear next to him and sits in the uncomfortable cheap cushion over plastic recliner.

Two knocks at the door and it opens, letting in the white pale light of the typical bland hospital hallway into a barley lit, less than basic hospital room reserved for the disenfranchised and downtrodden of the German people. The room brightens for mere seconds until Jason closes the door once again. With the aid of the thick drawn curtains the room once again plunges into darkness.

Jason Priest walks in wearing his traditional priest attire of black suit with, black shirt and white collar holding two cups of coffee. Without pause he passes one to Isis before taking a seat in a solid wooden chair that may have been manufactured sometime during the Second World War.

"You look awful; you need to actually get some sleep at some point before you drop."

Isis takes a sip of the coffee. "I look that great, huh?"

Jason rocks back in his seat and takes notice of the condition of the room. "He should be over at the military hospital. This place is deplorable. It's no wonder he hasn't regained consciousness, he'd wake up in this place and go into cardiac arrest when he saw the fright this place would illicit."

A snicker breaks out of Isis. She wipes her tears away and laughs again this time louder and more boisterous, but quickly catches herself and keeps the laughter to a whisper. Jason joins her and laughs at his own joke.

"His superior wanted him here. Kovac said it was a blessing that he was found with no identifying clothes or markings. Otherwise, the Chinese would have had him labeled terrorist and put to death. He says it's a relations nightmare. Tensions over this debacle could raise to that of conflict. And don't worry about the care, the doctors tending to him are from Landstuhl. Kovac made sure of that."

Isis reaches over and grabs the forearm of Jason and squeezes tightly. "Thanks for calling me, Jase."

"You were the first once I found out what happened."

Jason gets up and looks over Jericho. He eyes Jericho's wrist band and reads the name "Douglass Moody. Oh, God that's awful. "Douglass Moody is the best you came up with?" Jason said breaking into laughter again.

Isis seeing him laugh makes her laugh too, this time harder. "It was the best I had on short notice."

"You must not like my boy very much," Jason says as he keeps laughing.

As their laughter dies out they both just look at Jericho.

Sliding out of his chair, Jason kneels down in front of Isis' chair to meet her gaze at eye level while grabbing hold of her hand. "You know he's going to be alright. He's one tuff sumofabitch!"

Isis smirks. "Language, father."

End.

EPILOGUE

Mist of Purgosia

J ericho finds himself naked walking through endless mist. He doesn't know why, but here, being naked is not an embarrassment, quite frankly, just the opposite. Outside the fact that he's naked, he's more out of breath as he'd been calling out for hours until finally he acquiesced and remained silent.

A shadow catches his attention. Without hesitation, he begins to make his way following the shadow. After walking for what seemed to him half past forever he finally gained enough ground to see that the one shadow was actually two. Using the mist, he trots closer until almost earshot of the conversation of the two. The shadows both stop and one of the two quarter turns as if aware of Jericho's presence. Slowly, the shadow figure turns and faces Jericho.

Already hidden, Jericho crouches down further in an attempt to hide himself further in the mist away from the eyes of the shadow. Crouching, he slowly moves left and watches as the shadow's eyes follow him. *So, it can see me then!* Jericho no longer finding a point to remain concealed stands and begins to walk toward the mist and the glaring shadow. The shadow seeing him approach begins to walk toward Jericho as well.

As Jericho and the shadow closes in on one another, he realizes the shadow looks familiar. The long, knee-length trench coat becomes recognizable. It hits him. The man in black that was in the Congo and at the Embassy. Jericho starts to quicken his pace toward this familiar specter, this man that he thought was nothing more than an apparition in the jungle of the Congo. Jericho begins to part his tongue when he's grabbed about the shoulder and forced to turn away from the shrouded mystery of the man in black.

Gabriel turns Jericho towards her and hugs him tightly. She releases her grip and looks him in his eyes. In his heart, he's relieved to see her, but he has to know who the man in black is. He starts to turn back toward the shadowy apparition, but Gabriel grabs Jericho's chin and turns his face to fixate on only her.

"You have stumbled on a path in the dark that you don't belong, Jericho," Gabriel tells him. There is nothing for you this way but Death. It took me awhile to find you here lost in all of this cognitive mist."

Jericho tries to move his face, but Gabriel holds it in place keeping his gaze. "You have to listen to me, Jericho, those who speak to him here are not to return to the land of the living. You but just utter one syllable on this plain and your life will cease. Do you understand?" Gabriel nods at him. "Think of Isis, who even now wait for you to find your way from the dark back to her."

Jericho stops at the sound of the name he cherishes above any other. "Okay... Okay," Jericho yields.

Gabriel releases him but doesn't lose the compassionate gaze that she looks upon him with. Jericho looks into her eyes and just falls to his knees relieved that he's found a familiar face in the endless mist. However, it's not just familiarization alone that brings him down but also bearing the weight of being beaten by Imperial. Seeing Gabriel's face reminds him of the hope that she placed into him, and when it mattered he failed. Tears starts to stream from his eyes.

"Shh! It's okay, you hear me. It's okay." Gabriel helps Jericho to his feet and encloses her wings around him. A white beam of light strikes behind them. Gabriel backs into the light and is transported to the edge of sanity and reason. Her wings open releasing Jericho. Instantly, he can hear Isis and Jason talking. Gabriel points him in the right direction setting him on the path home, the path to consciousness. He follows the sounds of his friend's voices to a grayish void. He notices that there the mist has lifted.

Hearing Isis' voice creates a Cheshire grin exploiting his deep dimples. He looks back and sees Gabriel now standing next to Michael. Gabriel waves him on to step through the void. He doesn't hesitate he starts to run, but quickly stops himself and returns back and hugs Gabriel tightly. She hugs him back soothing his consciousness with peaceful suggestion. He releases the embrace.

"I'll put an end to him." And with those words spoken Jericho nods to Michael, not knowing who he is and takes off headed toward the void. Just before he enters he takes one last look at Gabriel and enters the void.

Michael stares at the void. "When he awakens the world will have changed greatly from the way he remembered it a few weeks ago. He's returning to a world where myth and legend has manifested within Imperial," says Michael. "In time it will be racked with chaos, anarchy, vengeance and wrath. Religions that have been established for thousands of years will fall, others will rise. The world that awaits him will be one of magnanimous eschatological cataclysm which I fear will be his road to perdition, it will become Jericho's bane.

Gabriel pulls her hood over her head and turns quickly causing the tail of her coat to flail. She starts to walk away, but decides to turn back to Michael. "This new world you speak of Captain, it will find him ready."

Kaiserslautern, Germany:
St. Joseph Krankenhaus Medical Center

Gasp! Jericho startles awake eyes stretched wide. "Isis?"

EXCERPT FROM BOOK II

Jericho's driver's side window shatters from incoming rounds. He's hit two times, once in the head the other in the chest. His heads rocks back as if he's taken a punch. The force of the round stuns him enough that he loses control of the vehicle and slides off the road into the store clerk's parked vehicle.

As Trina was in the midst of situating herself after jumping into the back, she makes the fatal error of not buckling her restraints. The sudden impact of the car collision ejects her from the backseat past Jericho and out through the front windshield.

Shaking off the effects of the crash, Jericho sees Trina's lifeless body mangled in the twisted metal that was once the front of his car. Disoriented slightly, he looks in the rear seats and sees that Jackson is on the floor boards of the vehicle, still bleeding out. Jericho knows if he doesn't find medical assistance for him soon, he'll be joining Trina.

More rounds crack off from the convenient store that he was passing at the time when he was struck by the stray rounds. Another round hits his vehicle. Jericho unbuckles himself and exits the vehicle looking for cover to get a glimpse of what the hell was going on.

Xavier's hit multiple times by the officers returning fire. The rounds for the most part find their target, but a few rounds find the plate glass window behind the gun toting criminal shattering the glass behind him as rounds that miss him strikes through it. Xavier's dead body falls backward through the store's window. As his body falls backward, Verminesk walks through the broken glass and looks menacingly at Raphael.

"Pull the strings and watch them dance, eh, Raph?" Vermin says while laughing.

Officer Cardenas walks over to the bullet riddled body of the thug with her gun still trained on him. As she checks his vitals back up units begin to arrive along with medics.

Verminesk pulls a blade from underneath his cloak slowly. Raphael pulls his as well. The two slowly closes the distance raising their blades overhead readying themselves for what they believe will be their final conflict.

Cardenas unsure that the thug is dead she kicks the weapon away from Xavier's body and then runs back to check on her partner. As she falls to her knees to check his vitals, unbeknownst to her, the angel and demon lock blades.

A metallic face plate generates from the neck line of Raph's armor, because he knows that Verminesk is a worthy foe that could end him. The two push opposite of each other with such force it breaks them apart. Vermin extends wings and brings them together in a thunderous clap. The shock wave throws Raphael past the responding units and ambulances out into the street. With backward roll he's on his feet again as Vermin meets him. They exchange a furious number of blows and slashes cutting and stabbing each other until exhaustion. They both swing nearly missing the clash of swords decapitating each other.

"You just won't let up, will you, Arch?"

Exhausted, Raphael face mask degenerates. Spitting blood from his mouth. "Never. A lot of brothers fell to that blade you hold. It's time I collect it."

Vermin catching his breath "That they did, little one. It seems that one more is to fall this night to it as well."

The two collide in combat again. A series of blades are thrown with just as many blocks and near misses. In an attempt to end the fight Raphael stabs for the chest. Vermin sidesteps and slams his blade on top of Raph's head. Raph, feigns the attack and throws himself backward letting the blade roll downward. Vermin blades falls through to the ground finding no target and leaves him exposed. As Raph pulls back to finish a striking blow, he hears a whistling sound.

As if a bomb has been dropped, another demon lands creating a circular shock wave. The ground crumbles in a crater fashion. The officers and their vehicle, along with all others on the scene are thrown from the epic center. Gas pumps are blown free from the ground.

Raphael and Verminesk are equally affected and thrown by the wave. Vermin is thrown through the front of the convenient store portion of the gas station. Raph collides into side wall of an ambulance. The ambulance rolls over three time with medics still inside. When it lands, a critically injured medic falls out the back.

From the smoke and dust-filled crater, Imperial emerges. His wings slam forward dispelling the dust from vehicles wreckage. Jericho witnesses Imperial. His vision is hazed and blurred, but he can see the majesty that is him and feel the fear rise within himself remembering his last encounter with the malevolent force.

Cardenas' partner, Coleman, is broken and bleeding as he crawls through the rubble He's overshadowed by wings of Imperial. Standing over Coleman Imperial steps on his arm pinning him down. "Weak, desolate, and cowering in the dirt. That is how I see all of you. Worthless! Do you profess Arcane deity?"

Coleman stares up at Imperial and smiles. "Fuck, no! I'm an atheist… But, if I had to choose, I'd have to roll with my man, Christ… asshole!"

Death perches on the gas station's roof. His face is covered by the shadow of his hood. He watches the exchange between demi god and mortal.

Imperial draws his blade and slides it smoothly into Coleman's chest unsatisfied with his response.

Raphael emerges from rubble slowly shaking the dizzying effects of being slammed with an ambulance. As he gets to his feet, he finds Imperial. The two lock in eye contact.

"Not since before the destruction of man have I seen a creature of your like. I killed scores of your kind back on the shores of Sarin," Raphael says as he extends his arm telekinetically calling his blade to his hand; is how it would appear to a lesser species. His gear has been upgraded to include weapon locater. "Your kind has been expelled from existence. Michael was right, you're an abomination that shall be stricken from this life."

Imperial removes the tip of his sword from Coleman's chest. "Understand, angel! My quarrel is with all of your kind, but not this night. I'm here for a charge under my command. If you interfere, I will give you my full unadulterated attention."

Verminesk emerges from the gas station.

Raphael looks past Imperial and places his sword to his face and then into a low guard combat stance saluting his enemy. "Come, Vermin, I welcome you."

Verminesk intense hatred for the celestials sends him running towards Raphael ignoring the presence of Imperial. As he covers the distance toward Raph, Vermin also extends out his hand, telekinetically claiming his weapon to it.

Imperial looks toward Verminesk. "Stay your hand!"

Verminesk ignores him.

Jericho starts to crawl from the wreckage when suddenly he's unable to move. From the corner of his eye he sees the entity that laid waste to his team and left him for dead in Germany. His anger wells up within him, but it's being displaced by the lingering fact that he can't move.

Death has placed his knee on Jericho's back pinning him down. He places the knee directly over a disabling nerve rendering his body inert. Death places his finger to his lip. "Shh!" he whispers. "Play dead, lest you draw attention of gods down upon you. This fight is not yours this night… Remain ever so still if you wish to fight another time more advantageous to your plight."

Jericho reluctantly acquiesces and lies still.

Raphael expands his wings and blasts toward Vermin, but changes his course at the last possible second to inflict harm on Imperial. In an instant, he's upon him. He goes to strike a blow but find he can't swing. He spins around for a midsection slice and freezes again.

BEHIND THE SCENES SKETCHES
AND
ALTERNATE COVERS

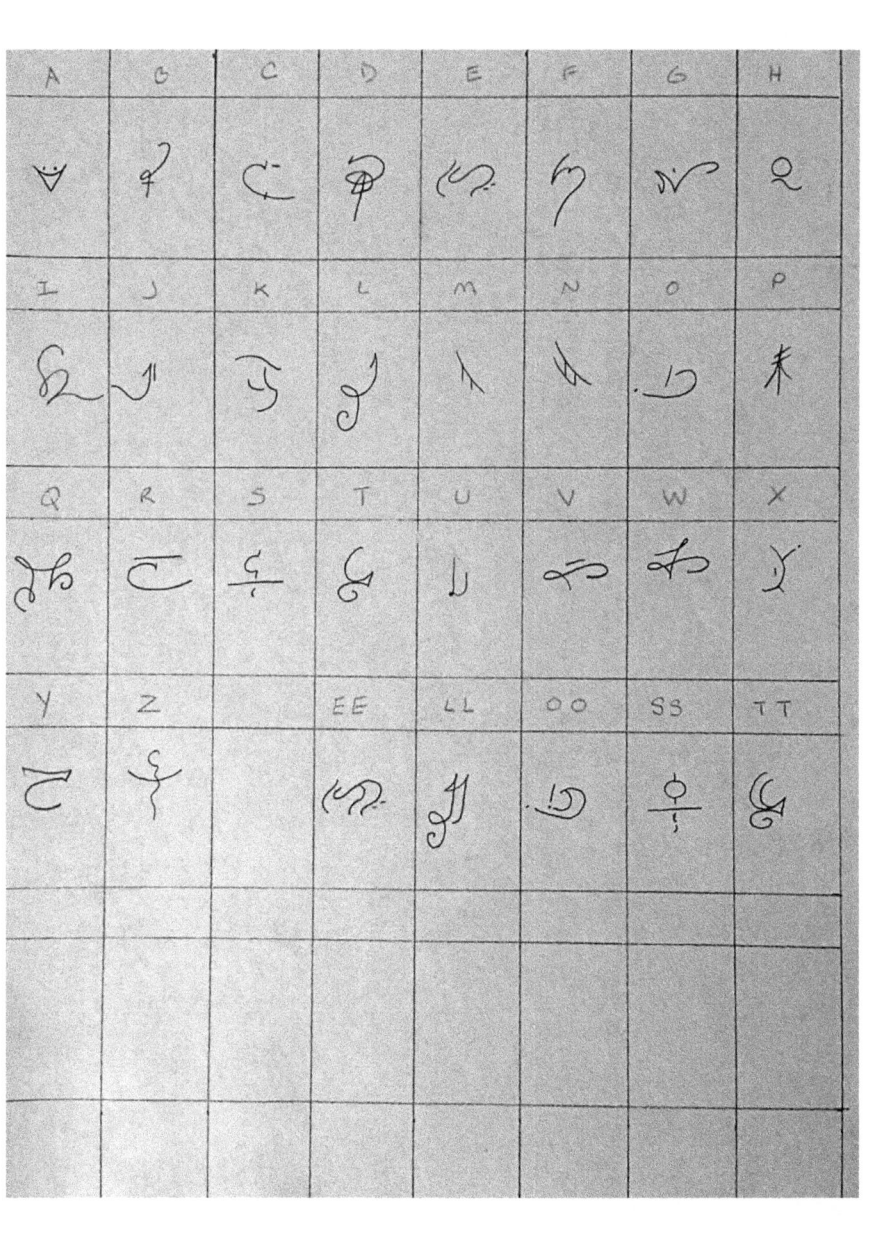

JERICHO'S BANE

IMPERIAL PROTOCOL

BY JAMES HOWARD

JERICHO'S BANE
IMPERIAL PROTOCOL

BY JAMES HOWARD

ArrowJKnight.com

Follow me on Instagram: 67rejections

Follow me on Facebook: Arrowjknight

Follow me on Goodreads: James L. Howard

Lightning Source UK Ltd.
Milton Keynes UK
UKHW040011060620
364507UK00001B/12